HEAT OF HYDRATIO

HEAT OF HYDRATION
A THRILLER

To: Lisa - I hope you enjoy the book... If you do, please leave me a review on Amazon! Thank you!

DWIGHT MORGAN, JR.

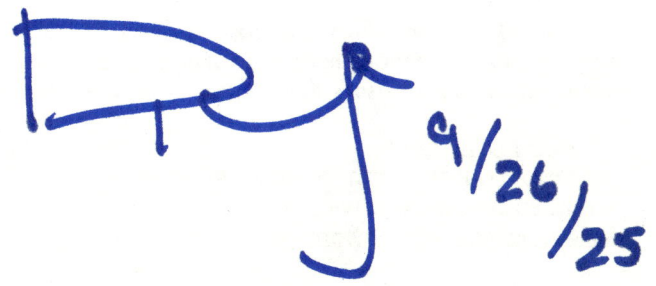

9/26/25

Black Rose Writing | Texas

©2025 by Dwight Morgan, Jr.

All rights reserved. No part of this book may be reproduced, stored in a retrieval system or transmitted in any form or by any means without the prior written permission of the publishers, except by a reviewer who may quote brief passages in a review to be printed in a newspaper, magazine or journal.

The author grants the final approval for this literary material.

First printing

This is a work of fiction. Names, characters, businesses, places, events, and incidents are either the products of the author's imagination or used in a fictitious manner. Any resemblance to actual persons, living or dead, or actual events is purely coincidental.

ISBN: 978-1-68513-538-6
LIBRARY OF CONGRESS CONTROL NUMBER: 2024949511
PUBLISHED BY BLACK ROSE WRITING
www.blackrosewriting.com

Printed in the United States of America
Suggested Retail Price (SRP) $25.95

Heat of Hydration is printed in Book Antiqua

*As a planet-friendly publisher, Black Rose Writing does its best to eliminate unnecessary waste to reduce paper usage and energy costs, while never compromising the reading experience. As a result, the final word count vs. page count may not meet common expectations.

PRAISE FOR
HEAT OF HYDRATION

'Best Pitch' award at Atlanta Writer's Conference May 2023

to patti

ACKNOWLEDGEMENTS

I started writing Heat of Hydration in 2010 with the goal of just writing a novel. My wife Patti gave me a self-help book at Christmas 2009 on how to write a book. I did not understand very many of the concepts outlined in this tutorial, so I just forged ahead with writing what I thought would be an entertaining story. I have always read a lot of thrillers by a variety of different authors and know what I think makes a good thriller. The goal was to write a page each night, a chapter per week. I finished the manuscript two years later, and it tipped the scales at 215,000 words.

I sent query letters to agents and tired quickly of the two words "no thanks" or in many cases I received no response at all. In 2017, a good friend, David Hynes, suggested I join the Atlanta Writer's Club. I did so. Over the next six years, I received some excellent coaching and advice on how the industry worked and learned much more about writing skills concerning character development (not mine), character arc, point of view, scene setting, etc. and that my genre (thrillers) were normally around 90,000 words. I had to 'peel the onion' quite a bit to get from 215,000 words.

The chain that goes from starting a novel to getting books on the shelf is long and the following people contributed individual links for me getting published. I am so thankful for their help and patience: Betty Collins, Bob Collins, Harvey Collins, Glen Jackson, Brian Lett, Craig Mitchell, Dick Parker, Bryant Wright, David Hynes, Chad Rhoad, Mari Ann Stefanelli, George Weinstein, Reagan Rothe and the biggest encourager of all, my wife Patti.

HEAT OF HYDRATION

CHAPTER 1
TAJ JILANI

April 1998

Taj Jilani sat in his desk chair, gazing out the window, flipping an unopened envelope back and forth that he kept with him always. The office he shared with Wang Soo was in a renovated, WWII, half-moon shaped aircraft hangar at the campus of the United Kingdom's top-secret military research facility. Despite the updated interior, the place still had an old, musty smell. The desk phone rang, breaking his stare. He laid the envelope down and picked up the receiver.

"Hello."

"Taj, it's Oliver. What time does Wang leave on holiday?"

"In a few hours."

"Notice anyone showing an extra interest in Wang's trip?"

"No. What's going on?"

"Nothing specific. Just precaution."

"OK." Taj frowned as he hung up with Oliver Thomas, his British MI-5 liaison. He liked Wang a lot and hoped it really was just a precautionary call, but they usually weren't.

Taj worked for Pakistan's intelligence agency, ISI, and moved temporarily from Karachi, Pakistan, to Salisbury, England. Highly classified info related to Wang's research was being leaked, and he was there to discover if Wang was involved. After six months of living and working with Wang, he found no evidence that the Cambridge educated scientist was distributing classified material.

ISI recommended him for this assignment for two reasons: he was a foreigner like Wang, and he could hold his own in discussing practical and theoretical applications of laser technology because of his multiple degrees in electrical engineering. In addition, learning MI-5 investigative techniques could be beneficial to ISI. His move or absence did not please his newlywed wife, but she was extremely proud of his promotion. As few compliments had ever come his way growing up, he cherished her praise.

Taj acknowledged Pakistan was only involved because the ISI had borrowed, well stolen, progress documents of Russia's laser program. To improve relations with the West, ISI gave this intelligence to the British and, by extension, the Americans. The information was a wake-up call for both, revealing Russia's unexpected advancement in laser weaponry. However, Wang's successful research models, proving the theory of ultrashort pulse lasers, were even more sophisticated and powerful than what the Russians had developed.

The office door opening behind him interrupted his thoughts. He too quickly placed the unopened envelope in his jacket pocket.

"Why you jumpy and secret acting?" asked Wang in his broken English.

"Have you ever tried knocking before entering?" asked Taj.

"You know we share office, right?"

Taj smiled when he looked up. Wang's thick, horn-rimmed glasses, black hair cut straight above his eyebrows and the gap between his front two teeth amused Taj. Standing, Taj grabbed two yellow post-it notes that were stuck to the edge of his desk. He placed them together on the bulletin board, then used a small level to align the yellow squares evenly.

"Why you do that?" asked Wang.

"Unlike *some* people, I like things neat—and organized," said Taj while looking at his office mate's messy desk. "Why aren't you at the apartment packing?"

"Done. Just came to say good day."

"You mean goodbye, not good day."

"Right. Goodbye."

"Question for you: did you tell anyone you were leaving sooner than the boss announced?"

"No."

"Or that you were going to Taipei instead of Paris?"

"No. You think I'm dum-dum?"

"No." *Whatever a 'dum-dum' is.*

"Listen to me. I make copy of my travel routes and put in drawer of bed-side table for you."

"Got it. You have a great trip."

"Thank you, please."

"You don't say those two phrases...never mind. See you later."

Wang left, appearing very excited about his time off.

• • •

Late that night, Taj arrived back at his and Wang's apartment. As he was in bed and drifting asleep, he sat up suddenly. His intention was to secure Wang's travel information. Rushing, he threw off the covers and went to Wang's bedside table drawer, opened it, found it empty. Taj grabbed his mobile phone and made a call.

A groggy voice answered, "Hello."

"Oliver—Taj. Wang told me he left a copy of his itinerary in the drawer of his bedside table. It's gone!"

CHAPTER 2
INTELLIGENCE OFFICER

The Next Day

The high-ranking intelligence officer was furious after the call he had just received. He screamed and strung together consecutive curse words in his native language, while slamming a notebook down on the table in his hotel room. One day, he would find out and take care of whoever exposed that they had the scientist's travel itinerary. Currently, he had to concentrate on the present. He had to assume that they also knew the location of the exchange. It certainly wasn't his people that screwed up. It had to be on the Russian side—sloppy—they were sloppy operators and probably leaked this information.

The day before, he completed a deal with a similar-in-rank Russian intelligence officer. He committed to give them the laser scientist, that would be responsible for the West jumping ahead of Russia, in laser weaponry. This was a secret, 'off the books' side job for him, though he used his country's resources to get this accomplished. The Russians finally satisfied themselves with who Wang Soo was and what he was working on. He had invested some of his and a close associate's money to get this information about Wang and his research. Time to get reimbursed, and then some. The Russians had agreed to the three-million-dollar price tag for the exchange. He could leave this business and retire—if they were successful, *and* the Russians paid.

He dialed a number. Someone answered the call immediately.

"Yes?"

He spoke in Mandarin and did so fluently. "Lang—my local British contact just informed me that both American and British intelligence agencies are expecting the scientist to be taken once he arrives in Taiwan. I doubt either can mobilize quickly enough to intervene, but you need to be prepared."

"Who do you think they would send? British SAS? Navy SEALs?"

"I don't know."

"I can handle either of them."

"This isn't a skills match, Lang. Just be ready. Are the locals you hired prepared?"

"Yes."

"Let me know when it is done."

The intelligence officer hung up. He's used Lang for many successful operations in the past. Against the Navy SEALs or British Special Forces, he would hold his own. He hoped there wasn't enough time for anyone to mess up this deal.

CHAPTER 3
COLTON GRAY

"Last one," Knox McKenna said. With veins bulging around the neck area, Colton Gray grunted and slowly exhaled, locking his arms out. Knox guided the bar and plates, totaling 400 pounds, safely to the bench supports.

"Glad I was here to coach you through that last rep," said Knox.

Colton nodded in mock agreement. "Yeah, you were a big help."

They finished their workout in the ship's gym and headed back to their respective quarters to shower. While drying, someone tapped on the door. He swung the door open and standing there was a young sailor.

"Sir, please go to Captain Anderson's quarters immediately."

Colton quickly dressed. As he headed up the steep stairs, his soles scratched and gripped the gritty rust on the floor's surface. The humble exterior presented a beaten-down freighter yearning for retirement but was in stark contrast to the modern interior and upgraded, powerful engines. She served the Navy SEALS and other U.S. Special Forces in the East and South China Sea. Currently, they were positioned 20 miles off the northeastern coast of Taiwan.

He and Knox were best friends and Navy SEALS. They had grown up together in the northwest Atlanta suburbs. Both were outstanding athletes and attended, played football, and graduated from the United States Naval Academy. This was their first mission together.

Colton rapped on the door of the captain's quarters. He heard Captain Anderson shout, "Come in."

He lowered his head and shoulder when he came through the opening. Seated around a small round table were the rest of Colton's team: Nick King, Jeremy Town, and Knox. Colton turned a chair around and rested his elbows on the chair's back.

Captain Anderson continued, "Orders just received instruct the immediate deployment of your team for an extraction. Today, British Intelligence informed us that a Taiwanese scientist, who is working on our joint laser program with both us and the Brits, was abducted near his family's home in Taipei. He is being transported to a warehouse roughly five miles northeast of the city. We believe they will hand him over to the Russians tonight and then he is gone forever. There is only one road into this industrial park where the warehouse is located. We must reach him first, before the Russians. Questions?"

Colton raised his left index finger. "Is there a reason British Special Forces aren't involved?"

"They don't have a team that can mobilize to this area soon enough. It's fortunate that we are so close."

Knox checked his watch. "How much time do we have?"

"About four hours from now. You should be able to make it to the suggested intercept point in 90 minutes."

Colton followed with, "Who are the abductors?"

"Not sure. We know a Chinese ex-Special Forces operator named Lang leads them. His name translates to wolf in English, and he served in the Chinese Assassin Corps with twenty-five confirmed kills before he was 18. His only description includes a wolf tattoo on his shoulder and an x-shaped scar beneath his right eye. He cut himself to celebrate his first kill."

"For simplicity, we will call him Wolf, and he sounds like the right guy to have around if we need to carve letters into our faces," Colton said, shaking his head. "Ground transport?"

"The Brits have organized that for you. These briefing packets cover what I just told you, along with a map of the local area. You guys need to confirm the suggested intercept point is the best one." Captain Anderson handed out the briefing packets. "Last, the truck that's transporting the scientist is currently being tracked by a local British asset on a motorcycle. Location updates are being reported via cell phone to your truck driver, also a British asset."

Colton nodded his head. "We'll get to it."

In the limited time they had, Colton and his team finally grew comfortable with their plan, although 'plans' rarely unfolded as they designed them, due to too many unknowns. They climbed into a rigid hull inflatable boat (RHIB) that would carry their team at almost 40 knots, roughly 46 mph. They should arrive at the extraction point with one hour to spare.

Colton was pleased how quickly they reached the shore because of calm water. They had a couple of daylight hours remaining. As they approached, he scanned the beach area with powerful binoculars and found what he was looking for. By the beach road, there was an old army truck with produce painted on the doors.

Upon landing, they trotted until they were within twenty yards of the truck and stayed spread out with their heads on a swivel for anything that might be a threat. Colton walked to within ten yards of the truck.

A short, older Taiwanese National with long, thin, black hair and a green baseball cap, who matched the description in the briefing documents, got out of the truck and introduced himself as Yu. Colton nodded to Jeremy who walked to the truck and motioned for the driver to open the flaps of the canvas top. He looked inside, nodded, and then walked around and peeked into the cab.

"All clear," said Jeremy.

They pulled the tail gate down, pulled out a map, and Colton explained their strategy to Yu. Yu's English was passable. Yu hopped in the driver's seat. Jeremy joined Yu up front, while Colton, Knox, and Nick sat in the back on a floor of old, worn-down lumber bolted to the truck frame.

The asphalt road they were on was rough and broken and it seemed Yu hit every pothole that was available. Colton checked his watch. Twenty minutes had passed. Colton continuously tapped his right leg with his hand. He noticed Knox's gaze shift from him to his hand, followed by a nod. Yu pulled off and parked on the opposite side of the road near the chosen sharp curve, among a stand of trees. Colton got out and checked the map. He gestured for Yu to go deeper into the trees. Yu did so and positioned the truck with its hood pointed toward the road. Daylight was changing to dusk.

Just beyond the end of the curve in the road, Colton watched as Nick and Knox laid a military spike strip that spanned the entire width of the road. Jeremy, the group's expert in long guns, provided 'over-watch' from higher ground inside the curve on the opposite side of the road. Beyond the curve, the grade sloped down at a 45-degree angle for about fifteen feet. Enormous trees were at the bottom of the slope.

It was unknown if the truck, used by Wolf's team, would stay on the road, or veer off when the tires blew. The truck's speed would determine this. Colton, Knox, and Nick concealed themselves on the left side of the road. Yu whistled for their attention, cell phone to his ear, and raised one hand, signaling five minutes before the truck would arrive.

Five minutes passed. They heard the truck slow slightly around the curve, saw the headlights, then a loud blast as all six tires blew. Swerving right, the truck barreled down the slope and crashed into a tree. Smoke escaped from under the hood. Jeremy left his position and joined Nick and Knox as they rushed the truck with weapons drawn.

Colton circled to the cab. The driver was unconscious and slumped over the steering wheel. A person wearing green camo suddenly leapt out and fled. Odd, thought Colton. It looked like someone had tied his hands together.

He came back around and joined Knox, Nick, and Jeremy. Everyone pointed their weapons at the truck door as Nick counted down with his fingers, then yanked it open. All yelled "out" in Mandarin. Colton specifically asked Yu for that word.

Three men wearing green camo appeared from the back, visibly shaken from hitting the tree, with hands raised. A fourth, dressed in street clothes and wearing a ski mask with his hands cuffed, followed, fell, got up and slowly made his way toward the back. They quickly disarmed the three soldiers and zip tied their hands and ankles. Colton and Knox quickly assisted the masked man out of the truck and hurriedly guided him up the hill. Jeremy and Nick lifted the soldiers into the truck, shut and zip tied the door. They then ran up the hill.

"Yu, bring the truck down," yelled Colton.

Jeremy joined Yu in the front as Colton, Nick, and Knox loaded the masked man in the back.

Colton yelled, "Go!"

• • •

They returned the same way they came. After a few minutes of riding, Knox reached to remove the ski mask. Nick aimed his flashlight at his head. He pulled it off and tossed it.

Colton, Knox, and Nick were shocked because the face they saw didn't match the photo of the scientist they had received. Staring back were dark eyes punctuated with an x-shaped scar under the right eye—Wolf!

"American fools," he hissed.

He snapped the fake handcuffs apart and ripped out, in one fluid motion, a knife hidden in his left boot. He plunged the knife into the right side of Knox's chest.

His other hand produced a second knife from within his sleeve and as he leaned to dive toward Nick, the truck hit a bone-jarring bump, causing Wolf to miss Nick's chest. He embedded the knife in his right shoulder. Wolf's shoulder crashed into Nick's head and Nick dropped his flashlight and fell back, not moving.

As Colton raised his pistol to end Wolf's life, Wolf leaped at Colton, looking like an enraged animal. He straightened his leg at the last second and planted the side of his heel into Colton's chest. Colton fell backward, losing his grip on the pistol, which slid into a corner. The truck continued barreling down the road, which, for the moment, was level and smooth.

Wolf lifted and straightened his leg high level with his head to bring down a powerful axe kick to Colton's head, using the back of his heel as the weapon. Flat on his back, Colton instinctively rolled to his right and swung his left leg to kick Wolf just above the ankle on the one leg he was standing on. As Wolf fell, Colton jumped on top of him and delivered a crushing elbow strike to the nose. Wolf grabbed Colton, and they rolled to the back of the truck, each trying to get some advantage over the other. When the rolling stopped, Colton was on top, but both of their heads hung off the truck's back.

Wolf squirmed and kicked while trying to get his thumb into one of Colton's eyes, but Colton had the height, weight, and strength advantage that allowed him to hold Wolf securely. The truck hit another huge pothole, and Colton's pistol slid back toward his hand. As Colton reached for his pistol, Wolf wiggled his body farther off the truck. Colton grabbed one of his legs as he was going over the edge. As Wolf slipped out of his grip,

Colton placed his pistol against the inside of his knee and pulled the trigger. Wolf's knee exploded, and he screeched in pain. Colton lifted his leg slightly as he let go so Wolf would fall headfirst onto the road. He bounced hard and then rolled to the side, his head at an odd angle to his unmoving body. Colton lay on his back, breathing hard, adrenaline at its peak in his veins. Suddenly, Colton's thoughts returned to his team.

Nick was conscious now and was leaning over Knox, wrapping bandages from his backpack around the knife that protruded from his chest. They would not remove the knife, as that could make it worse. Blood was everywhere. Nick looked up.

"Colt, it's not good. I've stopped the bleeding, but he needs help fast."

The truck slowed and came to a rolling stop. They had arrived back at the beach.

"How about you?"

"I'm OK. Shoulder's throbbing, but I have stopped the bleeding."

Colton leaned against the truck and shook his head. Two SEALS suffered injuries, one critically. No scientist. Mission failure.

Swiftly, Jeremy hopped out and sprinted towards the truck's rear. His face showed instant concern when he looked down at Knox. He then looked at Colton. "Some good news. Yu received information the British asset on the motorcycle picked up the scientist. The scientist was the passenger in the front seat that ran into the woods."

Returning his gaze to Knox, Jeremy asked, "What happened? Who was under the mask?"

"Wolf. He did this to Knox and Nick. Knox is critical. Got to go!" said Colton.

They all quickly went to the beach and carefully placed the unconscious Knox in the RHIB.

Colton turned quickly to Yu, nodded, and shook his hand. Colton jumped into the boat and stared down at Knox while thinking: *Mission accomplished, but his best friend might not make it.*

PHASE I

CHAPTER 4
TAJ JILANI

20 years later–April 2018
It had only been a month since he had buried the scant remains of his wife and daughter. Along with Nick King, they were all killed in an explosion—the same explosion. Three different explanations were given to him. One, a car bomb. The second, a blown gas main. His personal investigation found no evidence of either and felt the local authorities were lying. He queried ISI associates from his past. They said, though not confirmed, the preliminary intelligence reports leaned toward an errant missile launched by an American drone. This is what he believed.

It had destroyed the local marketplace where his wife and daughter were shopping. Devastation consumed him. Heartbroken. Competing internally with his sadness was anger. He would avenge his loss. Having a family of his own was his ultimate life goal. Now someone took it from him. He now had a new goal.

He pulled into the parking lot of Norky Funeral Home in Flint, Michigan. They were managing Nick King's burial arrangements. It was no longer raining, so he turned off his windshield wipers. He parked his rental car, got out, and walked through the bright, red front door. The powerful smell of cleaning solution hit his nostrils as he made his way to the front desk. A short, plump woman with gray hair wound in the shape of a beehive removed her reading glasses and greeted him. A co-worker was behind her sorting mail.

"May I help you?" she asked.

"Yes, I was hoping to get some information about the deceased, Nick King."

"I will help if I can. What is your name, please?"

"Taj Jilani. Can you tell me how Mr. King died?"

She leaned in like she was about to share top-secret information. "I heard he was killed in an explosion somewhere in Pakistan—or maybe it was Afghanistan. It's not safe if the country rhymes with 'banana stand' is my motto," she finished with a nod.

That statement annoyed him, but he concealed his feelings and pressed on. "I wish to express my sympathy to the widow. Is she here?"

No, everyone came for a closed casket viewing, but they've gone to the graveside service now.

He wasn't sure what a 'closed casket viewing' was. "May I ask her name and how I can contact her?"

The other staff member joined in. "Anniston King is her name, and she works at a hospital—Flint General."

"Thank you both. Can you tell me when the service starts and the location?"

The women spoke simultaneously. Taj finally pieced together enough details for the correct address and time. He got into the car, and without thinking, touched his left breast pocket to feel the unopened envelope. He drove to the cemetery, following the information he had typed into his phone app.

• • •

Concealed by a large maple tree, Taj watched the already in progress ceremony through small binoculars. A gentle mist fell upon a group of around thirty individuals. Because of umbrellas being opened, there was space between each person. All eyes focused on a man in black holding an open book. Ten minutes later, the service concluded. People briefly milled around, hugging a woman in a tan raincoat before leaving for their cars. He assumed the woman was Anniston King. After most had left, two tall men stopped for a few minutes and then each hugged her. As they left, one man handed her what looked to be a business card.

Unfortunately, this was bad timing on his part and didn't realize the funeral was scheduled for the only day he had available to ask Anniston King about the details she had been given regarding her husband's death. With a quick glance at his watch, he realized he had to leave now for Detroit for his flight back to Pakistan for an important meeting.

CHAPTER 5
TAJ JILANI

The Next Day

It was early morning when Taj checked into his hotel and unpacked. Because of the long flight from the U.S. and multiple connecting flights to his destination, Islamabad, he felt tired. Undressing, he laid his watch, car rental key, wallet, fountain pen, and unopened envelope, now yellowed with faded writing on one side, on the dresser.

Glancing at his face in the mirror after showering, his forehead suddenly had more wrinkles. Because of the loss of appetite, he appeared even thinner than usual. Despite proper eating and regular exercise, he became thinner while maintaining a healthy weight. His pencil-thin, black moustache and nose hair required some quick snips, which he took care of immediately with the small scissors he carried in his shaving kit. His mahogany brown eyes looked tired and swollen from the lack of sleep. Being a faithful Muslim, he believed it was Allah's will for this personal tragedy. However, it provided no solace for the emptiness and loneliness he experienced.

He dialed a number from his notes. Someone answered it immediately.

"Yes?"

"Confirming today at 2:00."

"Yes, that is correct. We will talk at 2:00."

In the several weeks following the burial of his family, he immersed himself in researching organizations that hated America. Through some networking and information provided by certain websites he knew, sort of, a man called Accem (pronounced ah-seem), although he doubted this was his real name. Written backwards, it spells Mecca, the holiest city in the Islamic faith. Although, in some ways, it felt like Accem had found him.

They exchanged introductory emails, through a secure website, and then talked twice in Arabic and set a date to meet to discuss working together. Based on accent alone, he thought Accem was from Saudi Arabia.

• • •

He parked his rental car and walked down the street toward a block of office buildings. On his right, he passed a coffee shop, a hardware store, and a Chinese cleaning company. As he crossed an alley, a small, Chinese man struggled to get his cleaning cart's wheel out of a large crack in the pavement. Stopping to assist, Taj helped him push what turned out to be an incredibly heavy cart out of the fractured pavement. The man nodded in gratitude and continued his way down the alley.

Taj continued walking and turned the corner and stopped when he reached the fourth building on the right. He climbed the three steps to the door and entered the numbers he had been given into the keypad. The lock clicked, and he entered. The hard tile floor was a lime green color. Ten feet in front of him was an unpainted masonry wall constructed across the room. The wall held a window, with a speaker vent at its center. The glass appeared very thick, most likely bullet proof. A table, level with the window frame's bottom, held three folding chairs. The room beyond the glass was dark.

He sat in the middle chair and waited about five minutes when he heard a voice speak in English. "Good afternoon."

Taj could barely make out a human form behind the thick glass.

"You are Accem?" Taj spoke in English as well.

"Yes, but I prefer to hide my physical identity."

"I see." *Well, maybe not.*

"We will always speak in English. I will get right to the point. I represent an organization that wants to destroy the West and their poisonous values in the name of Islam. We are politically connected to a variety of countries who share this vision. The U.S. is our current target for the next two to five years. The aim is to create a catastrophe larger than the U.S.'s 9-1-1, affecting both the U.S. and the world. But first, does this interest you?"

"What is the name of your organization?"

"It is best that you don't know."

"How are you financed?"

"We are required to have a different funding strategy for each mission."

Taj sat silent for a few moments, thinking. *He didn't exactly answer the question, and he said 'mission'. Maybe military or intelligence background.* "I am interested. You know of my recent loss. I put the blame on America."

"Yes, and I sympathize with your situation. Remind me again of your educational background?"

"I have a doctorate in Electronics Engineering and added a master of Structural Engineering last year."

"Any government or military service?"

"Fifteen years with ISI, Pakistan's intelligence agency, followed by three years as a professor at the University of Karachi. After my family's murder, I resigned from my faculty position."

"Other immediate family?"

"Mother and eight siblings."

Accem was quiet for fifteen seconds. "Your educational background and government experience will make you a great asset to our organization. We will compensate you at the same rate as your professorship and reimburse any expenses related to your work for us. Do you accept?"

Taj rubbed his chin. *I need the money.* He nodded and said, "Yes."

"Good. Your first assignment is to research and recommend an unconventional method to destroy a building, bridge, or road. This is to be accomplished by creating a system or network of explosives using building materials commonly used in the construction process."

"OK."

"You need to purchase 50 burner phones for now and use a new one every time we schedule a call. I will give you a new number for me after we talk. Everyone in our organization gets assigned a name and number. Yours will be 'Pakistan'. When you call me, I will ask for a number. Yours is '32'. Do you have questions?"

"No."

"You have six months. We will meet back here on September 11 at 2:00 p.m. for you to present your research and recommendation. I'll reach out if I require something before that time. Otherwise, we will have no contact."

"What if…" he heard a click. *What if I have a question for you?* is what he intended to ask, but the sound he heard made it seem the conversation was over. Taj sat there for another five minutes. All was quiet. He leaned in and listened. Nothing. He left the same way he came.

CHAPTER 6
HASSAN MUSTAFA

In Cairo, Egypt, a meeting was about to start in the back room of a mosque. Hassan Mustafa, a reputed 'street thief', was in attendance in his finest robe. Near the back, he lurked by the exit. This certain mosque was an Al-Qaeda recruiting station. They advertised today's meeting as an 'Enlightenment Seminar' for the Koran, Islam's holy book. People filled the room. Standing behind a small podium, the mullah appeared to be in his late thirties, with a warm smile that displayed white, even teeth. Hassan's friends told him that the mullah had a gift—charisma and that Hassan should hear him speak.

The mullah cleared his throat to get everyone's attention. "My job is to educate you in some of the finer points of the Koran—points that are sometimes unclear and may seem hidden in our sacred scripture." He talked for another twenty minutes with his deep voice booming at certain phrases.

He then closed with, "You are here because Allah has chosen each of you. You will commit yourself to a mission of extraordinary personal sacrifice—" he hesitated for effect and intentionally and slowly looked into the eyes of several attendees. "—that of a suicide bomber! And you will receive a reward of 70 virgins for your pleasure." He smiled and winked at them. "Your individual place of honor will be incredible." His presentation caused the young men to become stirred in a frenzy.

Hassan was interested in joining al-Qaeda, but as a warrior, not a sacrificial stooge. His goal was to lead a significant mission and advance within the organization. The mullah finished, and slightly pulled the sleeve of his ornate, ceremonial robe to glance at what appeared to be a gold Rolex. He said he had to leave as he had another important appointment in furtherance of Allah's work. The mullah's sales pitch was persuasive, as measured by the ten men that left to meet in another room. Hassan slipped out the opposite way. His journey would be different. The mullah's sales pitch did not move him. Hassan was 'street smart' and there was something fake about this guy. Outside, he approached a corner of the mosque but suddenly stopped short. He heard two men talking. One voice he recognized immediately — it was the deep voice of the mullah.

"I've got to go. A European will be in my hotel room in thirty minutes. You know how much I love being with someone new," laughed the mullah.

The other man shook his head. "I understand, but traffic is chaotic now. You were very convincing today, and you can collect your payment later tonight."

The men shook hands, and the mullah promptly departed in his black Mercedes.

Hassan hurried back to his beat-up motor scooter. Positioning his robe around his waist so it would not touch the hot, dirty muffler, he pushed the button to start the motor. He could safely tail the Mercedes thanks to the gnarled traffic. The mullah pulled up to a five-star hotel near the pyramids, tipped the parking attendee at the outside podium, and handed his keys over. Hassan quickly parked his scooter and rushed through the lobby, joining a crowded elevator with the mullah and other passengers. Several people, including the mullah and Hassan, got off on the third floor. Hassan followed the mullah to a door in the hallway. As Hassan walked by, the mullah tapped his keycard and opened the door. A beautiful blond wearing only a bath robe, grabbed the mullah and put her lips to his before the door could fully close. Hassan returned to the elevator lobby and positioned himself where he could see the mullah's door.

* * *

Two hours later, the woman exited the mullah's room, wearing a headscarf. Hassan watched as she counted her earnings. He followed her from the hotel to a black sedan parked on the street, spanning 100 yards. She climbed into the back seat. As he walked by the car, he stole a quick glance inside. She removed the scarf and pulled her blonde hair completely off her head. *She was a 'he'!* The wig and makeup had obscured his short black hair and rugged features. The sedan suddenly sped away. Islam forbids this type of sexual activity. The discovery of someone's secret had value. He hoped it would be useful someday.

CHAPTER 7
TAJ JILANI

Six Months Later – Sept 2018
As Taj was preparing for his meeting today, his thoughts drifted to his family. He promised his wife, Amal, he would leave ISI if they ever had kids. After years of trying to start a family naturally and then with various medical reproductive technologies, they believed it was not Allah's will for them to have a child. Then one day, Amal announced she was pregnant! He was speechless. Allah must have just been testing them. But that was nothing. When Sana was born – what a miracle! Finally, the family he had dreamed of. But everything changed that fateful day seven months and three days ago.

His phone rang. He recognized the ring tone. It was his 65-year-old mother's weekly 'cheer-me-up call'. He tapped the answer button, "Hi Ammi (mother)."

"Taj, I was just thinking about you."

"I'm OK, Ammi."

"My heart aches for you."

"I know it does. I will be OK."

"Taj, I haven't told you enough how you helped our family survive. You were the oldest but a child yourself. Helping raise your five brothers and three sisters was a blessing to me and them."

"Thanks Ammi. It was necessary for all of us."

"You worked so hard for us. You made our family so proud! Your situation will improve."

"Thanks Ammi. Hey, I've got to go. I have a meeting soon. I love you."

He hung up the phone. It was indeed tough growing up. They lived in the slums of Karachi. His father abandoned them after his youngest brother was born. His classmates ridiculed and mocked him for being poor, constantly poking fun at his shoes, which were three sizes larger than what he needed. It was embarrassing, but he endured it and grew strong from it. As the household's unofficial head, he had to work after school to earn money and provide food. After helping others with homework, he studied late into the night to complete his own. This forced him to become an excellent time manager. He vowed it would never be this way when he had his own family.

• • •

He parked, walked to the building, entered the keypad, and went into the room. Sitting in the middle chair, he waited. He had not talked to Accem in six months. Hearing a faint click he then heard a voice. "Greetings Pakistan. I look forward to your presentation. Begin, please."

"OK. It has some technical points, but I will try to break it down into simple pieces. I approached my assignment by researching non-military structures or buildings that are designed to withstand missile attacks or detonated explosions, and I landed on nuclear power plants. I focused on why the design of this type of facility includes concrete construction."

"Intriguing place to start."

"So, some general info on concrete. In its most basic form, concrete comprises four ingredients: cement, sand, gravel, and water. When mixed, the molecules of water and cement create a chemical reaction called hydration which produces heat. 'Heat of Hydration' is the industry phrase. It aids concrete in curing and progressing from a fluid to a solid."

"I understand. Continue."

"Researching the internet, I discovered that the Tennessee Valley Authority (TVA) in the U.S. has some of the safest, most efficient, and destruction-proof nuclear power plants in the world. TVA's website also revealed they have a patented process for repairing cracks when they occur in their concrete structures without shutting the plants down. They save a tremendous amount of money by keeping the plants on-line during scheduled maintenance and emergency repairs. They offer technical help free for countries that want to use their process for repairs at their nuclear plants."

"Why would they offer it for free?"

"The technical engineer I spoke to said to ensure the process is performed properly. My guess though, is that it enables the U.S. to monitor the operating conditions and emerging technologies of other country's nuclear power plants."

"That's an astute observation." Accem's cell phone rang. "I need to take this call." Accem was gone for ten minutes. He returned and said, "Continue."

Taj explained that TVA's technical department had worked for years on a procedure using high amperage electrodes and steel powder mix to fix concrete stress cracks in the walls of the main concrete structures. The trials produced this result: when the electrodes received too much electricity, the concrete would increase its hardness and become brittle to the point of failure.

"So, am I to understand that these special electrodes restart the hydration process of the concrete and that causes the concrete to become weak?" asked Accem.

"The hydration process is not enough. But, when the heat generated by the electrodes exceeds a certain maximum, the combination of the two will cause the concrete to fail," said Taj.

"How quickly?"

"TVA says they experienced concrete failure from three hours to five hours after the maximum current passes through the electrodes."

"How does this apply to a concrete building structure?"

"This will require more study. But I think if we can apply enough electricity to metal items cast into concrete, such as reinforcing steel or electrical conduit, we can cause the concrete to become brittle and fail. But the mass of a building differs from what TVA has evaluated. I have another viable solution in case the amperage requirements aren't met."

Accem was silent for a few moments. When he spoke, there seemed excitement in his voice, "I like this. I like this a lot! What's the next step?"

"I need to go to Chicago in ten weeks and attend a trade show for emerging technologies in solar and other construction systems. Something useful may await us there."

"You have done excellent work."

"Thank you."

"I need more time to discuss further. Please return tomorrow morning at 10:00 with the details for your trip to the U.S., and I will manage those arrangements."

"I will be here."

Taj heard a soft click. Accem had signed off. He paused as he pushed his chair back to leave. A noise made him place his ear against the slot in the thickened glass. *It sounded like two people walking away!* It was too dark to see anything. Rising, he walked to the front door, pressed a button, and departed.

CHAPTER 8
TAJ JILANI

Next Day

The next morning Taj arrived early for his meeting with Accem. He stopped at the small coffee shop next to the Chinese laundry. A strong, mixed aroma of different coffee beans was prevalent in the small space. He ordered an espresso. The wooden chair he plopped down on had a red, plastic vinyl seat that was ripped in the middle. The chair frame joinery was so loose, it wiggled under the weight of his 6'0" frame. Through the large window in the coffee shop, he saw the same Chinese man pass by pushing his cleaning cart. *I hope he doesn't get stuck in the crack again, mused Taj.*

A young boy, appearing to be about seven years old, approached his table with a wooden box and asked if he could shine his shoes. The boy's clothes were so big, they draped over his little body like a tent. He saw himself in the boy. His clothes, for many years, had been larger because they were hand-me-downs. The money also was probably going to the boy's family. Agreeing to the service and enduring his chair shaking the entire time his shoes were being shined, he paid ten times the amount he was going to be charged. The boy's face was one big smile as he thanked Taj calling him 'Maalik' (boss).

He finished his coffee and walked around the corner to Accem's building. He entered the building and saw two men seated at the table. They turned and looked at him.

"Come in Pakistan," said Accem. "I want you to meet the leaders of Jihad's Blood. They will perform the operational part of our mission and assist with the fundraising. To your left is

Hassan Mustafa, the leader of Jihad's Blood. On your right is Saleem Adel, his second in command."

Following Pakistani tradition, he walked over to shake hands with both men and placed his hand over his heart. He felt the outline of the unopened envelope through his jacket material. He noticed Hassan had a paper pad with a page filled with handwritten notes.

"Let me conclude my conversation with Hassan and Saleem and then we will talk," said Accem.

"Of course. I will wait by the door," answered Taj.

Taj could barely hear the conversation between Accem and Hassan.

"When can you provide the list?" asked Accem.

"Three to four months," answered Hassan.

Taj watched Saleem jerk his head to Hassan with his eyes wide-open like Hassan's commitment shocked him.

"Make it 100 days. Contact me on the number I gave you when the list is ready. We will not speak again until then. Your organization will get instant credibility and all glory will go to Allah when the mission is complete!" finished Accem.

Hassan and Saleem pushed back their chairs and headed towards the door. Taj opened the door for them and nodded as they passed through. He overheard their conversation before they got too far away.

"Impossible! How will we get the list?" asked Saleem.

Hassan responded, "I have a plan. Don't worry."

Taj waited a little longer as he watched them turn the corner. Saleem's hands continued to gesture, and his mouth moved quickly, as if engaged in a lively one-sided debate. He returned to the table and sat in the middle chair.

"This list seems important," said Taj.

"It's for the financing piece of the mission," said Accem.

"Why did you choose them?"

"They are new and need us more than we need them. They seek relevance and see us as a path to get that. We can guide them to take care of our needs."

"Tell me about leader Hassan."

Rustling papers reached Taj's ears through the window. "We did some checking on him. Al-Qaeda recruited him from his hometown in Cairo about six months ago. He has a remarkably high I.Q. with psychopathic tendencies as it relates to Islam. Hassan was outspoken on what he believed was a lack of leadership at the top of al-Qaeda. He strives to lead his own group of fighters and impact the world for Islam."

"So, no concern from al-Qaeda of his inside knowledge of them?"

"When he split with al-Qaeda, they were relieved as they thought he was a liability. My liaison confirmed he was not involved in any operational planning at the time which probably saved his life."

"Good assumption."

"Now—I am ready to reveal what we have been tracking as our next target. The United Nations recently announced they will construct a new headquarters building in New York. Do you think what we discussed yesterday would destroy this building?"

Taj nodded his head back and forth as he pondered the question. "Possibly. I know nothing about the building. Creating a practical weapon demands significant research, testing, and investment. The building's design may need to be influenced to match our weapon's capabilities. For example, the building structure should be concrete, not structural steel."

"I understand. After your trip to the trade show, put together a cost and implementation plan. If persuasive, I'll request approval of the funds. Leave your travel requirements on the table. Write my next cell number."

Taj wrote the number on the pad in his leather portfolio he had with him. He then removed the itinerary he had typed out for Accem. As he laid it on the plastic topped surface, he heard the click. Meeting over.

CHAPTER 9
HASSAN MUSTAFA

Hassan had two objectives for the meeting with his brother warriors tonight. It was midnight, the building was in a low rent area in Rawalpindi, a few miles south of Islamabad. The restaurant belonged to one of his men's brother-in-law, who worked there during the day. Saleem and he entered through the iron gate, which served as the back door, and went to a room near the kitchen. His men sat at two small tables. Each table had only two fat candles. Paint was peeling off the walls. The room reeked of cigarette smoke provided 'free of charge' by the kitchen staff during their breaks.

Hassan greeted everyone and started right in.

"Brothers, you know why we are here tonight. We have an incredible opportunity for our organization. The rewards will be extraordinary," said Hassan. He then told them the target that was chosen and their responsibility for destroying it.

"The last item I want to discuss is our role in helping raise the funds for this mission." Hassan described how they should produce the list and explained its intended use. He looked around to observe the reaction to his explanation. No emotion was apparent on any face. It was quiet — too quiet. His men were processing what they'd heard.

Finally, one man spoke. "I've never heard of anything like this. Are you sure it will work? Who develops the list? How can that even be done? I'm not liking this plan." Heads around him nodded in agreement and while others whispered to each other.

"I have an idea on the list. Assume I get the list handled. Let's discuss the more important item. What do you men think about us taking out this incredibly, significant target? Jihad's Blood will get all the credit for advancing our duties as Muslims in the name of Islam," said Hassan.

The room suddenly buzzed with conversation, and Hassan allowed it momentarily. Energized, Hassan spoke again. "We all need to work together for this to succeed. It will be a glorious prize for each of you individually. Is everyone in agreement?"

They looked up at Hassan and nodded. He noticed Saleem's wide smile. Now, Hassan needed someone's help to generate the list. He had a thought.

CHAPTER 10
COLTON GRAY

Colton sat in the UN conference room on the 23rd floor. A Human Resources person and consulting psychologist from Interpol were on their way to interview him for an investigative agent position in their headquarters in Lyon, France. Colton wore a blue suit, white shirt, and a gold and blue striped tie. He sat in his chair tapping his thigh while he waited. A man and woman arrived at 10:00 a.m., entering through an open door.

Colton stood to shake their hands. "I'm Colton Gray."

"I'm Cynthia Sandstrom, Director of Recruiting and this is Dr. Lev Bargo, our third-party psychologist." They took turns shaking each other's hands.

"I'm pleased to meet you both."

"We have looked forward to meeting you. Let's jump right into it. We have a flight back to Paris at 2:00. Your application and curriculum vitae (CV) you sent were informative. I will walk through your resume quickly and then we will have Q & A following. When Interpol was established in 1923, it chose Lyon, France as the location for its headquarters. Interpol, as you know, stands for International Criminal Police Organization and one of its primary duties is to track crime trends around the world for its 190+ member-countries," said Cynthia.

"Thank you for that introduction. I am familiar with Interpol," said Colton.

Cynthia put on reading glasses and opened her notebook with many colored tabs. "You graduated from the Naval Academy in 1996 and then served four years in Special Operations. Leaving the Navy in 2000 you went to work for

Beers Construction in Atlanta for six years, holding various positions until becoming a Project Manager. After your departure from Beers in 2006, you joined the FBI's Special Services Division investigating human trafficking. You remained with the FBI for six years in the Atlanta office and departed from the FBI in 2014 and moved to New York joining the United Nations newly formed Human Trafficking Division. This brings us up to date. Is this correct?"

"Yes," said Colton.

She further shared that she had read his performance assessments with permission from Division Director, John Hill. All were excellent reviews. She also mentioned being impressed when she read the 'Other Comments' section, discovering that Colton excelled administratively in running the best, organized meetings among everyone Mr. Hill had assessed or had ever worked with. Operationally, an investigator that successfully changes the direction of an investigation by stringing together seemingly unrelated information.

She continued, "When talking to Mr. Hill, after reading your reviews, he said, you are a... let me think of the word, 'weisenheimer'."

"John is nicer to me than he should be, and he is probably correct about me being cocky. He is a great boss and friend," said Colton.

"What languages are you fluent in?"

"English, French, and German though some of my New York friends might debate that I speak English. I hold a minor in languages from the Academy."

"Good. If Interpol hires you, how would Mr. Hill feel about losing you?"

"It was John who alerted me about the open position in Interpol. He shares my belief that a change of location would be beneficial."

"Why is that?" asked Dr. Bargo.

"Because human trafficking is emotionally draining. I could share stories that would bring you to tears. I've dealt, by choice, in the trafficking of women. Their handlers are so cruel and abusive that it is a constant reminder that evil is real. We made a small impact, but additional work is necessary. It is discouraging. As soon as we close one trafficking cell, another opens."

The doctor nodded his head. They then moved on and discussed at length the responsibilities of an Interpol investigator. The doctor went through a dozen different 'what if?' scenarios and took notes after Colton gave his answer.

"Your CV stated you are unmarried?" asked Cynthia.

"Yes. And my girlfriend of twelve months ended our relationship a short time ago. I will be transparent in saying this slightly figures in to my wanting to make a location change."

Dr. Bargo spoke. "Thank you for mentioning and being candid about that. Do you mind telling us why she broke off the relationship? I'm interested if it tracks with some results of the psychological tests, we had you to take."

"I do not mind at all. She says our relationship progressed until it hit what seemed like a wall. I will admit that has been a similar complaint from previous girlfriends as well. I have a tough time 'opening up' to someone or even letting my feelings get past a certain point," said Colton.

"Was your father abusive?" asked Dr. Bargo.

Colton was silent. *I did not see that coming.* His hand started tapping his right thigh. He saw Dr. Bargo's glance quickly toward his hand. He nodded and spoke, "Yes, he was. To both my mom and me."

"I wondered if that was the case. This showed up in some of your answers to certain questions. You may be experiencing what is called 'Attachment Disorder'. The way your father treated you and your mom can cause some of these symptoms. It affects personal relationships as you have described. Consider meeting a specialized psychologist to unload old baggage. This does not affect your hiring outcome, just some friendly advice."

"Thank you," said Colton.

Cynthia looked at her watch. "Last question for you. Professionally speaking, what desired outcome drives you?"

"To never, ever let the 'bad guy' get away. It happened once. Never again. That is my passion."

She nodded and closed her notebook. "Thank you. We enjoyed our conversation and will be in touch in the next few weeks."

They all stood, shook hands, and said their goodbyes. Colton sank into his chair, lost in thought briefly. He was relieved it was over. He grabbed his phone and touched a name in his 'Favorites'.

Knox answered, "Hey, I wondered if the interview was over. How did it go?"

"I think well. They are supposed to let me know something in a few weeks," said Colton.

"Look, I haven't told mom and dad that you are thinking of a job change. You need to be the one that calls them if it happens. Leaving the country will be hardest on mom as you know," said Knox.

"I know. I know. I'm so grateful for the kindness of your parents. After my mom died, they took me in and treated me like I had *always* been part of your family."

"Stop it – I got an instant brother I could push around. That was all I cared about." They both laughed.

"When I hear something, I'll call you. Later." Colton hung up.

CHAPTER 11
HASSAN MUSTAFA

The man briefly peeked through the slightly ajar door. He shut the door gently and noiselessly when seeing the mullah exit the elevator. Judging by his facial expression, the mullah seemed excited as he hurried toward the door of the hotel room. A meeting had been arranged for the mullah and the room's occupant to spend some private time together. The man heard a knock and cracked the door.

"Come in," said the man in a quiet voice.

The room was pitch black, except for a candle's dim glow on a table near the outer wall. Sensual, soft Arabic music played in the background. The mullah shut the door behind him. As he turned around the man with the quiet voice stuck a big knife against his throat.

"Turn around and put your hands behind your back!" barked the man.

"This is a mistake," said the mullah and did not obey the order.

"If I tell you to turn around again, you will have made the mistake," hissed the man.

The mullah slowly turned around.

"Do you know who I am?"

No answer was given. The mullah's wrists were zip-tied. He was led to the table with the candle.

A chair was pulled out for the mullah. "Sit." The mullah sat.

"Listen carefully." The man explained what he wanted the mullah to do.

The mullah shook his head. "That does not interest me."

The man pulled out a file and opened it so the mullah could see the contents.

The mullah's confident, smug expression evaporated. "How did —?"

The man cut him off. "If you don't do as I say, I will send these sex photos to the police and your al-Qaeda liaison. The authorities will imprison you if al-Qaeda doesn't kill you first."

The mullah looked down—defeated. He nodded. The man slid another file over, and he retrieved the first file.

Upon getting up, the man instructed, "Follow my guidelines and keep me informed on a weekly basis until you finish. My contact number is in the file. You have four weeks."

With that, Hassan wheeled around and left the room, leaving the mullah to figure out how to unbind himself.

CHAPTER 12
TAJ JILANI

December 2018

Before dawn, Taj departed from his apartment. As promised, Accem took care of his travel arrangements. His flight to Chicago's O'Hare International would take nineteen hours. Expecting wintry weather, Taj packed accordingly. In his travel packet, Accem included five preloaded credit cards for expenses. The show 'Innovative Construction Solutions,' highlighted advances in solar and state-of-the-art products for the construction industry.

After landing, he went through passport control for non-U.S. residents and collected his suitcase at the baggage claim carousel. He went outside to bitterly cold December Chicago weather. He quickly put on his overcoat. After locating the taxi stand, he got a cab and instructed the driver to take him to the Drake Hotel.

• • •

Fifty minutes later they reached The Drake Hotel. Taj studied the revolving door for a moment but did not navigate it properly. He ended up sharing the compartment with another person. It caused them both to shuffle with little steps. Taj quickly apologized to the other occupant. He walked over to the front desk.

"May I help you?" said a young lady.
"Checking in."
"Name?"
"Taj Jilani. Wow! It is cold in Chicago."

"It is. I'm moving to Florida one day."

After a few minutes, the clerk handed Taj a key card. Thanking her, he headed to his room located right above Michigan Avenue. He admired the winter scene outside - the snow, lights, and Christmas decorations were incredibly beautiful.

A room service menu was in the bedside drawer, and he ordered a salad. Afterward, he opened his conventioneer information packet and pulled out the dog tag placard that identified him and tossed it on the bed. The trade show lasted from 9:00 to 5:30 p.m. for three days.

• • •

The next morning, he dressed in a dark gray, pinstriped suit, white shirt with French cuffs and a solid royal blue silk tie. He grabbed a taxi and arrived at McCormick Place a little before 9:00. He could not believe the expanse of products under one roof. Rows and rows of displays filled the space. His goal was to visit one-third of the displays daily, starting with the left side that displayed heating and solar innovations.

He stopped at the display booth of B & I Radiant Heat Systems. Taj looked carefully at the enlarged color diagrams that made the system easy to understand. A man emerged from the booth, greeting him with a handshake.

"Hi, my name is Thomas Jawarski, but call me TJ. How can I help you today?"

"Can you explain how your system works?"

"Sure, before pouring the concrete floor, we install round metal tubes that comprise the radiant floor system. After the concrete is poured, the tubes are covered up and now hidden. At one end of the floor, a hook up point sticks outside of the concrete and connects to the tubing inside the slab. The hook up point is connected to a hot water source. Hot water flows through the tubing. The floor absorbs heat from the tubes and radiates it, warming the room."

"Is this system used in commercial buildings very often?"

"On parts of the building. The cost is prohibitive to be used in the entire building."

"Has the water ever gotten so hot that it caused the concrete slab to weaken and fail?"

"I haven't heard of that ever happening."

"OK, thank you." said Taj. He shook hands and wandered on. *The tubes present some options!*

He continued to wander around the great expanse of products until he had a sense that someone was following him. Halting abruptly, he scanned the immediate area behind him, but he didn't spot anybody.

He then stopped at the Roegge & Roegge Curtain Wall display. He wasn't sure what curtain wall was, but he picked up some literature and started reading.

The brochure said that curtain walls are made of glass and attach to aluminum support members. It serves as the weather-tight exterior wall of a building and is "non-structural," meaning it only supports itself. He further read they had developed a curtain wall system that incorporated solar cells that produced electricity.

A tall, slender man dressed in a gray suit and solid red tie held out his hand.

"My name is Tafton Jenkins but call me TJ. May I help you?"

Taj smiled. *Another TJ?* "Yes, I am interested in your RR9000 system."

"It's the most advanced system on the market. The brochure you picked up has all the technical info on the back page."

"So, are the solar cells embedded between the layers of glass?"

"Yes, and our next generation curtain wall will include a shading feature that darkens or lightens the curtain wall glass in individual rooms for further comfort but still allows the glass to produce electricity."

Taj nodded, shook Taft's hand, and thanked him.

Taj spent the rest of the day examining the displays but found nothing that held his interest. As he was returning to his hotel, his cab driver stopped at a traffic jam in front of an incredibly tall tower that looked like it had X's going all the way up the building.

"What's this building?" Taj asked, pointing at the tower.

"It's the John Hancock Building. It's 100 stories high," answered the cab driver.

"Please let me out here."

Taj paid the driver and stood in awe of the tallest building he had ever seen. He resumed walking and turned right at the next street, which was Walton, and stepped quickly into the corner building's entrance. Again, he sensed someone was following him. Waiting and observing, no one turned the corner who seemed interested in him. He went to his room, took off his shoes and lay on his bed for several minutes, feeling energized about the products he had seen today.

• • •

During the next two days, Taj browsed but couldn't find anything else that held his interest. It was time to make a call. Taj dialed a number that was answered after the first ring.

"Number?" asked Accem.

"32," said Taj.

"Update?" "

"Two products have potential, but owning the companies is necessary."

"Hold." After a minute Accem returned. "I've received advice that you should contact the law firm of Callahan and Mezzaro, who specialize in mergers and acquisitions and are reputed to be the best in Chicago. Ask for Jack Callahan. This is my next cell number. I will always give you a new one after we talk."

"I will call tomorrow," said Taj as he wrote the new number. "Accem?" Taj listened a few more seconds and concluded the call had ended. *Strange.*

CHAPTER 13
TAJ JILANI

After viewing their website, Taj learned the legal practice of Callahan and Mezzaro was on the forty-third floor of the prestigious sixty story AT & T tower in Chicago's downtown loop. John "Jack" Patrick Callahan III was the managing partner of the fifteen-person firm and had earned an undergraduate and then law degree from Northwestern University. Their website stated they differentiated themselves by studying carefully why mergers and acquisitions were or were not successful. Culture differences and unrealistic revenue growth were two of the most common breakdowns. They had developed several tools that would fully examine those issues and basically predict compatibility of the purchaser and the acquired. They did not engage in 'hostile takeovers'.

He called the firm and asked for Jack Callahan. He gave the receptionist his name. A few seconds later, Jack came on the line, "Taj Jilani? Did I pronounce that correctly?"

"Yes, that was very good," answered Taj.

"How can we be of service to you?" asked Jack.

"There are a couple of companies I might like to purchase. Can you check if they're interested in selling?"

"Who are they?"

Taj provided the names of two companies and explained their business activities. "I'll be in Chicago for the rest of this week. If you can arrange it, I could meet with these companies."

"I'll make calls and then update you. At what number can I reach you?" asked Jack.

"I'm staying at the Drake Hotel. I will call you," said Taj.

"That's fine." said Jack.

• • •

The next afternoon Taj called Jack Callahan.

"I have some good news for you," said Jack.

"What did you find out?"

"I talked to both owners, and both said they will meet."

"This week?"

"Yes. I set up meetings Wednesday with B & I Radiant Heat Systems and Thursday with Roegge & Roegge Curtainwall. I will courier information on both companies to you tomorrow morning. Also, I've made hotel reservations for us on Tuesday and Wednesday nights. I will pick you up tomorrow afternoon at 4:00 at The Drake. I drive a black Tahoe and it should be about a five-hour trip."

"Thank you. I look forward to receiving the information and will be ready to go at 4:00."

CHAPTER 14
TAJ JILANI

Taj wasn't sure what a Tahoe looked like and waited inside by the revolving door. It was bitterly cold outside. The overhead heater felt good where he stood, and the decorated evergreen trees by him smelled good.

Jack's photo was on his company's website, so he knew who he was looking for. A black car pulled in front. Taj noticed 'Tahoe' written on the car. He left his warm sanctuary as the passenger window lowered. He saw it was Jack. Jack waved and signaled towards the rear with his thumb as the cargo door lifted. As Taj loaded his luggage, he noticed an interesting-looking vehicle across the street with a small blade sign on top of the car that read 'TAXI'. It was yellow and tank-like with rounded features. A red racing stripe adorned car from hood to trunk and tires that featured mag wheels. He opened the passenger side door, stepped in, and shook hands with Jack.

"What kind of taxi is that?" he said, pointing across the street.

"The old Checker cabs were once prevalent in the city, but not anymore. It's rare to see one. Individual operators might use them now as a limo service, but I have never seen one fixed up quite like that."

Jack put the Tahoe and gear and pulled away. Taj fastened his seatbelt and checked the side mirror, and he noticed the red-striped cab pulling out behind them.

"Did you have time to review the material I sent this morning?" Jack asked.

"Yes. You put a lot of information together in a short amount of time."

"We have a good research team."

They drove along the Lake Michigan shoreline until they left the Chicago area and headed north to Michigan.

"Whom will we meet first and what shall we discuss?"

"Chandler Boyd with Radiant Heating Systems, in Traverse City. At introductory meetings, people rarely discuss money and terms. We will all introduce ourselves and our backgrounds. They may inquire about your intentions for acquiring their company, how you discovered them, potential name changes, your objectives, and similar matters."

"How do you think they will react to a foreign owner?"

"They know you are, yet still wanted to meet."

They arrived in Traverse City approximately 8:45 that evening, checked into their hotel and had a quick dinner with Taj asking a lot of questions about American business practices.

• • •

Late that night, Taj realized he'd left his briefcase in the Tahoe and went outside to retrieve it. Luckily, the door was not locked. As he closed the door, a car passed by. Its headlights bathed over a yellow Checker cab with a red racing stripe, parked across the street. Because of the cold, exhaust fumes caused a smoky cloud behind the cab. He started across the street for a closer look. As he got nearer, the cab turned its lights on and sped away. Taj stood there a minute watching the taillights of the vintage cab. He walked back to his room now sure he was being followed.

CHAPTER 15
COLTON GRAY

Colton sat in the passenger seat of the Ford Crown Vic and trained his binoculars on the window of the front bedroom of the ranch-style house. It was nighttime, cold, and they were near the town of Kingston, NY.

"You were right," said FBI agent Chester Lagod. "Instead of container transportation, they moved women in small boats up the Hudson and offloaded them in Kingston. How did you figure that out?"

"Experience, intelligence, my good looks, experience, intel..." Colton was interrupted.

"I say you were lucky, but here is the fifty bucks I owe you for our bet," said Chester as he opened his wallet and fished out two twenties and one ten.

"Like taking candy from a baby," uttered Colton as he snatched the money away.

He looked back through the binoculars. "Whoa, guess who's there? The Russian boss himself, Big Zeus!" *Where do they come up with these names?*

Chester grabbed the field glasses from Colton and looked. "It sure is! Why is Ivan 'Big Zeus' Ivanov here? If we arrest him, it'll be a game-changer." Chester spoke into his wrist mic and alerted his team of who was in the house and to be ready to move. He handed the eyeglasses back to Colton.

Colton watched Ivan depart while a woman and one of his men returned. He opened his hand and slapped her. She staggered, and he followed her slapping her again. She fell and then he kicked her, not once but twice.

"I've got to go."

"Where?"

Aggressively, Colton said, "She's being beaten!" His hand started tapping his thigh.

"Wait until we are in place."

"You better hurry or I'm going in."

Chester spoke into his mic and asked his tactical team leader if he was ready. "OK, on your signal." He turned to Colton. "About to happen."

Suddenly Colton saw ten FBI agents swarming the house. Four stood in front, four moved to the back, and one guarded each side, watching the windows. Bursting through the front door, the agents stormed in and quickly spread throughout the house, shouting commands.

The window he had been observing suddenly broke apart as someone threw a chair from inside. With a leap, the abuser jumped out of the window. He got up and took off running. Colton jumped out of the car.

"I've got him," Colton yelled to Chester as he took off running after the man. He knew it was unlikely the man could outrun him. Even at 42, he maintained his fitness and speed. Running down the street, he saw the man glance and notice he was being chased. Turning right, he ran up the driveway of the next house. He jumped the wood fence that surrounded the back yard. A dog in the yard barked as the intruder kept running. Colton leapt over the fence, gaining on the man. Crossing the backyard, the man slowed as he approached the property's rear fence. That is where he made his mistake. As he started over the fence Colton caught him, pulled him back and threw him on the ground. Rolling over, he was suddenly on his feet with a knife in his hand.

"Put the knife down," ordered Colton.

The Russian thug cursed at Colton and started coming toward him. Colton pulled his pistol from behind his back and aimed it at the man. "Drop it," said Colton.

Defiantly, the man stared back at him briefly before tossing his knife aside. He cupped his hands and moved all his fingers as one towards his body in a motion for Colton to approach him for close quarter combat. "You not so tough without gun, American man."

That was all Colton needed as he re-holstered and fastened his gun. He had watched that man hit and kick a helpless woman. That brought up deep, old emotions. Colton didn't wait and talk. He attacked. He started running toward him and executed a jump front kick into the Russian's chest which knocked him down. Colton straddled him and continuously slapped the man's face, back and forth. It was like a relief valve opened and suppressed anger flowed out as he beat the man more. He felt someone grab him from behind yelling his name, "Colton, stop! He's done. Colton…"

Colton turned. It was Chester. He glanced at the Russian and noticed his red, swollen face with blood seeping from his nose and mouth. "I'm good, I'm good," exclaimed Colton as he got up, breathing heavy and stepped away.

"You, OK? I've never seen you like this," said Chester as he snapped cuffs on the man.

"Yeah, sorry. A man beating a woman—gets all over me."

"OK—it's OK. We got Big Zeus and saved ten women. It's a great night!"

• • •

The next day, Colton was sitting in his office and explaining to his boss, John Hill, about the events of the previous night. "That was a big catch. Ivan controlled a lot of the east coast," John said.

"Yep. Could not have happened soon enough. The FBI seized his computer, potentially getting valuable information."

The phone rang at Colton's desk. John told him to answer it. Colton picked up and talked for about five minutes. He said he would consider it and respond soon.

"Sounds like a future employer conversation," said John.

"It was Interpol, and they have offered me the job."

"You going to take it?"

"Yes. I believe I will. Thank you so much for your recommendation."

"That was easy, but we will miss you."

"Me too. They want me to start in three weeks, January 2."

"This place will fall apart," John said and smiled as he stood to shake Colton's hand.

• • •

That evening Colton touched Knox's name on his phone. "What's up?"

"I got the offer from Interpol and I'm taking it," said Colton.

"Wow, that's awesome. Congratulations! When do you leave?

"Soon, like three weeks."

"Probably tell mom and dad at Christmas. It will be a *great* present."

"OK, there's something else." Colton shared with Knox about the previous night and how he allowed the trafficker to manipulate him into a fight. "I lost control and punished him myself," finished Colton.

"Man—I saw you do that once in college when we went to that hole in the wall bar. That guy was arguing with his girlfriend and pushed her. It took several of us to pull you off him. You even scared me! You became a different person."

"I remember."

"Look, Colt, maybe you need to talk to someone professionally about your thigh tapping and how to control what triggers your rage."

He sighed, "Yeah, maybe so."

"Hey! Don't let last night spoil the great news."

"Thanks. Talk later."

CHAPTER 16
TAJ JILANI

At 8:00 a.m., Taj was already sitting when Jack came up to join him. They ate from the buffet. Jack started the conversation.

"I received a voice message from Chandler Boyd. He mentioned he had invited his Chief Financial Officer (CFO), Gerry Weezler, to join us. He explained that Mr. Weezler is the nephew of his retired partner, Griffin Ingraham, and holds a minority ownership stake in the firm."

Taj thought Jack didn't look happy. "You seem troubled by that call?"

"My experience with CFOs on previous acquisition deals is they want to impress you that their abilities are more robust than just a 'numbers guy'," Jack said. "Several times CFOs became an obstacle to getting a deal closed."

They spent a few minutes discussing how to conduct the meeting before getting into Jack's Tahoe. Shortly after, they arrived at a small industrial complex and parked their vehicle. It was a brick, one story building with big block aluminum letters spelling B & I Radiant Heating Systems. A large warehouse, with a loading dock, stood on the building's right side.

A cheerful receptionist greeted them and showed them to a conference room located just off the lobby. She asked if she could get them water or coffee. They both asked for coffee, black. She went to a nearby table, poured their coffees, and mentioned that Connor and Weezler would arrive soon.

Moments later, two men walked in. Taj stood and extended his hand as the taller man introduced himself as Chandler Boyd.

Chandler had dark hair graying a little and a wide, friendly smile framed by a goatee.

"I'm Taj Jilani and this is my attorney, Jack Callahan."

"Thank you both for coming to see us today." Chandler turned toward the other man, "And this is Weezler, sorry, Gerry, our CFO."

"Call me Gerald, please," said Gerald.

Taj saw Connor glance over at Weezler when he corrected his name. He thought it slightly amusing that both the receptionist and Chandler called him Weezler. Weezler was shorter than everyone by at least eight inches and his small hands worked extra hard to have a handshake that was excessively firm. His eyes momentarily tracked Weezler as he strutted over to the credenza for coffee as everyone sat down. *I understand why Jack was worried now.*

The meeting was about to start when the receptionist pushed the door open and gave Jack and Taj a quick look. "Excuse me for interrupting. There's a yellow cab parked on the street. If that's your cab, it's fine for him to park in our lot."

"No, we drove here in my car," Jack said.

"Does it have a red stripe?" Taj asked.

"Yes, it does."

"OK, thanks," said Taj. *That cab is for me.* He continued, "I have asked Jack to get us started if that is OK with both of you," said Taj.

Both men nodded their heads.

"Let's go around and introduce ourselves and share any thoughts about today's meeting. I will start. I've had the privilege of being involved in many deals and discovered that a successful merger involves three key elements: trust, fairness, and open communication. If you can figure these out, you will know if you are a good fit," finished Jack. He then looked at Chandler.

"That's good advice Jack. I started this business fifteen years ago with a partner that recently retired. We grew fast and fortunately have been very profitable. When my partner retired, he took half of the equity out of the company, and this has hurt our ability to increase our revenues further. Your call was timely as we need an investor to infuse additional capital to maintain our growth goals," said Chandler who then looked at Taj.

Weezler interrupted Taj's attempt to speak by clearing his throat, pushing back his chair, and by accident picked up Taj's cup of coffee. With a serious and troubled look, he sipped, smacked his lips, and circled the table. Taj noticed Chandler staring intently at Weezler. "So, I have a few thoughts I would like to share," started Weezler. "Our new patented devices set us up for extraordinary growth. I..." Standing up, Chandler interrupted a possibly long speech.

"Thanks, Weez...um...sorry, Gerald for that intro but let's let our guest, Mr. Jilani, finish speaking as he started a minute ago."

Weezler sat down and took another couple of sips of Taj's coffee.

Taj nodded. "Thank you for agreeing to see us on such short notice. Those I represent have a keen interest in investing in emerging construction technologies as they see this as an industry that has promising growth potential."

Chandler stood again. "Do you want to see our operation before discussing mutual benefits?" Both Taj and Jack nodded their heads quickly. Chandler then stared at Weezler. "And *Gerald*, please pour Mr. Jilani another cup of coffee as you have been enjoying his for the last few minutes."

Taj smiled as he looked at Jack who was chuckling. They got up to go as an embarrassed Weezler scurried over to the credenza to prepare another cup of coffee.

• • •

They returned to the conference room a few hours later. Jack spent the next thirty minutes outlining what he thought should be the next steps.

"Go to the next step?" asked Jack.

Everyone nodded.

"Great. Please send me your most up-to-date financials and we will get started."

They stood, exchanged handshakes, and parted ways. Jack and Taj climbed in Jack's Tahoe.

"How do you assess this first meeting?" asked Taj.

"It went well, and I like Chandler. Weezler can be a problem, but I think Chandler will manage him fine," said Jack.

"I liked Chandler too. I will have some more questions, but I think I understand their products and services."

"Chandler did an excellent job of explaining what they do and what he needs. That's a good sign."

"I agree. On another subject, I saw the Checker cab outside our hotel last night. And now it followed us to our meeting. Do you find that odd?"

"Yes. I didn't know you saw it at our hotel. Strange. I will call my partner, Ben Mezzaro, and get him in touch with one of the investigation firms we use."

Taj noticed Jack frequently checking the rear-view mirror as they headed to Grand Rapids for their next meeting.

• • •

A few hours later Jack received a call and transferred it to speaker mode. "Hey Ben, I have Taj Jilani in the car with me. You have an update?"

"Hello Mr. Jilani."

"Nice to meet you Mr. Mezzaro," said Taj.

"I had our private investigation firm use their contacts to get the Michigan State Police involved. They stopped the cab about an hour ago. The driver's name is Bob Collins. He was alone but said his customer paid him generously for a couple of days of work. He drove the customer where he wanted to go. They asked if he was told to follow anyone. He said he was told to follow a black Tahoe. He wasn't given a reason for anything they did. They lacked sufficient grounds for detainment. That's all I have," said Ben.

"Thanks. I will talk to you later," said Jack.

Taj sat there wondering who would be interested in his whereabouts. Only one name came to mind.

CHAPTER 17
TAJ JILANI

After driving a little over three hours, they checked in at the Holiday Inn Downtown in Grand Rapids around 4:00. They had plans to have dinner with the Roegge brothers at 7:00 that night. Jack and Taj agreed to meet at the bar at 6:30 and wait for the brothers to arrive.

Taj and Jack arrived at the bar simultaneously and chose a table overlooking the lobby. Jack pulled out a thin manila folder with what research his firm had pulled together and reviewed it with Taj.

"Please pronounce their last name, again," asked Taj.

"Row-ghee," said Jack.

Jack explained the Roegges were fraternal twins and had taken over the business the previous year when their father retired. While checking out their company, he'd also learned that both Roegges had played football at the Naval Academy.

"Why choose our hotel for the meeting?"

"They didn't want any rumors to get back to their employees. If they or we are not interested, then no harm done."

Shortly thereafter, two tall, lean men walked up to their table and introduced themselves as Alex and Ryan Roegge. After exchanging handshakes, they sat down at the restaurant.

Alex had an amiable smile while his brother Ryan seemed quieter and more reserved.

"I understand you both played for the Naval Academy," Jack said. "When was that?"

Alex responded. "We both played from 1981 to 1984."

"I remember those years. You had an excellent quarterback, Knox McKenna, and a great running back, Colton Gray. He was lightning fast."

Ryan nodded, "Both tremendous athletes."

Alex pivoted from the small talk. "If you don't mind, we are a little uncomfortable about this meeting and would like to get right to the point. Why are you interested in our company?" he asked, looking at Taj.

"Those I represent want to invest in emerging technologies within the construction industry as they see that being the next market with huge growth potential. We believe if the product is good, the best return on our investment occurs early on. I met your sales engineer recently, and he mentioned you were developing an advanced shading feature for your curtain wall system," said Taj.

"That's Ryan's area of expertise. I will let him speak to that," said Alex.

"We have a design engineer dedicated solely to working on the next generation shading feature. We need additional testing to achieve a balanced electrical charge, preventing glass fractures and explosions," finished Ryan.

"Very interesting. Does it use DC or AC power to activate the shading?" asked Taj.

"That's an excellent question. We found that using AC power accelerates the shading over four times faster than DC, so we are doing all testing and research with AC. DC is a more efficient method as our panels generate DC power, but it is a lot slower."

Taj nodded his head, opened his leather portfolio, and made a couple of notes and circled one.

Jack asked, "Did you discuss the idea of selling your business?"

Alex drummed his fingers on the table and glanced over at his brother. "We had never considered selling our business until you called."

"We don't have a proposal prepared yet, but we like your products and want to explore your company further," Jack said.

Taj requested Jack to explain the process to them. Jack did so for the next hour. Alex expressed candid reservations about selling the company.

After discussing the main points, Alex pushed his chair away from the table. "We really appreciate your interest. We need to think about it," he said.

"I understand completely," Jack said. "May I call you in a week?"

"That would be good," said Alex.

Everyone stood and shook hands.

• • •

Taj returned to his room for a good night's sleep. He felt drained. He turned on the light. Someone had been in his room! His clothes were slightly out of place and the drawers not fully closed.

He dialed Accem. *That's the name that comes to mind that would have me followed.*

"Number?"

"32."

"Update?"

"Two good meetings. Waiting on more information, but I believe they can help us accomplish our goal."

"Excellent, Pakistan."

"One other thing. Someone is tracking me. A cab driver followed me from Chicago to my first meeting and tonight someone broke into my hotel room. Any idea who it might be?"

"I will check into it." He hung up.

CHAPTER 18
TAJ JILANI / ACCEM

Taj returned to Karachi. He worked on the report he was preparing for Accem. Polishing it to its final form, he was still missing one piece of information, and that was how much it would take to buy both companies. Jack answered on the second ring and after thinking about it for a minute, gave him a number to use but emphasized it was only an experienced guess.

Taj arrived for the meeting scheduled with Accem. He approached the door, entered the code, and went inside. He took his regular seat.

Taj heard a click, "Pakistan, please slide your proposal under the window," said Accem. Suddenly the window rose as silently as a car window for about two inches. Taj slid his report under. The window closed promptly. "Come back in thirty minutes," said Accem.

• • •

After thirty minutes passed, Taj returned to his middle seat. He heard a click. "I read what you gave me. I am fascinated with the potential," said Accem.

"Me too. The radiant tube system gives us flexibility in several ways because there will be a system of pipes inside the concrete. If we can't generate enough heat through the solution that is put in the pipes, we may use electricity instead."

"Explain that."

"The radiant tube system uses heaters to heat the blended water solution that is pumped inside the pipes. This warms the concrete floor and provides heat in the room. If the heaters can't produce enough heat to make the concrete brittle there is option two. We connect electricity, produced by the solar panels embedded in the glass of the window wall system, to the metal conductors in the concrete floor that consists of the radiant tube system and reinforcing steel. Enough electrical energy could make the concrete slab explode. This is using technology no one would easily suspect."

"I see. Your report makes more sense to me with that explanation."

"Now, a third option. Instead of the water blend, we could use an explosive liquid if heaters and electricity do not create the catalyst to make the concrete floors break apart. This is a much riskier method and creeps outside the parameters you gave me of using common materials in commercial construction."

"Ahh…true, but a reliable solution. I'll explore options for the third choice."

"Very well."

"Next steps with the two companies?"

"Mr. Callahan followed up with both companies a week ago and they both want to proceed. I included an estimated cost in my presentation."

"I saw that. Last question for now: What construction skill sets would Hassan and his men need to install the heating tube system?"

"We need the skills of an electrician or plumber."

"OK. You have done excellent work here. I am certain that this strategy is both unique and clever, and I will present it for funding approval. Anything else?"

"Yes. You said you would have someone investigate who was following me. What did you find?"

"Our local representative checked it out but found nothing."

A frown formed on Taj's face, "That's not good." *Maybe that's because it was the 'local representative' that was following me.*

Taj heard a click. He got up and left.

• • •

Accem watched the door close. He flipped a switch and soft lighting came on chasing away the darkness. He glanced back at the man seated behind him. "Did what he say match with what you observed in Chicago?"

"Yes," the man answered.

"Good." *If I can pull this off, I will retire as a national hero!*

CHAPTER 19
ACCEM

Accem left Islamabad early in the morning. He was to have his first meeting with his government liaison to get approval for his mission funding. He assumed it would be a bank loan from their bank in Casablanca, Morocco, because of the hefty sum. This was the norm in recent years. The funding strategy he would present would repay the loan.

The plane landed on schedule and Accem grabbed a taxi to his hotel. He checked in and went straight to his room. He got his presentation materials out and sat down in one of the comfortable chairs. His liaison, 'General', was a senior member of their country's intelligence agency. The name was not a title, but an inside joke from a past operation. They had many joint successes together, with only one failure in the thirty-odd years they had worked together.

At noon, someone knocked on Accem's door.

"Good to see you General," said Accem as he shook hands.

"I have been looking forward to our meeting," General said.

"I think you will like it. Let's have lunch at a place I know you will like," offered Accem. He knew General loved Chinese food, and that's where they went.

They left by cab and arrived a couple of minutes later. Accem requested the back room for a private meeting. Someone led them there and closed the doors.

Accem began by saying that Pakistan (Taj Jilani) had earned his respect as being efficient, reliable, intelligent, organized, and motivated, but he was still having him watched. His briefing was in three parts: Phase 1 covered the selection of Jihad's Blood and how the funds were to be raised. Phase 2 outlined how they had to manipulate and successfully guide the design of the new UN building. Phase 3 laid out Pakistan's idea for an incredibly effective weapon once the building gets under construction.

General sat quietly for a minute. He steepled his fingers and then nodded his head seemingly in appreciation of what he had just heard.

"I didn't expect you to come up with this idea. This is a brilliant!" said General.

"Thank you," replied Accem.

"What's the investment request?"

"$9 million."

Accem explained the allocation of the money for purchasing companies, living expenses, influence money, etc.

General nodded his head. "I approve. Let me know through secure channels when you need it."

"OK."

General glanced at his watch, stood, and made his way to the door. "Excellent work," he turned and told Accem. "Can't spare time now, but curious how you created your funding scheme. This is completely new to me."

Accem nodded and shook his hand, "Thank you."

He shut the door and stood for a few seconds. *Now the list— it starts with the list and it's due now!*

CHAPTER 20
ACCEM

Accem sat at his desk behind the thickened bullet proof glass. He received a call from Hassan, as instructed, and this happened the day after he arrived back from his meeting with his boss. It was a timely call as Accem was getting impatient. As he waited for Hassan, a beep sounded, and the front door latch retracted. In walked Hassan and Saleem and took a seat at the table.

"As-Salaam-Alaikum (peace be upon you)," said Accem in Arabic.

"Wa-Alaikum-Salaam (and unto you peace)," responded Hassan.

"You completed the list within the time limit I requested. Excellent work," said Accem now in English.

"Thank you."

"Pass the list under." Accem touched a button, and the glass raised two inches.

Hassan slid the 8 1/2" x 11" envelope through the gap. *The long-awaited list!* Accem closed the window. Hardly able to contain his excitement, he carefully removed seven sheets of paper from the envelope, read and then re-read each one carefully. It had all the information he had requested in their previous meeting with the correct amounts. He turned his microphone back on.

"You are sure of the accuracy?"

"I am," said Hassan.

"Why?"

"Because a man's life depends on it being correct and he understands that."

"OK. Ensure that all seven agreements contain the information you have provided me with here. When payment is required, call me at this number and I will have the money wired." Accem read out a number.

"I will."

"When we last met, I agreed I would cover the amount you said you needed for you and your men's living expenses monthly. I will arrange a different drop point for future disbursements."

Accem raised the window and slid an envelope filled with cash through the opening and then lowered the window. Hassan stuffed the envelope in his pocket.

"So, next is the operational step using the list. I will manage this part but when can it start?" asked Accem.

"In three months — the end of March," answered Hassan.

"I will count on that."

"OK, anything else?"

"Yes. You and your men need to get jobs as electricians or plumbers. It's the key to your success. It is our plan that you will help build the target you intend to destroy." Accem noticed Saleem's head jerk towards Hassan with a look of confusion. He pressed a button, causing a click that showed the microphone was off. He turned and handed the envelope to the man sitting behind him.

CHAPTER 21
CK / ACCEM

April 2019

The plane carrying the contract killer (CK) arrived on time at Leonardo da Vinci-Fiumicino Airport near Rome. He only had a leather carry-on which he rolled behind him. Standing just under 6'0", he had a lean, muscular build. And though in excellent physical condition, he walked with a slight limp. He was fluent in six languages, including Italian, and had no religious or political leanings.

There was, however, loyalty to the country or organization that hired him. The most profitable contracts typically came from the Middle East. He enjoyed a successful living doing what he did best, killing people. However, to him, taking a life was merely a transaction without pleasure. His enjoyment stemmed from the process—devising an incrimination-proof strategy and reaping financial gains from its successful execution.

He was old-fashioned in the way he accomplished his trade. Disguises, notes, and elaborate schemes were his trademark. His fee for this assignment was $50,000 per kill. His goal for retirement: *100 kills. Current total: 91 kills.*

CK grabbed a taxi to the railway station and purchased a ticket from Rome to Venice, with a stop in Florence. He walked over to Track 5. The peanut smell was strong from the oil used to clean the train's brake shoes. The car he entered was clean and he settled onto a worn but uncracked vinyl-covered bench seat. Only he was in the car. Placing his bag overhead, he settled into his seat. He pulled out the tourist pamphlet he picked up in the station and read about Florence: *Julius Caesar established this city in 59 BC as a settlement for retiring soldiers.* The city contained many beautiful buildings, bridges, and plazas that were shown with pictures and descriptions. He appreciated all historical buildings because of the excellent craftsmanship and careful planning that went into creating these works of art. Like his craft he thought.

Briefly, CK admired the scenic countryside through the window. Standing, he removed a folder from his bag and studied the contents for the next hour until the train coasted into Florence. Getting into a taxi, he handed the driver an address. He sat back and observed the incredible architecture that spanned several eras displaying the extraordinary skills of the master builders of those periods. The taxi sped at a speed CK judged unsafe considering the narrow width of the cobblestone streets and the heavy pedestrian traffic.

After many close misses with cars, scooters, and pedestrians, they finally turned onto Ponte alle Grazie (The Bridge of Grace) that carried them over the Arno River. He had reservations at a boutique hotel located nearby. The taxi stopped at what was formerly a grand residence. He walked through the large wooden door and a woman with a cheery smile greeted him. She located his reservation card and reminded him that payment was due in advance in cash. He pulled out his wallet and paid the full week's rent.

She guided him from the house to a former carriage house in the back. She opened the door to a spacious bedroom.

• • •

Later, CK changed into some running gear and left to locate the apartment building he was seeking. After 15 minutes, he stopped at a corner café that allowed a full view of the apartment building and sat outside. A server greeted him and handed him a menu.

"I would like chocolate gelato."

The server returned quickly with the order and CK ate while watching the building. Around 9:30 at night, a young man swiftly ran past his table. He had dark features and was unmistakably Middle Eastern.

The file that CK had contained information on his prey and was marked #1 on the tab. He had carefully studied the photograph and other info as he always did. *The Arab was slender, 5'6" tall, and 23 years old. His photograph, with his name on it, showed a face with a beard, minus the mustache, a large beak nose and closely cropped hair. The non-physical details, CK required, were also listed. He ran late in the evening, six days a week. Not being able to swim, he was terrified of water because of a near drowning incident at age six. He fled his home county of Egypt after being accused of attempting to force himself sexually on a 15-year-old girl. Video had proven the accusation was true.*

He watched the young man slow to a walk. His hands were above his head as he gulped in big breaths of air. He then turned around, walked 50 yards, turned left, and continued halfway over the Ponte alle Grazie bridge and then stopped. He leaned forward and placed his elbows on the sturdy stone rail and stared down at the river Arno while he cooled off. CK watched him from the end of the bridge. After 15 minutes, the man walked back toward his apartment building. CK walked in the opposite direction and passed within a few feet of him. He looked at him carefully. Indeed, it was #1. CK waited briefly, then jogged back to his room. He showered and lay in bed drifting off to sleep when suddenly, an idea popped into mind. After pondering the idea briefly, he fell asleep content with his strategy.

• • •

The next night CK waited near the same small café across the street. He was wearing a hooded nylon jacket tonight. He had watched #1 leave his apartment at the same time as the previous night and waited.

Number One came running approximately 40 minutes later and performed the same routine as the previous night. He started walking with his hands above his head, breathing in big gulps of air, towards the Ponte alle Grazie bridge. CK expected him to do this for the next five minutes, thus he began walking towards the bridge on the opposite side of the street.

Number One stopped at his regular spot on the bridge, leaned forward and supported his elbows on the stone rail and continued to breathe hard. CK crossed to the same side of the street and headed towards #1, soon passing close to him. There was no traffic crossing the bridge.

As CK passed #1 he twisted 90 degrees, bent down, grabbed #1 by his ankles and physically hoisted him over the stone rail in one quick, fluid motion. As his weight was already leaning forward, #1 continued in a flip as he headed downward. He shrieked out of surprise and desperation. His arms flailed out of control as he was in a free fall. He hit squarely on his back and sank into the watery grasp of the Arno River.

Just as CK resumed casually walking down the other side of the bridge he heard a man yell, "Basti!" (stop) "Basti!" (stop) followed closely by "Polizia!" "Polizia!" Someone on the café side of the bridge must have seen it all happen. CK was surprised. He had seen no one. He started sprinting. Running on some short, curvy streets behind the main road he then circled back to his street. Tossing his hooded jacket in a nearby resident's trash can, he walked calmly back to his room, showered, and lay in bed, savoring the satisfaction of completing his work so quickly and cleanly. *New total: 92 kills!*

• • •

He woke up the next morning and felt completely rested. He placed his belongings in his leather case and went to the main house for breakfast. Morning paper on table, he quickly found what he sought. The police reported pulling the body of a 24-

year-old Arab man from the Arno. Because of an eyewitness account, his death was being investigated as a homicide.

After breakfast, CK approached the woman at the front desk and asked for a taxi to the airport. The taxi arrived, and CK instructed the driver where to drop him off as he was catching a flight to Paris. CK paid and walked inside the terminal building.

He confirmed the taxi's departure, then promptly hailed another one that would take him to the train depot. Upon arrival, he quickly scribbled and mailed a postcard he had picked up earlier. Waiting a few minutes in line, CK purchased a round-trip ticket to Pisa with cash. Taking a seat on a bench, he unzipped the front large pocket of his leather suitcase and pulled out a new manila folder marked #2.

• • •

Reaching its destination, Accem quickly retrieved the postcard from the rest of the advertisements and periodicals. Michelangelo's 'David', a frontal view, was on the postcard. He flipped it over, saw 'Number #1' with the date written beside it. The man shredded the postcard. He drew a line through the name next to #1 on a small pad he kept with him.

CHAPTER 22
TAJ JILANI

Weeks ago, Jack Callahan had phoned Taj and requested his presence in Chicago to complete agreements with both firms. Taj agreed and asked if the U.S. company had been established. The reply was yes. After landing at O'Hare, he told the cab driver to bring him to The Drake Hotel. He was tired from traveling but had agreed to meet Jack for dinner at 7:30. He checked in, unpacked, then rode the elevator to the lobby where Jack waited. They shook hands.

"Hello Taj. Good to see you!"

"Thank you, Jack. It is good to be back."

He was glad to be here and meant it. Enjoying his last visit, he looked forward to assembling the pieces of their grand plan.

They departed the hotel and headed east towards the nearby Rosebud Steakhouse, just a few minutes away. The server seated them at a table near the kitchen. The dining area had a crowded and loud atmosphere. Taj could also intermittently hear and smell meat sizzling on the grill when the door swung open near their table. After ordering food, Taj asked Jack about the meeting schedule for the next few days. Jack suggested staying a week to ensure enough time for negotiations and closing both deals.

Jack pulled out a sheet of paper, put his reading glasses on, and started down the agenda.

"Those are thick glasses, Jack."

Jack laughed, "Yep. They seem to get thicker every year."

"I'm kidding of course. Mine are the same." Taj lightly patted his jacket pocket, pretending that the glasses were housed there, but he felt the outline of the envelope he always had with him.

"Anyway, we have arranged a meeting with Chandler Boyd and probably Gerry Weezler tomorrow at 11:00 a.m. I have arranged a conference room at The Drake for us. Did you have questions about the term sheet I emailed you?"

"No. It was satisfactory. But your email mentioned there is one open item. What is it?"

"I'm not sure. Chandler told me he would like to make one slight change. He assured me though that the deal would get closed," answered Jack.

"What about the other company?"

"I scheduled a meeting in two days to allow ample time for completing B & I."

"Understood."

"There's one thing I'm curious about."

"Yes?"

"Is there any significance with the name of the company I set up for you, Trebor & Rallim, LLC?"

Taj laughed. "Yes, Trebor and Rallim are brothers that have been my best friends since childhood. Both families' poverty led to classmates teasing us, and we had to defend one another."

"Got it, thanks."

"I've been meaning to ask you. If I wanted to find someone's cell number, how would I do it?"

"I have an app on my phone that I pay a small annual fee for. Whose number do you need?"

Taj gave him the name and Jack read the search result out to him. They finished eating and returned to the hotel. Taj went to his room. He breathed deeply and dialed Anniston King, the widow of the man who perished in the same blast as his family members. The phone rang four times before going to her voice mail. He started to say something, hesitated, and ended the call.

A live conversation trumped a random voice message. If he had time this week, he might travel to Flint and introduce himself.

• • •

The next morning, Taj received a call from Jack telling him which conference room he had reserved. Taj told Jack he would meet him there shortly. The conference room had dark paneling, a large mahogany conference table and six cushy, leather swivel chairs. A credenza contained soft drinks, a pot of coffee with steam rising from it, water, glasses, coffee cups, and a bucket of ice. Taj walked into the conference room shortly after Jack. Both wore sport coats and slacks. Jack was at one end of the table, and Taj took a seat next to him. Not long after, Chandler Boyd and Gerry Weezler came through the door. Chandler chose casual attire, while Weezler opted for a stylish seersucker suit, white shirt, cuff links, and solid crimson bow tie.

They all shook hands.

"Gerald, your suit outshines us all," Taj said.

"Thank you," Weezler said as he picked some lint off his coat sleeve.

"Good to see you both," Chandler said, facing Jack and Taj.

After some comfortable small talk Taj suggested they get started and nodded to Jack.

"Please help yourselves to the coffee and drinks behind us. I put each person's name on a coffee cup to avoid any confusion," Jack said with a smile. Chandler laughed loudly, slapping the conference table, and looking at Weezler.

Jack continued, "Let's go through the term sheet point by point and see if there are questions." After Jack finished, he asked, "All good?"

Taj turned to Weezler when he heard him clear his throat.

Chandler raised his hand to silence Weezler. "I've had second thoughts about selling the entire company. To maintain my status as an owner, it's important that I still own a minority portion, as I think it will matter to my employees. My suggestion is that the ownership be 90% you and 10% me. We can adjust the buyout amount," said Chandler.

Taj nodded, to show Chandler he understood why he was concerned. Jack leaned over and whispered something quietly to Taj. Taj nodded his head in agreement.

"Do you mind if Jack and I discuss this a few minutes outside?" asked Taj.

"Not at all," said Chandler.

They returned a couple of minutes later.

"Jack, please tell them what we discussed," said Taj.

"Certainly. We have a counteroffer for you. You keep ten percent ownership, and we reduce our offer proportionally or you keep five percent, and we keep the offer the same," finished Jack.

Taj observed Chandler as he seemed to consider it.

"That's very fair. I appreciate and accept the five percent ownership offer," said Chandler.

"Then that's it—it's settled! I'll make the changes and prepare a formal agreement for your review and signature," said Jack.

Everyone stood, congratulated each other, and shook hands.

• • •

Taj returned to his room after a few hours of celebration with Jack, Chandler, and Weezler.

He punched in a number. The call got answered after one ring.

"Number?"

"32."

"Update?"

"We closed the first deal with the company that provides the radiant heating system."

"Excellent Pakistan. Next company?"

"We meet in a couple of days. When will you wire the six million to Trebor & Rallim's bank account?"

"Tomorrow. Remember, the bank requires my approval on any disbursements."

"I remember."

Accem hung up.

CHAPTER 23
COLTON GRAY

Colton sat at his desk facing his formidable assistant, Colette, who was rapidly reading out loud his schedule for the week. He had spent about twelve weeks in Lyon, France. The older woman across from him seemed to have authority. She served four investigators or vice versa and kept things hopping in their department. From what Colton observed so far, she was pretty darn efficient.

"Cool-taan. Are you listening to me?" asked Colette.

Colton hadn't gotten used to the way she pronounced his name just yet. "Yes, of course I'm listening to you. What did you say?"

"I said Chief Inspector Du'boe wants to meet with you at 10:00."

"I just got here. Am I in trouble already?"

"No Cool-taan, no. Your comment in the meeting caught his interest, and he wants to talk to you about it. This is a big deal. Chief Inspector rarely talks to the investigators. He's an important man, you know."

No, I didn't know. "OK, since he is *important*, I will see him," Colton said, and he winked at Colette.

"Is something in your eye?"

"No, I...I would be happy to discuss my idea with him."

"OK, 10:00." She then took a step forward and slightly leaned over the desk. "And Cool-taan, I've been meaning to tell you something. The girls on 4th floor find you handsome with your white hair, bright blue eyes, and adore your left dimple." She touched her left cheek to demonstrate.

Colton smiled, "Thanks, Colette. I'm not open for business just yet."

She returned the smile, shook her head, and left, closing the door behind her.

After completing the mandatory eight weeks of training, Colton received his first assignment in last week's staff meeting. An influx of cocaine was coming through the southeastern corner of France from Italy. Located sixty miles north of Turin, Moncenisio is a town on the border just before entering France. To investigate the involvement of two countries, the French government submitted the formal request to Interpol. Chief Inspector assigned Colton this recent case, requesting a strategy to investigate drug flow.

Hearing a knock, Colton glanced up and checked his watch: 10:15. Close to 10:00 thought Colton. Probably Chief Inspector Du'boe.

"Come in," Colton said as he leaned back in his chair with his feet on his desk.

Chief Inspector entered through the opened door. "Sit down. Please, sit down", said Du'boe waving his hand in a down motion.

I am sitting down. "Yes sir. Thank you, I think I will."

He was short of stature with a thick, black moustache, enormous nose, and French captain's hat. Inspector Du'boe looked like one of the Mario Brothers video game characters. He sat down.

"Time ran out during our meeting. I am interested in something you said, but not sure I understood. You mentioned you solved a case in New York by checking out new business permits. How did it connect?" asked Inspector Du'boe.

"In our investigation, we studied the human trafficking trade from upstate New York through Canada's border. We discovered the traffickers were also using the women as 'mules' for transporting heroin but we couldn't uncover the method they were using to transport the heroin. So, we reviewed the business licenses new companies applied for over the last twelve months in towns near the border. Out of fifteen permits, thirteen businesses manufactured pottery. We then discovered they were producing double walled ceramic tea pots and hiding the heroin in the space between the layers," finished Colton.

"Ah, I understand now."

"That was how I planned to start my investigation."

"Brilliant, Cool-taan. We are lucky you are here."

CHAPTER 24
CK / #2 / ACCEM

CK boarded the train going to Pisa and stored his carry-on bag overhead. He had never visited Pisa and looked forward to seeing the tower. He skimmed a tourist pamphlet. The pictures showed detailed and beautifully crafted exterior arches and columns. Five years after construction started, the tower started leaning because of poor base soil and an undersized foundation. Strangely, the identity of the Master Architect was unknown.

After the train left the station, he stood up, unzipped the front of his bag, and withdrew his file on #2. *Number Two's physical description: Middle Eastern, 5'7", 285 pounds, 23 years of age, pock-marked face, crooked teeth, wide nose, and long, scraggly sideburns that stopped just short of his mouth.* He pulled out the full-size photo of a young man, with his name written on the back, and confirmed the description.

CK flipped the page over to "Other Details" and found a lot written: *Gambles and drinks heavily. Has an outstanding debt of $40,000. Pressure was being applied to repay the debt.*

The reason #2 was in Pisa to begin with is the Master Architect, that designed the Taj Mahal in India, was a direct ancestor of #2. Sketches discovered in the family vault, believed to date from the 12th century, closely resembled the Tower of Pisa. Number Two was researching the possibility that his ancestor designed the Tower of Pisa.

And last, many of his life decisions, including his history of betting, excessive drinking, and intimate relationship with other men, disappointed his family. CK started planning for this next assignment.

The train pulled into Pisa Centrale rail station at noon. CK returned the file and wheeled his luggage to the street. He quickly entered a taxi and requested the driver to go to Hotel Francesco. CK paid cash for the ride and walked through the hotel's front doors.

Hotel Francesco's location was within a short walking distance of the leaning tower. After checking in and dropping his bag, he left the hotel and walked until the famous tower came into view.

Pausing, he observed a long line of tourists waiting to climb to the top. The ornate, freestanding bell tower, as he read, measured 180 feet in height and had 300 steps. Upon purchasing a ticket, he patiently waited his turn. After about one hour, he entered the door leading to the steps of the tower, noting that one lock and chain solely provided the security for the massive door.

He joined a family of four, comprising parents and two young children. They had a 30-minute window to ascend and descend the tower.

CK asked the dad, "Do you mind if I go ahead of you. I want to run to the top."

The man nodded his head, making way for CK to go ahead.

CK took off running up the stairs. The steps were steep and not consistent heights. When he finally made it to the top, he bent over, sucking in air and rubbing his bad knee. He looked at his watch and saw that he had covered the vertical distance in just over 2 minutes. After five minutes, he strolled back down passing the family he left below.

"Did you make it?" asked the dad.

"Yes, but I must get in shape," CK responded.

After reaching the bottom and exiting, he surveyed the entire area, noting the roads and the lay of the land.

Around 5:00 p.m., he got back to his hotel room and took a shower. He could feel soreness already in his thighs and butt. He laid down for a brief rest and woke nearly thirty minutes later feeling refreshed. After stretching his muscles, he left the hotel.

He had two things to do. First, he wanted to see #2 in person. Second, he needed to observe the leaning tower at midnight.

Out of his hotel, he turned right and walked nearly half a mile to the address listed in #2's file. CK took an outside table at a small café across the street from #2's residence. At 11:00 p.m., a taxi arrived, and a young man clumsily exited. It was #2. He handed over payment to the driver and staggered up the steps to the front door, appearing clearly drunk.

CK left and arrived at the tower just past midnight. Despite the streetlights, there were many dark areas around the tower. One padlock was the sole obstacle to entering after hours, he confirmed once more. Satisfied, he walked back to his hotel, undressed, and climbed into bed. He was content with his plan and fell asleep quickly.

• • •

CK woke the next morning around 6:00. On the floor, he stretched for about 20 minutes to relieve his muscles after sprinting up 300 steps. CK left the hotel and returned to the main street, searching for a hardware store and gift shop. He hadn't gone far when he found a gift shop. He went inside, bought a couple of things, one being a greeting card. After paying cash for the items, he asked the clerk for directions to a hardware store. Two streets over he found the store and purchased a padlock and duct tape. He needed to finish some work before going to #2's office during their lunch break. CK was confident that #2 did not miss many meals.

He went back to his hotel and emptied the items onto the small desk. Opening the card, he wrote in caps:

IF YOU WOULD LIKE TO HAVE YOUR GAMBLING DEBT PAID OFF, MEET ME AT THE LEANING TOWER OF PISA TONIGHT AT 2:00 A.M.

Signed, A BROTHER IN ISLAM.

CK put the note in the envelope and wrote #2's name on the outside. He put the envelope in his pocket, checked the address and office number in #2's file, and walked to #2's office building, arriving a little before noon. After ten minutes, he saw #2 leave. CK went inside the small office block, and a short distance down the hall was lettering on a door that read, 'Architectural + Art Research, RM 107.' He slipped the card through the mail slot in the door and promptly left.

Anticipating that he would complete his assignment that evening, he then walked to the railroad station and made reservations for 7:00 a.m. to Florence. Upon returning to the hotel, he rested briefly.

In the evening, he rose, dressed in dark casual clothes and tennis shoes, packed a small backpack, and left. It was about 1:15 a.m. when he got to the tower. He stood in the cathedral's doorway alcove, next to the tower, ensuring no one was nearby. CK went to the doors of the tower, slid off his backpack, and removed a penlight and some lock picks he always carried with him. Turning on the penlight he held between his teeth, he picked the lock and removed it from the chain. He put the old lock in his backpack to dispose of later and then waited in the shadows inside the entrance hoping #2 had taken the bait. At 1:50 a.m. a taxi's headlights bathed the tower. Number Two stepped out, settled the fare, and lumbered over to the tower entrance. The door was open with the chain hanging from the door. CK flicked the light a few times and #2 walked through the door. CK stepped out of the shadows.

"I'm glad you came," said CK as he walked past #2 and slid the new lock through the two ends of the chain and locked it.

"Who are you?"

"People call me CK," answered CK.

"Did you send the note?"

A knife suddenly materialized in CK's hand. "Not important but this is. I will probably end your life tonight, but I will give you some hope. I will allow you to race me to the top of the tower. If you win, you continue living and have enough money to pay off your debt. If you lose, well—you are still debt free."

Number Two stared at the man and appeared stunned at what he was hearing. He whined, "Look at me. Do I look like I'm in shape?"

"Nope. It's only eight floors. It should take you about four minutes to get to the top," said CK. "I will give you a 3-minute head start. And here is $10,000 to show you I am serious."

He pulled a neat stack of bound bills out of his backpack and handed them over. Number Two began bending at his waist and almost completed a half squat, to loosen up.

"Where is the remaining amount of money?" asked #2.

"In a backpack at the last stair landing," answered CK.

Number Two's face showed slight excitement, seeing a way to escape debt. With the belief that he could accomplish anything in four minutes, this challenge seemed attainable to him.

Thunder rumbled in the background as it sounded like a storm was imminent. Number Two followed him to the start of the stairs. CK pulled a small miner's headlamp from his backpack and handed it to him.

"Whenever you're ready."

• • •

Number Two squeezed his enormous head into the elastic strap, clicked the lamp, and took off. He moved with surprising quickness for a man his size. He started up to the first floor. The headlamp cast an erratic beam that created menacing shadows as his heavy footsteps pounded the stone treads. He made it up the first flight of steps and headed toward the second floor. As he reached the second floor, he felt his feet grow heavy. Where he had been almost jogging, he had now slowed to a fast walk. He started up to the third floor and his breathing was raspy; he found it harder to get enough air, but he had to keep going. Pushing past the third floor, he was doing everything he could just to move his feet. He was having a tough time breathing but made it to the fourth floor. His muscles were screaming for relief, but he kept moving, one step after the next. At the fifth level, he stopped just for a few seconds to catch his breath.

A voice echoed in the stairwell.

"Here I come."

He heard shoes pounding against the steps below. Redoubling his efforts, he started toward the sixth floor. His lungs were like over-inflated balloons ready to pop. His whole body ached, but he was determined to win. He got to the sixth floor. The footsteps below were getting louder. He could not stop now. He willed himself to keep going but he could barely lift one leg ahead of the other. Somehow, he kept moving and made it to the seventh floor. Now he was light-headed, his vision blurred. The footsteps were closer. He heard the man announce that he was passing the sixth floor. His legs wouldn't move. He began crawling, determined not to give up. The man below announced he was at the seventh floor. How did he get that close so quickly #2 wondered?

He kept crawling. Two more steps. Footsteps sounded right behind him! Number Two, despite his condition, did something extraordinary. He dove—like a belly flop into a pool, onto the stair landing. A loud whoosh burst from his lungs through his mouth. *He made it! He won!* But he could not lift his head and find the backpack of money. He couldn't breathe. He couldn't move. What was happening? The floor seemed to move up and crush him. His chest hurt so much. His heart was pounding out of control. Stars flickered in his eyes. Everything went black.

•   •   •

From a few steps away, CK watched. His plan had worked, causing enough stress and panic that #2's body just couldn't take it. Had he not died of a heart attack, CK's backup plan was to stuff a sock in his mouth and wrap duct tape around his head to secure it as he would be completely exhausted.

He grabbed the headlamp and the $10,000 that #2 still held. CK used the headlamp in his right hand to search the man's pockets and locate the note he wrote. Satisfied, he jogged down the stairs.

He unlocked and relocked the padlock and started walking back to his hotel. His fingerprints were surgically altered many years ago, so he wasn't worried about leaving a clue. The clouds opened and drenching rain poured over him. By the time CK reached his room, the rain had completely soaked him. He stripped off his wet clothes and took a nice, warm shower. Content, he was asleep in minutes. *Kill count: 93.*

•   •   •

Awaking early the next morning to catch his 7:00 a.m. train, he checked out, paid in cash, and got a taxi. They couldn't find the body of #2 immediately as removing the new lock will take some time.

He reached the train station a few minutes afterwards and retrieved a small package. He put plenty of postage on it and dropped it in the mailbox. At 6:50, he waited on a bench near the tracks and used the remaining 10 minutes. He unzipped the front of his luggage and pulled out a file labeled…#3.

•   •   •

Four days later the small parcel arrived. Accem opened the package and pulled out a 3-inch-tall ceramic Leaning Tower of Pisa. On the bottom of the base were words #2 and the date, written in black ink. He took the ceramic statue to his workshop, picked up a hammer and smashed the replica into many pieces. He then swept the pieces into a wastebasket. He opened a small note pad and struck #2's name.

CHAPTER 25
TAJ JILANI

Taj met Jack in the Drake lobby just before their 2:00 p.m. meeting in the same conference room.

"Alex Roegge just called with some troubling news. They've decided not to sell their business. Instead, they have an alternative they hope will be appealing," Jack said.

"Did he say what it is?" asked Taj.

"No."

They headed up to the conference room where the Roegge brothers were waiting. They shook hands and took a seat.

Jack started the meeting and faced Alex. "You mentioned on the phone an idea you had to work together?"

"Yes, we have developed some innovative technology with solar and shading technology but don't have the funds to build a research and development laboratory to further refine it. Would you consider loaning us the funds to accomplish this? In return, we would share all our results with you and work out a licensing agreement for you to use for your own purposes."

A few seconds of silence hung in the room.

"How much will it cost to build the research facility?" asked Taj.

"Two million and eleven months to build," Ryan said.

Taj requested a few minutes to discuss their request. The Roegges left the room.

"I like the idea of a new research facility," said Taj.

"Why," asked Jack.

"Because I believe solar is the future. What kind of deal would be attractive if, with my background in electrical engineering, I could help with the development of solar and shading."

"Maybe give them a loan interest free. Pay back occurs after the new technology is producing revenue."

"That's a great idea. And we split the profits 50/50?"

"Yep, sounds good. Would you get paid?"

"No, that's part of the deal."

"Sounds fair to me. Let's see what they say."

Jack went out and asked them to return. They sat back down.

Taj said, "I would like to propose that I loan you the $2 million, interest free, to build your research facility. I think you remember I have a PhD in electrical engineering. I will work with your engineers, at no cost to you. In return, we split 50/50 any profits made from any solar and shading technology from now on. Once profits are being made, we will develop a debt retirement schedule."

This time, the Roegges excused themselves. They came back a few moments later.

"We like it, and we accept. So, will you work in our office until we complete the research facility?" Alex asked.

"Yes," answered Taj.

"Excellent," Jack said. "I will draw up an agreement covering everything and send it to your attorney this evening."

They shook hands, and the meeting adjourned.

• • •

Later that afternoon Taj called Accem.

"Number?"

"32."

"Update?"

"The second deal is closed. I will send you the details once we sign the agreement."

"Good, Pakistan. Excellent work!" The line went dead.

Taj put his phone in his pants pocket. The pieces were falling into place.

CHAPTER 26
CK / #3 / ACCEM

Arriving at the train station early, he heard the constant squealing of brakes and a banging noise from train cars being coupled and de-coupled to prepare for a new day of travel. CK boarded the 7:00 a.m. train heading back to Florence, where he would change trains for Venice. Hoisting his luggage in the storage area above his seat, he sat back for the short ride from Pisa to Florence.

The clickety clacking rhythm of the wheels on the track was relaxing. He closed his eyes and dozed. When the train arrived in Florence, he glanced at his watch and noted that it was nearly opening time for the Tower of Pisa. Number Two was the smoothest kill of his career.

After retrieving the file on #3 from the front pocket of his carry-on, he boarded the train to Venice. *The description showed a 23-year-old man, 5'11", 165 pounds, with a slightly rectangular clean-shaven face and black hair. He had dark, brown eyes, a narrow nose, medium lips and white, even teeth. All physical attributes added up to a handsome young man.* The photo of #3, with his name written on the back, confirmed the description.

In the "Other Details" section he read that the man's father was *extraordinarily wealthy and an Islamic fanatic. He funded non-profits accused of providing capital to terrorist groups. He had encouraged his son to take an interest in the cause, but he was indifferent to it all. Number three's description included being an excellent student with the gift of a photographic memory. He did not practice Islam and angered his father when he admitted he had developed a keen interest in Christianity.*

He had refused to attend an Islamic university in the Middle East. Finally, his parents allowed him to attend a private university in Munich. He pursued a mechanical engineering degree and would graduate in a few months. He had become friends with several students, also with wealthy backgrounds, from different European countries. His closest friend was from Rome and was to be married in Venice during their two-week spring break that started yesterday. Number Three was arriving a few days early. He had been tasked to organize and host a pre-wedding reception, on behalf of the groom's family, for 60 guests and family members. They all were staying at the same hotel which had a ballroom large enough to accommodate 100 people.

As was his pattern, CK opened a tourist information book he purchased in the train station. The summary paragraph on the first page read: *Romans fleeing from barbarians built the city of Venice in the heart of a lagoon in northeastern Italy bordering the Adriatic Sea. Roughly 117 islands compose it, connected by over 400 bridges spanning over 150 canals.* He did not know Venice was mainly small islands joined together. In the table of contents, he found: 'The Mysterious Curse of Palazzo (Palace) Dario' on page 32. He flipped to that page and read that Palazzo Dario, which was built in 1487, faces the Grand Canal. *According to history, anyone who owned this famous palace, as well as their relatives, experienced personal ruin, murder, or suicide. This pattern started with the members of the original family. Euro Investments, S.R.L. now owns the palace and regularly rents it for extravagant parties and balls.* On the page's bottom half, there was a picture of the palace and the leasing company's number for Palazzo Dario. He toyed with an idea for the rest of the way to Venice.

As they arrived in Venice, CK returned the file to the zipper pocket in his carry-on. Grabbing his carry-on, he walked out of the train station and down a series of steps to a wide walkway by the water. Boarding a water taxi, he instructed the driver to head towards Giudecca Island, the largest island in the lagoon.

Just like #3 and most of the wedding guests, he had successfully made reservations at the upscale Hilton Molino Stucky.

Once the boat left the pier, he sat back. A DHL delivery boat passed them followed by an ambulance vessel with its siren blaring. Coming from the opposite direction was a police boat cruising along. His boat pulled up to the pier outside the Hilton. CK jumped off and rolled his bag into the grand lobby. He checked in and asked if a friend of his (#3), had arrived. The receptionist looked at her computer screen. Not yet. Taking his key card, he went to his room, on the sixth floor. Sitting at the small desk he started making some calls. He'd landed on a strategy but needed more information.

His first call was to the real estate company named in the tourist guidebook that manages the Palazzo Dario.

"Venice Properties Limited. This is Claudio, how may I be of assistance?"

"I am a friend of the groom's family for a wedding this Saturday but would like to remain anonymous. I would like information on leasing the Palazzo Dario for one night for a large party of 60 guests."

"Our most popular choice is a masquerade ball. We can provide the traditional masks and costumes and musicians for this event for up to 75 guests. Each guest will receive entrance tokens, like an invitation, to enter the party. We also need addresses for all guests, so we can deliver the costumes. We then retrieve the costume the next day. To lease the Dario, cater, provide staff to manage the event, deliver and pick up costumes, and provide an orchestra is $25,000 per night. We need 24 hours advance notice."

"Thank you."

CK sat silently for a moment as he digested the information. It was most helpful finding out about the 'entrance token'.

He called Venice Properties back and told Claudio he would like to reserve the Palazzo Dario with their masquerade ball package.

"How would you like to pay?" asked Claudio

"I will wire the money," said CK.

Claudio gave him the wiring instructions. CK was confident the alias he had for his bank account would not allow an investigation to lead back to him. CK then gave him the name of a young man who would call and manage all the details.

He then sat down and scribbled a note to #3 to leave at the front desk. It told him a masquerade ball at Palazzo Dario had been arranged for the pre-wedding reception. It gave Claudio's name and number at Venice Properties for him to call for details. He signed it 'Friends of the Groom'.

He walked down to the pier and caught a water taxi to Piazza San Marco. After a quick ride across the water, he retrieved a map of the city and walked around for several hours.

After he'd familiarized himself with the layout, he walked back to Piazza San Marco, caught another water taxi, and returned to his hotel. Many people stood in line at the front desk, perhaps friends and family of the couple getting married. He took the elevator up to his floor and went to bed.

• • •

The next morning, he took the water taxi back to Piazzo San Marco to buy his own authentic mask and costume. Winding his way down the narrow cobblestoned streets he had asked for directions twice before finding the shop. The shop had costumes and masks of all different colors, styles, and sizes. He ended up buying a traditional Venetian, burgundy-colored costume with a pasty, white mask. The shopkeeper assured him that his costume was commonplace. He paid for the costume and left.

CK dialed the number for Venice Properties Limited.

"This is Claudio."

CK reminded Claudio they had talked yesterday and confirmed Venice Properties had received the money he wired. He then asked, "Could you leave a couple of extra tokens outside your front door in an envelope just in case someone loses theirs? I'll be by later to pick them up."

"Certainly. I'll place them under the flowerpot by the door myself," Claudio said.

CK was relieved he had easily solved his entry problem to the party. Now he needed to find a hardware store. After about an hour of asking directions and taking some wrong turns, he found it. It was 8:00 p.m. when he arrived at Venice Properties and found the two tokens Claudio promised. He pocketed the tokens and walked to Piazzo San Marco to catch the water taxi to his hotel. In his room, he laid everything out—one costume and mask, two metal party tokens with the date imprinted on them, some electrical devices, filament tape, a screwdriver, a 6-pound hammer and a jump rope.

• • •

In the morning, he put the screwdriver and electrical devices in his backpack and headed to Piazzo San Marco. Using his map this time, he could find Dario without getting lost. CK walked around the building and found that the main power panel was within easy reach and hidden from public view. With his screwdriver, he removed the panel's face and swiftly attached a device from his backpack to the main breaker switch. He screwed the face plate back on the panel box. With remote control operation, the device will turn off all lights by pushing the main breaker switch to the off position. That is when he will take care of #3. Satisfied, he left and checked out several cafes near Dario until finding one that would serve his needs.

Around 7:00 that night, he returned to the hotel and began modifying the jump rope. After removing the wooden handles, he cut the rope down to a 30-inch piece, then tied each end to the handle and wrapped the knot with filament tape. The finished product was a garrote. He pulled on both handles several times to be sure the connection would hold. Satisfied, he rolled it up, placed it in his backpack, and went to bed.

• • •

The next day, in the late afternoon, it was time to prepare for the 7:00 p.m. ball. He packed his costume, mask, two tokens, hammer, screwdriver, remote control device, filament tape and garrote in his backpack. Then he donned his newly purchased red baseball cap with Venice on the front and sunglasses and caught a water taxi over to Piazza San Marco. After a forty-five-minute walk to the café he had chosen the previous day, the hostess showed him to a table. It was now 6 p.m. Not long after, he gave his order to the server.

At 6:35, he signaled for the bill, paid it, and then made his way back to the toilet. After changing quickly into his costume and mask, he placed the garrote inside his coat pocket. He opened the small window and dropped his backpack, now containing his clothes, cap, sunglasses, and other items, into the small alley. He closed the window and walked out of the café, noticing that many patrons were smiling at his costume. Now headed toward Dario, a gigantic clock showed it was 7:05, which would put his arrival no later than 7:15. Perfect.

He walked through the courtyard and spotted many guests in costumes waiting in line to greet the bride and groom, who had not yet dressed up. An usher from Venice Properties stood

20 feet away, checking tokens at the door. CK patted his pocket to be sure he had both tokens. He pulled one out and handed it to the attendant and kept moving. An orchestra was playing lively music on the second floor. Intrigued by old craftsmanship, CK explored the rest of the house. Food aroma drifted from several tables in a spacious room. The flooring was colorful, patterned tile. In one corner a bartender was busy serving drinks. Climbing the grand marble staircase, CK reached what appeared to be the ballroom. Up on the third floor, he discovered mainly sitting rooms. The fourth-floor housed bedrooms. Intricate crown and base moldings framed every room. The fourteen-foot-high ceilings made it feel grand. In admiration, he stood gazing.

Hoping someone could identify #3, he returned to the first floor and waited by the bar briefly. He asked a man dressed in a ghoulish-looking costume standing next to him.

"Who arranged this grand party?"

"The young man standing over there in the corner talking with the event company attendant," answered the voice behind the mask as he quickly pointed toward the corner.

"Oh, I see."

The costume #3 wore was amusing, comprising a mask with a long beak measuring at least nine inches, a red frock coat, and black pants. CK walked by and #3 was deep in conversation with someone from Venice Properties as the stitching on their shirt confirmed. CK confirmed #3's identity from physical details not covered by the mask.

Guests continued to arrive, and the ground floor filled rapidly. The orchestra stopped at 7:45. CK heard voices upstairs, calling everyone to the ground floor for a quick welcome and evening introduction.

After the guests came down, #3 stood on the portable bar and got everyone's attention with a mobile microphone unit. He introduced himself and began talking about the evening.

"Thank you for being here this evening. Our intention was for the groom and bride's friends and family to mingle before the wedding. Friends of the groom's family had a great idea for a costume ball at a famous, potentially cursed palace."

Oohs and aahs came from the crowd.

"But, please have a great time tonight and remember — your very presence honors Michael and Sophia."

The guests cheered and clapped.

Number Three continued, "Before this party really gets started, I'd like to make a toast to Michael and Sophia."

Everyone raised their glasses.

"Congratulations and may your marriage be for eternity, Salute!"

He lifted his glass slightly higher, and everyone echoed, "Salute!"

• • •

Music resumed on the second floor, prompting guests to disperse to both floors. Wandering up to the second floor, #3 felt like everything was going as scheduled. He stood around the ballroom listening to the music as the orchestra played hits from the 1970s, 1980s, 1990s and beyond. The orchestra was excellent.

Suddenly two arms wrapped around him from behind. A head pressed sideways against his back. Then, a quiet female voice spoke in his ear.

"I would like a slow dance. I can hardly wait until Saturday," Sophia whispered as she lightly kissed his neck.

"Sophia, tell Michael, not me," said #3.

Sophia let go quickly and stammered, seeming to be very embarrassed. She laughed while apologizing, laughed some more and apologized again.

"You two are wearing similar costumes. I thought you were Michael!"

"I'll keep this to myself for as long as I can, but it is my duty to alert him you were hitting on me," #3 joked.

She hugged him again and told him what a splendid party it was, promising to talk with him later. Now, she had to go find Michael.

• • •

CK climbed the steps to the second floor where most of the 20 to 40 aged crowd was hanging out. He spotted #3 near the orchestra with a drink in his hand talking with several costumed women. They appeared to be having a grand time, but that was going to end soon. He gradually made his way over to within about four feet of #3 and pretended to be watching the crowd on the dance floor. They lowered the lights as soon as the orchestra hit their stride. CK felt a tap on his shoulder. He turned around and a woman wearing a pale, white papier mâché mask asked him to dance. He politely declined and said he was too old. She laughed and went on her way. CK turned around, but #3 was gone. Glancing around, he noticed #3 had moved to a corner, talking to a young woman. He moved within a few feet of #3.

He slowly positioned himself closer to #3. With a press of the remote, CK turned off the lights. Grabbing the garrote from inside his coat, he moved to the corner where #3 was. Light from the streetlamps shining through the windows enabled CK to spot that ridiculous long, beaked mask. The beak posed a challenge for wrapping the garrote as desired, leading CK to opt for a direct method. He raised the garrote over his victim's head like a jump rope, looped it around the victim's neck, crisscrossed the handles, and pulled them in opposite directions with all his strength. He crushed the trachea immediately. Then he turned around and pulled #3 onto his back, snapping his neck. He laid the body on the floor and hurried toward the stairs.

Guests were getting impatient and started turning on their cell phone lights while others yelled to turn on the lights. Finding the stairs, CK quickly descended, shouting that he would go outside and check the main electrical panel.

Swiftly, he left the property, passed through the square, and followed the street to the alley with his clothes. He found the bag and changed. In the distance, police and ambulance sirens wailed. CK put his costume and weapon into the backpack and walked casually to an unlit segment of the water's edge near Piazza San Marco. He scanned the surroundings. Finding no one, he let the backpack sink into the water. The weight of the 6-pound hammer would take it to the bottom. He caught a water taxi back to the hotel. After arriving at his room, he showered and promptly drifted off to sleep.

• • •

His cell phone alarm rang precisely at 7:00 a.m. After dressing and pulling his red cap down just above his eyes, CK headed toward the elevator. The doors opened right away. He pressed "L" for the lobby and the car slowly dropped but then stopped at the second floor.

The doors opened and in walked #3. Stunned, CK's eyes opened wide. Number Three glanced at his face and stepped aside. Regaining his composure as the elevator doors closed, CK stole quick glances at his face and noted the swelling around the eyes from lack of sleep and tears. *Unbelievable—he had killed the wrong person!*

When the doors opened, they both left. CK walked a few steps behind him until they arrived at the desk. After checking out, he waited at the pier for the water taxi that would carry him back to Piazza San Marco. On the way to catch his train, he stopped and bought a key chain with a medallion of a gondolier rowing along a canal. After ripping the medallion from the chain, he put both pieces in an envelope, addressed and stamped it. He found a mailbox and dropped the envelope in.

He looked for a newspaper to find out whom he had killed. After paying, he found a vacant bench. The front-page headline read: 'Curse of Dario Lives On', accompanied by a picture of the groom who, according to the article, had been murdered the previous night at his own wedding party. CK shook his head.

Unable to shake off his failure immediately, he pondered a side trip to Munich, where #3 lived. However, he needed to reach his next target. He reached into the compartment of his luggage and extracted a file marked #4 while thinking: *Kill total: still 93!*

• • •

Days later, Accem received an envelope by mail. When he opened the envelope and saw the key chain broken, he cursed out loud. Failure! Most unusual. He tossed the broken key chain parts in separate waste baskets and left the room. He put his notepad back in his pocket.

CHAPTER 27
TAJ JILANI

The next morning Taj decided he would go to Grand Rapids and get some information on housing, since he would move there to work with Roegge & Roegge. The agreements were done, so he had a free day. From there he would travel to Flint and attempt to meet Anniston King.

He asked the concierge for help with transportation. The concierge said he would take care of it. Soon after, the phone rang in the room. The concierge said transportation will arrive in 30 minutes at The Drake's entrance.

When Taj walked out, he was surprised to see a Checker Cab with mag wheels and a red stripe down the middle. The driver rolled the passenger side window down and asked if he was the client going to Michigan. *Yes, and I have some questions for you.* Taj nodded and hopped in the back. The driver, Bob Collins, introduced himself and inquired about Taj's desired location.

"Grand Rapids first, then Flint," Taj said.

"It is $1000 for the day plus meals plus tip," said Bob.

"OK. Did someone tell you to pick me up today?"

"You specifically? No. I hold the first position for limo service on trips exceeding two hours from downtown Chicago. I live close by, am retired, and a day trip pays good money."

"Do you remember me?"

"No. Should I?"

"You followed me to Traverse City several months ago."

"Oh yeah, I remember. I didn't know it was you I was following. I was instructed to tail a black Tahoe."

"Why?"

"Captain, I don't know why. Kind of weird fellow. He talked little. I did what he asked, and he paid me double rate."

"What did he look like?"

"He wore a baseball cap, wraparound sunglasses, even at night, and had a bushy, black beard. He may have been Hispanic or Asian but had no accent. I thought he was from the area."

"He never explained why you followed the Tahoe?"

"Nope. I stopped trying to make conversation or asking questions. He never responded. Only told me what to do. He was intimidating."

• • •

Three hours later they arrived in Grand Rapids. They stopped at the Chamber of Commerce in Grand Rapids for housing information. Taj returned shortly with a large folder and said to Bob, "Let's head to Flint."

• • •

A couple hours later, they arrived in Flint. Taj told Bob he was looking for an employee that worked at the hospital named 'Flint General'. They stopped for a late lunch. After they finished eating, they drove to the medical facility.

Taj walked up to the front entrance of a yellow brick building with the name 'Flint General' in big, silver, aluminum letters above. He continued through the automatic doors. He asked at the front desk for Anniston King. The receptionist said she would ring the floor desk where Ms. King worked. She talked briefly and turned to Taj.

"She is off today but back tomorrow."

"If I leave a note, would you make sure she gets it?"

"Yes, I'd be happy to."

Taj borrowed a piece of paper and wrote a note. He handed it to the receptionist and thanked her. He climbed back in the Checker and returned to Chicago. *Bad timing again!*

CHAPTER 28
CK / ACCEM

CK studied the file containing #4. *The young man was described as an Arab, 24 years of age, 5'11", slight but muscular build at 175 pounds. He had a narrow face with short, straight, black hair.* CK examined the photo, with his name on the back, briefly before placing it back in the file. He read the remaining part of the brief which showed *#4 also spoke Latin and Italian. Number Four began vigorous martial arts training at age seven and was an expert. He took part in the illicit pornography industry, acting in videos and selling the films he starred in. This angered, frustrated and disappointed his parents.*

His sole purpose for being in Rome, however, was to locate and destroy a document, known as **Secreta Edictum** *(Secret Manifesto) that proved the Vatican helped to create Islam. Credited for the founding of Islam, Muhammed signed the document along with the Pope. Secreta Edictum's content was unknown to #4, and only a select few within Islam were aware of its existence. Publicizing this document could spell disaster for Islam, contradicting its recorded creation in the Koran.* The brief did not say who hired him.

The train pulled into Rome station. He returned the file and stepped out of the car. The station, crowded and smelling of garbage, greeted him. The waste cans overflowed, and trash was strewn about. Entering a taxi, he provided the driver with the address of a Bed-and-Breakfast in a monastery near the Coliseum. Number Four lived in an apartment nearby.

They rode past the Coliseum and a couple of blocks later pulled up to a huge stone monastery. CK paid the driver in cash and walked up stone steps to the front iron gate and pressed the intercom button. Moments later, someone let him in. A priest led him through winding staircases and narrow halls to a room at the end of a hallway. The door swung open and revealed a twin bed, a bathroom, and a window. The room was clean and sufficient for his brief stay.

With his bag stowed beneath the bed, he set off to scout the area. Walking along a wide boulevard, he arrived at the famous Coliseum. Tourists crowded the surrounding plaza and gelato booths were everywhere.

Continuing, a little while later he came to the address listed for #4. It was a simple building with six apartments. He walked past and came upon a specialty coffee café and stopped for coffee and a pastry. He opened his tourist guide. One attraction he always wanted to visit, immediately caught his eye: the Sistine Chapel. What he read next heightened its appeal. *Michelangelo painted the chapel's ceiling and front altar wall. Over time, the ceiling aged and became grimy. It was finally cleaned years back and one small patch was left untouched to show tourists the contrast between the newly scrubbed plaster and the old.* This gave CK an idea. He called, made reservations for a tour, and returned to his clean room at the monastery.

• • •

Early the next morning, he took a cab to the Vatican. He walked to the tour meeting spot and the tour guide asked for his name. CK gave him the fake name he had used for the reservation and joined the five other guests that were standing together in a group.

"Welcome. Our company is the oldest and most experienced for Vatican tours. With our preferential tickets, we can skip to the front of any line. Everyone is here now so we can begin the tour," announced the tour guide.

They visited the main museum first, stayed there for over an hour and then entered the Sistine Chapel. The Chapel was so crowded it was difficult to move around. However, that didn't seem too bothersome once you saw the walls and ceilings. The colors were bright and vibrant and the artwork details extraordinary.

The tour guide mentioned what he had read: *"They restored and cleaned the paintings on the ceilings and walls in the 1990s, leaving a small 12" by 12" area on the wall unrestored to show the contrast from unclean to clean."*

CK left before the tour ended. CK headed back to the monastery and found himself amazed at the Roman relics he passed that were everywhere. Not noted for any significance, they were public structures still standing and showed the ingenuity of the builders of that time. *Fascinating.*

• • •

Almost an hour later, he sat down at his small desk and composed a note for #4:

MEET ME AT THE COLISEUM TONIGHT AT MIDNIGHT. MEET INSIDE THE 4TH ENTRANCE ON THE SOUTH SIDE FOR INFORMATION ON SECRETA EDICTUM.

A FRIEND

Folding it carefully, CK delivered the note to #4's apartment block. Arriving, he walked up the steps and placed the envelope through the mail slot and left. CK scouted around the coliseum studying the layout carefully. He stopped at a nearby restaurant and had dinner. After eating he left and went to his room, showered, and set his alarm for 10:00 p.m. and took a nap.

• • •

He awakened before the alarm went off. Dressed in all black, he walked outside and down the street toward the Coliseum. He found a spot to watch people coming and going at the Coliseum's south side. Not waiting long, he observed #4 heading toward the meeting spot CK put in his note. Number Four had his back to him when CK walked through the archway entrance.

"Who are you?" asked #4.

"Friends call me CK," answered CK.

"How did you know of my purpose in Rome?" asked #4.

CK looked around to be sure no one had entered behind him.

"That's unimportant," answered CK.

"Where do you think the document is?" asked #4.

"Secreta Edictum is in the Sistine Chapel. The altar wall has thicker plaster than the ceiling. After placing the document between two pieces of glass, they sealed the edges and Michelangelo worked it into the wall. The agreement is hidden in an unrestored wall patch. The Vatican cleverly explained that it was important for the public to see the contrast between the unrestored and restored artwork," lied the CK.

"That is not where it is," sneered #4. "It is stored in a vault under St. Peter's Basilica."

"Your information is wrong."

"What is your interest in this document?" asked #4.

"I have no interest in the document. Your death does interest me though."

Number Four seemed momentarily surprised.

He suddenly attacked. He took several running steps and leaped executing a jump front kick. As #4 was in the air, CK quickly sidestepped and brought his arm out straight and connected with #4's throat. It put #4 on his back immediately.

Surprisingly, from his position flat on his back, #4 raised his legs, pushed with his arms and he was suddenly on his feet. CK watched as he circled bouncing on the balls of his feet. Getting in a defensive position, CK wanted to end this quickly and silently. Number Four executed a series of kicks…front kick, side kick, and then jumped to get more distance using a turnaround back kick. CK shifted his strategy, moving sideways instead of backing up for the last kick. He brought his elbow down squarely on the side of #4's thigh as his leg was extended out horizontally.

Number Four did not fall but was now limping. His face appeared contorted with anger. He screamed, "You die!"

Reaching behind his neck, he withdrew a knife. Approaching CK, he dove at him with his arm raised and screaming at the same time. Having practiced this defensive move so many times, CK side stepped again, and with both hands grabbed his wrist holding the knife and followed him to the ground. He rolled #4 over and slowly forced the knife directly into his heart. CK pushed hard on #4's hand as #4's eyes closed. Dead.

CK looked around and confirmed they were alone. He left the knife in the body. Not long after, he arrived back at the monastery. The shower was amazing, and he felt invigorated from the combat. *Kill count: 94.*

• • •

When the alarm clock woke him at 6:30 a.m., he showered and paid cash for the room he had occupied over the last few days. The young priest called for a taxi. CK instructed the driver to go to the airport. After arriving, he went to the British Airways counter and bought a round-trip ticket knowing he was only going to use the leg from Rome to London.

He stopped at a kiosk and picked up a small ceramic medallion with a painted coliseum on its surface. He placed it in a small box, addressed it and deposited it in the mailbox with plenty of postage. As he waited for his flight, he opened the front zipper pocket on his luggage and looked inside. Three files remained — #5 London (*kill-95*), #6 Paris (*kill-96*) and #7 Madrid (*kill-97*).

• • •

• • •

A package arrived at the address that was on the label. Accem took it into his workshop and opened it. It was a ceramic replica of the Coliseum in Rome. Turning it over, he saw in black ink #4 written and the date. Nodding, he took a hammer out and smashed it into tiny pieces, swept them up and then disposed of them. Taking out his notepad, he crossed through #4.

CHAPTER 29
TAJ JILANI

Taj met Jack for breakfast at the Drake. While they were waiting for their food, Jack had Taj sign three original agreements for each of the deals he made with the Roegges and Chandler Boyd. He signed all six, kept two and returned four to Jack. He then pulled a slim, long wallet from his inside coat pocket. The yellowish, unopened envelope was stuck to his wallet as he pulled it out. It fell beside Jack.

"I got it," said Jack as he leaned over, grabbed it, and handed it back to Taj.

"Thanks, I would not know what to do if I lost it," said Taj as he put it back in his breast pocket.

"Looks old. I bet there is a good story behind it."

"Yes, to both statements." *Not a story I'm sharing though.* "These are the two checks for each company."

"Each will receive a contract and a check via overnight mail."

"Thank you, Jack. You did a magnificent job managing all this."

They finished breakfast and said their goodbyes. He wondered if Anniston King had gotten his note. He went outside and hopped inside a cab. "O'Hare," he told the driver.

• • •

At the airport, Taj dialed Accem.

Accem answered, "Number?"

"32."

"Update?"

"Both deals are done."

"Good." Accem hung up.

CHAPTER 30
COLTON GRAY

December 2019

Colton sank down in the soft, leather chair at the desk in his boutique hotel room. The construction of the hotel in 1820 included the use of rubble stone and timber structural elements. The room smelled industrial because of recent oiling of the wood beams, but it was clean and modern after being renovated a few years ago. For his 6'5" frame, the full-size bed wasn't big enough, but the soft mattress made up for the dimensional limitation. He was in Moncenisio and aimed to expose the drug trafficking into France. He hoped to find out tonight.

After many calls and on-line research help from Anna Monet, in Interpol's research department, Colton discovered seventeen companies got new licenses last year in the thirty-mile radius south of the French border. Eleven were related to the manufacture of candles. He pulled up the summary worksheet on his computer and checked one more item. After making an alteration, he hit the 'print' button for a copy and was now prepared for his meeting with his law enforcement partners in a few hours.

• • •

Colton sat in the backseat of an unmarked sedan with two Guardia di Finanza police officers. It was cold outside but inside was getting stuffy from the car heater on high. Of the eleven businesses, this building was the largest. It had a metal warehouse attached to the stone office building. The small factory was dark at 1:00 a.m., except for light leaking through the front office glass from the back of the warehouse. For now, this was the only building that Guardia di Finanza petitioned the court to allow them to enter and search due to observing vans and trucks, from the other ten locations, making deliveries here.

"You guys ready to roll?" asked Colton.

"Yes," Luca Rossi replied, cutting off the engine.

"Go to the side with the loading dock. There is probably a man door beside the big garage doors," said Marco Romano seated in the front passenger side.

They left and quickly found the personnel door at the loading dock. Colton watched as Marco removed a pick set from his coat pocket and went to work on the lock. He had it open in less than fifteen seconds.

"That was fast," said Colton.

"I wasn't always in law enforcement," replied Marco.

Luca laughed. Quietly, they entered the room, carefully closing the door. The overpowering aroma of different scented waxes made it hard to breathe. Each had flashlights and switched them on. Colton scanned the wall and zoomed in on an alarm panel with a small, rapid flashing red light.

"We tripped a silent alarm. We got to move!" said Colton.

Marco and Luca looked back and nodded their heads.

"Over here. Everyone takes a different candle," said Marco.

Colton and Luca ran to different tables. Their rubber-soled shoes made a squeaking noise on the polished concrete floor. Each picked up a round, scented candle. They ran to the man door, went and out and sprinted back to their car. They drove for a few seconds and Colton noticed Luca checking the rearview mirror. "Two black SUVs just pulled into the lot. Maybe their security," said Luca.

"Got away, just in the nick of time," said Colton.

Luca and Marco glanced at each other. "The *'nicky'* what?" asked Marco.

Colton laughed, "Means we just barely got away."

"Ah, yes, we did. Let's get back to your hotel and check these candles out."

• • •

Thirty minutes later they arrived at Colton's room. They each put their scented candle on the table.

"This is brilliant. Dogs can't smell cocaine because of the fragrance," said Marco.

"Who's first?" asked Colton.

"Me," said Luca. He opened his knife and cut all the way through the candle in one-inch increments starting at the wick end of the six-inch candle. Five slices later, solid pieces rolled apart. No cocaine. Luca handed his knife to Colton.

Colton repeated the procedure he watched Luca perform. No round circle inside of the slice and no cocaine. "Two down," said Colton as he handed the knife to Marco.

"I will start in the middle for good luck." He pushed down hard, and the knife stopped after it penetrated one-half inch. Marco pushed harder but it would not go further. He circled the candle with the blade and pulled the candle apart. There, in the middle, was a two-inch diameter by four-inch-long glass cylinder filled with white powder.

"We got'em!" yelled Luca. Fist bumps went all around.

• • •

Colton returned to Lyon the next day and back to his office. He had been in Moncenisio for two weeks, yet it felt longer. He was tired but enjoyed how his first assignment turned out. Colette popped her head in, "Chief Inspector Du'boe is on his way to see you."

"Does my schedule allow it?" asked Colton.

"Yes Cool-taan, you always set aside time for the Chief Inspector. He is a very important man."

Colton smiled. "Then I will see him since he is *important*."

Colette shook her head and closed the door.

Shortly after, he heard a door knock.

"Come in," said Colton. Inspector Du'boe walked in, sat down, and leaned forward.

"Cool-taan, congratulations! I just got word that Guardia di Finanza made thirty arrests, confiscated two tons of cocaine, and recovered over $3,000,000 in cash. At least for now, the drug supply chain has been disrupted at the border. Splendid work! Your strategy was successful. Very smart."

"Thank you, sir. Anna and Colette were a tremendous help. It was a team effort."

"Yes, good. On another subject, your previous boss, John Hill at the UN, called me on Monday of this week. He had a proposal he wanted to run by me before talking to you. He explained the potential benefits for us both. I don't want to lose you; I'll try to make it work."

"What is it?"

"I will let Mr. Hill explain, so please call him."

Colton frowned a little. "OK, I will."

"In the meantime, please study your next assignment." Inspector Du'boe slid a file folder across the desk. "I will allot you additional help. We have a college graduate that we hired a few months ago. I would like you to train him. Determine if there's a connection between the murders. They happened quickly, and the victims were all young, Arab men."

"OK. When do I get the new kid?"

"In four weeks. Again, well done, Cool-taan and let me know how the conversation goes with John Hill." Chief Inspector rose and for the first time, extended his hand.

Ughhh...a limp handshake. "Yes sir, I will."

Colton waited a few minutes until the Chief Inspector had left. He glanced at his wristwatch and did the calculation that it was before noon in New York. He punched John's name in his phone.

"John...Colton! How are you doing?"

"Good, Colt. I am hearing remarkable things about you from your Inspector Clouseau," said John.

Colton laughed. "It's Du'boe, not Clouseau. It rhymes, but that's it."

"I know, just kidding. He spoke highly of you. Did he explain anything to you?"

"He promised to make it work and asked me to call you for specifics."

"I'm glad to hear that he said that. Listen, the UN has approved building its new headquarters at the old Brooklyn Navy yard. They want a board, made up of different country representatives from within the UN, to oversee the project's design and construction. The name of this group will be the 'Steering Committee'."

Colton interrupted, "So what's this got to do with me?"

"Since the U.S. contributes 22% of the UN budget annually, an American will chair the committee and have two votes. I recommended to our ambassador that you be the chair. You have excellent meeting skills and construction experience. She is a friend of mine and will appoint you if you say yes."

"But I have a job."

"Come for a few days every month. We will cover all expenses, and you will receive a $75,000 salary as a UN employee. You can bank all that salary as Interpol will still pay you as well. The Chief Inspector agreed to this as he does not want to lose you. It is an excellent opportunity."

"Wow, I wasn't expecting this."

"I will email you a one-page briefing summary. Read it, think about it and get back to me tomorrow."

"I will John. Thanks for thinking of me and great to talk to you."

Five minutes later an email pinged from John Hill with an attachment. Colton printed it out, put it in his briefcase, and left for the day.

CHAPTER 31
COLTON GRAY

Colton was glad it was Saturday. After an intense investigation, it took him at least three days to unwind and relax. He sat at the small kitchen table in his apartment with a hot cup of coffee, opened his briefcase and retrieved the one-page memo John had sent him.

<u>Memorandum</u>

To: The U.S. Ambassador to the United Nations
From: Staff
Date: December 01, 2019

I. **<u>Background</u>**: UN Facilities hired a local consulting firm to evaluate the most cost-effective method of providing a new headquarters for the UN. Facilities chose the following option: Make a deal with a real estate development firm for a piece of property within the city and do a land/building swap. They decided to keep the UN at its current location until they completed the construction of the new building.

II. **<u>Budget:</u>** The Consultant prepared a cost model for the above option which amounted to approximately $2.5 billion. This included $1.0 billion for construction with completion of the project in 30 months. The balance would pay for remaining soft costs such as the property, design, FF& E (furnishings), relocation, etc.

III.   **Development:** The Consultant requested proposals from real estate firms. The chosen firm agreed to purchase 16 acres at the Brooklyn Navy Yard from the City of New York. Once vacated, the existing UN building would undergo conversion into high-end residential, retail, and fine dining establishments.

IV.   **Steering Committee:** The Consultant suggested setting up a nine-member Steering Committee to represent the UN in negotiations and management. The Steering Committee would have independent decision-making powers, with a majority rule format, and would report directly to the Head of Facilities of the UN. It would execute all agreements with any firm involved in the project. It was to ensure the project stayed on budget and met its 12-month design and 30-month construction schedule. The U.S. negotiated and agreed to contribute 22% of the budget, aligning with its annual UN budget percentage. It was understood that the U.S. would lead the committee and possess two votes. This enabled a tiebreaker when voting. That changed the need from having nine members to eight. In the end, representatives selected by the Secretary-General were: United States, Japan, United Kingdom, France, Germany, Italy, China, and Saudi Arabia.

V.   **Staff Observation/Notes:** China guaranteed a hefty contribution. Saudi Arabia made an even larger one. It was understandable why China would want to be part of this elite committee, but Saudi Arabia's investment was puzzling to staff.

Colton re-read the memo three times and thought about it. He pulled out his savings account statement. Not much there. A great way to save money, he thought. He punched a name on his phone. "Hey, you awake?"

"No," said a groggy Knox.

"Sorry. Listen. I have the chance to lead a board overseeing the new United Nations headquarters. I plan to work at Interpol and fly to New York monthly for the project. Both Interpol and UN are good with sharing me. What do you think?"

"Do it. Mom will really be happy."

"True. I did not think about that."

"Now, leave me be and let me know when you are coming."

• • •

Colton waited until 3:00 p.m. local time to call John Hill.

"Hey John. I'm in. Thanks for this."

"Awesome, Colt. I will inform the Ambassador of your decision. Look forward to having you back!"

CHAPTER 32
ACCEM

A Term Life Insurance Policy is a contract between the person buying the policy and the insurance company issuing the policy. The person buying the policy gives the names of who is to be insured and who is to be the beneficiary. The beneficiary will only receive a cash payout if the named person dies.

• • •

Accem cut out the following articles and taped them to plain, ruled paper. He and General sat down in his hotel room for an update:

- *Dunbar Life Insurance and Investments reported a payout of $2,000,000 to the named beneficiary for of the death of Abbi Saddiqi, 24. Death Certificate on file. Death is being investigated as murder in Florence, Italy. (#1)*
- *Egyptian - Arabian Mutual Ltd. recently released a cash payment of $2,000,000 its beneficiary in the death of J. Mafada, 23, of apparent heart attack in Pisa, Italy. Death Certificate on file. (#2)*
- *Cairo + Eastern Insurance Plc. transfers by wire $2,000,000 for policy holder A.K. Matish, 24, who died in Rome, Italy. Death being investigated as murder. Case still open. Death confirmation received and on file. (#4)*
- *Arabian Oriental Insurance and Services Ltd. approves payout of $2,000,000 of Policy #23AX537, in the death of S.S. Suleman, 25, in London, England. Death record on file. Local authorities investigating as potential murder. (#5)*

- *Iranian Mutual Insurance pays $2,000,000 because of the death of R. Mati, 25, in Paris, France on April 29, 2006. Death certificate on file. Death under investigation by local authorities. (#6)*
- *Abu Dhabi Insurance & Investments Plc. releases a hold on the claim of $2,000,000 in the death of policy holder K. Hussein, 23, in Madrid, Spain. Death certificate on file and being investigated by local authorities. (#7)*

Accem took a copy out of his file and slid it over to General.

General looked over the sheet and asked, "How is the money disbursed?"

"Total insurance companies' payout is $12,000,000. Six families split $3,000,000 equally, leaving $9,000,000 for us. This will pay off the $8,500,000 loan from Sterling + Mark, the investment firm in Casablanca that covers the investment into the two companies, the contract killer fees, and other operational and influence expenses. You know how the remaining $500,000 is disbursed." Accem winked at General.

"Great! Phase I was a success."

He stood up to go and proceeded to the door. He stopped abruptly and slowly turned around.

"I almost forgot to ask."

"What?"

"How were you able to persuade seven sets of parents to buy term life policies on their sons for the *sole purpose* of having them murdered?"

PHASE II
INFLUENCE THE DESIGN

CHAPTER 33
TAJ JILANI

January 2020
Taj left all his belongings in Karachi and brought only a suitcase of clothes knowing that he could lease a furnished house, a vehicle and could purchase the winter clothes he needed in Grand Rapids.

From Chicago, he drove his leased Jeep to a small, furnished two-bedroom cottage near the campus of Aquinas College. Arriving, he was glad to find the driveway cleared of snow. Opening the front door, the heat from inside the house smacked him as he walked in.

Having unpacked, he sat at the kitchen table with coffee and a notebook, jotting down thoughts on his priorities. He was eager to get started on creating the most sensational disaster ever!

Taj's reason for purchasing Connor Back's company was the radiant tubing that is installed in the concrete slabs. If they could get the water that circulates through the tubing hot enough to crack the concrete that would be the simplest solution. However, intuitively, he felt they would need to substitute an explosive liquid to cause the concrete to fail which would make the building collapse.

There was one other technology the Roegges presented he was keenly interested in, but that would require further research.

• • •

Later that evening, Taj dialed Accem.
 "Number?"
 "32."

"Update?"

"I am in a rental in Grand Rapids. Do not forget that we need certain specific building components implemented into the design for our strategy to be successful."

"I remember but need more specific information when you have it. We have invested in and secured a position on the newly formed UN Steering Committee, which oversees the project. This will yield the influence to ensure that will happen," said Accem.

"Good."

No response. Accem had hung up.

CHAPTER 34
COLTON GRAY

Once again, Colton examined the file on the deaths of six Arab men within four weeks. The killings stopped just as abruptly as they started. It was a curious pattern and a newspaper clipping had been added to the file that read of the murder of a young Italian in Venice. It didn't fit with the other murders. The young man wasn't Arabic, and the story had a haunted murder mystery vibe. The file included it as it occurred nearby and during the same time as three of the deaths.

He looked at his watch to confirm he had a few minutes before meeting the newbie Chief Inspector Du'boe was sending him. He took a moment to look at a black-and-white photo on his desk, depicting Knox McKenna, Jeremy Town, Nick King, and himself. Someone took a photograph shortly after Knox had been discharged from the hospital following his near-fatal stabbing by the Chinese assassin during their mission many years ago. Inside his desk drawer he kept a copy of a military artist's sketch of Wolf. He and Knox had given him the details, and he drew it.

His desk phone's intercom buzzed, "Cool-taan, your appointment has arrived."

"Send him in," said Colton.

Ali Masada's file showed he graduated from a university in Germany. Interpol hired Ali as an interpreter of written Arabic. He spoke three languages fluently, English, German and Arabic, his native tongue. The photo and enclosed showed a handsome young man with a clean-shaven face, dark hair, and mahogany brown eyes.

Ali came in and introduced himself. They shook hands. *Firm handshake. Good.* He let Ali tell him what he had been doing for Interpol and then asked if he knew why he was here.

"I understood you needed some administrative and language help on a case you were working on," said Ali.

"This assignment will include some travel and long hours. That work?" asked Colton.

"Yes," answered Ali.

"Good. Read this tonight and we will discuss it at 8:00 am tomorrow," mentioned Colton as he slid the file across his desk.

"I will."

• • •

The next morning Ali arrived at the reception area outside of Colton's office. Colton's assistant was not there, so Ali walked over and knocked on Colton's door.

"Yes?"

Ali opened the door.

"Mr. Gray, it's Ali." asked Ali.

"Come in but call me Colton."

Ali came in and sat down. He handed back the file Colton had given him.

"So, what's next?" asked Ali.

"You will get to witness first-class detective strategies that I will provide. Work with Colette on travel arrangements to London, Paris, Madrid, Florence, and Rome since those cases are being investigated as murders. Delay visiting Pisa since investigators haven't labeled the death as foul play. Here are the names and contact info of insurance reps and local police. You need to call and arrange meetings with both and then ask Colette to make our travel plans accordingly. Use the power of Interpol's name to get commitments to meet. Anyone with minimal talent could arrange these meetings within a few days."

Colton winked, knowing it would take much longer.

Ali laughed, "OK."

"I'm traveling to New York for a few days but will be ready to begin upon return. Questions?" He handed Ali the sheet of paper with the itinerary.

Ali stood, glanced at the list, and handed it back to Colton.

"No, you can keep that," said Colton.

"I've got it. I have a photographic memory," said Ali.

Colton cocked his head and looked at Ali. "Hmmm, I'll test you later."

Ali smiled briefly and remarked, "No questions, but there was a separate article about a murder in Venice." He remained silent; his gaze fixed on the floor.

"And—?" asked Colton, drumming his fingers on the desk.

Ali cleared his throat and looked visibly disturbed. He hesitated and then looked directly into Colton's eyes, "I was there."

Colton frowned, "What do you mean you were there?"

"The person in the article was my best friend. I planned the reception where the murder took place. The lights went off and when they came back on, he was lying on the floor dead."

"What did the investigation find?"

"Someone strangled him. It changed my life. I pursued a career with Interpol hoping the skills I learn may one day help solve my friend's murder."

Colton shook his head, "Wow, that's tough." *Colton knew how it was to lose a close friend. When Nick King died on a SEAL mission in Pakistan, it was very painful.*

CHAPTER 35
TAJ JILANI

Taj's office at Roegge & Roegge was small with a gray metal desk, an overstuffed vinyl-covered chair and one straight back wooden chair for guests. The walls had off-white paint and were bare. Taj was assigned to collaborate with their Chief Engineer, Wilbur Fledderjohn. Everyone called him 'Chief'. He was 70 years old. He had a round, pasty, white face with red blotches; white hair and a wide nose that supported oversized glasses with thick lenses. Standing a whopping five feet tall, his steady diet of donuts created an expanded waistline. He held structural and electrical engineering degrees and accompanying licenses, which was a perfect fit for this firm.

The technology that fascinated Chief was 'smart glass'. When an electrical charge was applied, the glass had the ability to transform from clear to opaque, tinted, or even darken to the point of appearing black.

"The key lies in the volume of electrical current. Applying more amperage causes the glass to change colors faster, but it bursts violently outward," Chief said.

"How do you control that?" asked Taj.

"I don't know yet, but you and I will figure it out."

"OK, sounds good."

He left Chief's office and called Anniston King and got her voice mail. Re-introducing himself, he left his number. After that, he worked on some mathematical equations deep into the night.

•   •   •

After arriving at home after midnight, he called Accem.

"Number?"

"32."

"Update?"

"My calculations have confirmed we need an explosive liquid inside the radiant tube system to bring the building down."

"I will take care of that. Anything else?"

Taj started to speak. *Accem had already hung up. Annoying.*

CHAPTER 36
COLTON GRAY / THE FRENCHMAN

Mid-January
Colton's flight landed Monday at noon at JFK International Airport. Reservations were made for him to stay at the Westin New York Grand Central, located a quarter mile from the United Nations building. His first meeting was at 1:00 p.m. the next day in a conference room on the 34th floor at the UN. Tonight, though, he had organized a heavy hors d'oeuvres mixer for the new members of the Steering Committee at his hotel so they could at least meet each other before tomorrow's meeting.

• • •

That evening, Colton waited just inside the door as members started arriving. Colton greeted each person at the door, and they greeted him back. One was missing. It was the French representative. Colton waited five more minutes and then called for everyone's attention.

"Welcome everyone. I am Colton Gray and I want to welcome each of you as members to the special Steering Committee for the new United Nations. Our role was explained to you before you were selected, but to state our responsibility simply, we need to control the budget and ensure that we design and build the project over the next..."

Suddenly the door opened, "Excusez-moi. Je suis Phillipe Devereaux."

"Welcome, Mr. Devereaux. Come on in. As I was saying, it is imperative that we manage the budget and ensure this project gets designed and built in 42 months. Communication will solely be in English, and decisions will be determined by majority vote. You each have one vote and I have two votes. Now, please introduce yourself and the country you represent starting over here." Colton extended his left hand to show where to start. He would mentally tag a descriptive word for each of them as they introduced themselves.

"Jocko Straw, United Kingdom." *Straw colored hair.*

"Qing Pow, The People's Republic of China." *King.*

"Hiroko Suzuki, Japan." *Motorcycle.*

"Phillipe Devereaux, France." *Late.*

"Mario Carboni, Italy." *Mustache.*

"Otto Schmidt, Federal Republic of Germany." *Bald — Colonel Klink.*

"Mustafa Jazerra, Kingdom of Saudi Arabia." *Jazzy Bathrobe.*

They socialized for a few hours before calling it a night. Colton thought it went well and enjoyed talking with everyone. One thing he learned — he was the only one with any construction experience.

• • •

The next day, the group sat in a mahogany clad-walled conference room. They were waiting on one more person. Ten minutes later, Phillipe Devereaux walked in. Late. Again. Phillipe carried his head slightly raised as he walked by Colton to his high-backed, black, leather chair. Colton could smell his cologne. He may not have showered and — offered no apology.

"Thank you to those who arrived punctually. We have three items to discuss today. One, sign the agreement with the real estate developer for a land swap, two, interview and vote on hiring an advisor for this committee and three, for the next meeting in February, bring your recommendations for an Architect. This should be a firm that has experience designing a commercial building greater than 35 stories high with approximately one million square feet or ninety-three thousand square meters," said Colton.

Colton then signed two copies of the real estate agreement, returned them to a file folder and slid them to the side. "I've invited Jim Rattler for an interview. I hope you read the resume I emailed each of you. He will be glad to answer questions about his abilities and the service he will provide."

Colton stepped outside and returned with Jim. "Guys, this is Jim Rattler. I will introduce everyone in the room. Then Jim, kindly summarize your experience and how you can be of help."

After Jim finished, followed by a few minutes of Q & A, Colton asked if there were any additional comments. Everyone shook their heads. Colton thanked Jim for coming and said he would be in touch. Colton thought Qing Pow asked the best question concerning which building codes were to be used because of the independent status of the United Nations.

"OK, let's vote. Those for hiring Jim Rattler, please raise your hand."

All did but one.

"All opposed."

Phillipe Devereaux raised his hand.

"The minutes will show the majority has voted to hire Jim Rattler as an advisor this group."

Suddenly, the Frenchman got up and left the meeting. *Come late and leave early*, thought Colton. He ended the meeting a couple of minutes later. Everyone trickled out of the room. The receptionist gave Otto Schmidt a small envelope in front of Colton. His reaction after reading the note appeared to be one of surprise as he rubbed his bald head twice. Making a call, he talked briefly and hurried off. Colton looked in the direction the German was walking and saw someone partially hidden behind a large plant in the hall. The Frenchman! And he was watching the German. *What is going on here?*

• • •

You see, Phillipe Devereaux thought he had been discreet. He had a weakness for attractive American women but hadn't acted on his desires yet. If the chance came, he wouldn't let being married get in the way.

After his selection to serve on the prestigious Steering Committee, a celebration occurred at a popular bar. A beautiful woman approached him. She was tall, with dark hair, dark brown eyes, and full lips. She was a model from Texas. That's what she said, anyway. He turned on the charm and took credit for the speed at which intimacy developed between them. They wound up in bed in her hotel room.

He thought he had been so careful and secretive until a small parcel marked 'Confidential' arrived at his office that contained a note with a thumb drive containing all the details of their evening together. The cowboy hat, she had encouraged him to wear while he was naked, looked silly now.

The note read: *To preserve the confidentiality of our* rendezvous (like my French?), *vote as instructed while serving on the Steering Committee. If not, the thumb drive's contents will be emailed to your wife.* He was told to vote against hiring Jim Rattler. He did.

• • •

Later that evening the Frenchman made a call and described how the German reacted after reading the note the receptionist had given him. He was told he did a good job.

CHAPTER 37
TAJ JILANI

Early Monday morning, Taj left for Traverse City to meet Chandler Boyd. He parked in a visitor's parking space. He put his hat, coat, and gloves on before getting out of the car. The receptionist greeted him with a smile.

"Chandler and Weezler are located in the conference room."

"Thank you." *Funny—still calls him Weezler instead of Gerry.*

Chandler jumped up to greet him as he entered the room. Weezler normally had a grave 'all business' look on his face, but it was something else that caught his attention. Weezler had a black eye.

"When we met last, I told you I would have our business plan for the upcoming year prepared for you. I'll go through each tab and explain the contents and answer questions you have," said Chandler. He slid a black notebook over to where Taj took a seat. A few hours later they finished.

"Excellent presentation, Chandler," said Taj.

It was noon, so they went to a diner that served comfort food and sat at a round table with red-checkered covering near the back.

"So, what happened to your eye?" asked Taj looking at Weezler.

"My girlfriend's ex-boyfriend, Butch Braxton did this. Big guy, like 6'3". He followed us back to her apartment one night, was drunk, and grabbed my girlfriend's arm. He yelled at her about some past event. I intervened, and he punched me in the face—nearly knocked me out," answered Weezler.

"I told him to contact the police for assault charges, but he won't listen," said Chandler.

Taj asked a couple of details about Butch and then let it drop. Taj could sense that Weezler felt embarrassed about the whole affair. After lunch, they returned to the office to walk through the warehouse. Taj declined a dinner invitation and went to his hotel. He entered his room, made calls for information, and noticed a missed call with a voice message. Anniston King's message said she was returning his call and would like to meet. That was great news!

He departed the hotel and drove to a tavern across town. Sitting in a booth, Taj waited to see if Butch Braxton would come in. The fifty-dollar bill he gave to the bar tender was for handing a note to Butch. Finally, a tall man entered and sat at the bar. He wore work boots, blue jeans, a flannel shirt, red down vest, and crowned his head with a Budweiser hat. Sitting at the bar, he appeared to laugh at all his own jokes as he harassed different patrons.

As soon as the bartender slipped Butch the note, Taj slid out from his booth seat and went outside and waited by a red, jacked-up, four-wheel drive, pickup truck Weezler described to him. Butch strutted over and cursed at him and asked the meaning of the note.

"Do not bother Gerry Weezler or his girlfriend again," said Taj.

"Who?" asked Butch.

"You heard me."

"He had better stay away from my girlfriend."

Taj moved so fast Butch was unprepared for what happened next. He jammed the end of his thumb into Butch's throat. Butch turned to the side grabbing his throat and gasping for breath and Taj kicked the side of his knee. Butch fell to one knee. Grabbing one of Butch's hefty wrists with both of hands, he twisted it behind Butch's back, forcing him to go face down on the cold, cracked pavement.

"You are not to bother them anymore. Do you understand?" Taj asked as he applied more pressure to Butch's wrist.

"Yes—yes—let go! Yes! Let go!" yelped Butch.

Wheeling around, Taj left Butch face down. *He hated bullies.*

• • •

Later that night, Taj dialed Accem.

"Number?"

"32."

"Update?"

"Question. Did you solve the liquid in the tubing?"

"Almost."

"Any further votes pertaining to the Steering Committee?"

"Yes, including our man, we now have four."

"How?"

"We hired a prostitute and videotaped the French representative spending the night with her. We threatened distribution of this material to his wife unless he cooperated. The German delegate's wife oversees the Anti-Drug program for Germany but also has a debt problem her husband is unaware of. To resolve her debt, we convinced her to deliver cocaine. We taped the entire delivery and hand off and told him we would expose her to the public and the police if he didn't vote as instructed. Last, ten years ago, the Italian member picked up a woman at a bar. He was drunk and while driving them to his apartment late that night, hit and killed a homeless person. There were no witnesses. His wealthy father paid the woman to keep quiet. We found her and got her to confirm the story. In return for his vote, we told him we would not expose this to law enforcement."

"Did…?" Taj started to ask a question, but Accem hung up.

CHAPTER 38
COLTON GRAY

Colton returned from New York on Friday. Ali pleasantly surprised him by arranging meetings over the next ten days with law enforcement and insurance representatives. He scheduled London, Paris, Madrid, and Florence for now, and Pisa and Rome a few weeks later in February.

• • •

On Monday, their first stop was London. He and Ali landed at Heathrow Airport outside London on schedule at 10:30 am and grabbed a taxi.

"Driving or riding on the wrong side is something I can't adjust to," Colton expressed.

"It is a matter of perspective," said Ali.

"Nope, it's just strange."

They arrived at the precinct and were shown to a conference room. Despite the long-standing ban on smoking, the room had a noticeable odor of baked-in cigarette smoke. The walls needed paint and none of the chairs matched. It was like other law enforcement conference rooms Colton had been in before. The insurance investigator had already taken a seat. Entering through the side door, a detective carried an evidence box and file. They introduced themselves, exchanged cards, and took their seats. Colton thanked them for their time and elaborated on Interpol's involvement in the case.

The detective placed both the file and container on the table.

"May I see the box?" asked Colton. The detective slid it over. He removed the top and found the victim's passport, cash, and a ticket stub.

"We both interviewed several witnesses, and they told similar stories. The deceased stood near the platform edge at the London Underground. As the train approached, someone tripped and fell headfirst into a blind man, who was directly behind the victim and knocked him onto the train tracks. Neither the blind man nor the person who tripped have been located," finished the detective.

Colton and Ali thanked the men and proceeded to the railway terminal. Returning to their hotel, they debriefed over some fish and chips for dinner.

"I agree with the detective's initial synopsis. The 'blind man' possibly faked his blindness and hired an accomplice. It makes little sense to me how he left so quickly without being caught," Colton speculated. They discussed their next stop, Paris, and then called it a night.

• • •

The next morning Colton met Ali in the lobby. Colton started complaining right away.

"These elevators are the size of a phone booth. I could barely get in with my luggage."

Ali laughed. They hailed a taxi for the airport and flew to Paris's Charles de Gaulle International Airport. Even after getting directions, it was still extremely difficult finding their way around the airport. They finally picked up their bags and headed to their hotel.

"If you were a criminal and wanted to hide, come to this airport. The authorities would never find you. It's awful trying to navigate this airport," Colton complained.

"I agree," said Ali.

The city sanitation workers were on strike so there was garbage in large piles both in the airport and everywhere they drove. The stench was pungent. They checked into their hotel, dropped their luggage, and came back to the Lobby. Colton grabbed a cab and asked the driver to take them to the Arc de Triomphe. The driver couldn't drive them around the ring road because of many accidents and insurance coverage exclusions for the circular road. They arrived near the Arc and the driver pulled over and parked. Twelve avenues radiated outward from the loop road like spokes of a bicycle.

"Why are we stopping here tonight?" asked Ali.

"I wanted to look for myself before our meeting in the morning," answered Colton.

• • •

They departed their hotel the following morning and reached the police station. Garbage was stacked high outside of the entry stairs. They entered an interview room where the insurance investigator and French detective were already seated. Everyone introduced themselves.

"When do you think the garbage strike will end?" asked Colton.

"Soon I hope, or it won't matter. The smell will kill us all," said the detective.

The French detective opened his file. "It was a hit and run — simple as that. We found the scooter and dead body on the ring road. They found the truck that hit the scooter a few streets away, with the scooter's paint on it. The truck had been reported stolen, and the keys remained in the truck. They did not find any evidence, including fingerprints, in the truck. We estimate this occurred around midnight."

They chatted briefly, then the French detective rose, signaling the meeting's conclusion. "I'm very busy and have another meeting. If someone had witnessed the event, we might have already solved it. If I find out more, I will contact you."

Colton and Ali came back to their hotel, grabbed their luggage, and left for the airport. Colton complained about signage at the airport being confusing again. It was Thursday evening and their flight to Madrid was scheduled to leave at 5:00 p.m. On the plane, Colton read a brochure about Madrid and the Running of the Bulls because Ali discovered, after talking with the insurance investigator, that the young man had died from a bull during the run.

In the 'Running of the Bulls', men race ahead of six to ten bulls on a barricaded route to a bullring. There are gaps in the temporary fence every so often to allow a runner to slip through for safety. While not usually life-threatening, injuries occur at every 'Running of the Bulls' event.

They arrived in Madrid and checked in to their hotel. The weather was cool but pleasant for January. Their boutique hotel was sleek, modern, and thankfully, did not smell of garbage.

• • •

The next morning, a taxi took them to their meeting with the detective and insurance investigator at the Police precinct. They shook hands and sat down. The detective showed them the file he had on the death.

"The deceased joined the run, tripped, and as he got up, was skewered by a bull's horn. All we have is his passport copy and a few interviews," the detective said.

"Did anyone witness the man trip and fall?" asked Ali.

"Yes, but only one person commented on the cause of the fall. Do you suspect foul play?"

"We haven't gotten that far yet. We are investigating potential links to recent deaths elsewhere," said Colton.

He skimmed through the report until he located the desired page. "Here it is. Among the young men, a woman noticed an older man with a slight limp. But, once running, he ran as fast as the young men. The older man grabbed the young man's belt, yanking him backwards. Then, he released him, causing him to fall," the detective concluded.

Colton made some notes in his notebook. "Anything else?"

Both men shook their heads. Colton thanked them both for their time and he and Ali left.

• • •

It was Sunday morning. Colton put on a white dress shirt, tan slacks and a navy, blue blazer and headed back down to the lobby. Ali was sitting there reading the paper.

"Where are you going?" asked Ali.

"Church."

"You're Christian?"

"Yep."

"Can I go?"

"Of course, but I thought you were Muslim," said a somewhat surprised Colton.

"Not anymore. My best friend, the one that was murdered, was instrumental in me converting to Christianity. It created a big divide between my dad and me and we have not spoken since."

• • •

Later that day, they departed for the airport to catch their flight to Florence. They arrived that evening and checked into a boutique hotel right off Piazza della Signoria, the beautiful square in the center of Florence where a replica of the statue of Michelangelo's David is located. People were bustling about, and motor scooters buzzed constantly. Even Colton found the history and architecture surrounding the square impressive. They found a small restaurant and ate crispy, thin crust pizza that was delicious. They finished and went to bed.

• • •

The following morning, they reached the inspector's office. The insurance investigator hadn't yet arrived, but they started talking about the case.

"Someone saw the murder," the inspector stated, giving them the witness statement.

Colton read the report. "This eyewitness report is the most detailed I've ever read. Is it possible to talk to him?" asked Colton.

"Maybe — I will try to get him," answered the inspector.

While the inspector was gone, the insurance investigator arrived and after introductions, Colton brought him up to speed with his and the inspector's discussion.

The inspector returned. "He agreed to briefly stop by at noon."

He and Ali visited the bridge where the man was killed, then they returned to the station before noon. The eyewitness was there. Colton started by thanking the man for coming over. Colton walked the man through the events, which aligned precisely with his report. The man started to leave but abruptly spun to face them.

"I just remembered something I left out. You asked me if he had a limp and I told you I did not see him walk, only run. As a runner myself and an orthopedic surgeon, frequently I observe others running and noticed when the suspect ran away, his stride was unnatural," said the eyewitness.

"How do you mean?" asked Colton.

"Just like someone who underwent knee surgery."

Colton controlled his excitement. This case was getting interesting.

The surgeon left. Colton and Ali thanked both remaining men and returned to their hotel. With clues in hand, they planned to analyze them when they returned to Lyon.

CHAPTER 39
TAJ JILANI / ANNISTON KING

Taj was looking forward to meeting Anniston King. She had given him the name of a restaurant in Flint and agreed to meet him there at 7:00 p.m. He left his house in the afternoon so he could stay focused on the snowy, road conditions in the light of day. Arriving in Flint, he found the restaurant and parked in the back. He walked around to the front and went inside and immediately enjoyed the warmth inside the building.

His gaze drifted across the room until it locked onto the eyes of a woman sitting. She got up, walked toward him, and introduced herself as Anniston King. Dressed in black slacks and a royal blue sweater, she caught everyone's attention. As they shook hands, she smiled at him, revealing white, even teeth. Anniston was tall and had the curves an athletic body produces. Her beauty was stunning.

"Our table is ready," said Anniston.

"Excellent and thank you for arranging this," said Taj.

The hostess guided them to a table in the corner, promising their server would arrive soon. The tables were arranged so a private conversation would go unheard, and the dimmed dining area created a comfortable atmosphere.

Following casual conversation, the server arrived, inquired about prior visits, and described the evening's specials. Shortly afterwards they ordered. After that, they both spoke at the same time and laughed. Anniston asked Taj to go first.

Taj started with where he was from, what business he was in, where he lived and moaned sufficiently about the cold temperatures in Michigan. He then asked her about her job.

Anniston explained what she did as a nurse. She traveled frequently to Chicago, usually once a month, to visit her parents. They tried to get her to move permanently to Chicago, but she liked her job, church, and friends who had helped her through a dark time in her life.

Their food arrived, and they continued making small talk until they finished eating. There was silence in the air momentarily. Anniston broke the silence.

"I really appreciate you driving over here tonight. I still have the note you left for me at the hospital."

Taj nodded. "I wondered if you thought the note was just a hoax."

"Not at all. Your note said you had information concerning my husband's death."

For a moment, Taj hesitated, his eyes on her. "Several years ago, I was married and had a beautiful young daughter. My wife and daughter were visiting relatives in northern Pakistan and an explosion in the local shopping market killed them and—your husband."

Taj saw Anniston's eyes tear up immediately.

"I'm so sorry," she whispered as she looked down.

He continued. "They gave me several explanations of how they died, but I didn't believe any of them except one. What were you told?"

Anniston looked away. "Just that he died in an explosion. Do you have other details?"

"Yes. I finally confirmed, from friends within Pakistan's intelligence agency, that an errant missile launched by a U.S. drone caused the explosion."

Both were quiet momentarily. Suddenly, Anniston tilted her head with a puzzled look on her face. She opened her lips to say something but paused.

"What?" asked Taj.

She shook her head. "It is hard for me to talk about it."

Uncomfortable silence lasted a minute. Taj changed the subject as it was emotional for both. Thinking it was a good break point for the evening, Taj thanked Anniston for agreeing to meet him. He walked her to her parking spot. They shook hands, and she thanked him for dinner and climbed into her SUV.

• • •

Anniston sat in her car, not moving. She let it warm up and could finally feel some heat from the vents. She was reeling from the conclusion she had drawn. The details the military gave her was that Nick King was a hero as he died trying to save a little girl from a suicide bomber—*a female suicide bomber*—which could only have been Taj's wife!

CHAPTER 40
COLTON GRAY

Mid-February 2020

The next meeting of the Steering Committee was to include Jim Rattler, their advisor. Colton let him know the committee had approved his hiring and had forwarded a consulting agreement for him to execute.

Colton called the meeting to order. "Anyone have questions or comments on last month's meeting minutes?"

All in attendance shook their heads. He moved on as the door opened and the Frenchman, arriving late, entered. He was wearing a dark gray suit and royal blue tie. The Colton had to admit he was a sharp dresser, except for the four-panel strip of toilet paper that was following him, stuck to the bottom of the heel of his shoe.

"I invited Jim Rattler here today to outline a strategy for hiring the professionals to design and build the project. I also requested each of you to bring your recommendation for an architect to this meeting. We will get those names later."

Qing Pow, from China, raised his hand. Colton nodded toward him. "Mr. Rattler, could you explain the professionals' roles? We are not in this business."

"That's an excellent suggestion. In the South, we call that exercise, 'who's who in the zoo'? Jim, do you mind doing that?"

"Not at all." Jim laughed seeming to find Colton's comment funny. He went to the whiteboard and drew four boxes: the top box he wrote in the name 'Owner' and underneath Owner wrote, 'UN/Steering Committee'. Three boxes below in a row he wrote the names: 'Architect', 'Preconstruction Firm', and 'General Contractor'. He explained each box below the Owner:

"The design team, led by an Architect, hires engineers to complete the different components of the building, including the structural, HVAC, plumbing, electrical, civil, landscape architect, and specialty consultants. The Architect is like an artist who first rough sketches on canvas what he intends to paint. He gradually adds details to the rough sketch. After he is satisfied with the details, he applies the last colors to complete the painting. Like the artist, the design process goes through four phases: programming, schematic design drawings, design development drawings and final construction drawings."

"So, the Architect only designs the building?" asked Mario Carboni from Italy.

"Yes, and ensures that it is built properly," said Jim.

Jim explained that the Preconstruction Firm provides estimating and cost analysis for each of the four phases during the design period. The reason for this is to show that the design and cost are in balance. And finally, the entity that manages construction of the project is the General Contractor. They will use twenty to thirty different specialty contractors called subcontractors. Subcontractors typically provide the labor and materials for the project.

"So, we hire all the professionals?" asked Mustafa Jazeera, the Saudi delegate.

"Yes, that is correct. Anyone else?" No one spoke.

"So, how do you recommend we proceed?" asked Colton.

"First, let's interview all the design firms and choose one. Let's schedule them for April's meeting. This gives them enough time to prepare a presentation. Second, we hire a preconstruction firm. I know three capable firms that I can request a proposal from based on some general parameters of the project. I can make sure they are ready for March's meeting. Then when the design is 100%, we advertise the project to the construction industry. We select three contractors that we feel are most qualified and let them submit a price. We choose the one with the lowest number."

"I like that process and timetable. Should we consider anything else?" Colton inquired.

"Yes, if you choose an Architect from a foreign firm without an office in New York City, I recommend that the selected Architect hire a local New York City architectural firm to complete the design after the schematic phase. This is because foreign design firms do not know the local codes. Now, because of the UN's sovereign status, it does not have to follow local codes if they choose not to. But my recommendation is you adopt the local codes. This allows us to have inspections performed by the City of New York building inspectors and the fire marshal which is important."

"OK, that makes sense to me. Now, let's see who everyone has selected for the design firm competition. Jim, your handwriting is excellent. Write the names on the board as we go," Colton said.

"Will do," said Jim. Each delegate spoke their choice starting with the United Kingdom:

1. U.K.-Dunhill St. James
2. Italy-Studio Minnelli
3. France-LeGrand Cartier
4. U.S.-Blackstock & Davis
5. China-Woo Sung
6. Japan-Tanaka
7. Germany-Dietrich + Helmutt
8. Saudi Arabia-Sayedd Architecture

"Thanks Jim and thank you all for choosing the design firm as I requested last meeting. I will send a formal letter to each firm congratulating them as a shortlisted design firm for our project and request they each make a presentation to us in April's meeting. Does everyone accept Jim's suggested process for both the preconstruction and architectural firms' selection?" asked Colton. He looked around and everyone nodded. "Good, I will see you in March. Thank you for your input."

Everyone left except Jocko Straw, the British delegate. He motioned to the Colton to wait a minute. After the last person left, Jocko closed the door and faced Colton.

"I've got a bit of a problem, mate."

"You seemed a bit distracted today. What's happening?"

Jocko explained he received a phone call earlier in the week and the caller threatened to expose some information that would cause a disaster for him and his family unless he agreed to vote as instructed.

"What does he have on you?" asked Colton.

Jocko told Colton an incredibly heart-wrenching story.

CHAPTER 41
TAJ JILANI

Taj had settled into a routine. He spent most of his time in Grand Rapids working with Chief on the shading technology and the thin film laminate that would be embedded in the curtain wall glass to produce electricity.

"So, what do you think about my latest calculations?" asked Taj.

"I haven't looked at them yet," said Chief.

Taj hit the print button and walked a copy over to Chief. "I believe my computations close the gap."

Chief looked at the paper and frowned. "I think you're onto something. This should balance the electrical current and prevent fracturing. And it still allows the glass to achieve maximum speed transitioning from clear to dark! This is a perspective I've never considered before."

"It will work."

"I can't wait to test it." Chief hurried out of Taj's office seemingly upbeat.

Taj's cell phone rang and saw it was Anniston King.

"Hello Anniston."

"Hi Taj. Once again, I'm calling to bug you about my friend Miriam Clarke. I believe you would enjoy meeting her."

"I'm sure I would." *I'm not sure I would.*

"Can you come to Flint in two weeks and meet at my house?"

Taj looked at his calendar and sighed. "Yes, I will."

"7:30 p.m. OK?"

"Yes. Text me your address. I look forward to meeting Miriam." They said their goodbyes and hung up. *Like normal people do.*

• • •

It was late Friday night when he closed a manila file folder and locked it in his desk drawer. He checked his watch, 11:30. He dialed Accem.

"Number?"

"32."

"Update?"

"None, but a question. Any progress on the liquid explosive?"

"Yes. I will give you more information once we have a source. Also, we have secured the fifth and final vote to control the Steering Committee — the British member, Jocko Straw."

"How?"

"Straw was an inspector for Scotland Yard for most of his career. His brother committed suicide and left a note requesting Straw to care for his infant daughter. His wife died giving birth. Straw asked the authorities to label his brother's death as a murder because their mom couldn't cope with the news of one of her sons taking his own life. A lot of money and resources were spent investigating the death as a murder. Since Straw and his wife had no children, they were delighted to become the child's legal guardians but still had to go through the adoption process with the National Foster Care Agency. The last interview, for final approval, is scheduled for this May. Exposing the cover-up leads to Straw's arrest and the child's placement in National Foster Care. She has been living with them for four years under temporary order. We threatened to expose him—he quickly agreed to vote as instructed." Accem hung up.

Taj sympathized with the Englishman's predicament and—*Accem hanging up abruptly was getting old!*

CHAPTER 42
COLTON GRAY

Colton gave Anna, his research assistant, all the descriptive data they had gathered from their trip. She entered this into Interpol's robust database for matches—height, weight, hair color, knee injuries, crime, and terror organization affiliations, etc.

"And, Anna, I'm expecting excellent results. This entire case rests on you," Colton said kiddingly as he stood over Anna.

"I get my best results when someone isn't hovering over me like a drone," replied Anna as she typed and entered the information Colton had given her.

"I'm lurking here solely as an advisor and coach."

She shook her head.

Within minutes after Anna hit the search button, the system generated a list of fifty-one names. From that list, Ali vetted all the names. By doing a lot of calling, e-mailing, texting, he crossed off all but two.

Colton amended their travel plans to Rome and Pisa to include making a visit to interview the two remaining names on the list. One was in Frankfurt, the other in Zurich. Colton and Ali flew from Lyon and arrived in Rome for their meeting with the inspector and insurance investigator.

The inspector started, "We've made no progress. There were no clues that led anywhere. We found a young man with a knife in his chest but there were no fingerprints on the knife and no eyewitnesses."

"Time of death?" asked Colton.

"Late night, early morning is best guess."

They chatted briefly before wrapping up the meeting in under an hour. Colton and Ali came back to the hotel and made plans for dinner. Their train left at 6:20 a.m. to Pisa. Colton did not expect to learn much in Pisa, but the two additional cities they had added to their itinerary might prove productive.

• • •

Colton and Ali's train arrived in Pisa. They had scheduled to meet at 3:00 that afternoon. They arrived and someone showed them to a small conference room. The room appeared clean, with matching chairs, and Colton noticed a paint smell, suggesting that the room had recently been refurbished. The detective and insurance investigator were already sitting. Everyone shook hands as they introduced themselves.

Colton thanked both individuals and stated the meeting would be brief. The detective opened his very thin file and recapped the interview with the employee who found the body. Upon arriving at work that morning, he discovered his key did not fit the lock. He cut the lock off with bolt cutters as tourists were lining up to visit the tower. The employee hurried up the stairs to collect the trash and discovered a body. The Medical Examiner estimated death between 1:00 and 2:00 a.m., attributing it to a heart attack.

"Can you describe the deceased's appearance?" asked Colton.

"Severely overweight," said the detective.

"No personal items?"

"Nope. Clean."

"Why was he there late night?"

"Don't know. It makes little sense."

After asking a few more questions, Colton thanked them both. Upon returning to Florence by train, they subsequently took a flight to Frankfurt and later checked into their hotel.

•   •   •

The following morning, they went to their meeting. The station captain greeted them and led them to the meeting room. Before entering, the captain stopped them to give some background on Hans Luger.

"We know Luger well because he used to be one of us. Commanding the 'Red Viper' unit, he handled drug and weapons enforcement. Unfortunately, the bribes he received was used to aid the drug business instead of stopping it and got him seven years in prison."

"Thanks, that is helpful to know."

Colton and Ali showed up, and someone directed them into an interview room. Two officers sat with Hans Luger. They introduced themselves, and Colton provided a vague description of their interests.

"Were you out of the country between April and May 2019?" asked Colton.

"No, I was working at my uncle's flower shop. I can't travel out of the country as part of my parole agreement," answered Hans.

"Have you ever injured your ankles or knees that required surgery?"

"No."

"Would you mind pulling up your trouser legs?" He did and Colton did not observe any surgery markings of any kind.

"That's all I have. Thank you all for your time."

Colton and Ali left and crossed the street. Colton wanted to observe Luger walking. Luger emerged from the station and headed straight to the bus stop at the end of the block. Neither man detected a limp. Satisfied for now, they went back to their hotel, picked up their bags and caught a taxi for their train departure to Zurich. Arriving in Zurich early evening and they checked into their hotel.

• • •

The next morning, they met for breakfast to review the file and photo of their next person of interest. They each had a copy and re-read the information:

Jacques LeClair was a sniper in French Special Ops. Upon leaving the French military, he transitioned into an independent contractor role, allegedly working as an assassin-for-hire in the Middle East. Local authorities haven't arrested or even suspected him of committing any killings. In a small auto repair shop, he worked as a mechanic. He has lived in Zurich, Switzerland for the past five years.

Colton and Ali made it to the local police station and a police captain came out to greet them. He told them he sent a car to collect Jacques LeClair this morning, but he was not at his apartment. He left a note with the doorman that he would meet them at the Blue Lizard Bar that evening at 6:30.

• • •

Colton and Ali arrived at 6:30 and the bar was mostly vacant. They sat in highchairs, ordered beers and Colton casually asked the bartender what time Jacques LeClair normally comes in. The bartender said he was not familiar with that name. He looked at his watch and was a little annoyed that the police captain's officers had not arrived yet. Trouble approached as three men walked over and formed a semi-circle around them.

"Why do you ask for Jacques?" asked the one in the middle.

"We are Interpol agents and have a few questions for him, but we can come back," answered Colton calmly.

Ali slid off his highchair, but the man nearest Ali gave him a hard push. Ali landed flat on his back. Everything happened so quickly after that—.

Colton swiftly struck the leader's nose with his palm. Blood spewed everywhere as the man's head snapped back. He collapsed to one knee screaming. Immediately after his hand left the man's nose, he landed an elbow strike, using the same arm, on the snout of the thug standing to his right. Again—lots of blood—another man down. The guy who pushed Ali hesitated too long. Colton pivoted 90 degrees and kicked him square on the kneecap, then grabbed his head and brought it down to meet his rising knee. Three men down, just like that.

A man entered, pointing a pistol at Colton. His face matched the photo they reviewed earlier—Jacques LeClair!

"Very efficient monsieur, very efficient," said LeClair.

"Drop your weapon!" screamed a police officer as he and his partner entered the room, with their guns drawn and pointed towards Jacques LeClair. Jacques LeClair turned, reversed the gun, holding it by the barrel and laid it carefully on the bar. The two police officers walked quickly over and handcuffed him.

One officer turned to Colton, "Do you wish to press charges?"

"No, it's OK," said Colton.

The same police officer spoke harshly to the three men still sitting on the floor nursing their wounds. He told Colton to meet him at the precinct. Arriving there, the captain, Colton, and Ali went into the interview room to talk to Jacques LeClair.

Jacques was leaning back in his chair, slouched with legs spread and a toothpick sticking out the side of his mouth. They all sat down.

"In April and May of last year were you in London, Paris, Pisa, Florence, Madrid, Rome, or Venice?" asked Colton.

"No."

"Can you prove it?"

"Yes, my employer will have payroll records showing I was working at his garage."

"Have you ever injured your knees to the point of requiring surgery?" asked Colton.

"Of course—I played football, or 'sockeer' as you say, and my last knee injury ended the possibility of playing professionally."

He pulled up one of his pant legs and showed a knee surgery scar. Colton became very interested. He raised the other pant leg and showed he had surgery on that one as well.

"With operations on both sides, I don't limp anymore," he chuckled.

After a few more questions, Colton finished and stood up to leave. As he swung the door open, the Frenchman called out to him.

"Monsieur, I am not the murderer you seek. I will tell you something that might interest you. I deal with many organizations in the Arab world, so I learned to speak, write, and understand basic Arabic. On my last assignment I overheard chatter about a colossal disaster being planned in your country. Since you didn't press charges against my men, I am giving you this information for free."

"I will pass it on," said Colton.

"The way you handled yourself in the bar impressed me. What was your training?"

"The U.S. Navy trained me."

"Ah—a Navy SEAL."

Colton did not respond, and they left. Colton and Ali crossed the street in front of the police station and watched as Jacques came out. There was no limp.

Colton's cell phone rang. It was Anna.

"I have something unbelievable to show you when you return."

"What?"

"Just trust me it is best to wait."

"OK."

. . .

The next day, Colton stopped by Anna's office first thing. As usual, she was already hard at work.

"So, why the secret code talk on the phone?"

"Sit down and I will explain." He sat.

She continued, "The murder in Venice never made sense to me. It did not fit the pattern. On a hunch, I developed a list of all the life insurance companies that mainly do business in the Middle East, seventy-four total, and then called each one. I asked each if they provided a policy for a certain name. One did, Abu Dhabi Life, PLC. They said the policy expired." She slid a file over to Colton. "Look at this. They emailed me a copy after I explained we were in an active investigation."

"What am I looking for?"

"I highlighted who the insured was."

"OK" He stopped at the yellow highlighted words. "Ali Masada!"

"What if Ali was the intended victim at the wedding?" Anna asked.

"Whoa, I never thought of that. Unbelievable. How could a father do that?" *Although—I could see my dad doing that to me!*

CHAPTER 43
TAJ JILANI

Chief seemed very excited. On Monday, they would commission and turn over the new research facility to him. Taj and Chief walked back to their offices after inspecting the new facility.

"One last thing remains for me to do, to bid farewell to this old office," Chief said.

"What is that Chief?" asked Taj.

"I'll show you in a minute."

Taj returned to his office, located a few doors down from Chief's. He heard what sounded like furniture feet scraping the floor when being pushed. He assumed Chief's packing had begun. Suddenly, the quiet was interrupted by a loud explosive noise accompanied by the sound of shattered glass. Taj raced down to Chief's office. He cautiously swung the door open expecting the worst. Smoke filled the room.

"Chief! Chief!" yelled Taj.

Emerging from the smoke, Chief laughed so hard he wasn't making a sound.

Taj, concerned about Chief, asked irritably, "What's funny?"

He finally slowed down enough to speak and point toward the wall in the corner. "I have finally done what I wanted to do for almost 40 years," said Chief.

The smoke cleared, and Taj directed his gaze towards the corner of Chief's office where a glass assembly stood. The wall behind the glass assembly had long, jagged shards of glass sticking into it. It looked like a professional knife thrower at the circus had thrown the glass. Long shards pierced a poster board featuring a crude human body sketch and a photocopy of a woman's head atop it. The long shards were the object of Chief's laughter.

"Who is on the poster board?" asked Taj.

"My mother-in-law!" howled Chief as he removed his thick, safety glasses and dabbed his eyes with a handkerchief to soak up the laughter tears.

"How did you do that?"

"On the shading dial, I cranked up the electricity up to the maximum current."

"Wow, it really blew apart."

"Yes, more than I expected, actually,"

They departed from the office, wishing each other a good weekend. Taj's thought drifted to tomorrow when he was meeting Miriam. He had to admit he was anxious.

• • •

Later that night at home Taj had a blazing fire going in his fireplace. He glanced at his watch and gave Accem a call.

"Number?"

"32," said Taj.

"Update?"

"We need to get our products included in the building's design."

"Be specific," said Accem.

"The Architect should include in the drawings and specifications a requirement for only using our radiant tube system and electricity generating curtain wall on the project. This will ensure that we provide our systems. We need the radiant tube system to carry the liquid explosive. The electricity generated by the thin solar film in the glass of the curtain wall will detonate the liquid in the tubes."

"OK, as I mentioned before, our voting majority on the Steering Committee should be able to make that happen. Get me the technical information for both systems."

"I—." Accem had already ended the call. *Again!*

CHAPTER 44
COLTON GRAY / UNIDENTIFIED COMMITTEE MEMBER

Mid-March 2020

The Steering Committee gathered early in the conference room to prepare for the preconstruction firm interviews and selection. Everyone showed up on time and took their usual chairs.

Colton started, "Good morning, everyone. I'm looking forward to today's interviews with the three preconstruction firms Jim Rattler recommended. I received each of the preconstruction companies' proposals confirming the scope of the engagement and the amount each will charge. The process I would like to use is this: let's go through the interviews and rank the firms in order: 1, 2 and 3. Then let's see if their bid amounts sway our thinking. Any objections or questions before we get started?" There were none.

After spending the full morning listening to all three preconstruction firms' presentations, they said their goodbyes to the last firm.

"We will break for lunch and meet back here at 2:00 to discuss and select the firm we think will best serve us," said Colton. "Any comments before we break up?"

Mustafa raised his hand. "Firm C's in-house mechanical and electrical experience impressed me. Only they had that capability."

"Good point," said Colton. "Anyone else?" All heads swiveled no.

• • •

All returned from lunch just before 2:00. After everyone sat down, Jim Rattler summarized the chief strengths of each firm.

Colton stood up and said, "Now it's time for each of you to write your choice on a sheet of paper, fold it and pass it down. After tallying the votes, Jim will share each firm's proposed cost."

Everyone wrote their choice and passed it to Colton. The Consultant wrote vertically on the board Firm A, B, and C. Colton then read the letter on each sheet of paper. When finished Firm A had 1 vote, Firm B had 0 votes, and Firm C had 7 votes.

"Well, based on their presentation and first impressions it looks like Firm C has the most votes. Now, please write each proposal amount beside the corresponding firm," said Colton.

The consultant opened a sealed envelope from each firm and scrawled the values on the board. It looked like this:

- Firm A-$1,775,000
- Firm B-$1,825,000
- Firm C-$1,700,000

After a brief silence, Colton announced, "If there are no objections, we choose Firm C, EstiReady. Jim, please formally notify each firm of our decision and thank the two unsuccessful firms for their time and effort."

"Will do," said Jim.

"We will interview design firms one month from today. We sent out a schedule showing dates and times for each presentation a week ago. Please follow up and double-check that the firm you recommended is prepared for the interview. Thanks for your time today and I will see you in a few weeks."

Everyone left except Colton and Jocko.

"Have you heard anymore from the mysterious blackmailer?" asked Colton.

"Yes. He told me to vote for Firm C," answered Jocko.

A knock on the door interrupted them. The administrative assistant looked inside.

"Come on in. What's up?" asked Colton.

"While I was gone momentarily, someone dropped off an envelope addressed to Mr. Straw," she answered. She handed it to Jocko and left.

He opened it, read it, and then immediately slammed his hand on the conference room table. "Whoever this is knows the names of those who were part of the cover up I orchestrated when my brother killed himself. He had said he would show me. I thought I was the only one who knew everyone involved, but he has them listed on this sheet of paper!" exclaimed the Brit.

Colton pondered briefly before speaking. "I wonder if any other members have been compromised? But I can't think of a good reason we shouldn't have selected Firm C."

• • •

One of the Steering Committee members wasn't surprised when the president of EstiReady (Firm C) called to thank him for choosing him. Only the member and the president knew that he would secure the most votes from the interview alone. But that was not enough. He needed to have the best price to make it foolproof. He was asked how much money would ensure EstiReady's bid would be lowest. The president said pay him $200,000 and he would lower his price by $200,000. They agreed his firm would receive payment after they were awarded the contract. In return, EstiReady was tasked with ensuring that certain building systems would be included in the design. EstiReady had the most experience in mechanical and electrical systems of the three firms and this experience would give credibility to their recommendation for using the radiant tube system and the solar curtain wall.

CHAPTER 45
TAJ JILANI / ANNISTON KING

The next day, Taj was to meet Anniston's friend, Miriam. He really wasn't looking for a relationship, but out of respect for Anniston and her persistence, he agreed to meet her friend.

He checked his handwritten notes once more from what Anniston had told him. *Miriam Clarke. Born in Pakistan. Mother was Pakistani. Father was English. Lived in Pakistan until she was ten and then moved to London. Between high school and college, her dad's job transferred him to the United States. Attended the University of Michigan. Degree in nursing. Was married, with no children. Husband died of pancreatic cancer. Great sense of humor. Attractive.*

He parked his Jeep in Anniston's driveway. After switching off the engine, he got out of the car and headed towards the front door. He wore tan slacks, a blue and white, striped button-down shirt, and a blue blazer that held the unopened envelope in the inside breast pocket. He tapped on the door. Anniston swung the door open and greeted him with her engaging smile. She showed him in and closed the door. The sitting area was warm, thanks to the blazing fire in the fireplace.

Miriam stood up from the chair she had occupied. She was tall like Anniston and had long, dark hair. Her skin was a little lighter than Taj's. She had a smooth forehead, a proportional nose, and amazingly bright blue eyes, obviously from her father's side. She was stunning! Her blue eyes were unlike anything he had ever seen.

He crossed the floor and shook her hand as Anniston introduced them. They all sat down.

"Our dinner reservations are at 8:00 so we have a few minutes before we need to leave," said Anniston. Several minutes passed with no uncomfortable or forced conversation.

Taj looked at his watch. "Should we go?" he asked.

Anniston answered, "Yes."

They all got in Taj's Jeep and drove to the same restaurant where he met Anniston previously. The dining area was at capacity, but not noisy. They waited ten minutes before being shown to their table. A few minutes after the menus were handed out, the server arrived and took their dinner orders.

"Anniston told me you moved to London at the start of high school. Why did you move?" asked Taj.

"My mom and I converted to my father's religion, Christianity. It caused many problems with my mom's family and friends. We even received death threats. My father requested a transfer. They not only agreed but offered a big promotion if he moved back to London. He accepted. I learned about the death threats much later, but it must have been tough for my mom. She never talks about it, though. Anyway, that's my story. Tell me yours."

Taj shared his childhood experiences and the hardships of growing up in poverty. There were eight kids. He was the oldest and performed well in school and got an academic scholarship. He earned his undergraduate, master's, and doctoral degrees from the International Islamic University in Islamabad. Upon graduation, he worked for the government for fifteen years and later became a professor of electrical engineering at the University of Karachi. He resigned when he lost his spouse and child.

Taj discovered a shared commonality among them—they had all experienced the loss of a spouse. However, this topic remained unmentioned as they conversed throughout the evening, enjoying the excellent food. After dinner he drove them back to Anniston's home. Anniston invited them in for coffee. They sat around for an hour longer talking about a variety of subjects.

Taj said he needed to be getting back. Anniston stood up and hugged him. He felt surprised when a woman he barely knew hugged him. Miriam said she would walk with him to the door. Anniston took the coffee cups and left. Taj turned at the door and Miriam stepped in and gave him a hug. He returned the hug and held her tightly for just a few seconds. They looked in each other's eyes for just a moment — and then another moment.

"I really enjoyed this evening and want to see you again," Taj said.

"Me too," said Miriam.

Taj let go of her, opened the door, and hopped into his Jeep. Taj felt an excitement he hadn't felt since he met his late wife. Just as quickly though, he became remorseful — she is Christian, and I am Muslim — no way that works. And then the envelope he always kept with him. He could never forget that. Despite the internal struggle, his attitude brightened at the possibility of her maybe, just maybe returning to Islam. Anyway, he wanted to see her again.

• • •

"Well?" asked Anniston playfully.

"I really enjoyed tonight. He was everything you described," said Miriam.

"I thought you would like him. Do you want to see him again?"

"Yes! The sole concern I have is our religious beliefs. It's a significant obstacle for me."

• • •

Later, Anniston lay in bed unable to go to sleep. She wondered how Taj would feel if he knew his wife was the suicide bomber that caused her own death, the death of his daughter and Nick. After further contemplation, she decided she would contact one of Nick's old SEAL teammates, to see if there were any more details concerning Nick's death. At Nick's funeral, she briefly met him and could only recall his height. His name is Colton something—she thought a minute. She had his card somewhere and remembered he had written an email address and said she could send a message anytime. Getting up, she went to Nick's old box in the closet, carefully searching until she found what she needed.

CHAPTER 46
COLTON GRAY

Mid-April 2020

The Steering Committee met Tuesday morning at 7:30 to discuss the next few days of interviews. After everyone arrived, Colton handed out an information packet for each member. He urged everyone to dress formally for the upcoming interviews. Although he wasn't sure of what to expect, the outcome didn't disappoint him. Mustafa Jazeera's flamboyant gold and crimson robe stole the show. Standing at five-foot eight and very round, a lot of high-end fabric was required to cover that body.

Colton went quickly through the packet and asked if there were questions about the day's interviews. They proceeded to the conference room because no one asked questions.

The order of the presentation was:

1. China
2. France
3. Germany
4. Italy
5. Japan
6. U.K.
7. U.S.
8. Saudi Arabia

The Chinese firm of Woo Sung was ready when the Steering Committee entered the room. After introductions, a video began by showing a bird's-eye view of New York City and then dramatically zoomed in on a cluster of buildings superimposed on the location of the new UN Headquarters. They presented a sleek complex of rectangular buildings interconnected by elevated bridges. The plan included lots of glass and solar panels. When they were done, there was a healthy session of Q&A. When finished, Colton thanked them for an excellent presentation.

• • •

After a break for lunch, France presented. The LeGrand/Cartier partner introduced his team. He presented color renderings showing a layout of four, 10-story triangular-shaped buildings. Between the buildings was a cobblestone plaza and shading the plaza was a huge geodesic dome supported at the fifth floor of each building.

After the Q&A session, Colton thanked the firm and informed them that a decision would be made soon. Colton asked that the committee stay behind a minute.

"Any other comments before we adjourn for the day?" asked Colton. "None? OK, tomorrow we have Germany and Italy. See you then."

• • •

Wednesday, the German firm Dietrich + Helmutt started the morning. Colton observed the Germans sitting rigidly straight in their chairs. Their presentation was dry and dull just like their conceptual design, which was a square, thirty-story building that accomplished everything the UN would require. Q&A followed but not for very long.

The Steering Committee took a break for lunch and returned shortly before Italy was to present. The presentation by Studio Minnelli was well-done and similar in content to France's presentation. Once Studio Minnelli departed, the Steering Committee quickly debriefed and concluded the day.

• • •

Thursday, Japan's selected firm, Tanaka, used technology to its fullest. Japan, a recycling leader, could incorporate recycled materials in 30% of the building. They presented a sleek, futuristic design for the building and overall had a very impressive presentation. After answering questions, they said their goodbyes and the Steering Committee broke for lunch.

• • •

When they returned, United Kingdom's Dunhill St. James, were all standing in a line in the conference room.

Stepping forward, they firmly shook all the committee's hands. They wore conservative blue suits with red and blue striped rep ties, except for the Managing Partner, who wore a solid red tie. They were a professional-looking group.

"Welcome gentlemen," said Colton. "We will get seated and please start when you are ready."

"Thank you," said the Managing Partner. He introduced his firm and told a very colorful history of the 200-year-old firm, including the Tower Bridge that crossed the Thames in London. He believed they had created the perfect design for a new building.

They wheeled in a rolling cart draped with a tablecloth that covered a tall vertical object. The Managing Partner removed the cloth like a matador and revealed a scale model of their proposal. It was extraordinary! Exposed to view was a tall, cylindrical glass tower with a hole in the middle and the top angled at 45 degrees. The wall on the outside and inside of the cylinder and the 45-degree sloping roof was glass curtainwall. At the round, open space at the ground floor of the cylindrical-shaped building was a plaza. Underneath the plaza was the Grand Meeting Hall, which was designed like an amphitheater. He pulled the model apart vertically and showed a dome in the center of the plaza with a radius of 50 feet in all directions above horizontal. This was to be the VIP conference room. Then, he showcased how this domed meeting room floor could retract and become an open skylight for the Grand Meeting Hall below.

The presentation clearly impressed Colton and the Steering Committee. The Managing Partner concluded by saying if they were fortunate enough to be chosen, they had already decided their stateside partner would be the New York office of Blackstock & Davis. There was an extensive Q&A period. They then exchanged handshakes and bid their farewells.

The Steering Committee debriefed for almost 30 minutes, mostly about the model, and it was clear to Colton that the British firm had won a lot of favor. Also, he thought, it was a skillful move to include Blackstock & Davis, his choice for the United States, to be their local partner. The Managing Partner was clever. They figured getting my two votes would ensure that the U.S. firm I recommended would be involved. *Excellent strategy.*

• • •

Friday, the final interview day. The U.S. firm of Blackstock & Davis made a solid presentation and stressed they had the experience of getting the drawings in compliance with local codes. The afternoon was then spent interviewing the firm from Saudi Arabia, Sayedd Architecture. They noted that most of their work was in the Middle East and Europe, having offices in Riyadh and London. Both firms addressed all the items they were asked to cover. The Steering Committee debriefed quickly, and Colton requested they reconvene at 10:00 on Monday morning to vote.

• • •

Monday morning, Colton began by saying, "Good morning," while everyone was seated. "I want to commend everyone's selection of an architect. All eight firms were very capable. Please state the best attribute of the firm you suggested, and then we'll proceed with voting."

They started in the same order as they presented. So, China was first.

"I liked the connecting bridges between buildings and the artful use of solar panels," said Qing. Colton nodded to the French representative.

"I think the most beautiful buildings are in France," said Phillipe.

Colton frowned. *Not what I asked you to comment on.* "OK, next."

Otto stood up. "The German design was simple and likely the most cost-effective."

Colton nodded to the Italian member.

Mario remained seated. "I think Dunhill St. James had the most comprehensive and attractive design of all."

Hearing that response, Colton sighed. *France and Italy don't know how to play this game.* "OK, Japan."

Hiroko Suzuki stood and bowed. "I believe Tanaka will use the most recycled materials in their design which is great for the environment." Colton nodded to Jocko.

"I agree with what the distinguished member from Italy said about Dunhill St. James," said Jocko.

Colton smiled slightly, "Got it," *Distinguished member from Italy? What a politician.* "I think Blackstock and Davis differentiated themselves with the knowledge of local codes and processes." He then looked over to Arabian delegate and nodded his head.

"Sayedd's Arabian design elements gives an international flair to the building," said Mustafa.

"Thank you. Let's vote," said Colton.

Colton reviewed the voting protocol. Everyone had one vote except him—he had two votes. Passing everyone a sheet of paper with all the firms listed he told everyone to circle the name of the firm they wanted, fold it in half and he would collect them. Writing all the names on the white board, he then read each vote aloud and marked a vertical line by each name receiving a vote:

Woo Sung - III (3)
LeGrand / Cartier
Dietrich + Helmutt
Minnelli
Tanaka
Dunhill St. James–IIIIII (6)
Blackstock & Davis
Sayedd

Colton looked at Jocko, who showed obvious signs of satisfaction with the outcome.

"Congratulations to Dunhill St. James and to the *'distinguished British member'*," Colton said the last part with sarcastic emphasis.

Everyone clapped, except the Frenchman. All got up and left. Colton stayed and motioned for Jocko to do likewise.

"I think it worked out in your favor all the way around," said Colton.

"It bloody well did. I hope my blackmailing friend keeps his word as I have an important event happening soon—and I appreciate your two votes for Dunhill St. James. That helped seal it," said Jocko.

Colton nodded, "It worked out like it was supposed to." *He voted as instructed, resulting in two out of three votes for Woo Sung.*

• • •

That evening Colton hit the call button.

"What's going on?" answered Knox.

"Hey, leaving tomorrow back to Lyon. We chose an architect for the new building. I think Beers should take a crack at building this project."

"In New York…ughhh. I'm not sure about that."

"It will be a fantastic project for the company."

"I will talk with dad about it again. When would it start?"

"In fourteen months, so you have plenty of time to prepare."

"OK, we'll discuss it."

"Talk later."

• • •

Later that night Colton finally relaxed from the exhaustive process of choosing the architect and felt it was a success. They selected Dunhill St. James because they had the best presentation. Also, Blackstock & Davis were assured of involvement. Despite the Secretary of State's call urging him to vote for Woo Sung, he remained confident that Dunhill St. James would win. The Secretary of State believed that voting for their firm would benefit her relationship with her Chinese counterpart. It ended up better than that. The Secretary could now say she helped Woo Sung become a finalist. And, he had helped someone high in the U.S. government which could be helpful in the future.

CHAPTER 47
TAJ JILANI

Taj dialed Accem.
"Number?"
"32."
"Update?"
"I need an address to send to you the written descriptions for the radiant heating, curtainwall and shading technology."
"Send it registered to this address." Accem read it out.
"Got it." They both hung up.

Taj sat at his computer and opened a blank word document. Typing a heading for each system, he then added bullet points under each that included a system description, technical data, performance requirements, and any applicable model numbers that only B & I and Roegge & Roegge's products would meet. He wrote the address on the outside of the envelope, sealed it, and planned to drop it off at the post office next week.

He had to get ready as he had to leave shortly for Flint for his first solo date with Miriam. Prior to leaving, he shaved, showered, and wore slacks and a jacket. As he placed the unopened envelope in his pocket, he noticed that it was worn through and splitting. He laid it flat on the dresser, then got scotch tape. He put half the width on one side, folded it over the top of the envelope, and smoothed it out on the other side. Satisfied, he put the envelope in his breast pocket and left for Flint. They had a date at 7:00.

• • •

An hour and a half later, Taj's GPS delivered him to Miriam's townhouse. He pressed the doorbell. Miriam opened the door and stepped toward Taj and gave him a quick hug. He caught a whiff of her perfume and liked it.

"Come in," she said. She was wearing a blouse that had stripes in blue and white. The blue matched her magnificent eyes.

"You look great," Taj said.

"Thank you. Sit down and let me get my jacket."

Taj sat in a very comfortable chair and enjoyed the smell of a scented candle. The tasteful decoration of the room helped create a pleasant atmosphere. Miriam came back a couple of minutes later. "You ready?"

"Yes."

He held the door open for Miriam and walked around to the driver's side.

"I asked you to pick a place for dinner. What did you come up with?" Taj asked.

"Do you like Mexican food?" replied Miriam.

"I've never had it."

"Would you like to try it?"

"Yes."

She gave him directions as they drove. They pulled into a crowded parking lot and found a space in the back. They walked around the brown, plastered building and through the arch in the front to get to the entrance door. Three mustachioed men in black pants and short black and gold, sequined jackets produced loud music. On their heads were colorful, oversized brim hats. Their music competed with the laughter and conversation of a full dining room.

"How many?" asked the hostess.

"Two," answered Taj.

"This way."

They followed her and took a seat at a booth that had just been cleared. They sat facing each other as a server placed the menus there. Immediately, a server brought hot chips and two bowls with thick sauces: one red and the other green.

"What's that?" asked Taj pointing to the bowls.

"Salsa. The red is hot, but the green is hotter. Either goes well with the chips. Try it."

Taj grabbed a chip and dipped it in the red sauce and chewed it a few times. "I like it. It's good."

Taj said he would have whatever she was having. She ordered two cheese enchiladas, rice, and refried beans. They ate chips while they waited. Their food came out surprisingly fast with the warning that the plate was hot. Taj enjoyed all of it. Miriam asked a lot more in-depth questions about Taj's upbringing and life in Pakistan. This made him very comfortable as he hadn't been out with anyone since his wife's death. She was an excellent conversationalist, quick-witted and looked him in the eyes as he talked. Taj checked his watch. Two and a half hours had passed quickly.

"Maybe we should get going," he said.

"OK," said Miriam.

Taj paid the bill, and they left. They drove back to Miriam's and Taj walked her to the door.

"Do you want to come in for coffee?" she asked.

"No thank you. It's late, so I had better get going. I really enjoyed the evening and would like to see you again." he replied.

Miriam replied with a smile, "Me too."

He was nervous. Having not kissed a woman since his wife, he wasn't even sure Miriam wanted to be kissed. Miriam turned to face him. Playing it safe, he stepped in, gave her a quick peck in the cheek and hugged her. She returned the firm embrace. Releasing her, he stepped back and said, "Good night, Miriam."

"Drive safely," said Miriam.

Taj got back into his Jeep. He sat for a second and touched the outside of his coat, feeling the outline of the envelope. There were several emotions he was struggling with at once: sadness, guilt, and excitement. He really enjoyed being with her.

CHAPTER 48
COLTON GRAY

Colton returned to Lyon after a long week in New York dealing with the selection of the architectural firm. Looking at the file on his desk, the only new information regarding the murder was Anna's revelation of the term policy naming Ali as the insured and his dad as the beneficiary. Colton also passed on the information Jacques LeClair had given him about a major event taking place on U.S. soil, but there wasn't enough detail for any action to take place.

Colton's phone intercom buzzed interrupting his thoughts. "Cool-taan, it's the Paris detective you met with a few months ago. He said it is urgent. Also, the Chief Inspector wants to see you in thirty minutes," said Colette.

"I'll take the call, but unsure if I have time for the Chief Inspector, Colette," Colton said, smiling, knowing it would provoke her.

"Cool-taan! You must see the Chief Inspector."

"OK, I will work him in, but I will talk to the detective now."

Colton spent twenty minutes on the phone with the detective. The detective informed Colton that they had arrested a prostitute for solicitation a few hours ago. She told them she could help solve a murder case in exchange for the charges being dropped. They cut a deal with her. Witnessing a truck ramming a scooter, she followed the man driving the truck to a hotel and took a picture of him the next morning. It was dated the day after the murder and at the time she had told them. They were running the picture now through their database and would gladly send it to Interpol. Colton confirmed his email address.

"I want to interview her," said Colton.

"We will make her available to your schedule," said the detective.

"Thank you. I will get there this afternoon."

His computer pinged, letting him know he had a new email. He hurriedly opened the attachment and saw a grainy photo of a man's face wearing a red baseball cap with the word 'Venice' on its front panel. Something about him was familiar to Colton, but he couldn't pinpoint why.

After pushing the intercom button for Ali's extension Colton barked, "Ali, we might have a break in our case. Get us two round-trip train tickets to Paris for today and let me know when we leave."

"Yes sir," answered Ali.

• • •

Ali called back a while later and gave Colton several options. Colton then touched the reply button and sent the detective a return email telling him they would arrive today at around 2:00 p.m. Colton immediately emailed the photo to Anna and asked her to run it through their system for matches. He packed his briefcase with a copy of the photo. He stood to leave and was about to tell Colette his plans and in walked the Chief Inspector.

"Please," said the Chief Inspector motioning his hand downward. "You don't have to stand for me."

"Thank you, sir. Please sit down," said Colton as the Chief Inspector had already taken a seat. Colton sat back down.

"Cool-taan, I am thinking of closing our involvement with the European murders. There's not been much progress and I have something new for you," said the Chief Inspector.

"Chief Inspector, I just got off the phone with the detective in Paris I connected with a few months ago. We have a picture of the potential murderer in Paris, and I am set to meet the witness later today. Also, I need to tell you something else."

Colton told him about Anna's discovery concerning Ali and the leads that it might produce if his father cooperates. Colton noticed the Chief seemed to be taken aback by Anna's revelation.

"Incredible! OK, I will assign this new case to someone else," Chief Inspector said while shaking his head in apparent disbelief. He got up and left.

Colton pressed the intercom button for Anna. "Anna. Any matches?"

"No," answered Anna.

"OK, I'll call you right before I board a train to Paris," Colton said.

Ali was waiting for him when he arrived. He called Anna, who once again reported no matches found. Ali handed him a ticket, and they climbed aboard the train. Colton was glad to see that their car was nearly vacant. They sat facing each other with a small table in between. The train left on time for their two-hour trip to Paris.

After they settled in, Colton pulled out his file with the photograph of the killer with the red cap but left it unopened.

"Ali, tell me about your family."

"My parents live in Riyadh, Saudi Arabia. I am very close to my mom. I hope she will travel to visit me soon as I have promised a great tour of Paris," he finished.

"What about your dad?"

Ali broke the silence. "Our relationship is strained. He is a devout Muslim and things between us totally unraveled after my conversion to Christianity. And believe it or not, sometimes Muslims, who convert to another religion, are killed by a family member for their decision. He hasn't spoken to me in a couple of years now. I miss talking to him," finished Ali.

Colton held off for now Anna's discovery. He then asked Ali to go over every detail about the week he spent in Venice preparing for his friend's wedding. Ali described how he got a note saying a family friend of the groom organized the costume party. He went day by day. Guests enjoyed the elaborate costume party. But chaos started when the lights went out.

"Did anything happen that surprised you, or seemed out of place, at all?" asked Colton.

Ali pondered briefly before responding, "Three things: first, it was a relief that someone else arranged the event for me, but none of the guests confessed to orchestrating the party during the investigation. Second, during the party Sophie, the bride-to-be, mistakenly thought I was her fiancé because our costumes were very similar. And last, when I entered the elevator at my hotel the next day, this guy inside the elevator stared at me with a stunned expression. I'll never forget the look on his face," finished Ali.

"Is this him?" asked Colton as slid the picture over from the file he just opened.

Ali's eyes got wide. "Yes! And that was the hat he was wearing. Where did you get this picture?"

"From our detective pal in Paris. An eyewitness to the murder took this picture and we are going to interview her." *Confirms it. Ali was the target!*

• • •

Two hours later, when the train reached Paris, they took a taxi to the police station, and an officer guided them to an interview room. The garbage smell that had been so prevalent the visit before was no longer an issue. The detective shook their hands like they were old friends.

"I know you are glad the sanitation strike is over," said Colton.

"Yes, it was about to reduce the population in Paris. Enter and meet Jessie," the detective said.

They entered the room, and the detective introduced them. The young woman was petite, had short brown hair, intelligent green eyes, and dimples on either side of an engaging smile.

Colton asked her to retell her story again.

"I had a business appointment that night near the Arc. I was leaving and saw this truck slam into the scooter."

"How far away were you?" asked Colton.

"Twenty-five to thirty meters. Walking towards the man, the driver placed a hand on his neck, then stood and surveyed the surroundings. I ducked into the shadows, so he did not see me. He then got back in the truck and left. I hopped on my scooter and followed. The truck suffered severe damage, and he parked it a few streets over. The man got out and sauntered away. He turned the corner and entered a hotel. I parked my scooter and took a seat in the lobby out of sight of the front desk. It is a small hotel, eight rooms only. I waited all night. He checked out around 8:00 the next morning. I snapped a photo with my phone when he turned to leave."

Colton asked the big question, "Did he limp?"

"Yes, but it was very slight."

"How tall?"

"Maybe 175 to 180 centimeters." (5'9"–5'11")

Colton jotted a few more notes and thanked the woman for her help. He and Ali exited the room with the detective.

"Anything else pop up?" Colton asked the Detective.

"Yes, I just got this back. He registered at the hotel under the name Pierre Dumont."

After adding the name to his notes, Colton requested the detective to inform him if they discovered any additional information. Following that, Colton and Ali departed to catch a train back to Lyon. Colton contacted Anna and instructed her to get the hotel guest list of the Hilton in Venice for the specified dates and confirm if a 'Pierre Dumont' appeared on it. Anna called back and confirmed that no one registered with that name during the specified days. She was having the guest list sent anyway as there may be an alias that helps them later.

"Thanks Anna. Good work. No hits on the photo?" asked Colton.

"The most we got was a 20% match, but that was it," answered Anna.

• • •

An hour later, they boarded the train. The train got into a rhythm of rocking back and forth and Colton said, "Ali, there is something I need to talk to you about. It involves the Venice murder."

"Go ahead — shoot," said Ali.

Colton hesitated for a moment. "It is very possible that you were the intended target in Venice. According to Anna's research, someone bought a $2,000,000 insurance policy, naming your dad as the beneficiary and you as the insured. Your friend's fiancé was fooled because you were dressed similarly enough. It's possible that the killer was also fooled and made the same mistake during the power outage. I believe he was shocked to see you in the elevator because he thought you were dead."

Ali sat silently and then spoke, "I don't know what to say —"

"I'm sorry Ali. Nothing for you to say to me. I just wanted you to know everything."

CHAPTER 49
TAJ JILANI

June 2020

Accem assured Taj that the specifications and drawings would include the systems descriptions. Despite the great news, Taj had to convince Chandler, Alex, and Ryan to take part. He asked Chandler to come to Grand Rapids and discuss the opportunity. After explaining the project, all three vehemently rejected any involvement with New York or its unions.

"Look, I know little about New York or its unions, but I believe what you are telling me. However, this opportunity will give our products excellent marketing exposure on a national level. I have an influential relationship within the UN and the person who will lead the advisory board for the project is someone you guys know from the Naval Academy. Jack Callahan mentioned his name when we first met," said Taj as he glanced over at the Roegges.

"Who?" asked Alex.

"Colton Gray."

"No way," Ryan exclaimed, "I never would've guessed."

"Further, I was able to get the RR 9900 curtain wall system, the GS 1000 glass shading technology and the radiant heating system with the EX 250 heaters all specified as 'sole source' meaning the General Contractor must use our products."

"How did you do that?" asked Chandler.

"The preconstruction company the UN hired apparently showed significant operating and utility cost savings when using our products. I gave them rough technical data."

"Why didn't you tell us you were working on this?" asked Ryan.

"I should have and apologize for not doing so. I wouldn't bring it up now unless we were 'sole sourced', which I just found out has happened."

"What is the projected start date for construction?" asked Alex.

"A year from now."

"Has a General Contractor been selected?"

"No. I received information that they will select a shortlist of three in January, and they will submit pricing in April."

"Taj, that is incredible that you could get our products specified as 'sole source'. What if we wait until the General Contractors are shortlisted before we decide to be involved? Working for a bad GC can also kill us," said Chandler.

"I agree," said Alex.

Ryan nodded his head in agreement.

"Very well. We'll revisit when the shortlist has been determined. We'll explore scenarios to find one that makes us comfortable with the risks."

• • •

Late afternoon the next day Taj was getting ready to drive to Flint to see Miriam. He left his house, then promptly returned to retrieve his envelope. Guilt forced him to return after contemplating leaving it for the first time.

He arrived at Miriam's at 6:30. They had steadily been seeing each other since April and usually talked two or three times a week. Taj enjoyed her quick wit, which she used at his expense mainly with American slang and phrases limited to those living in Michigan.

He knocked on the door and entered without waiting for Miriam to open it.

"Hey," Taj said as he walked over and gave her a long kiss and hug.

"How's the drive over — good?" she asked.

"It was fine. Why do you add 'good' before I answer the question?" Taj asked smiling at his own poke at her phrase.

"I don't know exactly, but everyone does," she answered.

"What do you feel like eating a tonight?" he asked.

"How about the Mexican restaurant?"

"Good with me."

They reached the restaurant and were shown to a booth. The crowd and Mariachi band matched the liveliness from before. They ordered the same dish as before but instead of water, Taj ordered a Coke.

"I didn't know you liked pop," said Miriam.

"I didn't either. What's pop?" asked Taj.

"Carbonated drinks like Coke. The nickname 'pop' comes from the sound made by removing the cork. This was before metal caps replaced corks."

"Got it. Thank you for that bit of history." Miriam detected the sarcasm and laughed.

The server brought chips and green and red salsa along with their drinks. Water for Miriam and a Coke for Taj. Miriam's margarita would be out shortly, he said. They munched on the chips and Miriam reached for Taj's Coke and took a sip through his straw.

"I like pop, especially with these salty chips."

Their food came a short while afterwards along with Miriam's margarita. Enjoying the food, they stayed until closing time. It wasn't until they walked out that they realized how loud it was in the restaurant. Until well after midnight, Taj did not leave Miriam's townhouse.

CHAPTER 50
COLTON GRAY

July 2020

After signing the contract with Dunhill St. James and EstiReady, the preconstruction firm selected, Colton had monthly meetings scheduled starting in July and continuing until the design was complete the following March 2021.

"Fleming, what do you have for us today?" Colton asked, glancing at the architect.

"In June we completed the schematics for the site plan, building elevations, a section through the building showing floor heights, interior partition types, a door schedule, exterior, and interior material selections, and a written narrative for elevators, HVAC, plumbing, fire protection, electrical, fire alarm and security systems. We flipped it to EstiReady, so they could put together a Schematic Cost Budget in time for this meeting. We are prepared to go through our design and EstiReady can present the initial budget today."

"OK, let's see what you have."

On a large TV screen, hooked to Flemings's computer, he showed a virtual 3D view of the building exterior, and rotated the view as if a drone was circling the building. Then, he pulled up actual drawing components they had completed. This partial set showed the building design was moving along as agreed to in their contract.

"Are you interested in reviewing the narratives we have written on the various systems?" asked Fleming.

"I don't think so. Questions on the initial design?" asked Colton.

"Yes," said Qing Pow. "Is the roof constructed of the same curtainwall as the exterior walls?"

"Yes," answered Fleming.

"How is the water collected from the roof for reuse during a rain event?"

"Good question. We're unsure now, but we'll talk to the manufacturer for guidance."

That was a good question. "Anyone else before we get into the budget? OK...moving on. Where are we on the schematic phase budget?" asked Colton looking at Castle, EstiReady's representative.

"We have a sixteen-line-item breakdown that Fleming can put on the screen for us," said Castle.

The image came up and Colton's eyes went to the bottom line, $1.1 billion dollars. "We need to maintain a $1.0 billion budget," Colton said.

"Agree. The initial pass is always a little conservative," said Castle.

"Does having more detail, as the design progresses, result in a more accurate number," Qing asked.

"Yes, it does, but being over budget by 10% at the schematic phase budget is typical, so don't worry," replied Castle.

They spent the next couple of hours going line by line. Qing Pow and Colton continued asking the most questions. Qing's questions impressed Colton, considering he didn't have any construction experience. Colton ended the meeting and pinned down next month's meeting date.

• • •

That evening, Colton hit Knox's number. "Hey, so what do you and your dad think about pursuing this project. We will shortlist only three GC's."

"Surprisingly, dad has warmed to the idea but said I would have to move to New York to run it if we were to win it. That doesn't get me too 'warmed' to the idea," said Knox.

"Man, that would be outstanding. I can coach you on how to run a project properly."

"Ha. I would say we are in. I was going to call you next week, but you beat me to it."

"Look, I can't help you strategize on winning, because of my role as chair of the Steering Committee, but I have someone who can give you the lay of the land. Next month, we will advertise the Request for Qualifications (RFQ), but I will make sure that we send one directly to you. Talk later."

CHAPTER 51
COLTON GRAY / ANNISTON KING

January 2021
Colton was on his way to Chicago to meet Nick King's widow. Out of the blue, she had sent him an email last month asking some questions about Nick's death. She said it wasn't urgent but appreciated anything he could find out. At last, he found the people who could verify what happened that day. It wasn't much more than he already knew.

He answered Anniston and said he would meet her and tell her what he learned. She said her parents lived in Chicago and she would be there during Christmas holidays and if that were convenient, she would meet him there. They agreed to meet on January 2 for lunch at The Cheesecake Factory in the Hancock Building downtown. Colton would detour to Chicago before heading to New York. His committee needed to interview General Contractors and select three for a shortlist.

After landing, Colton grabbed his duffel bag at baggage claim and took an Uber to the Knickerbocker Hotel, located a few blocks from their meeting spot. He checked in and made it to the restaurant by 11:50. It was cold and his breathing created misty clouds as he walked fast. Upon entering, he immediately felt the comforting warmth. He observed a tall, slim woman with long, blonde hair facing away from him. He approached her.

"Excuse me—Anniston?" he asked.

The woman turned around to face him. Her beauty immediately caught his attention. Her eyes, gray and penetrating, were striking. She smiled showcasing perfect teeth surrounded by full lips.

"Yes, and you must be Colton Gray. I distinctly remember you and your friend from the funeral because you both were tall," she said as she extended her hand in a firm handshake.

"That friend would be Knox McKenna and for the record, I am taller than he is by one inch," Colton said with a smile as he returned the firm handshake.

She laughed. They sat down in a booth and a server immediately brought them menus. They quickly settled on what they were going to eat and placed their order. Colton stole a glimpse at Anniston while she was ordering and finalized his assessment of her: *strikingly beautiful!*

Anniston asked Colton about his activities after leaving the Navy. Colton went through his history working for Beers Construction, the FBI, and United Nations dealing mainly in human trafficking. His latest career move was a relocation to Lyon, France with Interpol with shared duty at the United Nations for their new headquarters building.

"So, Colton Gray, do you always catch the bad guy?"

"The bad guy got away once, and I swore it would never happen again so yeah, I usually get the bad guy. Enough about me. Tell me about you."

"Well, kind of boring compared to you. By attending Northwestern University on a basketball scholarship, I earned a nursing degree. In Flint, Michigan, I hold the position of head shift nurse at a hospital. I really love my job and am here frequently as I think I told you my parents live downtown."

After some more small talk Colton asked, "Why did you suddenly get interested in any additional facts surrounding Nick's death?"

Anniston was quiet for a second as she looked at her food. "A Pakistani man, now a friend, tragically lost his wife and daughter in the same explosion that claimed Nick's life. He told me that a U.S. missile had killed them. It was reported to me that Nick lost his life to rescue a young girl from a female suicide bomber. I could not understand why our stories were so different and deduced that his wife must have been the suicide bomber since only one man, one woman, and one child were killed. Because of the conflicting stories, I felt the need to dig further without mentioning it to him."

Colton shook his head, "Wow, what a tragedy. Can you share how you crossed paths with the man from Pakistan?"

She informed him he had located her and desired to compare notes about that terrible day.

Colton nodded. "I checked again, and you received the official story from the U.S. side."

"I really appreciate you doing that."

They had long since finished lunch but continued asking probing questions about each other. Anniston looked at her watch which made Colton look at his. It surprised him that three hours had passed. It was probably time to wrap it up, but he did not want to.

"You probably have a lot to do for your trip back to France," said Anniston.

"I am staying here tonight and then on to New York where we will interview General Contractors for the project, I told you about. After that, back to France."

They rose and went outside. Colton raised his hand to signal a cab. A cab pulled up shortly after. Colton swung the door open and before she got in, she turned to Colton, gave him a hug, and thanked him. She fit perfectly in his arms. He started to walk away but quickly turned around.

"Anniston?"

She stopped getting in the cab and looked up at him.

"I...well...will you have dinner with me tonight?" he asked.

She smiled, tilted her head, and then nodded, "Yes, I will."

Anniston couldn't find a scrap of paper, so she grabbed Colton's hand and with a pen wrote her cell number on his palm. "Don't lose that number. Call me."

She waved, and he returned one as he watched her leave. He looked at his hand. *That was hot!* He made his way back to the Knickerbocker, unbothered by the cold, excited and... he kept glancing at his hand adorned with ink.

• • •

Colton met her in the lobby of her parents' condo, and they rode to Giordano's on North Rush Street. The smell of pizza, the taste of a cold beer, the warm dining area and the beautiful woman sitting across from him created a very comfortable atmosphere. Colton considered it the finest deep-dish pizza he had ever eaten and expressed his satisfaction. The cheese under the tomato sauce and the chewy, thick dough was incredible. Their conversation was mainly questions and answers as they continued to probe slowly into each other's personal lives.

It had gotten late. They cabbed it back to her parents' condo building. He accompanied her in the elevator to the fortieth floor and walked her to the door. He asked Anniston if she would consider coming to see him in France. She said she would. They ended the evening with a long, deep kiss. He turned around, but quickly grabbed her again and shared another passionate kiss.

"OK, is this it?" she asked. "I just want to be prepared for the next surprise attack."

Colton smiled, "You are so beautiful—one more." He kissed her again. "Tonight was incredible. I want to see you again."

"Me too." She waved, slowly closed the door, but still peeked at him with one eye through the crack. Colton laughed, seeing her one eye only, and slowly pushed open the door and kissed her again.

He finally walked away dazzled. *Dazzled?* No one dazzles Colton Gray, unless her name starts and ends with Anniston King.

• • •

With her eyes closed, Anniston leaned back against the inside of the front door. She hadn't felt like this in a long time: tall, ruggedly handsome, cocky in a funny way, and that cute dimple. She never imagined feeling this way for someone other than Nick. Although she could never replace Nick, she couldn't wait to see Colton again.

• • •

Colton left the next morning and flew to New York. He reviewed the RFQ file on the plane. In last month's meeting the Steering Committee narrowed the field of respondents from fifteen companies to five based on: company balance sheet, bonding, previous high rises built, and experience working in congested, urban areas. The Steering Committee scheduled a meeting with the five this week.

After three days of interviews concluded, Colton called for a vote. "OK. Time to pick three top-notch General Contractors for our shortlist. Circle your choices on this sheet and pass it back," Colton remarked as he passed each one a piece of paper.

After ten minutes everyone handed their ballots to Colton. Colton asked Jim Rattler to write the votes by the names as he read them out.

Beers–9
Bovine–8
Chapman Bros.–0
DeWayne–3
Turnkey–7

"OK, the three general contractors we will ask to submit a proposal on April 15 are: Beers of Atlanta, Bovine, and Turnkey, both of New York City. Jim, please write letters to all five and inform the three shortlisted contractors of the process. Questions?" asked Colton. All shook their heads. "OK, see you next month for the final drawing review with the design team. Jim, can you stick around briefly?"

"Sure," said Jim.

Colton laid out what he was worried about and asked Jim for advice. Jim immediately came up with three unique tactics that would allay Colton's concerns. Colton told him to move forward. Jim left the room and Colton hit the button on his phone for Knox.

"Hey, the votes are in, and you guys didn't make the cut. Man, I'm sorry. I probably should have voted for you."

"What? Really? I thought the presentation went well."

Colton laughed. "Just kidding. My amazing powers of persuasion got you the most votes of anyone. Congratulations! You will hear from Jim Rattler on next steps and some strategies to navigate working up here."

"Hilarious, but that is great news. I will let Dad know and I look forward to hearing from Mr. Rattler. Talk later."

• • •

As Colton boarded the plane to Paris, he received an email from Ali requesting a month's leave to visit his family. Colton responded and approved it. "That's going to be an awkward confrontation with his dad," he muttered, shaking his head.

CHAPTER 52
TAJ JILANI

Taj set up a meeting with Chandler and the Roegges after being informed by Accem about the contractors. They met in the Roegges conference room.

"So, the three general contractors are Bovine, Turnkey, and Beers. Two are from New York, Beers hails from Atlanta. Do you know any of these contractors?"

"I know Turnkey and they are brutal on subcontractors. Not someone we should work for," Chandler remarked.

"I did not know who Beers was until Ryan and I got a call from Knox Mckenna recently. His family owns Beers, and he wants to discuss the project with us. He knew B & I and us were sole sourced and wanted to strategize if we were open to it. I told him we had a professional relationship with B & I and we were all meeting today about the project. Chandler—Ryan, and I played football with both Colton Gray, who is the Steering Committee chair, and Knox Mckenna who you just heard about. Both are great guys," said Alex.

"That's an excellent development." said Taj.

"We feel more comfortable now that Beers is involved. Knox told us he would manage the project if they were the selected General Contractor. We still want to avoid union dealings in New York. If we can supply all the material and let someone else locally install our material, Alex and I are in," said Ryan.

"I see it the same way. Having some people we trust, like your football buddies, is an excellent development but, Taj, I don't think you and I want to get involved with the unions in New York either," said Chandler.

"What if you trained me on how to install the radiant tube system? I will move to New York and supervise the installation. How many craftsmen would I need to manage?"

"Ten, maybe twelve. We would probably have to sign some sort of union agreement as well. But you would move and manage this for us?"

"Yes,"

"OK, I'm in," said Chandler.

Taj then lobbied for the Roegges to submit a price to furnish and install the special curved glass dome at the ground floor level. This would be the project's highlight, providing valuable marketing material for their company. Alex agreed with Taj's logic and said if Taj would take care of any union issues and manage the installation for them also, they would do it. Since Taj just made this same offer to Chandler, he agreed.

Taj brought up one other point. "Let's meet with Knox and see what his perspective is on our approach. One item I forgot to mention. When getting 'sole sourced' we must give all the general contractors a quote."

"I can see why that's required. And, Knox may have some ideas on how to mitigate our concerns that we haven't thought about," said Alex. Alex punched a button on his phone.

"Hey Knox, Alex Roegge. Catching up with you was great."

"Same here," said Knox.

"Can you come meet us next week to discuss strategy?"

"Yep. Next Friday work?"

Alex held the phone down. "Next Friday work?" Looking at the others. All nodded. "Friday is good," said Alex.

"Great, see ya'll then."

CHAPTER 53
ALI MASADA

Ali's flight landed in Riyadh. He decided it would be better to drop in instead of informing his parents about his arrival. Getting into a taxi, he provided instructions to the driver. The decorations and lights the taxi driver had adorned his taxi with were a source of amusement for him, although typical in Saudi Arabia.

The driver took him to the address. He went to the intercom at the gate in the enormous wall that surrounded his parents' palatial estate. He pressed the button and gave a traditional hello. His Mom asked if it was really him. Yes, he answered.

The gate unlocked immediately. Ali strode in and his mom came running out and hugged him as hard as she could. She said it was a joyous day. They walked in together. The house smelled of one of his favorite dishes his mom used to make for him.

"Why didn't you tell us you were coming?" asked his mom.

"I wanted it to be a surprise. Is that lamb stew I smell?" asked Ali.

"Yes, it is."

"Where is Dad?"

"He won't get home until later."

• • •

His dad finally came home at 8:30 that evening. Upon entering their home, he was stunned to see Ali. His eyes showed it all.

Ali did not move toward his dad. His lips trembled and his eyes watered with tears.

"Dad, I know about the insurance policy you purchased. How could —," His voice cracked, but he continued, "How could you have done that to me?"

CHAPTER 54
TAJ JILANI

February 2021

Taj, Alex, Ryan, and Chandler sat in the meeting space when Knox McKenna entered. His big hands produced a firm handshake. The Roegges and Knox caught up with a few Navy football stories. Knox told Taj and Chandler that Ryan was a strong safety who hit the hardest on defense, while Alex excelled as an intelligent and strategic center on offense.

They transitioned to discuss business from there. Alex laid out all their trepidations about working in New York.

"Believe me, I understand," said Knox. "Because you all are sole sourced, it can give us a distinct advantage if we plan it properly."

"How? Don't we have to give everyone a price?" asked Ryan.

"Yes, but not necessarily the *same* price," said Knox.

"Ah, I see," said Alex.

"A few things you should know. Our two competitors must use union subcontractors in the New York metro because they have union agreements. We do not have to use union subcontractors nor does the United Nations require it because of their independent status. However, protests by the unions because we use non-union subs, might affect the schedule. We don't want that to happen. So, we are meeting with a preferred list of union subcontractors, given to us by someone who knows the local market. We will tell them, if they give us better pricing than they give the other two GC's, we will use their numbers and forego using non-union subs. Finally, the United Nations can award this project to anyone they choose, regardless of price. We want to have lowest number to make it an easy decision, if possible."

"Are non-union subs less expensive than union subs?" asked Taj.

"I am told by as much as 10-20%. The required labor ratios, benefits, and dues drive up the cost of union hourly rates, however, a benefit is that their craft and safety training is excellent."

"Is your strategy collusive in any respect?" asked Chandler.

"No, and we wouldn't be involved with that sort of thing. We plan to make business deals with a select group of seven to ten subs and hopefully they will have the lowest number compared to their competition. Alex, what are you guys thinking?"

"Our plan is to submit a material only price for the curtain wall and a material and install price for the feature dome. Chandler will give a material and install proposal for the radiant tube system. You will need to get labor provided by a curtainwall subcontractor to add to our number. What advantage do we need to give you with our pricing?" asked Alex.

"Think of it like this. How much money is required for you to consider working for the other two GCs in New York? It provides a starting point for determining how much to include. We can discuss it further on the day we submit our cost proposal. That sound reasonable?"

They all nodded and then discussed a myriad of other items before finally adjourning around 8:00 p.m.

• • •

Taj drove to Flint after the meeting. He got there late and grabbed a motel room. He had been dating Miriam regularly for eight months. Unfortunately, Taj believed their relationship had plateaued and thought Miriam felt the same. They openly discussed some of the broad differences in their religious beliefs in a light-hearted manner, but he knew it was a deep divide between them. Tomorrow morning, they planned to discuss their religious differences and their relationship.

CHAPTER 55
COLTON GRAY

Colton was sitting at his desk reviewing the file on the murders and was looking forward to having Ali back. Colette rapped on the door.

"Come in," said Colton.

"Cool-taan, Ali just called and said he will arrive in five minutes."

"He's late."

"He's been on holiday. And Cool-taan, the girls on the fourth floor, remember?" She touched her cheek on the left side appearing to reference Colton's dimple.

"Thanks Colette. I remember. Send Ali in when he gets here, please."

After a brief period, Ali rapped on the door.

"Come in, you're late."

"Sorry boss."

"Sit. How was your time off?"

"Very emotional but helpful in the end."

"If you care to discuss it, how did it go with your dad?"

Ali briefly looked down and nodded. "When my dad saw me and I asked him how he could do this to me, his face showed shock and surprise."

"Who else was there?"

"My mom."

"What did she say?"

"She was unaware of the situation. She looked at dad and then me, but dad told her he and I needed to talk through some issues, and he would explain later."

"Then what happened?"

"We went into my dad's study, and he shut the door. The first thing he did was hug me and then started crying. It was weird—my dad never did that."

"I see why that could be surprising." *My dad never did either.*

"So, when I renounced my faith in Islam, he unloaded on several friends about this. One recommended he talk to some mullah in Cairo that could advise him on a creative way to handle the situation. Upon the mullah's persuasion, he became convinced that taking my life aligned with the teachings of the Koran. Dad then attempted to call it off, but was unsuccessful as he couldn't reach the mullah. Because he thought it was an insurance scam, he didn't call to warn me. My mom was still talking to me, so that confirmed it for him. It made me feel better he changed his mind, but I was close to getting killed."

"Did he know that someone murdered your best friend?"

"Mom did but never told him because of our strained relationship. I also chose not to tell him that I was targeted, as I didn't want to burden him with unnecessary guilt. He apologized and expressed his desire for a better relationship, admitting that he missed me."

"What did you say?"

"I told him I forgave him."

"Wow. It seems it worked out all the way around. Good. Your next job is finding the mullah. He may have something for us."

CHAPTER 56
TAJ JILANI

Christianity and Islam, the world's top two religions, rank number one and number two, respectively. Estimated numbers of believers for each: Christianity, 2.2 billion; Islam, 1.7 billion. Both believe in one creator. Christianity calls him God. Islam calls him Allah. Islam means 'submission to Allah'. Despite both accepting Jesus Christ's virgin birth and teachings, Christians view Him as much more. Both religions teach moral living. Both have sacred texts that the believer should obey in living their life. Christians follow the Bible and Muslims follow the Koran. Both believe in an afterlife where one's destination can be good or bad. They both believe in angels and Satan. Taj folded the sheet of paper he had printed from his on-line research comparing the two religions. He needed to be prepared when they discussed their different beliefs in the next few hours.

Taj picked up Miriam for breakfast and they were going to return to her townhouse afterward. She was wearing blue jeans, a lightweight sweater, and running shoes. They drove to an old log cabin that served the best breakfast in the area. They sat down, looked at the menus, and placed their orders. Miriam seemed a little nervous, maybe anxious. Taj knew she wanted to get things resolved between them. He did as well. Today was the day he hoped they could accomplish that.

• • •

They finished eating and drove back to Miriam's and sat down on the couch in her den. Miriam turned to Taj, "Okay, you want to get us started?"

Taj looked down at the list they had created together. After a moment, he selected a topic that he believed they would agree on.

"Islam believes in one Creator."

"Christianity believes in one Creator as well."

"Christianity allows for one wife only, correct?"

"Right and Islam allows up to four wives at one time—right?"

"Right," answered Taj. "However, I believe a man should have just one wife."

Taj watched as Miriam smiled briefly, but it was only briefly. He continued, "As I think you know, Islam's Allah and Christianity's God are the same," said Taj. He felt there was some wind in his sail and gaining momentum. Miriam surprised him when she shook her head no.

"Christians do not believe they are the same because of their unique character traits. They believe in the Trinity: God the Father, God the Son, and God the Holy Spirit. They are not three separate gods but one God that forms the Godhead, each with different roles. Christianity's God desires a relationship with humans."

"I don't really understand," said Taj.

"Though not a perfect explanation, one could compare God's triune nature to water: water exists as a liquid, turns into a gas (steam) when heated, and solidifies when frozen. Same water, different characteristics. Christians have a personal relationship with God through the person of Jesus Christ, the Son. Muslims believe knowing Allah personally is impossible because of his immense greatness. He is mysterious and aloof. That is why they are not the same."

Taj was in awe. It was accurate what she said about Allah. To his surprise, he discovered that his understanding of Christianity was more limited than he had thought.

Taj started, "Muslims believe in the virgin birth of Jesus Christ and that Jesus was a great prophet and teacher. Men corrupted Jesus' message from God and Mohammed came along and cleaned it up."

"We agree about the virgin birth but not about Jesus' message being corrupted. Christians believe Jesus is God and became a human for a short while. We speak of Him as the Son of God, but Son in this case means 'unique'. Christians believe the only way to Heaven is through Jesus," said Miriam.

"Is it narrow to believe that only Jesus can lead one to Heaven?" Taj asked.

"It may sound narrow but that's what Jesus said Himself—that's the *only* way. To become a Christian, simply admit you are a sinner, believe Jesus died and came back to life, and ask Him to be your Savior and Lord. You cannot earn your way to Heaven by doing good deeds or being a self-assessed 'good person'."

"I'm not sure I understand why Christians need a Savior," said Taj.

"The Bible says a single sin separates us from God, and consequently, we would die a second death, meaning, go to Hell. When we believe and trust in Jesus, His death on the cross takes the place of our second death. Jesus substituted himself for us and saves us from the second death," Miriam finished.

Taj nodded and tried a different approach—his ace card.

"What do you think about you keeping your beliefs as a Christian and me keeping mine as a Muslim?" However, he knew this went against Islamic principles.

Miriam was silent for a moment. "The Bible discourages such arrangements, which wouldn't suit me."

"It sounds as if you have decided," said Taj.

"Simply put, I will not convert to Islam. Consider becoming a Christian, but decide for yourself and for genuine reasons, not just for me. Short of that happening, our relationship can't continue."

Taj was stunned. There was no need for any misunderstanding. "So, let me be sure I understand. It is over between us unless I exchange my religion for yours?"

Miriam's eyes were tearing as she investigated his. She stared at him for a few seconds. Instead of answering, she nodded her head up and down.

With no words, he stood, hugged her, grabbed his coat, and left without looking back. He was heartbroken. He could not prioritize the different emotions he was feeling as he backed out of Miriam's driveway. She understood, more than most, the risks of his conversion to Christianity, knowing it could endanger his life and strain family relationships in Pakistan.

He finally admitted to himself that there was a great internal struggle going on. What he was involved with would likely kill a lot of innocent people. This bothered and nagged at him. His anger and pain, not Allah's promise of a reward, led him to this.

As he drove, he wrestled with other questions. If they were successful in their mission, what was his plan to get away? What if he got caught? How would his mother react? What would Miriam think? His involvement with Miriam was a mistake, but now he deeply cared for her.

CHAPTER 57
COLTON GRAY

April 2021

The day arrived for the proposals from general contractors. Colton sat in his office next to the conference room, waiting for the delivery of the bids that afternoon. He reflected on the last few months. The design of the glass cylindrical building was a work of art through the collaborative efforts of Dunhill St. James and Blackstock & Davis. EstiReady delivered their final estimate last month totaling $1.05 billion, a slight reduction from the initial budget of $1.1 billion. Colton hoped competition in the marketplace would drive the price down even further.

While many high-profile buildings in NYC used structural steel for the structure, this project was designed using concrete. EstiReady evaluated both frame systems during design and recommended concrete instead of steel for several reasons. After 9/11, it was determined that concrete structures were stronger and safer in the event of a terrorist attack and using concrete shortened the schedule.

All three general contractors turned their bids in by 2:00. They assembled in the meeting room as Jim Rattler opened each proposal and wrote the number on the board by each name. The numbers came in lower than EstiReady's final estimate and were within the budget:

- Beers—$987,000,000
- Bovine—$995,000,000
- Turnkey—$990,000,000

"The General Contractor with the lowest number is Beers. We will enter negotiations with Beers. Thank you all for your proposals," said Jim.

"We are going to file a protest because of the unfair advantage Beers had because they could use non-union subcontractors!" shouted the representative from Turnkey.

"I agree," said Bovine's rep.

"You may do what you want, but your protest carries no weight due to the United Nations special status. Thank you all for submitting proposals."

Everyone left the room except Colton, Jim, and Knox.

Knox fist bumped Colton and turned to Jim, "I really appreciate your advice and guidance. Everything you suggested, worked perfectly."

"You're welcome. Colton asked me to take part in a way that would withstand scrutiny," Jim said.

"You did, Jim, thank you," said Colton. "Let's go celebrate the big win!"

CHAPTER 58
ACCEM

It had been almost eighteen months since Accem last met with General. They met again in the same city and dined at the familiar Chinese restaurant. After clearing the dishes, the manager closed the sliding door of the back room and assured them he would not disturb them unless called.

General turned to Accem. "Old friend, I look forward to your report."

Accem explained how they gained control of the Steering Committee and selected the preconstruction firm. This also permitted them to choose the architect that would incorporate several key systems in the design and the preconstruction firm would confirm these components to be a cost savings. The two companies Pakistan purchased produces these two critical components. Hassan and Jihad's Bood will be the installation crew for the tube-based heating system. And, since they last met, they decided on using a liquid explosive, instead of water, to be injected into the radiant tubing system. Once ignited, it will bring the entire building down. In conclusion, he said he was handling all the logistics for the liquid explosives.

"Got it. "

"How do you get Jihad's Blood into the U.S. and into the work force," asked General.

"Key employees inside the Department of State received some influence funds, and they promptly granted visas for all six men. Then we purchased union cards, for $10,000 a piece," answered Accem.

"How is Pakistan doing?"

"He's smart and has performed well for us."

"Good work," nodded General. "I ran out of time when we last met. Question: how did you convince parents to be part of the insurance scheme to have their sons murdered for a payoff?"

Accem retrieved notes from a file folder and explained all the details to General.

"Truly incredible. I never believed it would be successful."

"Thank you," said Accem as he closed his folder.

"This will shake the world," General stated.

"Who in our government knows of this plan?" asked Accem.

The General fixed his gaze on him momentarily, apparently calibrating his response. "You're better off not knowing," the General replied.

The General then looked at his watch and stood to leave. They said their goodbyes.

PHASE III
BUILD THE BUILDING
THAT CREATES THE BOMB

CHAPTER 59
TAJ JILANI

June 2021

Taj attended the first official subcontractor meeting scheduled by Beers. Last week, he and a few subcontractors met with Beers' scheduling consultant for three days to create an agreed-upon schedule. Knox Mckenna and the Beers Superintendent entered the room and closed the door. There were roughly twenty-five subcontractors in this initial meeting.

"I want to extend a warm welcome to everyone at the meeting today. My name is Knox Mckenna, and I will oversee the project for Beers. To my right is the Project Superintendent, Jay 'Big Dog' Meyer. I wanted this initial meeting to introduce ourselves to each other. A sign-in sheet is circulating. Please sign with your email address and cell phone number for us. Now, starting on my left, please introduce yourselves, your company and what your scope is," said Knox. After that was done, Knox then used Dunhill St. James model, borrowed from the Colton, to talk about the project.

"The building from ground level is sixty stories on the west side but stops at forty-five floors on the east side. The building has been described as a thick-walled pipe standing vertically with the top cut off at an angle. You can see that glass curtain wall covers the outside wall, the sloping top, and the inside walls to ground level."

"Does the curtainwall act as solar panels?" asked the HVAC sub.

"Yes, embedded between layers of the glass," answered Knox as he looked at Taj.

Taj nodded, attentively, as Knox explained the one distinctive feature of their building was the Grand Dome, a curved glass structure in the middle of the interior plaza. The Grand Dome functioned as a skylight for the amphitheater and an executive meeting place. At ground level, movable floor plates extend and close the opening. It resembles pocket doors in a house but positioned horizontally instead of vertically. They would bring conference table and chairs into the room. The huge exterior plaza surrounding the building would contain a combination of park benches, grass, trees, and stone pavers. They will place flags from the 192 member countries around the building.

"OK, last, we will have subcontractor meetings every Friday at 9:00 a.m. A typical agenda is on the table. Meetings won't exceed 90 minutes. You come prepared; they will be efficient. The project schedule will be the focus. Questions?"

There were none. Knox thanked everyone for coming and the meeting lasted just under 90 minutes.

• • •

Later that evening Taj called Accem.

"Number?"

"32."

"Update?"

"Hassan and his men must arrive here in about ninety days."

"I will take care of it. There is an issue I must deal with immediately. One of Hassan's men leaked information about our plan to a French mercenary who is asking questions like an investigative reporter."

Then silence. *Hung up again with no warning, thought Taj.*

CHAPTER 60
COLTON GRAY

American flight #3232 landed in Paris right on time. Anniston and Colton planned this trip for months and the time had finally come. It couldn't come soon enough in Colton's opinion. Since their first date, he and Anniston had talked by phone three or four times a week and texted each other regularly. They had been on five more dates because of Colton being able to extend his stay around his monthly meetings in New York and transiting back to Paris through Chicago.

Colton was in the public area waiting for Anniston to clear Customs. It was early Friday morning. Anniston was staying until the following Saturday. Because of jet lag, he knew she would be tired and sluggish. While droves of people walked past him, he patiently waited. Suddenly, he caught sight of her. She was wearing blue jeans, a black turtleneck, and a brown tweed jacket. Her hair was tied back in a ponytail. She was radiant despite the long flight. She hurried. He wrapped her up and gave her a kiss. They walked holding hands to collect her luggage.

She looked at the carousel and pointed at her bags. Colton hoisted them off the conveyor, and they walked out of the terminal to Colton's parked car.

He pulled out his notebook and looked carefully over their itinerary. He took through Tuesday off work, but he had meetings on Wednesday and Thursday. Then, he was off on Friday.

"I will be your local expert while you are here. We'll stay in Paris until Tuesday morning, and drive to Lyon that afternoon. I've got to work short days on Wednesday and Thursday and then you have my full attention on Friday. Then, I will reluctantly bring you back here Saturday," said Colton.

She playfully frowned and made her mouth do an upside smile at the news of leaving on Saturday.

"Looks like you have it all planned. Have you been to Paris? Can you speak French?" she asked.

"I've been here on business. This is my first time as a tourist and if the French can speak it, I'm sure I can as well."

She laughed.

"So, let me get this straight. You are going to be the tour guide, but you've never visited Paris and don't speak the language. Is that what I am to understand?"

"That about sums it up. Are you excited?"

"Yes, this should be a fascinating trip. I studied French in college, so I can help if needed. But, I don't want to get in your lane," she said, as she smiled.

They got to the ticket booth to pay to exit. A small Frenchman, who looked to be in his late 60s, with a scraggly goatee, manned the parking exit booth. He took Colton's ticket, inserted it in a ticket reader and told him the amount.

Colton shook his head and asked Anniston, "What did he say?"

"Eight Euro," said Anniston laughing.

"His French was terrible," Colton said, after paying.

Their suite was not ready at the Hotel Napoleon. Built in the 1920s and furnished in Art Deco, it was located very close to the Arc de Triomphe. It was a beautiful, old hotel with intricate moldings of plaster throughout. They left their luggage in a baggage-check room and left walking to see the Arc de Triomphe.

They walked to the Arc and stopped to read many of the historical inscriptions. It was larger than pictures lead you to think commented Anniston. Motor scooters, small Peugeots, and

Smart cars buzzed around the Arc, continuously beeping their horns, and filling the circle road.

They walked a little further and stopped at a small, busy café. All the chairs and tables outside, which were small, were made of cast iron and painted green. One table was available, so they took it. As servers moved in and out, the scent of fresh pastries filled the seating area. They both ordered coffee, and a chocolate filled croissant. They watched people stroll by and Colton enjoyed sitting quietly with Anniston.

"There are two things I want to learn about you during our time together," said Anniston breaking the silence at their table.

"Sounds like an interrogation. You know, I'm the only one qualified to do that. What information are you seeking?" asked Colton.

Anniston laughed. "One, your childhood and two, why a marginally, handsome guy like you has never been married."

"Wow! Two deep subjects. OK, I will start with childhood at dinner."

• • •

They returned to their hotel a few hours later. The hotel owner had given him the 'Napoleon Suite' free as Colton and Interpol had saved him a lot of money by foiling an international money-laundering scheme involving his hotel.

Anniston loved the room and the view. Colton inquired if she was hungry, and she responded that she was famished. They walked 20 minutes to a restaurant named Le Fumoir near the Louvre Museum. Their reservations allowed them to be seated immediately. They ordered drinks and appetizers while they studied the menus that were written in only French. Anniston looked around the room. Imitation famous art covered the brick walls. The focused lamp above the paintings was the only room lighting besides the tall, lit candles on the table.

"Romantic," Anniston remarked, scanning the surroundings.

"Yes, it is," said Colton.

"Do you need assistance in understanding the food selection since the menus are written in French?"

"I will do just fine, thank you very much."

Anniston ordered and Colton agreed to do the same. Anniston laughed at his shortcut. "OK, tell me about little Colton," said Anniston.

Colton started with location. He grew up in a suburb just northwest of Atlanta called East Cobb. His father retired from the Navy, and he was an only child. Colton's hand started tapping his thigh as he was talking. Anniston looked down at his moving arm but quickly back to his eyes. He said the nicest part of his story was what he just told her.

"What do you mean?" she asked.

Colton looked away briefly as his hand kept tapping his thigh. "This is hard for me. My father was an alcoholic and used to beat my mom a lot and me some when I was young. When he came home late, mom would send me to my room and instruct me to cover my ears. I was so scared. The worst beating she got was when she blocked my room's door to protect me. He would sometimes come in my room, slap me around and call me a 'sissy' or 'momma's boy' and that I should wear a dress to school."

Anniston gasped with her hand over her mouth and said, "Colton, I had no idea. I—"

"It's OK. Starting at ten, he had me train in Tae Kwon Do, a type of karate, to toughen me up. Since Knox McKenna was and is my best friend, my mom would sometimes ask his parents if she could drop me by their house when she thought it was going to be an awful night. They always welcomed me. I think they suspected some abuse by my dad. Mr. Mckenna would ask me if there was trouble at home because he could help. I would always say 'no'. I was so embarrassed." His hand continued to tap his thigh.

"You don't have to tell me more if you don't want to," Anniston said with tears in her eyes.

"It's probably good for you to know. Knox and his family are the only ones that know my entire story. Mom told me to count to 100 when things got bad. I put one hand over one ear, I would tilt my head to my shoulder to cover the other ear, and I would tap my leg until I got to 100. When I feel anxious, I do that."

"I'm so sorry."

"Then, when I turned 14, I had a growth streak and shot up to 6'3", weighed 190 pounds and got my black belt that same year. One night my father started in on Mom, and something snapped inside me. I pushed him away from her. He swung at me, and I blocked his punch. I grabbed a baseball bat and swung as hard as I could and hit his arm just below his shoulder. He seemed surprised that I was standing up to him. He ran out of the room, holding his injured arm and I chased him out of the house. I yelled he better never come back."

Anniston was sniffling now with tears running down her cheeks. "Unbelievable how a father could act in such a way."

"Then, I went back to my mom, and I was crying uncontrollably. She tried to tell me it would be OK. I told her I was upset only because he got away."

"So, when you told me only *'one bad guy'* has ever gotten away from you, that was your dad?"

"You connect dots quickly. Yep, that was him. It's fortunate he escaped, otherwise I might have ended his life that night."

"Have you seen him since?"

"I don't know what happened to him, he never returned. My mom died a couple years later from cancer and Knox's parents welcomed me with open arms and treated me like I had always been a member of their family. It was my first taste of 'normal'."

"They sound incredible."

"They are. Sorry, I feel like I have dumped a lot on you."

"I'm glad you did and so sad this happened to you."

"I'm good now plus—I have you."

"Yes, you do."

Their meal arrived and Colton shifted the conversation about their plans for tomorrow. The food was excellent. They strolled back to the hotel holding hands. They talked little, and Colton enjoyed the silence. Being with Anniston was enough.

The next morning, they were up and out early to visit the Louvre. A long line formed for entry. Colton had purchased 'skip the line' tickets for about $100 each with a private guide. They walked around the line to a separate entrance. The attendant scanned the bar code and let them through the turnstile, where a young man in a black suit with a red tie greeted them.

"Welcome, I'm Daniel and will be your guide for the next two hours." Following introductions, Daniel led them on a museum tour, providing the history of the Louvre and its exhibits. Anniston asked many questions, but Colton found it boring. He had to act like he was enjoying himself because Anniston seemed to be. The last stop was Mona Lisa, surrounded by a large crowd. The painting was behind very thick glass for protection.

"I don't understand the interest in this painting," whispered Colton. "She's not very pretty."

Anniston lightly elbowed him and whispered, "Shhhhh—famous art. Listen and learn."

Shortly afterwards, they finished the tour and walked to the Eiffel Tower where they were to have lunch according to Colton's plan. Near the Eiffel Tower, they reached a small café that wasn't crowded yet. In the indoor seating area, the scent of fresh bread and coffee permeated the air.

"Why are the chairs tiny?" Colton asked.

"Maybe it's because you are so big," answered Anniston.

"Maybe. OK, the next agenda item you wanted to discuss was why a good looking, smart, funny, successful—did I mention 'good looking'?—guy like me has never been married. Is that correct?"

"I'm not sure that's what I said, but yes 'Mr. Good Looking', that is my interest."

"This story won't be as dramatic as last night, and it'll be shorter."

"I'm ready."

Colton said that there was a similar theme from several women he dated. They told him they felt he never totally committed. The relationship would reach a certain point, but Colton stopped it from progressing. He also admitted he's told no one what he shared with her last night.

"I appreciate you felt comfortable enough telling me everything."

"I've never felt at ease talking about it. When I interviewed with Interpol, the psychologist I talked to asked if my father abused me. He said my answers to some of their tests led him to wonder if I suffered from 'Attachment Disorder'."

"What's that?"

Colton explained it presents itself by not allowing people to get close. Another symptom is a person doesn't seek comfort from others or respond when they do. The psychologist said there were better coping mechanisms than leg tapping, and I should seek professional help.

Anniston grabbed both of his hands and said, "I strongly recommend it as well. Colton, I understand the feeling of having a soul mate, someone you share everything with. Your compatibility allows you to face challenges together."

Colton nodded his head and said, "Maybe I will. There is only one flaw left for you to know, and then everything will be covered."

"Only one?" asked Anniston with a smile.

"Yes. My temper flares up when I see a woman being abused. I physically intervene to an extreme."

"If you'd like, I can find someone in Chicago for you to visit and come along with you. When Nick died, I needed professional help. It was a blessing for me coping with his death."

"It's a deal."

They finished eating and walked to the plaza of the Eiffel Tower. Colton bought tickets, and they rode an elevator to the top. The cool breeze made them leave quickly, but they enjoyed the view.

"What an incredible structure," said Anniston.

Colton put his hand on one rivet at a steel connection. "I agree. It's quite a feat to hand drive 2.5 million rivets and complete construction in a little over two years. Impressive!"

Exiting the tower, they heard a voice say, "Mr. Colton Gray."

Colton whirled around. Jacques LeClair!

"Jacques, what are you doing here?" asked Colton.

Jacques walked over. Colton introduced him to Anniston. She held her hand out to shake his, and he took it and kissed it softly.

He looked at Colton. "She is lovely."

"Yes, she is," agreed Colton smiling at Anniston.

"Jacques—again, why are you here?" asked Colton.

"Looking for you. I have information on the target in the U.S." He looked around as he spoke. "Can you meet me later?"

Colton looked at Anniston and she nodded it was OK.

"Where?"

Jacques wrote the tavern name and address on a scrap of paper.

"Nine o'clock?"

"Nine o'clock works," said Colton.

Jacques turned and told Anniston what a pleasure it was to meet her. He wheeled around and walked away. Colton and Anniston left, returning to the hotel.

CHAPTER 61
TAJ JILANI

Taj finished his field supervisor training in preparation of moving to NYC. He was comfortable managing the installation of the radiant heating system and the Grand Dome in the center of the plaza. He strived to do well for both the Roegges and Chandler Boyd. It was helpful having Chandler at the scheduling meeting with Beers as he could commit to durations for the crews Taj would manage. The Roegges told him he should plan ten weeks to install the dome.

After rechecking some calculations, he confirmed, that assuming everything was manufactured and installed properly, the Grand Dome would function as designed. His heart still ached from not seeing Miriam. It had been five months since they had broken up and he wished things had gone differently.

• • •

Later that night Taj called Accem.

"Number?"

"32."

"Update?"

"I have secured apartments for Hassan and his associates near the project site."

"They will arrive as scheduled."

"OK." *Silence. Accem hung up already.*

CHAPTER 62
COLTON GRAY

At 8:30 that night, Colton departed from the hotel. The cab took him to an older, less touristy part of the city. The streets were narrow, and the area was dingy and run-down. Where streetlamps were working, the light washed over building facades showing them to be grimy with peeling paint. The driver came to a stop at the bar that bore the address Jacques had written on the slip of paper. People loitered around the sidewalks appearing to transact commercial deals ranging from drugs to prostitution.

Colton settled the fare with the driver and cautiously looked around before heading in. He entered a warm room filled with the heavy stench of cigarette smoke. It was almost 9:00. Despite looking around, he couldn't find Jacques anywhere. As Jacques line of business required a lot of trust, Colton believed him to be a man of his word.

Sitting at a table, he ordered a beer, and waited a few minutes for Jacques. Wearing tennis shoes, blue jeans, and a Naval Academy sweatshirt, Colton realized he looked out of place. He wasn't drawing any undue attention, but his senses were on high alert. Something didn't feel right.

He looked at his watch once more — 9:05. He would wait five more minutes and then check with the bartender. If he learned nothing, he would leave. Colton walked to the bar, paid for the beer he had barely touched and in perfect French asked the bartender if he knew Jacques LeClair. The bartender looked around and whispered quietly to Colton.

"Jacques was just here. Spotting someone, he hastily scribbled on this scrap of paper before promptly departing through the rear exit. That was just before you came in. He has not returned. He told me to look for a tall American that would be dressed like an American," finished the bartender as he handed Colton the note.

"Thanks. I'll look around." Colton said as he stuffed the note in his pocket.

Colton walked through a ragged curtain covering a doorway near the side of the bar. He entered a room, functioning as both storage and a makeshift office. By the worn, wooden desk, a door led out of the building. Colton pushed open the door and light flooded the darkened alley. Suddenly, a metal trash can fell to cobblestones about sixty feet away. Hearing footsteps in the opposite direction, he walked cautiously. His skin tingled. Next to the toppled trash can, he discovered a man lying face down. Colton discovered that the man was Jacques LeClair! A second man, not moving, lay five feet away. Light reflected off the man's face, exposing a bullet hole in his forehead.

Looking at Jacques, he saw a bloody knife in his left hand. Feeling for a pulse on his neck, Colton remained vigilant, searching for any signs of others nearby. His pulse was weak. He immediately dialed Emergency Services and gave an address and said it was a life and death situation. He turned his phone flashlight toward Jacques body and saw his sweater soaked with blood. Uncertain of his wounds count, it was imperative to stop the bleeding. Peeling back the sweater, Colton was relieved to find the Frenchman wearing a bulletproof vest. The protective shell had four slugs embedded, but his unprotected side had wounds. Colton took out his handkerchief and applied pressure the best he could. The sounds of sirens were getting nearer and nearer shortly.

Not long after, the tavern door burst open and several uniformed men with Emergency Services vests made their way to Colton. They got to work immediately. They applied bandages to stop the bleeding and loaded Jacques on a stretcher and hurried him off to a hospital. Colton remained behind and answered questions from the police. Colton asked where Jacques would be taken. Speaking on the radio, the officer turned to Colton and shared the hospital's name and address with him.

Colton walked a few blocks and waved down a taxi. He returned to his hotel with his thoughts on Jacques. Before leaving to visit Jacques at the hospital, he had to inform Anniston about the situation. It was 11:30 by the time he made it back to his suite. He quietly walked in. Anniston was lying on the couch sleeping soundly. Colton put a blanket on her and was careful not to wake her.

Prior to going out again, Colton tidied up in the bathroom. Upon removing his sweatshirt, a folded piece of paper fell out of the pocket. He had forgotten about the note. He opened it, glanced at what was written, and then left for the hospital.

The emergency room physician gave Colton a quick status report. Jacques was still unconscious and there was a massive amount of internal bleeding. It didn't look good, the doctor told Colton. They needed Jacques to recover so he could decipher the mysterious scrawl, which seemed to be a single letter. Colton couldn't determine if it was an 'M' or 'U'!

CHAPTER 63
CK

While getting his wound attended to, CK reflected on the day's events. From the highest point of the Eiffel Tower, he tracked Jacques LeClair's movements using powerful binoculars. He watched as Jacques spoke to a tall man and woman briefly. The tall man seemed strangely familiar, but he couldn't figure out why.

CK had found the man who informed Jacques about the impending disaster in New York. He made what he thought was a fair offer to the man. To remain among the living, he had to help silence Jacques LeClair.

That night, he planned to end Jacques's life. CK and his 'new' accomplice followed Jacques to the tavern and observed him for several minutes. Upon scouting the area, CK discovered an alley behind the building and promptly crafted a plan. He sent his helper into the bar through the alley door to draw Jacques out where he would hide for a surprise attack. When Jacques passed by, he stepped out behind him, but his shoe kicked a piece of glass making a tinkling sound. With lightning-like quickness, he saw Jacques bend, twist around and produce a knife that he used to slash deep into CK's abdomen. The Frenchman's counter was a surprise and effective. However, CK still unloaded six shots from his silenced pistol into Jacques' center mass, pivoted and put one in the head of his assistant.

CK remained calm as he had experienced injuries before. Calling his emergency number for Paris, he then drove to a veterinarian's darkened clinic. A man assisted CK into an examination room. The vet gave him local pain medication and worked on sewing up the deep cut. It took a hundred stitches to repair the wound. After verifying his blood type, the doctor started a transfusion for the lost blood. As he drifted in and out of consciousness, CK reflected on his kill total: *#98 and #99 — one more to go!*

CHAPTER 64
COLTON GRAY

Colton continued to check on Jacques LeClair. He remained stable, but in a coma. Colton was most impressed with this French mercenary that risked his life to get information he thought would save lives in the United States. Hopefully, he will wake up soon.

Taking Anniston back to the airport two days ago was a lot harder than he realized it would be. It felt longer than two days.

Colton knew she was the one for him. He felt no barriers to giving his entire heart and soul to her. For the relationship to grow, they must be together. Anniston clearly expressed that. Colton was stuck. Would she move here? Not likely. Could he move back to the United States? Yep, he could. Wanting to be close to her, he pondered ways to make it possible. Next month, he had plans to spend his entire two-week vacation with her. While there, Anniston agreed to set up a therapist session for him. A knock on the door interrupted Colton's strategizing to move to the U.S.

"Yes?" asked Colton.

It was Ali.

"Enter, but don't expect to consume much of my time. I'm deep in thought."

Ali smiled. "Sorry, I can't tell when you are thinking and when you are not. I received an email from my dad this morning. I asked him about the insurance transaction details. He agreed to check his notes. According to him, the insurance payout for my death would come via courier. The courier would have two checks—one in his name and another written as a joint check with his name and a company's name. He was to sign the joint check and hand it back to the courier. He thought the company name was something like 'Sirling & Match'. So, I searched the name and got a lot of hits on an investment banking firm called Sterling + Mark in Morocco. I came immediately to you."

Let's involve Anna in this. He punched a few buttons on his phone.

"Anna?"

"Yes."

"Please give me a briefing on a company called Sterling + Mark. See—"

Anna interrupted him. "I'm already working on it. Ali talked to me about this thirty minutes ago. Don't you guys communicate?"

"Fine. Hurry," said Colton and hung up.

"So, came to me immediately, did you? Sounds like I was the second person to hear about this," said Colton.

"Maybe."

"Any success in locating the mullah?"

"No, he has vanished!"

"Get out of here. I've got more deep thinking to do. Call me when the research is done." *How do I get to Anniston?*

CHAPTER 65
CK

July 2021
Nitromethane Should Only Be Handled, Stored, Or Used By Trained Personnel Who Fully Understand The Properties Of This Explosive Liquid read the label in a language other than English. CK saw these labels pasted on all drums. He had never used Nitromethane but what he remembered was a single five-gallon bucket has a fatality range of 42 feet and could cause extensive injury or damage at a range of 300 feet. His assignment was to ride with the first load for the entire way to the storage location as a test run. They would adjust the route based on this trip. He was moving carefully because of his stomach wound. His biggest disappointment of late is he learned Jacques LeClair survived six bullets to the abdomen and was currently in a coma. He must have been wearing body armor. A nurse in the hospital agreed to keep him up-to-date on Jacques's condition. Nothing to do now as Jacques may die on his own. If not, he would kill him later. Kill count: *back to 98.*

He was in a neglected industrial area, in a remote part of the country. An eighteen-wheeler was backed up to the loading dock. Its cab had rust spots. He stepped up, grabbed a metal rung, and peered into the window. Duct tape covered several tears on the worn smooth vinyl seat. The truck driver, Gus, resembled his truck—old and run-down with weathered skin holding creases around his forehead and eyes.

CK stared at the order document. It showed approval for 750 drums of nitromethane destined to a port in southern Pakistan. They would load all barrels onto a ship bound for Venezuela and warehouse them there. Next, they would bring 100 drums at a time into the U.S. via the southern border. After loading the last pallet, CK helped Gus tie down the canvas. Seven additional trucks were loaded and ready to follow Gus. The wind was blowing from the east and dark clouds rolled past. A bolt of lightning lit up the sky. CK was ready to get the wheels in motion. As large raindrops splattered the windshield, Gus started the truck, put it in gear, and left driving slowly.

• • •

The next morning around 11:00, the crew secured all 750 barrels of nitromethane in the hold of the cargo ship. They also attached new labels that read 'Industrial Lubricant'.

CHAPTER 66
COLTON GRAY

Colton spent his two-week vacation with Anniston in Flint, Michigan and then Chicago. It was Thursday and his flight to New York was on Monday morning for an afternoon Steering Committee meeting. They would spend these last four days in Chicago. Tomorrow morning was his meeting with the psychologist Anniston had set up for him. He lacked enthusiasm for this meeting.

He never felt such intense emotions for any woman except Anniston. Colton was the first to share explicitly his feelings, confessing his love for her on several occasions in recent months. She would nod and say, 'I know.' Even though he hoped for a reciprocal response, she explained she still carried some guilt about being with anyone but Nick. He wanted to marry her. However, her participation and consent were necessary. They had dinner that evening at Giordano's.

"Do you remember when you were visiting me, and I agreed to be the tour guide?" asked Colton.

"I do. Your inability to speak French was exceeded only by your failure as a tour guide. I did most of the interpreting and guiding if I remember correctly," answered Anniston.

"Maybe. But I'm about to admit something—a deep, dark secret."

Anniston sat up erect in her chair. "Go."

"I happen to be fluent in French and several other languages."

"I see, I see. Does that include or exclude English?"

"You're hilarious."

"I'll test you."

She rattled off a long-winded question concerning the historical significance of the French Revolution. He, in French, eloquently explained that it was news to him that this was a significant event. Switching to German, he informed her that one day she would love him so much he would—no promises though—consider marrying her and what a lucky woman she would be.

She started laughing. "Your French is quite good. You changed to German, but I'm not sure what you said made sense to me."

Colton smiled. "I will interpret it for you one day."

• • •

The next morning Colton left to meet the psychologist. Anniston went with him. Signing in, he sat down in the waiting area. Fifteen minutes later, a staff member showed him to the doctor's office.

"I'm Dr. Greenburg, it's nice to meet you, Colton."

"Thanks for seeing me."

"So, reading your chart here, you think you might suffer from attachment issues, is this correct?"

"Yes. When I was going through their interview process at Interpol, the psychologist conducting the tests asked if I had experienced abuse when I was younger. My answer was 'yes'. My dad was violent to both my mom and me. He brought up the phrase 'Attachment Disorder' and recommended I investigate it further with professional help. So, here I am."

Dr. Greenburg invited Colton to join him in his sitting area. With a pad and pen, he asked around 50 questions, leading to tense conversations. At the end of the 90-minute session, Colton felt like someone had interrogated him.

"Colton, I have four recommendations for you: one, when you feel anxious and start your hand tapping, do the 4-7-8 breathing technique I showed you. Breathing and exhaling will calm you considerably. Two, when you witness a woman being abused or mistreated, intervening should be your sole satisfaction. Leave the punishment phase to someone else. Three, having a deeper-rooted romantic relationship is significant progress for you. Being comfortable enough to tell Anniston your background shows you trust her, and by doing so, you lowered the internal barriers you've had in place for a long time. Four, what your father did to you and your mom is not your burden to bear. Think about all the sadness, fear, hate, and anxiety as pieces of junk appliances you will dump at the recycle center. Not yours to worry about ever again."

Colton nodded his head. He wrote the four items on his own pad. "Do you need to see me again?"

"If the four items we talked about make sense to you and you feel progress is being made, then no. If you struggle to make headway on any of the four, consider revisiting me or someone like me. I think your friend Anniston has already helped you significantly. Just get rid of the old stuff."

"Thank you, Dr. Greenburg. This was beneficial."

• • •

"How did it go?" Anniston asked, getting in her car.

"If he asked, 'How does that make you feel?' one more time, I think I would've strangled him. But he helped a lot. He pointed out some guilt I didn't realize I was carrying around. He gave me some suggestions on how to handle my trigger points differently."

"OK then. I'm expecting big changes out of you."

"He also said, since I confided in you about my childhood it was a big step in trusting someone and my feelings for you make me want to be close to you. You received all the credit."

"As I should. My hourly rate is probably less than his and I'm happy to help anytime."

Colton laughed. *She's as big a 'smart-alec' as I am.*

• • •

Their two weeks together concluded. As Colton was leaving to go to the airport, he kissed and hugged Anniston and quietly said, "I love you."

She leaned toward him and put her lips next to his ear, kissed and then tugged his ear lobe with her teeth and whispered, "I love you, too."

CHAPTER 67
CK

After their ship arrived, they loaded all the nitromethane into a warehouse next to the port property in Puerto Cabello, Venezuela. CK set a goal of ten days from Puerto Cabello to New York City. They loaded their leased 18-wheeler with 100 barrels and headed to Colombia. From Colombia, they went north through Panama, Costa Rica, Nicaragua, Honduras, Guatemala and finally Mexico. All border crossings were uneventful and smooth. But CK had received warnings about the stringent inspection program at the border checkpoint when leaving Mexico into the United States.

CK studied the map of the Mexico-U.S. border. There were two main entry points south of San Diego: San Ysidro and Otay Mesa. Otay Mesa was the crossing trucks were instructed to use. It was also one of the busiest. Two exits away from the border crossing they pulled off and briefly met a representative with Border Crossing, Inc., a firm specializing in providing proper documentation for products entering the U.S. He handed them a black booklet he said had all the documentation. He mentioned the possibility of a three-hour wait at the border checkpoint because of the peak season. He told them, "Good luck".

• • •

A few miles later, Gus exited the highway and drove into the Customs Export Compound. CK watched as Gus handed over the documents and showed both of their fake passports to the border agent who approached the driver's side. The agent examined the passports, focusing on the photo page and scrutinizing Gus and CK. A moment too long thought CK.

"Proceed left for screening," the agent instructed.

Gus hesitated.

"Sir, move your vehicle to the building I just directed you to," said the agent with a forceful tone in his voice.

Gus pulled into a large warehouse with big letters that read 'Screening Facility'. Five or six agents suddenly surrounded the truck. The agent closest to the driver spoke first, requesting them to step out of the truck.

After exiting the cab, CK and Gus were escorted to a small waiting room. CK observed an agent climbing on top of the trailer and unscrewing the top caps from what seemed to be randomly selected barrels. A different agent followed him, using a small ladle to take a sample from each barrel. Two hours passed. Finally, a border agent walked through the door and gave them permission to cross. CK and Gus climbed back in the cab and followed the arrows that led them across the U.S. border.

"How were the barrels changed?" asked CK.

"A standard 55-gallon drum is thirty-five inches tall with a diameter of twenty-three inches. Twelve inches down from the top another top has been welded and sealed solid. They poured industrial lubricant in the top twelve inches. They drilled a new fill port fourteen inches from the top and pumped the nitromethane into the lower twenty-three inches. This disguise has also worked at European checkpoints."

CK nodded his head.

• • •

They drove five days more and arrived in Poughkeepsie, NY, a couple of hours outside of New York City, where Hassan had rented storage space in a fenced warehouse facility. There were ten, single-story buildings in the compound. Each had five units with a single car width garage door.

As they stopped at the front gate, CK's phone buzzed. He received a text that he immediately responded to. "After we finish here, I need you to drop me at JFK Airport," CK informed Gus.

"OK."

CHAPTER 68
COLTON GRAY

It was Wednesday morning. Colton had returned to Lyon yesterday and asked Colette to arrange a meeting with Ali and Anna for 9:00. He requested a status report on the various items they were involved in. His absence from the office seemed longer than two weeks.

"Cool-taan, welcome back," said Colette.

"Thanks Colette. It's 9:05. Where are Ali and Anna?"

Voices behind Colette spoke up. "We're out here waiting."

They filed into his office and sat down in chairs opposite Colton. Colton looked at his notepad with questions.

"What is the status of Sterling + Mark, the investment company in Casablanca Ali's dad remembered?"

Anna opened her notebook and took out a piece of paper. "They were very secretive to start with. The director informed me they are a private company and have no obligation to provide information about their business. I reminded him that Morocco has been a member of Interpol since 1957 and if we needed to open a formal inquiry, we would. He then became slightly more cooperative."

"What did you ask him?"

"I asked if they provided loans to individuals or companies. Rarely, he said, and if they did, it was usually a friend of one of the board members or one of their big investors. These types of loans would be no longer than twelve months though. I inquired about the board's composition and prominent investors. He told me that was confidential information. I asked if they were co-beneficiaries on life insurance policies. Not that he was aware of, but they did own term insurance policies for their own board members."

"What did he send you?"

"I asked for loans made over the past thirty-six months and he agreed to send a summary print out, not including amounts of the loans, and hoped that would satisfy my questions. I agreed, and this is what he sent me." She handed Colton the piece of paper.

Colton analyzed it for a short period. "So, it looks like they made one loan to an American company named Trebor & Rallim, LLC, in Grand Rapids, Michigan. It shows the loan paid off six months after the killings stopped, which is plenty of time for insurance companies to pay off the policies. Great work Anna. Next, who is Trebor & Rallim and what do they do?"

"I'll get on it," said Anna.

Just then Ali's phone pinged with a text. "You will not believe this. Jacques LeClair is out of his coma!"

"Call hospital security now and execute the plan we set up. After that, get us tickets on the first available train to Paris. We've got to move!"

CHAPTER 69
CK

CK arrived at JFK, checked in, and rested comfortably in Business Class for the flight to Paris. The gift card of $500 he sent the administrative assistant that was assigned to the lobby front desk, bought him regular updates on Jacques LeClair's condition. CK was told it was unlikely Jacques would recover. She insisted he didn't have to pay her. It was the least he could do, CK explained, since he was out of the country and really cared about Jacques' status.

CK grabbed a cab, gave directions, and about thirty minutes later arrived at the hospital. He settled with the driver and walked toward and then around the 150-year-old building. It had an ornate exterior constructed of stone with large, slightly beveled, deep joints. After finishing the loop around the building, he needed to verify some details inside as he planned to return later.

Walking through the front entrance doors, he continued to the information desk. He asked where the dining area was. A name badge was prepared for him to stick on his shirt and directions given shortly after. The name tag, in his mind, gave him a license to wander around and check out each floor.

It was a successful scouting mission as he stole a set of hospital scrubs from the laundry room and stuffed them in the shopping bag he had with him. He found the electrical rooms on each floor, then returned to the reception and inquired about Jacques LeClair's room number. She entered the name in the computer and informed him that room 234 was flagged, and no visitors could enter without prior approval. He asked if she had a floor plan for the 2nd floor. She pulled out a small map and showed him where room 234 was located. He rotated the map to orient himself and saw it was an exterior room at the hospital's backside. What good luck! After thanking the woman, he left.

He walked to the stairway, went up to the 2nd floor, and stopped at the Nurses Station to ask about room 238. She pointed toward the room. Walking as instructed, CK noticed a police officer seated beside a door. Walking past the officer, he quickly cut his eyes and confirmed it was room 234. He expected security, but now he knew exactly what he was facing. Walking onward, he briefly halted at room 238, opening the door to briefly examine something. Continuing to walk, he eventually returned to the Nurse's Station and left the hospital.

• • •

It was 11:00 p.m. CK had a small doctor's satchel, a surgeon's cap, a mask, and a stethoscope around his neck. He entered the hospital and rode the lift to the second floor. Swiftly, he headed to the electrical room, skillfully picked the ancient lock, and stepped inside. Locating the electrical panel, he opened his doctor's bag and placed a small explosive on the conduit that brought power to the panel. He closed the door.

At 11:15 he walked down one floor and out the front entrance. Glancing around for onlookers, he casually walked to the hospital's rear. Counting the windows, he then navigated to the bushes beneath room 234. Connecting bungee cords to his bag, it became a backpack. He put on the sticky gloves he brought with him. Like a spider, he scaled right up the building putting his shoe tips and hands in the deep joints of the stone veneer. Each window had a deep ledge with a stone balustrade fronting the window.

CK could support himself to the side of the window while he peeked in. The room remained mostly dark, though a small lamp illuminated it slightly. The medical staff hooked up several IVs to the patient and strapped an oxygen mask to his face. *Wait, there's something else.* Sitting in the corner was a second security officer! His leg muscles were fatiguing as he processed this new threat. He pulled the remote detonator device out of his pocket and flipped the switch. The charge blew apart the conduit feeding the 2nd floor electrical panel knocking out the power to the entire 2nd floor. Battery powered lights for exit signs came on immediately as well as one or two corridor lights. The smoke generated from the explosion set off fire alarms and loud horns.

The officer left his chair, opened the door, and then stepped out quickly. CK stepped over to the balustrade, opened his bag for a small hammer, smashed one small pane so he could unlock the latch and push up the window. Climbing through, he quickly wedged the chair under the doorknob.

Earlier, when he went to room 238, he confirmed the doors had no inside locks. Reaching into his bag, he pulled out a knife, ran over to the bed and brought both hands down from an arc over his head and plunged the knife deep into Jacques LeClair's heart. He heard the door trying to be opened, but the chair held.

CK ran back to the window, crawled through, and jumped from the ledge. Landing feet first, he let his legs collapse as he rolled on the ground. Sirens pierced the outside air as a fire truck had pulled up to the front of the building. He swiftly reached the sidewalk and calmly returned to the hospital front. There, he witnessed the building's evacuation. Hailing a taxi near the entrance, he gave him his hotel address and sat back and relaxed thinking: *Heh, dead men don't talk!*

• • •

CK relished it when his informant relayed the bad news about the murder of Jacques LeClair. She was so sorry. After thanking her for all the updates and smiling about his ruse with her, he hung up. *Kill count: Back to 99!*

CHAPTER 70
COLTON GRAY

Colton and Ali made it to the hospital late that afternoon. Their plan included having a police officer hidden inside the room as a back up to the officer outside. *Dead men don't talk—which includes cadavers!* On loan from the morgue, that's what the assailant's knife penetrated. Colton had expected someone inside the hospital leaking information, so he set a trap to catch whoever got past the door guard. Ali put the plan in motion. Whoever wanted Jacques dead had moved quickly. Colton thought they had successfully baited the killer, but that person still escaped. However, they were still one step ahead.

The media would report the death of Jacques LeClair. It should allow some recovery time since no one would look for him. They planned to hold a funeral as well. The truly unfortunate event is Jacques slipped back into a coma before Colton and Ali could talk to him. He was alive and safe, at least for now.

• • •

The following morning, Colton and Ali took an Uber to catch their train to Lyon. Ali received a text that Jacques had just woken up for the second time. They directed their driver to head to a small clinic in an industrial area outside Paris. A security officer confirmed their identities and led them to the room Jacques was in.

Colton tapped on the door. He heard a voice say, "Come in." Colton opened the door to find Jacques sitting up in bed, happily sipping from a cup.

"My friend — come in."

Jacques was thin and pale. A stark contrast to the man Colton first met months ago.

"Ready to get out of here?" asked Colton.

"Yes," answered Jacques.

"How are you feeling?"

"Pretty weak. It will be a while before I return to my professional life."

"Do you remember the night someone shot you?"

"Yes. My attacker had his face covered with a ski mask. Although he got the jump on me, I cut him deep with my knife, but he acted like nothing happened. I was stunned and let my guard down for a second. He pulled out a pistol and started shooting. I was told he shot me six times and my vest stopped four of them. You saved me twice — once after the initial attack and again by replacing my body before the second attack. Thank you, my friend."

"You are welcome, Jacques. You are a life worth saving. What were you going to tell me that night we were supposed to meet?"

"The target is the new United Nations building in New York. I also heard insurance companies financed the operation. It made no sense to me."

Colton sat down and shook his head. *His project is the target, and the insurance scheme matches what Ali's dad said!*

CHAPTER 71
TAJ JILANI

September 2021

It was Friday morning and Taj had taken a seat and laid his notebook on the conference room table in the Beers office complex. The weekly subcontractor meeting was to begin shortly. Since he wasn't wearing a sports jacket to work any longer, he kept the unopened envelope in the side pocket of his notebook.

Taj looked at the four-week look ahead schedule Beers handed out. All the foundations and amphitheater concrete had been completed up to ground level. The concrete pour for the first elevated slab, bringing the structure above ground level, was scheduled for Tuesday morning. The meeting started off peacefully enough.

Knox first looked at the concrete subcontractor's project manager. "You guys ready?"

"Yes, we have two concrete pumps, a backup pump and an agreed to truck cycle with the concrete plant."

Knox glanced at the electrical subcontractor and asked, "What about you?"

"Nope. No way we'll be ready," said the electrical superintendent shaking his head.

Big Dog stood up and raised his voice. "Get more men, work longer hours or whatever you need to do. The slab will be poured on Tuesday with or without your conduit!"

The electrical superintendent crossed his arms and did not speak further.

"How about radiant tube system?" Knox asked, looking at Taj.

"We'll be ready."

"Plumbers?"

"Yep, ready," said the plumbing superintendent.

The meeting adjourned shortly thereafter with Big Dog asking Taj, the concrete, and electrical subcontractors to hang around for a moment.

"I don't take threats very well. We will get done what we can. You can't pour the concrete without our conduit." said the electrical subcontractor.

"This isn't a threat. We will pour on Tuesday. Taj and his crew have more piping in the slab and use a smaller crew than you, but he will be ready. Why can't you guys get it done?" asked Big Dog. Again, no response.

Taj left the meeting feeling pretty good about their preparation for the first pour. Hassan along with his team were working hard. There were six other local men from the union he hired to aid Hassan's crew. They had a negative attitude about working with men from the Middle East. He needed to monitor that situation.

His thoughts drifted to Miriam and his internal debate he had once a day. *Maybe he would call her just to see how she is doing.*

CHAPTER 72
COLTON GRAY

Colton emerged from the conference room at noon and greeted Knox, who had just left his subcontractor meeting. He pulled him aside and said that the Architect had introduced a new field inspector named Sal Rizzinni, who would be on site from now on.

"That's all we need, more help from folks that have no 'skin in the game'," said Knox.

"Yeah, I know. Also, one of his eyes is glass, so it's hard to know exactly when he is looking directly at you," said Colton smiling in anticipation of Knox's reaction.

"You're kidding, right?" said Knox.

"You'll see."

They entered the conference room; everyone had just grabbed a box lunch and was getting seated. Colton and Knox sat at opposite ends of the conference table.

"Before we get started, I have been advised that this project was recently added to the United Nations' counterterrorism watch list. There may be some upcoming security precautions we will have to institute. OK then—Knox please give us a progress report and 'look ahead' schedule while we eat."

Colton listened as Knox explained what Beers had accomplished in the last four weeks and what they planned on getting done in the next four weeks. Colton noticed no one ate their apple, except Sal, which drew attention because of the noise it generated and the juice squirting out with every bite.

"This coming Tuesday, we will pour our first elevated slab which will be the first floor. I just left our subcontractor meeting and looks like we are ready. Overall, we are on schedule," said Knox.

Colton then asked if anyone had questions.

Qing Pow raised his hand. "Two questions. Would additional security measures impact productivity and the timeline negatively?"

Colton answered, "Depending on what's required, it could. But Knox will figure out how to keep the completion date intact, right Knox? What's your second question?"

Knox smiled and shook his head.

"Our project being added to the 'watch list' — is this standard operating precaution or has there been an actual threat confirmed?" asked Qing.

"There has been a confirmed threat to our building," said Colton.

"Thank you," said Qing.

"Other comments or questions?" asked Colton.

"So, you really think you are on schedule?" asked Sal, looking down at his notebook but seeming to direct his question to Knox.

"No — we are actually ahead of schedule — by five days," answered Knox.

Everyone laughed, except Sal. "Well, a little bird told me that the electrical sub would not have his conduit installed in time for the pour on Tuesday," said Sal still not looking up from his notebook.

"Information from 'little birds' is unreliable. We'll pour the slab on Tuesday. Any conduit not installed will be surface mounted under the slab using rigid conduit," answered Knox.

"That OK?" asked Colton shifting his gaze to the Architect.

"That solution is acceptable," said the Architect.

"Good," said Colton. *Knox–1, Sal–0.*

That afternoon, Colton left for the airport to catch a flight to Chicago. He hit the button for Anniston's number. She answered immediately.

"I'm headed to the airport," said Colton.

"Are you on time?"

"Yep. Looks like it."

"Can't wait to see you."

"I can't wait to see you either. Bye." *Seeing her once a month just isn't enough!*

• • •

An hour later Colton stopped at a tavern inside the terminal and sat at the bar.

"What would you like?" the attendant asked.

"What do you have on tap?"

"Guinness, OK?"

"Guinness is fine, thanks."

Colton took a sip. A man's voice became notably loud in the restaurant's rear. The man loudly cursed at a woman seated opposite him. He stood up and opened his hand like he was going to slap her.

"Get ready to call the police," said Colton to the bar attendant.

Swiftly, Colton moved towards the back where the man persistently pointed and cursed at the woman. She was in tears. Colton stepped between the man standing and the woman sitting.

"Hey man, calm down," said Colton.

The man cursed at Colton, telling him to mind his own business.

"I'm not trying to cause a problem. You pulled your hand back, as if about to strike her."

"If you don't move on, that's what will happen to you."

I'm not in charge of punishment. "I'll return to my seat."

Colton walked away back toward the bar. He heard her scream, turned around, and witnessed the man shaking her. Rushing back, he slipped his arm around the man's neck and after a few seconds, gently laid him on the floor.

Punishment is not my job. "Stay," said Colton pointing to the man.

Turning to the woman he said, "Ma'am, are you OK?"

She nodded her head and was crying. Grabbing her purse, she passed Colton and said, "Thank you. This happens when he has too much to drink."

Two police officers arrived and quickly approached the man lying down. Colton backed away and let them do their investigation. He sat back down at the bar and did several repetitions of his breathing technique and was surprised at how quickly he calmed down.

"Good job, man," said the bar attendant.

"Thanks for calling security."

Before leaving Colton asked the two officers if they had questions for him. They informed him that he was cleared to leave. Colton felt good. He controlled his temper.

CHAPTER 73
HASSAN MUSTAFA

February 2022

It was 12:15 in the morning and 22 degrees outside. Hassan and Saleem sat up front in the beat up 1974 white, Ford Econoline van, where the most heat was being produced. Two more men sat in the rear. The van slowly pulled up to the storage complex. Their eighteen-wheeler was at the front gate, parked. Hassan pulled up by the truck cab and lowered his window to speak.

"Any problems?" asked Hassan.

"No," answered Gus.

"I'll unlock the gate and get you unloaded."

The truck pulled through and backed up to the garage door of the storage unit Hassan directed him towards. Saleem unlocked their unit door and rolled it up through the channel track in the ceiling. They had a portable electric forklift that could move each pallet with four barrels. It took them twenty-two minutes to finish.

Gus stayed in his cab the entire time. Once finished, he rolled down the window and remarked, "That's all." He put the truck in gear and slowly left the compound.

• • •

Later that morning, Hassan and his crew were dragging from their late night out. The other local union workers were grumbling with one saying loud enough for Hassan to hear, that they were doing all the work, and the 'Ragheads' were not doing pulling their weight.

Hassan considered them the biggest complainers he had ever encountered. Despite their lack of energy today, Hassan and his crew were still as productive as the six union workers.

They still got everything ready for concrete pour. Hassan, Jug, and their men were in their job shack, putting away their tools, as they had finished their work for the day. Jug, a big man, was the outspoken leader of this union crew.

"You and your people couldn't keep up today," said Jug looking at Saleem.

"We got the work done," replied Saleem.

Jug stood up, and it escalated from there. Jug unexpectantly swung his fist forcefully and punched Saleem square on the nose. Saleem left his feet from the force of the blow. One of the other union workers grabbed Jug. Hassan helped Saleem up and held him back as he tried to get to Jug. He walked Saleem out as he was still cursing at Jug in Arabic.

• • •

It was 10:30 p.m. Hassan and Saleem, with his bandaged nose, had followed Jug to Joey's Tavern. Dark inside, Hassan entered inconspicuously, wearing a cap pulled low over his eyes, and sat in the back corner. He overheard Jug retelling his worker pals about his big knockout punch on "Salami" or whatever his name is. His pals whooped it up with drunken laughter. He watched as Jug stood up, wiped his mouth against his sleeve and appeared to be asking for the bill. Hassan found a rear exit near the restrooms and hurried around to join Saleem.

They watched Jug leave. After walking several steps and looking around, he turned into an alley. Hassan nodded to Saleem. Saleem cranked up their white Ford van, parked across from the bar. He hit the gas and turned into the alley and surprised Jug while he was relieving himself. Wearing ski masks, they jumped out of the van with baseball bats.

Saleem swung first and hit Jug in the knee. Jug immediately went to the ground. Hassan cursed and violently beat Jug until he was motionless. The blows disfigured Jug's head, leaving a mess of flesh and bone. They quickly hopped into the van and drove away. Hassan laughed deliriously. He slapped Saleem's shoulder.

"What a night!" He removed his ski mask. "Killed my first *American*, and it feels great!"

CHAPTER 74
TAJ JILANI

Taj requested Hassan's presence in the work shack right after work. Everyone left, and it was about 4:30 when they sat down. Taj started by mentioning Hassan and his group were doing a good job and moved quickly to Jug's death.

"I overheard Saleem bragging about taking care of Jug. You don't have to answer whether he did but understand this: if he did, that puts everything we are doing at risk. Do you understand that?"

"Jug deserved to die," answered Hassan.

"I don't know if he deserved to die or not. I have informed Accem about this situation. He is not happy. I expect you to control your men and their emotions and don't bring needless attention to yourself." Taj detested unnecessary acts of killing. It weighed heavily on him.

Hassan glanced elsewhere momentarily before directly facing Taj. "I understand."

Taj continued. "Chop told me he knows Saleem is responsible for Jug's death and retribution is due."

"Which one is Chop?" asked Hassan.

"Chop is the one with red hair and sideburns the size and shape of a pork chop. He was Jug's right-hand man."

"They are all lazy and Chop better watch himself." Turning, he walked out of the shack.

Later that evening, after dinner, Taj stretched and then crawled into bed. He lay there thinking. *Would it be a problem if he gave Miriam a call just to check on her? Maybe he would see if she would like to visit NYC—just, maybe.*

CHAPTER 75
COLTON GRAY

Colton asked Knox to give the committee a briefing on the exterior wall system for the project. Understanding more, Colton believed the committee would be better prepared to answer questions.

"OK Knox, let's get started."

Knox started with the basics and explained the exterior wall system goes by several names: building envelope, skin, exterior enclosure, window wall and curtain wall. The main reason for the exterior wall system is to shield the interior of the building from intrusion of water, snow, ice, wind, sunlight, cold, and hot air, and any other weather-related forces. Other forces on the system include water vapor, thermal expansion and contraction, and structural movement of the building frame.

"Questions?" asked Colton.

Qing Pow signaled by raising his hand. "What is the system's main issue?"

"Making sure any flashing, which directs the water away from the skin, caulking, and any system related rubber seals is installed properly so it doesn't leak," answered Knox.

"How do you ensure that happens?" asked Jack Straw.

"Yes, please tell us how you plan to do that," added Sal.

"The best defense we have is Sal," said Knox looking at Sal. "When you perform your inspection, I am quite certain you will check, carefully, everything we do."

Everyone but Sal laughed. Sal appeared annoyed.

"Anything other questions?" asked Colton. *Knox–2, Sal–0.*

There were none. The meeting adjourned and Colton asked Knox to stay momentarily. "I've meant to ask you something. Anniston's best friend, Miriam, was dating a guy named Taj Jilani for a while. Anniston says he is involved with the project in some capacity."

"Yes, he is. He's the superintendent for one of the best subcontractors on this project—a pusher and a sharp operator. Small world we live in," said Knox.

"Well, it gets even smaller. The same explosion that killed Nick also took the lives of his wife and little girl. What Anniston was given did not align with Taj's account of their deaths. Anniston asked me to check if the official military version was the only version. I verified and found the military's record to be what we were all told. One guy suggested I talk with Pakistan's Intelligence Agency, ISI, which you probably didn't know stands for Inter-Services Intelligence."

"Yeah, yeah—keep going," smiled Knox.

"What was the name of that Special Ops agent from Pakistan we worked with? I can only remember his nickname—'2 S'."

Knox paused briefly. "Sada Suleman. What would Interpol do without normal citizens like me helping?"

Colton laughed, "It was on the tip of my tongue. Talk to you later."

CHAPTER 76
TAJ JILANI

Taj sat in his normal seat. Arriving early as usual, he studied the upcoming four-week schedule while the other subcontractors gathered for the weekly meeting.

Knox started the meeting. "Today may be a tense meeting. Several of you are behind schedule."

Big Dog shut the door when the last person arrived. Then for thirty minutes he grilledns is the three subs that were behind. Two cooperated. One did not — the electrical subcontractor.

When it was the electrical subcontractor's turn to receive Big Dog's wrath the electrical superintendent said, "You keep saying we are behind schedule and our work is affecting the critical path of the project. I don't think you even know what affects the critical path. We aren't holding anyone up."

Big Dog stood up and glared at the electrical sub. "You guys, more than anyone else, must be dragged to the finish line on every activity. You are high maintenance. My experience is this: the non-performing subcontractor determines the critical path. In this room, that is you! Some great examples of low-maintenance subs are B & I and the concrete sub. Why don't you ask them how they get it done!"

The electrical sub folded his arms and had no response.

Big Dog continued, "The three of you better develop a 'catch up' plan and show progress by next week's meeting."

"Next, Swindler, the elevator subcontractor has joined us," said Knox as he introduced both the project manager and superintendent.

"OK, you guys will be out here next week and start dropping lines for your rails, correct?" asked Big Dog.

The elevator project manager spoke up. "Not until our contract gets resolved."

"How long have you had your contract?"

"About six months."

"Don't you think that's long enough to review a contract?"

"Our corporate attorneys are busy," answered the project manager.

"Your industry acts like the world revolves around it. It doesn't. Be here next week or we will get someone else. Got it?"

The project manager quickly nodded his head, "Got it."

Big Dog glanced at his notes, addressed a few more matters, and concluded the meeting.

• • •

Taj left the conference room and went to meet Hassan at the job shack. They were alone and Hassan was sitting down when Taj came in.

"What's going on?" asked Taj.

"Chop is a problem. He consistently refers to my team as 'Ragheads' and accuses us of being lazy, illegal immigrants who should go back to our countries of origin. If he doesn't stop it, Saleem and I may adjust his attitude permanently. I'm giving you this warning. Handle it or I will."

"First, you don't need to warn me about anything. I don't care what Chop says. Do your job and ignore him. Don't be naïve. He's trying to bait you. I've already told you we don't need a side distraction. You talk to your men and get their attitude right on this. Keep the primary goal in mind. I will talk to Chop but don't expect a big change. Don't mess this up, Hassan. You understand?"

Without answering, Hassan got up and left.

• • •

That evening Taj called Accem.

"Number?"

"32."

"Update?"

"Hassan is stirring it up with one of the workers here. His hatred for the Americans is clouding his judgement."

"I'll handle it." Accem hung up.

CHAPTER 77
STINGER

June 2022
In a secluded industrial area, it was late at night. Stinger stopped what he was doing and watched the busy activity in the enormous warehouse. An Airbus A350 was being altered. Several supervisors wearing government uniforms huddled around drawings. They and twenty-five skilled workers like Stinger handled the retrofit, which was quite ingenious. Old barracks had been cleaned up and readied for their long stay.

The light from the arc welding stingers flashing intermittently caused the building to emit an eerie glow, like it was sending Morse code signals. Welders were working twelve hours each day, six days a week. A few weeks ago, the crew had finished hardening the underbelly of the Airbus A350 at the locations shown on the blueprints. They were now fabricating parts and pieces for the interior walls.

Stinger was a master welder and given the nickname 'Stinger' as he was one of the best arc welders around. Stinger was slang for the electrode holder that secures the welding rod to apply the weld. He had filled out an application on-line to be hired for this job. The wages were quadruple the going welder rate including the promise of a bonus equaling one-half his total earnings. Despite his dislike of being away from family, he believed it was the right decision because of their financial needs.

• • •

It was well past midnight. After working a long 12-hour shift, Stinger was exhausted. However, he could not go to sleep. He hopped out of his bunk bed and headed to the warehouse. He crossed the 50-plus yards to the makeshift manufacturing facility and opened the back door quietly. The overhead light at the back helped, but it was still dark.

Suddenly, he heard voices. *Who would be up at this hour?* He silently walked half stooped over and squatted behind a large wooden crate. Two bosses chatted with two other men. Stinger moved slightly closer, so he could see. An unidentified man in military attire resembled a general. Squinting, he spotted what seemed to be multiple bodyguards, vigilantly surveying the surroundings, outside the small group of men. The man by the military officer turned toward him — he was astonished. The man was his country's leader! He had seen his picture many times in the newspaper.

Stinger crept quietly until he could hear clearly. *He could not believe what he heard. Who could he tell or trust?* Undetected, Stinger silently exited. He had never felt such fear before.

• • •

The next day, Stinger quietly discussed what he overheard with another welder, BG. BG was short for 'Bubble Gum' because he chewed bubble gum while he welded. Both had similar backgrounds and eagerly accepted the chance to work on this project. Stinger always found it odd that someone flew them in the middle of the night with dark bags over their heads — corporate secrecy, they were told. Now, he understood why. No one knew where to go if they wanted to leave, as none of the workers knew where they were. For his plan to work, he needed another person. BG thought he was kidding at first.

"You heard me right. When we finish, they plan to kill us all," Stinger explained.

"Why?"

"I don't know."

"Do you have a plan?"

"Yes."

Stinger explained his strategy.

CHAPTER 78
COLTON GRAY

Colton received a call with his caller-ID showing a series of letters and numbers. "Colton Gray," he answered. Static filled the line.

"It's 2S. Sorry—long delay—getting back—assignment—been doing?"

"You're breaking up—can you hear me?"

"Yes—much better. I may lose you. I'm in the mountains."

Quickly Colton told him what he was looking for. He needed confirmation that a female suicide bomber caused the explosion he described. 2S promised to check and get back with him.

• • •

Later that night, Colton's phone rang, and he saw scrambled numbers and letters on his screen. 2S he guessed.

"Colton Gray," he answered.

"It's 2S." The connection was good.

"I have information for you. The official ISI record is the same as the U.S. military record. A blast from a vest bomb worn by a woman killed everyone. The woman was the wife of a former, respected ISI agent." The connection turned silent after static.

Colton called Anniston. He told her he had confirmed, through a reliable source in Pakistani Intelligence, that what she had been told by the U.S. military matched their records.

Silence followed on the phone until she finally asked, "Why do you believe he received different information?"

"I don't know. Just a guess, but maybe to protect him personally."

"Should I tell him?"

Colton was silent for a few seconds. "I don't see the benefit of doing so."

"What about Miriam?"

"Probably good if she knew the truth."

"I agree. Thank you for checking on this. Love you."

"Love you, too."

CHAPTER 79
CK / UNIDENTIFIED COMMITTEE MEMBER

CK regarded Hassan and Saleem as reckless amateurs. They planned to meet CK at 2:30 a.m. to move the remaining barrels of nitromethane to a different building on the property. This was a precautionary move in case anyone, including Gus, had witnessed barrels being loaded in the original warehouse location.

CK donned a disguise he used around them and waited in the darkness until he saw a headlight, the only one working on the white van, as it pulled into the parking lot. Hassan and Saleem unlocked the roll-up door to their rented space and began moving barrels into the van. CK walked over.

"You guys are late. Hurry! A security patrol will drive through here soon," CK said.

"If there is trouble, I'll take care of it," Hassan said with an edge to his voice.

"There's the issue. We don't want any trouble. From what I have seen so far, you guys continue to risk exposure with your sloppy actions," said CK.

Hassan opened his mouth to say something else, but Saleem told him they better get started. They rushed. Right as they were about to complete, a security guard appeared earlier than expected. As the car came to a stop, they were pulling down the door, and the guard activated the vehicle's yellow flashing lights. CK hid behind the white van and watched the disaster unfold. The driver got out. Suddenly, Hassan and Saleem both pulled out guns and ordered the guard to his knees.

"Please! I have a family with three little kids. Please don't do this!"

Hassan told the man that his kids would grow up without an *infidel* for a father and pulled the trigger, shooting the guard through the top of his head. He toppled over immediately. Hassan yelled, "Glory to Allah! Glory to Allah!" and started jumping around with his hands held high. Saleem was laughing deliriously at Hassan while slapping both knees as he bent over. CK swiftly moved in, cursing at both, demanding they leave quickly as the guard may have radioed his base station.

Hassan approached the van and glanced at CK. "I said I'd handle it," he sneered, getting in and closing the door.

Chanting in Arabic as they passed CK, Saleem hit the gas, and they spun their tires for almost 50 feet as the van fishtailed back and forth. CK made a call to Accem. It was not a pleasant conversation. He got specific instructions on what to do next.

• • •

A few hours later, a Steering Committee member pulled on latex gloves. Using different words snipped out of magazines and other periodicals, he glued and then placed the words, using a rusty pair of tweezers, on a piece of white copy paper, which he folded and inserted into an envelope. The note and the address both featured the same type of cutout words. The tape covering the sticky part of the envelope was removed and the flap securely pressed. He placed the envelope in his overcoat, pulled on leather gloves and walked out of the building and dropped the envelope into a corner mailbox. This note will be a shocker as an alternate plan had been developed.

CHAPTER 80
COLTON GRAY

November 2022

Colton had a quick meeting with his Steering Committee before they were to join the construction workers and other dignitaries for the 'topping out' ceremony.

"What exactly is the 'topping out' ceremony we're attending?" asked Mustafa Jazzera.

"It is a celebration for the structure being completed. It is customary to hold the celebration when they set the last structural steel beam or pour the final concrete floor. In steel structures, they paint the last beam white. Workers and invited guests sign it with a black marker. Sometimes, the construction crew places an evergreen tree at the uppermost point of the building to show that they have officially completed it. It is a major milestone for a high-rise project," said Colton.

• • •

Colton and his committee arrived at the site. He observed the ground floor lobby had been tidied up and now it had round tables. Three tables up front were marked as 'Reserved' with name cards at each seat. Red and white checkered tablecloths draped over the tables. Colton and his team found their seats and sat down. He watched as his best friend walked to the makeshift podium and asked for everyone's attention for just a few minutes. Almost 600 people hushed to hear the speaker.

Knox started, "I would first like to thank everyone for attending today's topping out ceremony. Also, I want to acknowledge the individuals who have contributed to the project's current success."

He named nearly twenty-five individuals, asking each to stand, then requested the workers in the crowd to acknowledge them with applause. He then talked quickly about the schedule, quantities of materials installed, and complimented the performance of several subcontractors. The crowd gave another loud round of applause. Knox said he would close with one last observation before the food was served.

"People often ask about the differences between living in New York and the South. I think I can sum it up this way. I visited the local zoo recently with my kids. All cages had a sign displaying the animal's name in English, with the Latin name below. In the South, cages display animal names in English and a recipe on how to prepare the animal for dinner, below."

The crowd gave a hearty laugh while clapping at the same time.

"Thank you for your hard work. Keep it up so we finish strong. Let's eat!"

Knox did a great job recognizing everyone, and the project was on schedule. They roped off lanes for ten serving lines ready to dish out the food. Guests received T-shirts featuring the new building's rendering and topping out ceremony date. It had been a fun day.

CHAPTER 81
TAJ JILANI

May 2023

Knox asked Taj if he would mind meeting Colton Gray at the construction conference room to answer a few questions. Taj arrived and took his normal seat. Not long after, Knox walked in with Colton. Knox made the introductions, including Colton's relationship with Anniston and highlighted Taj's excellent work as a subcontractor on the project. He then left the room. After a brief conversation about Anniston and Miriam, Colton, and Taj got straight to business.

"As Knox mentioned, I chair the Steering Committee for this project representing the United Nations. However, this meeting is connected to my work at Interpol, where I am employed full time. One case I'm involved in led us to a financial company in Casablanca named Sterling & Mark. Are you familiar with them?"

"They lent money to the company I established here in the U.S. for investing in two companies: Roegge & Roegge and B & I. Both are involved in this project."

"Who took out the loan?"

"I don't know exactly."

"How was the loan retired?"

"I was not part of the financial arrangements, so again, I don't know. Talk to the attorney I hired to help put all the deals together. He may provide some details, but I doubt he can answer the questions you just asked me."

"Is that Jack Callahan with Callahan & Mezzarro?"

"Yes. Jack's a great guy and I'm sure he will help you if he can. Have you asked Sterling + Mark? It would seem they could provide some answers."

"Yeah, we are working on it. OK, thank you Taj. If anything comes to mind related to questions I asked, please call, text, or email me." Colton handed Taj an Interpol business card.

"I will and please say hello to Anniston for me. She is a wonderful person."

"Thank you. I will. Oh, I nearly forgot. I received instructions to inform you that Miriam said hello. Anniston suggested you call her sometime."

"Thank you for remembering to tell me that."

Taj shook hands with Colton and felt uplifted by his comment about Miriam. Uncertain about Interpol's focus, he intended to notify Accem about the meeting.

• • •

Taj called Accem later that evening.

"Number?"

"32."

"Update?"

"I met with Colton Gray, who chairs the Steering Committee for our project but also works for Interpol. He was asking specific questions about Sterling + Mark's loan to Trebor & Rallim."

"What did you say?"

"I was unaware of the loan's details or its repayment."

"Good answers, Pakistan. I will ask our Steering Committee representative if the UN has Interpol involved in the project."

"You might also—Accem?" *Silence. Hung up.*

CHAPTER 82
COLTON GRAY

Colton and Ali walked to the construction project to meet with Knox. Ali came as Colton asked, to see the project he had been working on. Then, Ali was going to Chicago to handle Colton's latest assignment.

"How's Jacques LeClair?" asked Colton.

"He is doing well. Physical therapy was hard on him he says. He plans to purchase the garage business he works at and retire from his other extracurricular activities. Those were his words."

"Glad to hear. Jacques a good man. I need to call him."

Upon arrival at the project site, they entered the conference room and found Knox already seated.

Colton started, "I wish to introduce you to my understudy, Ali. Intending to save all of you helpless citizens from disaster, he has accompanied me here to aid my investigation. Despite his shortcomings, I've chosen to mentor him as a special project. He'll be here briefly to investigate a Michigan company that may affect our ongoing case."

Ali laughed at Colton's description of him and shook hands with Knox.

Ali said, "I have heard a lot about you, and meeting you finally is a pleasure."

"The pleasure is mine. You guys sit down," said Knox.

Colton's administrative assistant brought in three bottles of water and then left, closing the door behind her. Colton was there to inspect a note that Knox said he received.

"So, let's see the note you just called me about."

Knox pushed the note and envelope to Colton, who had put on latex gloves. Looking at the cutout letters that formed a sentence, he read it once. Then, read it aloud:

"The Building is A BOMB!"

"Did you know your lips still move when you read silently?" asked Knox.

Colton shook his head slowly and Ali laughed. "Any idea what this means?"

"No. We've constructed exactly what's on the drawings, with no significant changes."

Colton placed the note and envelope into a plastic bag, sealed it and stood up to leave.

"I've got to get this to the right folks. A task force will be formed with local law enforcement, Homeland, FBI, and other alphabet agencies. I am going to request Interpol station me here full time to stay involved in the investigation."

• • •

The next afternoon, Friday, Colton's phone rang while he was sitting in Knox's office. The screen showed Ali's number.

"What?" answered Colton.

"It's Ali."

"I know. I have your name and number in my phone. What did you find out?"

"Not much more than we already knew. Jack Callahan was very accommodating and discussed his interactions with Taj Jilani and the companies Taj invested in but said he knew nothing about a loan or the firm Sterling + Mark."

"Got it. Enjoy the weekend in Chicago. I will get there tonight, so plan on having dinner with Anniston and I on Sunday."

"OK, see you Sunday."

CHAPTER 83
STINGER

The team completed the modifications on the A350. Stinger was included in the final checkout of all the structural modifications. After multiple checks, they then checked once more. He witnessed the hydraulics testing as well, and all had been successful. No surprise, as the design was solid, and alterations were simple. They weren't using new technology—just a new application.

Stinger was looking forward to the huge celebration that had been promised for all the workers who had worked tirelessly to make all this happen. Whether they were working for the government, or a government-backed company was unclear. But that didn't matter. Someone had a sinister plan when the project was complete. Early tomorrow morning, someone told Stinger they would fly the plane to another location for flight-testing. Stinger and BG planned to be uninvited ticket holders on this flight.

• • •

Everyone expected an enjoyable evening. Pits had been dug and several animals prepared and roasted for hours in red coals. The food was excellent, and the alcohol flowed freely. At the event's start, they also announced that everyone had the following two days off. Loud cheers erupted. They consumed alcohol at an even greater pace now they had a couple of days to recover. The night was going to be amazing. The unexpected gift of no work in the upcoming days was a welcome surprise. People might not immediately notice his and BG's absence. This enhanced their chance of pulling it off.

He watched as BG drank another large mug of beer. Part of the plan was to appear like they had consumed too much alcohol. But the way BG was guzzling beer, it would not be an act. Stinger had to intervene. He would not allow BG's poor judgment to jeopardize their plan. Stinger staggered over like he was drunk and grabbed BG by the arm and told him to go for a walk, while he still could. They both laughed out loud and others with them at that comment. They moved beyond the crowd.

"What are you doing?" asked Stinger.

"What do you mean?" answered BG with a slight slur and a big smile.

"You're close to being drunk and it will screw up our plan!"

BG suddenly got serious. "I haven't been drinking at all—looks like my act is working."

Stinger looked at him and realized he was telling the truth. He shook his head in relief. They walked back and arrived at their barracks around 10:00 p.m. They did a quick check to see that they were alone. Months prior, they swapped bunks with colleagues, positioning themselves across from each other, in anticipation of tonight.

They found extra pillows and stuffed them in their footlockers. They tried their best to create the illusion of bodies in the bed and unscrewed the two closest overhead light bulbs. It would darken that end of the barracks for additional cover. They hoped their drunken act would make others from their barracks believe they had passed out in their beds. When they finished staging their beds, they grabbed a small laundry bag already packed with water, candy bars, bungee cords, a kitchen knife, and small personal belongings.

They quietly walked behind a long row of barracks, so they could arrive at the main warehouse virtually undetected. There, it would be tricky since one guard with a radio always watched the plane. They got to the warehouse entrance and carefully opened the door. They duck-walked to a spot behind a forklift and quickly checked for the key in the ignition. It was there.

BG's task was to start the forklift, drive it down an aisle, and create noise to distract the guard from the plane. Stinger told him he needed five minutes to get in position. This would give him time to open the bottom hatch to access the cargo hold. BG would jump off the forklift before it crashed, circling around to reach the access hatch just as the guard arrived to check out the racket.

Stinger quietly moved until he got within 30 feet of the Airbus. He glanced at his watch, noticing one minute remaining. The guard was sitting in a chair reading a book. He carried a long flashlight and a radio. Wearing blue coveralls, he had an ID badge on a chain around his neck. He looked up at the laughter, shook his head, and returned to reading.

Suddenly, Stinger heard a yell followed by laughter. Glass shattered against the concrete floor from a beer bottle hurled by BG. Those noises and the sound of a forklift starting yanked the guard from his relaxed position in the chair and he ran toward the noise. Stinger seized the moment, ran, and grabbed a ladder. He would pull the ladder up after BG joined him. He opened the ladder and ascended quickly to the hatch. Seconds later BG came running and stopped at the base of the ladder. There was shiny sweat on his forehead reflecting light. His head moved, searching for the guard or anyone else. He looked up at Stinger to check his progress in opening the hatch. Stinger tugged on the metal arm. It wouldn't budge. Stinger glanced up and noticed a padlock securing the arm to the hatch frame.

The forklift motor was no longer audible in the distance, showing that the guard had reached it and shut off the engine. They had limited time before the guard returned. Their plan was about to fall apart because of a padlock. Stinger grabbed the padlock in his hand—it hadn't yet been engaged! He opened the lock and pulled it off. BG whispered for Stinger to hurry. He pulled the lock from the hole, pulled the arm down, turned it clockwise and the hatch's latch disengaged. The door opened into the airplane. Stinger crawled into the cargo bay and motioned for BG to follow. He climbed the ladder like his life depended on it because it did. Stinger grabbed him and helped pull him through the opening. They both perspired because of the heat and humidity, and their adrenaline was supercharged. Grabbing the ladder, they pulled it up. It was constructed with aluminum, so it wasn't particularly heavy, just bulky. The telescoping legs of the ladder would drastically change its length upon once they got it inside the plane.

A few seconds later it cleared the edge, and Stinger carefully and quietly laid it down just as the guard walked back. Their only problem now was the open hatch. It was dark under the belly of the plane, so it wasn't immediately noticeable.

The squeaking sound of the guard's tennis shoes caught their attention as he left with a broom and dustpan to clear the glass. With the guard out of sight, Stinger locked the hatch from the cargo side of the Airbus. They collapsed the ladder and secured it with bungee cords. They moved through a door to the galley, where food was prepared. Upon closing the door behind them, they lay there for several minutes, sweat-soaked and finally able to relax for the first time since embarking on their escape. Success! They made it!

They planned to hide in the luggage storage area above the seats until the plane landed, then find a way home.

CHAPTER 84
COLTON GRAY

Colton hung up with Ali and looked at Knox.

"Any progress on the note?" asked Knox.

"Nothing. The note did not have any residue or traceable substance detected. It's confusing why someone would send a warning," Colton replied.

"Anything I should share with my team at this point?"

"Not yet. A site security plan with delivery checkpoints is being worked on. We will get it to you when done."

"OK. We are calling for a punch list inspection next week for the first fifteen floors. It's coming together."

"Wow, that's good news. Now starts the grind, right?"

"Right."

"I've got to go. As you know, I have important business in Chicago and then back at Interpol. Catch you in a couple of weeks."

They fist bumped and Colton set off for the airport. The slight bulge in his canvas computer bag was the primary reason he planned to see Anniston. He was ready to ask the important question to the woman he wanted to be with forever.

• • •

On Saturday, Colton said, as usual, he had a great evening planned. It would mirror their first date. They ate lunch at The Cheesecake Factory and then pizza at Giordano's. From there they walked to Millennium Park and stopped and sat on a bench by the Bean, the large, stainless steel art structure that was the park's centerpiece.

The night had turned pleasantly cool. They sat there quietly relaxing and observing the few folks that walked by. Colton was trying to disguise his 4-7-8 breathing technique, but Anniston picked up on it right away.

"So, what's with breathing? Does being with me make you anxious? I did not know I had that kind of influence over your behavior."

Colton turned to Anniston. "Ha! I have something I want to ask you."

Anniston looked deep into his eyes. "And what would that be?" she asked.

"Um, what's your opinion on marriage?"

"Finding the right person makes marriage great."

"Yeah, yeah—I know all that—I'm talking about you and me."

"So, what are you asking exactly?"

"Well, you know, about getting married—us."

"I see. I have an old-fashioned approach to things like this. Just for conversation's sake, if I was interested in getting married, I would like the man to get on his knee and ask me if I would marry him."

She's not making this easy. Colton suddenly moved from the bench and got down on one knee. He grabbed the little velvet box out of his pocket, opened it, and looked up to her.

"Anniston King, will you marry me?"

Anniston leaned down until her lips were next to his left ear and whispered in perfect German. "You told me one day I would love you so much and you would, no promises though, consider marrying me and what a lucky woman I would be. Is this correct?"

Colton was stunned. *She can speak German?* He stayed on one knee, unsure of what to say and feeling awkward. After a brief pause, she leaned back, smiled, and responded, "Yes, Colton Gray. I will marry you!"

Relieved, Colton slipped the ring onto her finger, stood up and hugged her swaying slightly back and forth for several minutes. He then looked at her, suddenly feeling confident again. "You never told me you could speak German."

"I planned to save it for the perfect moment. I found it very amusing when you were speaking German and thinking I couldn't understand you."

Colton laughed out loud. "And — some more news. With the case I'm working on with Interpol, it now intersects with my UN project. Until the case is solved, I will request temporary relocation to New York."

"That is wonderful!" said Anniston.

Colton grasped her hand and walked to catch a cab and share the news with her parents.

• • •

Later that night, Colton called Knox and asked him to be his 'Best Man'.

"I will be honored to serve that role. Now, just to confirm — she really said 'yes'?" he asked.

CHAPTER 85
TAJ JILANI

July 2023

Taj boarded his morning flight to Detroit and landed an hour and forty-five minutes later. Picking up his key for the rental car at the Enterprise counter, he drove to the offices of Roegge & Roegge. Arriving at 11:30, he went around back hoping to surprise Chief. Walking slowly to Chief's office, he peeked around the door frame. Chief sat with his back to the door studying some papers.

"Hey, Chief!" Taj exclaimed, walking over. When Chief turned around, his smile was big and his eyes were open wide. Rising to his feet, Chief wrapped Taj in his short, chubby arms, hugging him with such force that it nearly took Taj's breath away.

"Come, come, sit right here. How long are you here?" asked Chief as he cleared a couple of empty donut boxes off the wooden upright chair.

"Just until tomorrow. I've got to get back. Did they deliver the glass for the dome?"

"Yes, the last shipment arrived yesterday."

"Good. I want to verify that all the glass was properly manufactured."

"You can check it all out after lunch."

"I suppose I can take you to lunch—only if you are hungry though," smiled Taj.

Chief loved this all-you-can-eat pizza joint they used to go to. With tomato paste smeared all over his jowls, Chief told Taj all he had been working on. One twenty-four-inch pizza later, Chief finally slowed down eating but asked if Taj was going to finish that last bit of garlic bread that was on Taj's plate.

Taj smiled and slid his plate over to Chief as Chief sopped up some puddles of tomato sauce on his own plate. Taj looked at his watch which signaled it was time to go. They stood up and returned to the warehouse.

Taj took off his jacket, rolled up his sleeves, and began carefully examining each piece of rounded glass, one bundle at a time. It seemed like they accounted for every piece of glass, plus they included five extra pieces, one for each distinct shape of glass, in case any pieces broke during delivery or installation. Satisfied, he unrolled his sleeves and slipped his jacket back on. It was almost 5:30.

He locked the door behind him and retrieved his phone. He dialed Miriam's number and hoped she would answer. They hadn't talked since he had moved to New York. She answered, and he told her he was in Grand Rapids and was returning to New York tomorrow afternoon.

"May I take you to dinner? I could leave shortly and be there by 7:30."

"Yes. That sounds great."

By exceeding the speed limit, he reached Flint in just over an hour with his rental. Upon his arrival at the familiar motel, he quickly checked in and took a shower. As he transferred the unopened envelope from his notebook to his jacket, he dressed himself in gray slacks, a stylish white shirt, and a navy-blue blazer.

As he arrived at Miriam's house, she promptly emerged from the front door before Taj exited the car. She opened the door and got in. They hugged, and he kissed her lightly on the cheek. Taj drove them to what had been their favorite restaurant before he moved. The tables were lit only by candlelight. Dinner was splendid, and they comfortably caught up on their activities. They both refused dessert and Taj asked for the check. The small house's dining area was nearly vacant. Neither spoke. The delivery of the bill interrupted the few minutes of silence. Taj paid cash and gave the server a generous tip.

He then looked back to Miriam. "I have really missed you. You are always on my mind, and I wonder if we can overcome our differences?"

Silence.

"Am I the only one feeling this void?" Taj finally asked.

"No, but we can't ignore beliefs that are core to who we each are."

Taj hesitated a moment and then spoke with a slight edge to his voice.

"Miriam, there are some things I have never told you. I mentioned my wife and daughter died, but I never said how. A missile launched from an American drone killed them. Ever since that day, I hated everything about America and vowed to avenge their deaths. However, since being here, my hatred has lessened as I've made friends, and met you. But when you tell me I must convert to your religion for our relationship to continue, I get mad towards all things American."

Miriam appeared clearly taken aback by his tone and what he said. She glanced downward, silent for a moment. Slowly, she raised her head, looked into his eyes, and clarified, "I never asked for your conversion to Christianity. The choice is yours and yours alone. I have a say in my relationship choices, though. Certain things must align and that is one of them," replied Miriam.

That stopped Taj cold. She was right. All at once, he was combining several things together. She never asked to change his beliefs. He pressed what made it work for her. Taj felt instant internal conviction and guilt.

Taj spoke, "You are right. I apologize. You have been honest and upfront about everything. I have mixed things up a bit inside my head."

Miriam nodded her head in acceptance of his apology. She appeared to be contemplating something — and then she spoke.

CHAPTER 86
CK

CK punched in Hassan's number on his phone. "I'm ready to review your plan," said CK.

"Who is this?" asked Hassan.

CK ignored his comment and knew Hassan did not like answering him, but Accem told Hassan he was to do whatever CK told him to do. "You need to meet me tomorrow night. Write this address down."

• • •

Hassan and Saleem showed up at the motel later than CK had requested. From the window, CK witnessed their ascent up an exterior staircase to room 223. The place was a dive, with rooms rented by hour, day, week, and month.

Hassan pounded on the door. Wearing his normal disguise of glasses, a mustache, and a ball cap, CK pushed the door open and quickly checked for any observers. Satisfied, he opened the door wider and let them in. The room had bare walls, peeling paint, dingy linoleum floor and one double bed covered by a blanket that looked as soft as sandpaper. There was also a round table with four small chairs. The old TV had coin slots and CK turned it on with the volume moderately high.

"Nice place," said Hassan sarcastically while looking around.

"You are late," said CK.

"I don't control the traffic," said Hassan.

"Sit. Let's go over your plan."

"It's simple. We load the barrels of nitromethane out of the warehouse and move it to the project site and distribute twelve barrels to each level. Each floor has four mechanical rooms where we will store three barrels. We then pump the nitromethane into the piping system moving from one mechanical room to the next. Each mechanical room needs a detonator to ignite the nitromethane. We will conceal the detonators in a metal box with a built-in relay and set of contacts that will remain in the 'open' position. Remotely, using a wireless signal, we will simultaneously cause all the contacts to go from open to closed, which completes the electrical circuit to the detonator. The detonator then ignites the nitromethane, and the building collapses. We will perform testing to ensure the contacts close when receiving the signal. Got it?"

CK nodded. "I have a couple of suggestions. Conduct a trial run. Inform the General Contractor that you want to confirm the proper selection of pumps and are going to circulate a blend of water and cleaning solution through the piping on one floor. Buy three extra 55-gallon drums and transfer the nitromethane into those new drums for now. Pour water and cleaning solution in both compartments of the three nitro barrels. Place small stones in a sealed sandwich baggie and let it sink to the bottom of the top compartment. Since this is how and where you will hide the detonators, this will be an excellent test when the barrels are inspected. Second, black barrels look suspicious. Paint all your barrels green, an environmental color. It might make a difference. Finally, hire a trucking company to transport the barrels to the project site. You take them from the loading dock into the building. In case of a problem at the security checkpoint, your chances of avoiding capture are higher."

CK ended by telling Hassan to let him know when they were going to schedule the test run. Hassan and Saleem then left. CK overheard Hassan tell Saleem as they walked past the widow, "I don't like him, but he had some good suggestions."

"I agree," said Saleem.

CHAPTER 87
STINGER

Thousands of miles away, Stinger read an article in their village's local paper with keen interest. *A military plane crashed, claiming the lives of twenty-three craft workers, flying home from a special assignment. Relatives of the deceased have been notified. The plane's explosion upon impact prevented the recovery of any bodies.*

He suddenly sat up straight, startled by what he read next. They listed his and BG's names as two tradespeople who worked on the project, but their current location is unknown. *Why would they do that? To flush them out? They must believe the two of them escaped. He needed to act if he and his family were to survive. He needed to tell someone, but who? Who could he trust? He now knew his government was involved. They might be looking for them now. He had a cousin who once worked in government intelligence. He would talk to him.*

His wife interrupted his thoughts.

"Share once more your escape story now that you've been home for a while."

"Late one night, BG and I stowed ourselves in the overhead luggage bins on the plane we worked on. After it landed, we waited until 2:00 a.m. to leave the plane. Luckily, there was a town five miles away. We walked there and hired a car to get us here."

"Who is BG, again?"

"Short for 'Bubble Gum'. He always chewed bubble gum when he worked."

"I'm so glad you are safe. Are they searching for you?"

"I'm unsure, but I'll attempt to discover the answer. We may have to move in a hurry! Look what's in the newspaper today."

He handed her the paper, and she read the article. "This confirms what you overheard. I'm so glad you made it back to us."

"Me too. But it's not over."

CHAPTER 88
TAJ JILANI

"What if that was not the way your wife and daughter died?" whispered Miriam, her voice trembling slightly.

"Miriam, what do you mean? I know how my wife and daughter died!"

"Maybe you don't. Anniston was told by the U.S. Navy that her husband Nick died in an explosion — an explosion caused by a *female* suicide bomber. Given that only one woman died in the explosion, it is likely that your wife was the bomber."

That's not possible, he thought. He was suddenly sick to his stomach. So many conflictive feelings ran through him.

"It's just not possible! My wife would never — she wouldn't risk —" He stopped speaking and lowered his head in his hands and murmured, "How did Anniston come by this information?"

"Anniston told me you and she had different versions of what happened. Following that, she sought a man who had served with her husband in the Navy, Colton Gray. He verified the U.S. version through contacts he had within the Pakistani government — their intelligence agency. Anniston was not going to mention this you, and she only told me recently when Colton confirmed it with the Pakistani government."

Taj observed Miriam. *He believed her. He had to leave.*

"Miriam, let's go."

They left the restaurant and drove back to her house. They remained silent. Miriam exited the car, glanced back, and whispered, "I'm sorry." Taj nodded but looked straight ahead and did not speak.

He would sort this out. But how could his wife, his sweet wife, have done such a thing? The pain, loneliness, guilt, and confusion he felt were unmatched — unlike anything he had experienced before. His wife's potential role as a suicide bomber, Miriam still out of the picture, and his very personal struggle having a hand in the murder of many innocent lives, was overwhelming.

• • •

After a restless night, Taj woke up early. He made a couple calls while heading to the airport. At the terminal waiting area Taj heard a ping for a text. The text read: *Call me, Accem.*

"Number?"

"32."

For ten minutes Accem pressed, prodded, and asked Taj questions on one aspect of the operation.

"Pakistan — are you absolutely sure?" asked Accem.

"Yes."

"You better be." Accem hung up.

Was that a threat?

CHAPTER 89
COLTON GRAY

At his desk in Lyon, Colton was gathering a few items to get ready for traveling back to New York for Friday's Steering Committee meeting. He had asked Colette to schedule a meeting with Chief Inspector Du'boe for this afternoon at 2:00. She stuck her head through his door.

"Cool-taan, the Chief Inspector's office just called and said his meeting with you must happen now. He is very busy you know."

"I know he is busy. But does my schedule allow for this?"

"Yes, you always make yourself available for the Chief Inspector, Cool-taan."

"OK, then send him in when he gets here. Colette, did you inform the fourth-floor girls I'm off the market?" Colton tapped his left dimple.

"Yes. They are very sad."

Moments later, a tap on the door signaled the arrival of the Chief Inspector.

"Hi Cool-taan, thank you for accommodating my schedule."

"No problem. I wanted to give you an update on my case load and make a request."

"OK, go ahead."

Colton provided an update on the progress of the investigation into the deaths of the Muslim men, potentially connecting it with a fundraising scheme, Jacques LeClair, and the first mysterious note. The Chief Inspector followed up with a few questions when Colton finished.

"Alright. What would you like to request?"

"That I move to New York. I believe my investigation into the deaths and the threat to the new building intersect. I don't know how but I need to be there to get it solved. My remaining caseload can be easily reassigned."

"Does your involvement matter since many of your government agencies are involved in the investigation?"

"Yes. My role as the Steering Committee chair and personal knowledge will bring a perspective I think will help. Our contribution will also give Interpol some enhanced standing."

"I think you are right. Your request is approved. Send me a written update on the status of your caseload. I will reassign your cases to other agents, but I need you here to answer questions before you leave. What is the timing?"

"August 1, which is almost two weeks. Does that give you enough to time to distribute my current load?"

"Yes. I will make that work."

"Thank you, Chief Inspector. I will send you a brief before I leave this afternoon."

• • •

Later that night Colton called Anniston.

"Babe, I got approval to re-locate temporarily to New York. I will see you every weekend now."

"That is great news! I will see if my calendar is open on the weekends," replied Anniston.

Colton laughed, and they finished up shortly after. Colton prepared for his trip back to New York.

• • •

The following day, Colton sat in Knox's office as Knox pushed an unopened envelope with the eraser end of a pencil. Colton picked up the envelope with latex gloves covering his hands and removed the note.

"When did you get this?"

"Yesterday."

Colton read it out loud:

The Monster will sleep until BLOOD fills its veins

"The same form of cutout words used again. I doubt we will find any fingerprints. Any ideas?"

Knox shook his head.

Colton placed the note in the envelope, then in a plastic bag, and stood to leave. "I will turn it over to the experts. I'll talk to you later."

Knox asked, "When do you leave to see Anniston?"

"Because of the late afternoon meeting with the Steering Committee, I could not catch a flight until Saturday morning. Back here Tuesday."

"Can you come to the apartment for dinner tonight, around 7:00?"

"Sounds good. I'll see you guys then."

• • •

As Colton was leaving, his phone rang. It was Chester Lagod with the FBI.

"So, my boss just called and informed me I am now part of a task force related to your project. He mentioned that you specifically requested my inclusion."

"Yes, I did. We need you," said Colton.

"Happy to help. Who's leading this group?"

"A Special Agent from Homeland Security named Quade Shapiro. Do you know her?"

"Yep. She is originally from the French West Indies. She's smart, quick-minded, tough, organized—makes excellent decisions. I worked with her on another joint assignment a few years ago. She's a perfect choice."

"She should possess all the qualities you mentioned."

"Also, she is petite but can probably kick your butt and— she's *gorgeous*."

"Not sure the extra descriptive information was necessary. I'm not looking to spar with her or date her; she will have her hands full with what we are dealing with."

"Just sayin'."

"Anyway, welcome to the team. I'll see you at the first meeting."

• • •

That afternoon, Colton and all the Steering Committee members sat at the conference room table. He shuffled his papers and put them in a neat stack and started with the first item on the agenda.

"OK, project update. Currently Beers is working on punch list on the below ground level work and floors two through ten. They are delaying inspections on the first floor until the end because it is the entry access to the other floors."

"What's a punch list?" asked Japan's representative, Hiroko Suzuki.

"It's a list of items that need to be corrected. The Architect will inspect the work and create this list for Beers to fix. After Beers fixes the items, the Architect will perform a re-inspection to confirm their completion."

"So, the project still on schedule to complete in five months?" asked Jack Straw.

"Yes, and the additional security measures are working smoothly," Colton assured.

They discussed the furniture move in and the phased approach agreed to for relocating staff from the existing building. Last, Colton brought up the potential threat of a terrorist act.

"In my capacity as an investigator for Interpol, I am moving to New York. I will be part of a recently formed task force that will meet weekly that includes Homeland Security, FBI, Secret Service, ATF, NYPD, and NYFD and others. Regarding the threat, I discussed with the task force chair what I could share with you. She was OK with me, sharing the content of some notes sent to the job site that are being investigated. The first one, received in May reads, *'The Building Is A Bomb'*. The second, received just yesterday reads, *'The Monster Will Sleep Until Blood fills Its Veins'*. We should not share this information."

All started talking at once as it seemed the notes made this threat real.

Qing Pow extended his arm. "Seems odd. Why would someone be giving clues here? To help solve the threat or act as a diversion for something else?"

"Good question. We don't know at this point. It could be both. I'll keep you informed on updates I am allowed to give, but know these warnings are being taken seriously."

There were no further questions, and the meeting adjourned.

CHAPTER 90
TAJ JILANI

October 2023

Taj sat down for the Subcontractor meeting. Big Dog started the meeting off discussing the schedule. Work was progressing on the punch list on the top 25 floors. All punch list items on the floors below were corrected and signed off by the Architect.

"Is there any testing scheduled?" asked Big Dog.

Taj spoke. "We would like to test our pump tonight that will fill our radiant tube system. We will fill the tubes on the second floor using three barrels of blended water and cleaning solution. It won't take long, just a few hours."

"OK, I'll let security know you're coming. Make sure the manufacturer's rep is there," said Big Dog.

• • •

Around 5:00, a rickety, white Ford van with one headlight arrived at the gate. The sign on the gate said, 'ALL DELIVERIES THROUGH THIS GATE ONLY'. Taj and a representative from Peerless Pump were waiting for them at the security checkpoint. Equipment must undergo inspection and verification by a manufacturer representative. Hassan exited the van and approached the gate. Taj also walked over and introduced himself, the Peerless rep and what they were planning to do. The security guard checked his clipboard, found the entry, and glanced at Hassan.

"Five barrels of solution and two Peerless Pumps for testing?" asked the guard as he looked carefully into Hassan's eyes.

"No, we have three barrels and one Peerless Pump only for the test. Someone made a mistake," said Hassan.

"Happens all the time. You and your men stay by the guardhouse while we examine the barrels and pump," said the guard.

Taj expected a thorough investigation and believed the question with the incorrect numbers was a test. First, they searched under the van, then checked the wheel wells and eventually looked inside the van. Their attention shifted to three green barrels and a portable pump. They opened a barrel and discovered murky water. After taking a quick sample, they used a rubber mallet to smack the top back on the barrel. The engineer from Peerless removed the pump cover for an internal inspection. She put it back on and nodded her head that everything was OK.

The men rolled barrels around in the van, searching for anything odd. After satisfying themselves, they motioned for Hassan to drive the van to the loading dock. From the loading dock they moved all three barrels to the first mechanical room. After pumping all three barrels into the system, Taj recorded the time. It fit within the range he estimated.

Hassan reversed the pump, sucking the blend back into the barrels. Cleaning up what little spillage there was, they checked the strapping on the hand trucks to be sure the barrels were secure and rolled the three barrels back to the van. Taj helped them load up and Hassan drove to the gate, waited for the gate arm to go up and continued out the exit.

CHAPTER 91
COLTON GRAY

November 2023

The note arrived on Thursday at the Beers project office. Knox called and Colton left his UN office. Knox waited for him, shutting the door upon his arrival.

"Here it is," he said, now with his own latex gloves. From the first note onward, all mail went directly to Knox's desk, ensuring prompt attention. First note was from NYC, second from Chicago, this one from Pittsburgh.

Colton donned his gloves and carefully opened the note. He read it once silently and then aloud:

The TRANSFUSION begins SOON

"Are these notes viewed as someone trying to help or hurt?" asked Knox.

"Much speculation surrounds that subject. There's no consensus yet."

"Separate subject. How are the wedding plans coming along?"

Colton laughed. "We are on a roughly sixty-day countdown. Seeing Anniston every weekend is a dream, but my 'Things to Do' list keeps growing. Returning to work is necessary for me to rest."

"How many have agreed to attend this big event?"

Colton stood up to leave. "I'm not sure. I received Ali's RSVP last Friday, and he's bringing someone with him."

Knox acted like he was adding the numbers in his head and using his fingers to count. "So, that's two. My wife, Quinn, and

I are seriously considering coming ourselves so put us down as a 'maybe'."

Colton smiled and shook his head. "Quinn being there is most important. You play a part in the wedding so you got to be there. Anyway, I'll see you at the Steering Committee meeting tomorrow. I need to get this note to our team."

• • •

The next afternoon, Colton, the Steering Committee members, and Knox gathered in the meeting area.

"The project is almost complete. Knox, you guys have done a great job!" said Colton.

"First, thank you. Many people have worked hard to make it happen. The remaining construction work is in the plaza: landscaping and stone pavers. The architectural dome framing is being erected with the special curved glass arriving in the next few weeks," said Knox.

"Please make sure you finish the dome as scheduled. Heads of state from each nation of the UN Security Council will gather at the designated location on January 10, 2024, to celebrate the building's opening. Any problem with that?"

Knox shook his head and said, "Nope."

All individuals comprising the Steering Committee clapped at this. Knox thanked them and left the room. Colton closed the door, then faced the committee.

"We received another note yesterday. It reads, '*The Transfusion Begins Soon*'."

CHAPTER 92
TAJ JILANI

Taj was hard at work constructing the domed skylight which included the patented shading feature. This architectural feature served as a skylight over the main auditorium, but with the push of a button, hydraulics moved two floor plates to close the opening. Currently, the floor plates were locked in place and scaffolding has been erected to construct the dome frame. With all the glass checked, he expected no problems.

As the dome's completion was only weeks away, it reminded him of his part in ending innocent lives. Also, he still couldn't square internally his wife's role in the market bombing that killed her, their daughter, and Nick King. He still needed answers on that one.

• • •

That night he called Accem.

"Number?"

"32," said Taj.

"Update?" asked Accem.

"Everything is on schedule," said Taj.

"I've made a change in plans."

Change in plans? What was Accem up to? "What do you mean?" asked Taj.

"Nothing you need to concern yourself with."

Accem hung up.

CHAPTER 93
COLTON GRAY / UNIDENTIFIED COMMITTEE MEMBER

Mid-December 2023

"Does the mail come at the same time every morning?" asked Colton.

"Yep, around 10:30," answered Knox.

Colton eyed the envelope. "Hmmm—postmarked Des Moines, Iowa. Moving out west a bit. He cautiously sliced across the upper part of the envelope and retrieved the note. He read to himself and then aloud:

*"**Final Clue,** The Monster will DIE if **you** follow this code:* **JN 81399"**

Colton got up to leave. "I'll talk to you later." He left in a hurry.

Time was running out, and a fresh puzzle piece had arrived. Reluctantly, Colton admitted the lack of progress in uncovering the plan. Lots of theories, ideas, and discussions had been kicked around for months but honestly, nothing made sense—yet.

Colton left the Beers office and dialed a number on his cell phone. He spoke quickly to Special Agent Shapiro saying that a meeting had to be held immediately as he had just received another note.

Colton stepped into the conference room and saw all the usual attendees seated.

"Hey, Colton," said Special Agent Shapiro motioning him in.

"Quade, I've got a hot one here," declared Colton as he removed his coat.

"What do you have for us?"

Colton walked to the grease board and picked up a red marker. He wrote the message on the board exactly as it was in the note:

Final Clue, The Monster will DIE if you FOLLOW this code:
JN 81399

The room was quiet as each person read and absorbed the message.

"The envelope had a postmark location of Des Moines, Iowa," Colton added as he sat back down.

Special Agent Shapiro let a minute pass. "Any ideas or initial thoughts from anyone?"

Colton observed the room's brief, chaotic discussion that lacked a consistent theme. Gradually, agreement formed around two ideas: 'Monster' meant the bomb, and the sender aimed to expose the forthcoming occurrence.

Special Agent Shapiro continued, "OK, talk to your people. Let's get this figured out. Colton, anything happens, call me. Meeting adjourned."

• • •

Colton immediately started typing on his phone and sent a group text to his Steering Committee calling for a meeting in one hour. Colton went directly to the UN conference room and found everyone seated by the time he arrived. He unfolded the piece of paper he had written the latest message on.

"We just received another note and wanted to inform you of its content. It reads: *Final Clue, the Monster will Die if you follow this code: JN 81399*. Any ideas or thoughts?"

Everyone started talking just like in the meeting he just left. After five minutes, Qing Pow raised his hand.

"Yes Qing?"

"Could this be a license plate number? Are the numbers and letters the sequence used in the city?"

"I'm not sure. Why would you think that?"

"In one of my previous investigative roles in government, a series of numbers and letters turned out to be a license plate."

Colton looked at Jim Rattler. "Is two letters and five numbers a vehicle plate?"

"Yes, for commercial vans," said Jim Rattler nodding his head.

"Good eye, Qing! Guys, I've got to make a call. Meeting adjourned."

• • •

As soon as everyone left, Colton hit a button on his phone for Special Agent Shapiro.

"Quade, it's Colton. I just informed my Steering Committee about this latest note. One delegate asked if it could be a license plate sequence. Another attendee confirmed the sequence of numbers and letters used for commercial vehicles in the city. This may be significant."

"Got it. I will have the number run through the DMV database. Thanks Colton!"

• • •

Down the hall, a Steering Committee member stopped and entered an empty office to make a call. "It's out now. Prepare yourself, everything is about to unravel."

CHAPTER 94
HASSAN MUSTAFA

As twilight descended, it had turned cold. The temperature was around 22°F, with the sky covered in moisture-laden clouds. Once the rain began, it quickly transitioned into sleet. Hassan looked at his watch. The delivery truck was late. They had to load the last fifty barrels and take them to the site. He was pleased that they had successfully transported 700 barrels to the project and placed them in the mechanical rooms on all but the top few floors.

A loud horn broke his deep concentration. The truck arrived and backed up. Saleem was directing the driver. The truck driver stopped the rig on the command of Saleem's clenched fist and hopped down from the rig. "This it?"

"Yes. How are the roads?" asked Hassan.

"Nothing closed yet, but it's going to get worse later," answered the driver.

They loaded the rig in forty-five minutes. The driver pulled the canvas cover over the load and strapped it down. He got into his cab and pulled away. Hassan and Saleem jumped into their van to follow.

• • •

Three hours later, they arrived at the project site. Traffic congestion affected all directions of travel and authorities started closing roads. The weather had gotten worse. Hard sleet covered the roads, and the temperature dropped to the low twenties—a terrible combination. After security performed the standard inspection, the driver backed his rig in and waited for the forklift to unload the pallets of barrels. Everything had gone smoothly as the last pallet of barrels were loaded onto the freight elevator.

Tomorrow night they would start pumping nitromethane into the tube system. Over the next two and a half weeks, including working through the weekends, they would start at 4:00 p.m. and finish at 2:00 a.m. After pumping the barrels dry, they would load the van fully and take them back to the warehouse. The cycle they estimated was five trips each night. They would finish up on New Year's Eve.

CHAPTER 95
AGENT LAGOD / SPECIAL AGENT SHAPIRO

December 29, 2023

Just past midnight, the white van made its final barrel delivery to the warehouse, following the same pattern as observed by two FBI agents. It appeared the driver failed to notice the black Tahoe pull out and tail his van. The number sequence in note #4 belonged to a white van with a single working headlight.

"This should be it. It's the fifth trip tonight," said Agent Christian Furr who was at the wheel of the Tahoe.

"I talked with the security team at the delivery gate at length and everything appears to be in order. They have checked every delivery, tested the liquid in every barrel and have found nothing that would raise their suspicions," said Agent Chester Lagod.

"I want to check inside the storage space where they continue to deliver these empty barrels."

"I agree. Let's do it after they unload."

• • •

Agents Lagod and Furr left their Tahoe and watched from a vantage point behind another building in the storage complex. Both men moved easily and quickly. Snow fell heavily, as the driver positioned the van in such a way that its one headlight bathed the entrance to the warehouse with light.

He left the van's motor running, stepped out and after a few seconds located the right key in his key ring and unlocked the roll-up door and pushed it up. He laid the lock in the slushy snow beside the building. Unloading the barrels quickly, he grabbed the cord that was now slightly above his head, rolled the door back into place and relocked it. Stepping up to his seat in the van, he drove off.

After ensuring the van's departure, the agents walked towards the door. After picking the lock, Agent Furr raised and lowered the door behind them. They entered with flashlights, and each walked down a narrow aisle created by the stacked pallets. Despite the cramped space, they both made their way toward the rear of the building. An odor of paint mixed with what smelled like WD 40 lubricating oil was prevalent throughout.

Agent Lagod walked up to one barrel. He stepped back to read the painted words, that were upside down, and inadvertently knocked a barrel over, making a loud noise. Something felt strange about the barrel's weight and balance as he picked it up, as if it contained a gyroscope. He re-stacked it but felt puzzled. They engaged the padlock on the roll-up door and drove away.

• • •

Early the next day Special Agent Shapiro called Agent Lagod, "Chester, anything turn-up at the warehouse?"

"There's something odd about the barrels. Furr is sick but I'll take another look," replied Chester.

"Do it tonight. We are running out of time."

CHAPTER 96
HASSAN MUSTAFA

December 30, 2023

Hassan and his crew loaded into the van and headed to the job site. They merged into traffic and Hassan noticed a black Tahoe following them. Hassan arrived at the job site a few minutes later. His men got out near the delivery dock, so they could clear security while he parked the van. He parked and watched the Tahoe pass by and park down the street. He cleared security and met up with Saleem and the others.

"Tonight, we must finish pumping liquid and return the remaining barrels," stated Hassan.

"Do you want to wire the relays when we finish?" asked Saleem.

"No. Show me where you hid the detonators."

"Follow me."

They went to one of the mechanical rooms on the second floor. Saleem opened the door and closed it once Hassan had entered.

"Put your hand right here," said Saleem.

Hassan reached up, felt the Ziplock bag, and discovered the sealed detonator inside.

"Perfect. All detonators dry?"

"Yep."

Furniture on dollies was being moved in building, with lots of cardboard and plastic strewn throughout the corridor. Hassan and Saleem zig zagged between the movers and the debris and made their way back to the ground level. Hassan called the other four over.

"Finish pumping tonight. We have five days to complete the low voltage wiring, one day to test the connection to the contacts and one day to set all the detonators. That gets us done by January 7th."

All heads nodded.

"Saleem, I need you to come with me for the last trip with the empty drums. We were being followed earlier!" finished Hassan.

• • •

Hassan drove the van with Saleem upfront to the storage unit compound where they quickly unloaded the last of the empty barrels. They locked the storage unit door and left the compound. On a small side road beyond the entrance, Hassan parked the van and waited.

Thirty minutes later a black Tahoe slowly passed by and went through the entrance. He and Saleem climbed out and made their way on foot and hid behind the man's Tahoe, whose headlights bathed the opening to one of their units.

Hassan watched as the man picked the lock and then raise the garage door. The man walked over with what appeared to be a J-shaped walking cane. He dropped the cane on the floor and grabbed the nearest barrel in a bear hug and slid it off the edge. The barrel hit the concrete floor with a loud thud. He loosened and removed the cap on the barrel and stuck the walking cane down the hole. It stopped when it hit the hidden second top. Tapping the hidden top a few times, he dropped the cane, clapped his hands together once and yelled "gotcha".

"He's figured out there are two compartments," Hassan whispered to Saleem.

"I'll take him out," responded Saleem clutching his weapon of choice.

Engrossed in his discovery, the man was unaware of the approaching footsteps. Without warning, the aluminum bat connected forcefully with the back of his head. The man fell instantly. When they saw the letters FBI on the sweatshirt, Hassan looked at Saleem who appeared on the verge of panicking. Saleem glanced at the FBI agent, then Hassan, and back at the agent.

"Is he dead?" asked Saleem.

"I don't know but we need to hurry. Let's load him in his truck and drive to the van so I can have a moment to think."

The two men had to lift and place him in the seat. They loaded the man into the Tahoe, closed the garage door and relocked it. They then drove out of the storage unit compound and parked by their van.

Hassan turned to Saleem. "This is the plan. You drive the van and follow me. Right before the complex, the main road curves and descends towards the woods. I'm going to veer off and drive through the guardrail. I'll jump out, let the truck hit the trees, and move him to the driver's side. If he is not dead, he will freeze to death. It will look like the road was slippery, and he had an accident. Let's go!"

• • •

Hassan sped up, maneuvered the Tahoe, and forcefully broke the guardrail. He barreled down the slope toward a group of trees. Swiftly, he flung open the door and dove out of the truck, narrowly escaping the collision. A loud noise followed. A crisp V-shape in the bumper and hood resulted from the truck crashing into the twenty-inch diameter tree. Smoke billowed out from under the hood.

Hassan got up, brushed himself off and opened the passenger front door. He pushed the agent across the console. Satisfied with his work, he ran as fast as he could back up the slope, slipping and falling several times before reaching the top. He found Saleem waiting in the van. He hopped in and they drove off. It started snowing, which was timely, as it would fill in Hassan's shoe path in the snow. Hassan's plan was working out perfectly.

CHAPTER 97
AGENT FURR / AGENT SHAPIRO

January 5, 2024

It was early in the morning and Agent Furr sat holding the hand of a teary-eyed Jenn Lagod, Chester's wife, as the surgeon discussed Chester's condition and the backstory of how he got to the hospital.

"Two things favor his survival tonight: a helpful driver in a delivery truck and a thick wool hat protecting his skull. The truck driver has a regular route of eight round trips a day on the road where the accident occurred. On his last trip he drove slower because of the heavy snowfall. This probably allowed him to see a gap in the guardrail. He slowed to a stop and spotted smoke curling out of the vehicle and called 9-1-1. About thirty minutes later, an ambulance arrived at the scene and transported him here to treat head trauma."

"What exactly is his status?" asked Jenn.

"A CT scan confirmed intracranial bleeding, so we immediately went into surgery. We relieved the fluid build-up that was exerting pressure on the brain before any damage could occur and moved him to ICU. He is under sedation, but all his vitals are good."

"Thank God!" said Jenn, closing her eyes.

• • •

Later that night, Agent Furr was sitting near the UN building in a black Suburban. His cell phone rang. It was not a number he recognized, but he answered, anyway.

"Christian, this is Jenn Lagod. Chester just woke up. He asked me to call you with this message." She relayed the message.

Agent Furr slammed the truck in gear and called Special Agent Shapiro.

"Quade, Chester's wife just called. He just regained consciousness and is stable. She informed us that the barrel we recently observed has two compartments. I am going to get a barrel; send backup up to this address."

Furr rattled off the address and then concentrated on navigating the slippery road he was driving on at an excessive speed. He arrived at the warehouse complex and drove to storage unit 10C. With bolt cutters, he cut the lock, raised the door, and went to the barrel they had previously viewed. He loaded it and one other into the back of the Suburban. As he finished, another black Suburban came sliding up. Three FBI agents leaped out of the car. Agent Furr instructed them to follow him back to the FBI's lab building.

• • •

Special Agent Shapiro called an emergency meeting of the task force for 6:00 a.m. Everyone showed up a few minutes early. Seated, she glanced around the room.

"First, Agent Lagod will recover. His curiosity about the 55-gallon drums gave us the break we needed. By cutting two barrels vertically in half, the lab confirmed a top compartment and a bottom compartment. We found a harmless water-based liquid in the top compartment. They swabbed and tested the bottom compartment—it's nitromethane!"

There was a chorus of comments. She quieted the room. "Here's how we'll handle it." She opened her notebook and calmly assigned each alphabet agency what she wanted done.

She closed her notebook flap hard and ended the meeting with, "I want updates at the top of every hour. Go!"

• • •

Roughly 100 FBI agents received pre-prepared blue coveralls with a fictitious furniture name stenciled on the back at a warehouse outside the city. Special Agent Shapiro followed the communication protocol she had set up with the task force. Things had to happen quickly, and she would make sure they did. After completing all the steps, she sat back, took a deep breath, and thought, *'Game On!'*.

CHAPTER 98
COLTON GRAY

Saturday January 6, 2024

Colton arrived at Knox's office with Agent Furr and an explosives expert from the FBI straight from his 6:00 a.m. meeting. Knox and Big Dog had already sat down. After introductions, Colton explained what they wanted to check.

"Where does the liquid get pumped into the radiant floor system?" asked Agent Furr.

"Every level contains four mechanical rooms. The system pumps the blend from there. One mechanical room serves approximately 25% of the floor," said Big Dog.

"Could you take us to a floor and show us?"

"Let's go."

Big Dog took them to the second floor. Stopping at the first mechanical room, Big Dog pointed out the chemical's injection port.

"Are there tubes in all the cement?" asked Furr.

"It's concrete, not cement but yes, the tube system is throughout the entire floor," answered Big Dog.

The explosives expert walked over to a small box, opened it, and let his eyes follow the wiring. Looking at Furr he whispered, "The only thing missing is the detonator, and it's ready. They can initiate this remotely. The building floors will explode immediately."

Agent Furr and the expert left immediately without speaking further. Colton walked over and thanked Knox and Big Dog and then left. Colton told Knox he would talk later.

"What's going on?" asked Big Dog.

"There's a big problem. Stay tuned," answered Knox.

CHAPTER 99
HASSAN MUSTAFA / CK

That evening, Hassan drove to a location about ten blocks away from the job site. Using a small wireless remote, he toggled the switch from up to down.

A few seconds later Saleem called, "All contacts closed on the Ground floor."

The crew continued this process until they reached the sixtieth floor. When the sixtieth floor checked out Saleem yelled into the phone, "Praise Allah!"

"Yes, praise Allah," replied Hassan. "Tomorrow night we set the detonators."

• • •

Minutes later Hassan's phone rang. The annoying voice was on the line.

"Status?" asked CK.

"Remote control tests checked out. We set the detonators tomorrow night."

"Let me know when you are done."

"I will."

"If anything goes wrong before or after you blow the building meet me at the storage facility. I have a plan for you and one more person to leave the country."

"Why only two?"

"It will only work that way."

"What if there are three of us?"

"You will eliminate one or I will eliminate you. Either way, it's still two."

CK hung up.

CHAPTER 100
TAJ JILANI

Taj, over the past few weeks, had purposefully disengaged himself from Hassan's team while they pumped the fluid into the radiant system. It was easy and convenient because he was working on completing and testing the Grand Dome in the Plaza. He was unsure about the specific chemical but knew it would be powerful. And finally, he reached out to an old acquaintance in Pakistan's Intelligence Agency (ISI), telling him exactly what information he needed and requesting that it be done expeditiously.

Now to his task for the day. He arrived early at 5:30 am, when there was minimal activity in the building, and headed straight to a small electrical closet on the lowest level. Closing the door behind him, he switched on the overhead light, and he opened the notebook that contained the instructions for the alterations and then opened the electrical panel door. Puzzled, he rechecked his scribble. The panel was the same, but he didn't notice the red tape he had requested the electrical subcontractor to stick there for him. He may have written his notes incorrectly.

He decided to check the next floor up. Quickly leaving, he went up one floor and entered the electrical room there. Opening the electrical panel door, he saw the red tape marking the circuits feeding the dome. In a few weeks, they would install permanent labels identifying what each circuit fed. Using a flashlight, he examined it briefly and then looked at his checklist. After retrieving his tools out of his backpack, he got to work and finished an hour later. He packed his gear, turned off the light and returned to his apartment.

He showered, donned a bath robe, and sat down in his comfortable recliner. As he sat quietly by himself, sadness and guilt suddenly overwhelmed him, as all the things that were bothering him seemed to collide at once—his wife Amal being a suicide bomber, his failed relationship with Miriam, her strong and unwavering beliefs about Christianity, and his role in the killing of many innocent people. *He wasn't a murderer. Why did he allow himself to get in this messy predicament?* He mulled over his feelings briefly, then determined it was time— time to open the envelope.

Grabbing his notebook, he removed the yellowed, taped up envelope he carried around for twenty-six years. He held it for a minute and then took out his pocketknife and carefully slit one end. He removed the note carefully and started reading. His eyes teared up immediately.

CHAPTER 101
TAJ JILANI

Dear Taj,

If you are reading this letter, I am no longer with you. It makes me sad to even write this. So, no matter what happened, know that I loved you with all my heart, soul, and mind.

In moments of doubt, follow the path of doing what's right. You've always been a stable, reliable influence for anyone fortunate to cross paths with you. Your kind and generous heart attracted me to you.

And last, it is OK to fall in love again! Don't burden yourself with guilt. Keep moving forward as I wish only happiness for you. You are a wonderful man and even better husband!

My Love Always,
Amal

Shortly after they married, they both wrote letters to each other in the event one of them died tragically with no last words like an extended illness allows. It was mainly because of Taj being with ISI, but Amal insisted they both write notes. He could not open it after Amal's death, as he likened it to still having a piece of her with him and saving it for the right time. Though painful to read, the timing was perfect.

He made two decisions: to return to the project site and undo the recent alteration to the Grand Dome electrical panel. He had to figure out how to extricate himself from this whole mess. Grabbing his backpack, he arrived back at the project at 8:30 and observed an unusually large number of furniture movers in blue coveralls enter the building. He entered the electrical room, corrected it, and quickly left the building.

The second decision involved Miriam. When calling and asking her if she would see him tonight, he detected excitement in her voice when she answered 'yes'. They agreed on 7:00.

• • •

He pulled up to Miriam's drive in his rental car and she came right out. With a smile on her face, she genuinely looked glad to see him. She wore a heavy, gray wool sweater, along with blue jeans. Approaching Taj, she gave him a hug and a quick kiss on the lips. He closed the car door behind her.

They drove to a small, quiet restaurant a few miles outside of town that served excellent seafood. Dark wooden booths, almost like separate rooms, offered privacy. It was Friday night and crowded but Miriam had made reservations. Upon entering, the host quickly seated them. The server presented the specials for the night, shared which one was his favorite, and took their drink orders.

They finished an excellent meal. Pleasant small talk occupied dinner.

Miriam admitted, "I felt awful after your previous visit. I hurt your feelings, and I am so sorry. My mistake, sharing that information with you. Please forgive me."

Taj looked deeply into Miriam's eyes. "Apology accepted but not required. My sources in Pakistan will seek to confirm the story, but it may take time."

He went on. "Something unexplainable tugs at my heart when I think about our discussions on Christianity. I desire to convert to Christianity."

"I don't want you to become a Christian just to pacify me."

"Trust me on this. I'm not."

A moment of silence, then Miriam spoke. "It is easy. Sin separates us from God. Accept Jesus Christ as your Lord and Savior and He will bridge the gap between you and God. You pray for Christ to come into your life, and it will happen. All your sins; past, present, and future are forgiven forever."

"That's it?" asked a surprised Pakistani.

"That's it."

Extending across the table, she clasped both of his hands in hers. With him, she offered a simple prayer. She spoke, he repeated.

Filled with amazement, he looked up at her. A sense of relief washed over him as the burden of guilt and anxiety disappeared. He felt different. He felt a deep sense of peace unlike ever before. His next course of action was clear in his mind.

"Thank you," he whispered. He paused. "Now, I've got to tell you what I'm involved with."

For the next hour, he told Miriam everything. Miriam's face wore a look of disbelief and shock.

"I must prevent this. Who do you suggest I should talk to?"

Miriam was quiet. "Sorry. Give me just a minute. I'm just trying to catch up with you." She thought for a minute. "I think you need to talk to Colton Gray. He will know what to do."

"He gave me his card, but I left it in my notebook."

"I will call Anniston and get his cell number."

It was now almost 10:45 and Miriam dialed Anniston and got Colton's cell number. She told her she would explain later.

Taj called the number. It was 11:00. A sleepy voice answered the phone.

"Colton Gray."

Taj greeted Colton and quickly reminded him of their meeting several months ago. Taj asked if he could meet with him tomorrow. He was currently in Flint but had information concerning an upcoming disaster at the new UN headquarters building. Colton's voice changed and seemed way more interested in their conversation. Colton suggested a place at 4:00 p.m. and said he would see him then.

Miriam and Taj left the restaurant holding hands. Their meeting rekindled their relationship. Taj felt like a new person. But now he needed to stop the disaster. After Taj dropped Miriam, he drove back to Detroit and spent the night there. He booked a 12:05 p.m. flight to NYC but intended to arrive at the airport early to check if he could catch an earlier flight by going stand by. Getting back in plenty of time for his meeting with Colton was paramount.

CHAPTER 102
HASSAN MUSTAFA / AGENT FURR / CK

Sunday January 7, 2024

In the morning, around 8:30, Hassan and his crew entered the van. No need to wait till afternoon as they usually do. It was time to set the detonators. They drove to the project, parked, and cleared security. Hassan observed more men than usual wearing the one-piece blue coveralls with a furniture company name. He pondered that they probably needed more men to finish on time.

At the freight elevator, they waited for a short while. Their plan was to begin at the top and descend. Inside, Saleem pressed the button marked 60. Before the door closed, someone shouted, "Hold the door!" Four guys in blue coveralls got on the elevator with them. As they rode up, Hassan found it odd that none of the four men glanced at the button panel or pressed any buttons. How did they know we were going to the same floor?

The elevator tone sounded when they got to floor 60. Everyone got out. From a short distance, Hassan watched the four men enter an office. Minutes later, walking past the office door, he saw the four men unwrapping furniture. For the moment, Hassan felt satisfied.

He kept walking until he got to the first mechanical room where Saleem and his team were. In just five minutes, they located the detonator, removed it from the top of the duct where it was hidden, and securely placed it in the metal housing. It was now ready for detonation. The other three mechanical rooms followed quickly. They found the nearest stairwell and walked down to the next floor. They should complete setting all the detonators by early afternoon.

• • •

After Hassan walked past, Agent Furr walked to the door and watched Hassan go to the end of the hall and enter the mechanical room. He observed Hassan and another man exit the mechanical room shortly after. They walked a few steps, reached the stairwell door, opened it, and descended the stairs. Agent Furr came back to the office.

"Let's go. I think they are working their way down."

They split up, and each selected a mechanical room. The remaining three were explosive experts who instructed Agent Furr on removing the detonator from the box.

Agent Furr arrived at the mechanical room nearest his location. He knocked on the door, making sure it was empty. No answer. With the light switch on, he headed towards the metal box. Using a screwdriver as a lever, he popped it open and carefully removed the detonator from its cradle. Walking to the central area of the building, he joined the others. They simultaneously showed each other that they each had detonators. One man had taken pictures documenting its position before removal.

Agent Furr made a call to the commander below to start his men up. They decided right then to capture the terrorists on floor 50. Twenty agents took three mid-rise elevators to floor 48 and, from there, would walk up the next two floors using the stairs. Agents also remained at ground level.

Agent Furr and his team moved to floor 59 and headed to the designated rooms, which were identical on floors below. They removed the detonators and started down the stairs to floor 58.

• • •

Hassan still felt uneasy about the furniture delivery men. After they finished floor 56 and moved to 55, he took an elevator back to floor 60 to see what those guys were doing. He got off when the doors opened. The floor was quiet. He trotted to the office where he had last seen the four men. Nonchalantly, he passed the room as if heading down the corridor. He glanced to the left, finding an empty room. Halting in his tracks, he peered into the interior. The desk and credenza were still half unwrapped! Hassan understood what that meant and immediately ran back to the elevator. The doors opened, and Hassan pushed the floor button for floor 55. At 55, he disembarked and sprinted to the nearest mechanical room, where Saleem was working.

"We've got to go! Someone has discovered us. Go tell the others to finish this floor and meet me in the van. Do not use the elevators!"

Saleem ran down the corridor to tell the others. Hassan started making his own plan. Reach the van, then activate the switch for the detonators. It would be an exceptional explosion but would only damage the top floors. It would be a victory for Allah. A blast at a well-known building, like the new UN tower, would attract significant attention.

Anticipating men waiting on the ground floor, he opted to take the elevator to the second floor and began contemplating his next course of action. He texted CK, letting him know they had been discovered and asking him to meet at Unit 10C in the warehouse.

• • •

FBI agents were walking up to floor 50 when they heard sounds of feet coming toward them in the stairwell. They stopped at floor 50 and waited. The lead agent saw five men turn the corner of the stair the next floor up.

He shouted, "FBI! Get down on the floor!"
The men reversed course and sprinted up the stairs.

• • •

Meanwhile, Agent Furr and his team were working furiously to clear the remaining detonators.

• • •

Saleem and his four men went through the door on floor 52. On reaching the floor, they dispersed to locate any weapon available. They were determined to go out fighting.

FBI agents pushed the door open and entered in a calculated manner. Ten agents were now on the floor, searching for terrorists.

The men of Jihad's Blood armed themselves with screwdrivers, metal parts, wrenches, or anything else they could find. Once located, they steadfastly refused to back down or surrender. Instead, they aggressively confronted whoever had found them and the authorities shot them with precision. Saleem, the last casualty, took the same route as the rest, shouting, "Allahu Akbar."

• • •

The FBI transmitted the kill result over all their radios. The men at level G did not leave their position. All the other agents quickly ascended to floor 52. Medical personnel were escorted on the elevators to administer medical attention. It was a waste of time. None of the terrorists survived. Agent Furr called

Special Agent Shapiro and gave her the update. The team successfully cleared all detonators and eliminated five of the six terrorists. The sixth terrorist fled in the white van they were now pursuing. She praised him for his work and said call her when they got the last one.

• • •

Hassan moved quickly to a stairwell door and waited. Suddenly, he heard shoes pounding on the stairs and continued past his level. Waiting a minute, he cracked the door, but saw no one. Quietly, he slipped out and descended, hearing the footsteps above him growing fainter.

Reaching Level G, he skillfully maneuvered around furniture cartons, reaching the garage stair door without detection. Entering, he ran down the stairs and out to his van in the garage.

He opened the passenger side and reached into the glove box and pulled out the remote device. He opened the plastic bubble covering the switch and, with no further thought or hesitation, flipped the toggle to the 'On' position.

Nothing happened! Hassan heard no explosion and cursed silently to himself. *They must have cleared them all!* He started the van and slowly drove away as two men in delivery uniforms appeared suddenly with their pistols drawn ordering Hassan to stop the vehicle and get out. Hassan reached down and pulled out an AK-47 CK had bought for him and opened fire through the right side of his windshield.

The agents dove to the ground. One was hit. One was not. Hassan stomped on the accelerator and headed toward the agent who was rolling on the ground unwounded. He tried to run over him but missed him. The agent continued to empty his ammo into the van as it went by, but it did not stop the one-eyed white beast that now had a big hole in its windshield.

Hassan tires squealed as the van gained traction leaving the deck. He had to get to the warehouse. He got out of the city safely and did not see anyone following him.

• • •

An hour later, he pulled up to the warehouse complex and slowly drove to unit 10C. After hopping out of the van, he noticed that someone had removed the lock. Upon opening the door and as light chased away the darkness, he saw CK sitting on a barrel. CK motioned for him to close the door. Hassan lowered the door and turned the light switch on to illuminate the space. He turned around to speak to CK. He stopped and attempted to process what he was seeing—a pistol with a silencer on the end in CK's hand pointing at him. *What's he doing?*

• • •

CK looked directly into Hassan's wide-open eyes and calmly pulled the trigger twice. One bullet pierced Hassan's forehead and the next his chest. Hassan fell flat on his back. His life was over. CK turned off the light, lowered the door and left to take care of the next pressing assignment Accem had given him which involved leaving immediately for Flint, Michigan. But for now, he achieved his professional goal: *Kill Count: #100!*

• • •

Later that evening, Special Agent Shapiro received a call from Agent Furr telling her the last terrorist was found dead at the storage warehouse.

CHAPTER 103
TAJ JILANI

Taj took the noon flight and landed two hours later at JFK. He Ubered from the airport to the restaurant Colton recommended for the meeting. It was a small Italian eatery a few blocks from the job site. He arrived at 3:30 p.m. and took a seat.

He looked at his wristwatch again. It was 4:10. Thirty more minutes passed, and Taj called Colton's cell phone. It immediately went to voice mail. Taj left a message. After another fifteen minutes passed, Taj believed Colton wasn't coming, so he stood up and headed to the project site. Maybe Knox McKenna would be there and could locate Colton for him.

He arrived at the building to find it cordoned off with barricades and yellow plastic tape. NYPD officers and FBI agents stationed themselves at regular intervals around the building. Taj approached a barricade manned by an FBI agent. At the barricade, he informed the agent that he was a subcontractor with unfinished work. The agent told him the building was closed until further notice. He answered Taj's questions the same way and then asked Taj to move on. Taj left, returning to his apartment. He attempted to contact Colton once more, but failed and chose not to leave a message.

CHAPTER 104
COLTON GRAY

Monday January 8, 2024
Colton woke up at 7:30. He felt crummy and knew he had a slight fever and the digital numbers of the thermometer reported 100 degrees. Feeling achy and uninterested in any activity, he chose to lie in bed. As his meetings concluded last night at 11:00, he kept his phone switched to silent, just like it had been during the meetings yesterday. Special Agent Shapiro led the entire show with good, sound decision-making and had all the agencies well-coordinated and informed, including the White House.

Out of their many meetings, they derived a plan to remove the nitromethane into 55-gallon drums, transport the barrels safely, and store them. Over 500 emergency personnel would be used with the goal of completing the work by Tuesday at noon.

• • •

Two hours later, Colton awakened feeling much better. Walking to the kitchen, he grabbed some crackers and slowly munched on them. He picked up his cell phone and saw there were five messages. Two were from Anniston, two were from Miriam's friend, Taj, and one from Ali announcing his arrival for the big wedding event next week with Jacques LeClair in tow as his 'plus one'.

Punching Anniston's name on his phone, she answered on the first ring up and listened while he gave her an update.

"You better get well, mister. There is an important event that requires your participation this weekend."

"Believe me—I know. I'm feeling a ton better."

"Good. Remember, Miriam and I are going to a friend's house in Ann Arbor for a party they are throwing for me. We are staying the night. I'll be back tomorrow."

"I remember."

Next, he called Taj. He apologized for missing their scheduled meeting and asked if they could meet later this morning at 11:30 at the same location. Taj agreed and again told Colton he had information that he needed to hear.

CHAPTER 105
TAJ JILANI

The anticipation of meeting Colton in two hours made Taj both relieved and anxious. Taj needed resolution on what he had been involved in. After hanging up with Colton, his cell phone buzzed. The screen read 'unknown caller'. When the phone rang, Taj was surprised to hear Accem's voice.

"It is almost over. Did you make the alterations at the electrical panel serving the dome?" asked Accem.

"What's the reason behind your question?" answered Taj.

"Because Plan B is in play."

"What is 'Plan B'?"

"Yesterday, Hassan, and the rest of Jihad's Blood were killed."

That's why the lockdown occurred. "I still do not understand."

"Several events led my decision to change our strategy — mostly involved around the reckless behavior of Hassan's crew at the site and then one of them tipping off a French mercenary who warned Interpol. I sent four clues to the contractor so the authorities would uncover the activities of Hassan and his group."

Taj interrupted. "Why would you do that?"

"Very simple. We needed the main plot to be discovered close enough to the Grand Opening so the authorities would believe the threat was neutralized. Nobody expects another scheme. You convinced me of the destructive power of the Grand Dome you built. The 'Heads of State' of the countries belonging to the UN Security Council are going to have a private, celebratory meeting at 10:00 a.m. in the Grand Dome.

All will be killed! It will cause incredible mayhem and a vacuum in leadership like the world has never seen. Allah will have a special reward for you, my friend."

Accem had been way ahead of him. In an aggressive tone Taj said, "I follow Allah no more."

"What? What was that you said?"

"You heard me, and I will not go through with this. I will not be part of it."

"Doesn't matter. The plan proceeds, with or without you!"

"It's over. I will inform the authorities. You can't do anything about it."

Accem spoke harshly. "I've already done something about it. I often wondered if you would change your mind — and for that, you will be killed. The failure of the Grand Dome exploding will also result in the loss of your friend Miriam's life. You do not seem to be able take care of your women — just like your wife!"

CHAPTER 106
TAJ JILANI / ACCEM

"What? Why did you mention my wife? You know nothing about her!" said Taj angrily.

"You are naïve. In this chess match, your King is in 'check'. We recruited you because of your unique skill set but made you believe you found us. We needed to give you a personal cause to hate the Americans, so you would join us," said Accem.

"What are you saying?"

"While your wife and daughter were on holiday, we kidnapped your daughter. We told your wife if she wore a phony, bomb-laced vest in the public market to create a diversion for the bank robbery we planned, we would release your daughter. This was a lie, of course, but she agreed. We pointed your wife out to your daughter and then released her knowing she would run to your wife. She did, and we ignited the vest, as it wasn't a fake, right as your daughter got to her. We paid our contacts in ISI handsomely to float the possibility that it was an American drone attack."

Taj had a hard time absorbing everything he heard. His wife—his poor wife died thinking she was saving their daughter. He seethed with anger towards the monster on the phone. "Why? Why us?"

"Because you helped thwart an operation of mine a long time ago. I always settle the score with anyone who crosses me!"

"What are you talking about?"

"Years ago, you reported to MI-5 that the travel itinerary of the laser scientist Wang Soo had been stolen. Putting that mission in place required extensive effort on my part. It's the only one that has ever failed."

Taj said quietly with a steely tone, "Do not hurt Miriam."

"That's in your hands." Accem said and hung up.

Taj sat down with his head in his hands. He did not know what to do. He dialed Miriam's number, but it went straight to voice mail. Taj decided he had to get to Flint. He was going to do everything in his power to save Miriam. Leaving now, he would make the 11:00 flight to Detroit.

He needed help, but he would figure that out once he got there. During the cab ride to the airport, Taj called Colton and could not leave a voice message as his mailbox was full. He sent a text with four lines: *'Can't make meeting, headed to Flint, Miriam in trouble, call me, Taj'*. When the flight attendant announced phones must be turned off, he noticed he had a missed call. The area code was 312, Chicago. Not recognizing the number, he would worry about that later.

• • •

After hanging up with Pakistan, Accem immediately made a call to CK and gave the order—"Kill Pakistan!"

"Where is he?"

"He will come to you in Flint."

He possessed the skills to change the electrical panel himself, and he intended to do so. Plan B with the Grand Dome was going to be successful.

CHAPTER 107
CK / CHECKER CAB DRIVER

Two eyes tracked Miriam and Anniston's progress as they left the grocery store with a small cart filled with several plastic bags. The eyes watched as Miriam opened the hatch of her small SUV and unloaded the basket on wheels that contained flowers and bottles of wine. He observed Anniston rolling the cart to the buggy corral. Both women opened their front doors about the same time and climbed in.

"Alrighty, let's go. No work tomorrow. Fun night ahead. It is so nice of you guys to do this for me," said Anniston.

"Stop it. Everyone is excited about your wedding this weekend and having a pre-wedding party is a great way to celebrate. Hmmm, this is weird though."

"What?"

"I feel like someone has moved my seat forward. I am closer than I normally sit. Let me adjust it and we will get going."

No matter how hard she pressed on the seat adjuster, the seat wouldn't budge backwards. While checking for obstructions, she was stunned to discover a man's face peering at her. She screamed. Anniston's shock was obvious as she witnessed a knife to Miriam's throat.

"Quiet! Drive where I tell you to go," said CK.

Anniston started crying softly. Miriam was shaking. Anniston watched her put the SUV in gear and followed his directions to a small, wooden-frame house on the outskirts of Flint. Driving down the driveway CK instructed her to park inside the detached garage. Walking in front of him, he guided them to a bedroom that had an adjacent bathroom. He made them lie face down, as he zip-tied their legs and hands. After checking his work, he placed them each on the queen-sized bed.

After closing the door, he turned and spoke in a matter-of-fact tone, "If you cause me any problems, you both will die."

• • •

Across that same grocery store parking lot, hidden by a delivery truck, was a yellow Checker cab with mag wheels and a red racing stripe. It wasn't supposed to be there. In fact, the instructions given to him, after he dropped his creepy passenger, was to return to Chicago. Bob Collins witnessed the man breaking into the SUV and enter through the rear passenger door behind the driver's seat. This wasn't good. He followed the SUV at a safe distance and watched them turn down a long driveway. He scribbled the address in his notepad and then punched in a number—it went unanswered.

CHAPTER 108
TAJ JILANI

Taj arrived in Detroit at 1:15 p.m., rented a car and headed to Flint. His anxiety centered on Miriam. Despite leaving her five messages, he received no response. He needed help, so he called Colton.

Colton answered, "Taj, I got your text. Where are you?"

"Just leaving Detroit Metropolitan in a rental."

"What did you mean that 'Miriam's in trouble'?"

"I will get to that. Anniston's absence might mean she's in the same predicament."

"What? I'll call you back."

A few minutes passed and Taj's phone buzzed showing it was Colton.

"I called Anniston, and it went right to voice mail. What's going on?"

"I need to start at the beginning. You need to know everything, and I need your help!"

"Go ahead."

He started with the death of his wife, meeting Accem, and everything else that has occurred until now. He told Colton about his conversation with Accem last night, but Colton interrupted.

"You intended to meet me on Sunday to share everything, correct?"

"Yes, but you figured it out."

"We received notes giving us clues. Did you send those?"

"No. Accem told me last night he sent the notes."

"Where is Accem?"

"I don't know."

"I interrupted you. Is there more?"

"Yes. That is why he wanted you to figure out the liquid explosive. It became a diversion to mask what is still going to happen."

"What's planned?" Colton asked in an anxious voice.

"The Grand Dome's glass is specifically engineered to shatter. Acting like small missiles, the fragmented glass will shred anyone in the room."

"*Anyone* refers to the leaders of the countries that are currently part of the UN Security Council. They will meet at 10:00 a.m. on Wednesday."

"Who is part of the UN Security Council?"

"There are five permanent members: U.S., China, Russia, France and, the U.K. plus ten rotating members from other countries. What causes the glass to fracture?"

"The Grand Dome's glass has a shading feature. I worked and helped perfect this technology. If you over supply electricity to the glass, during the shading transition, it will make the glass explode sending shards of glass downward. The electrical panel that feeds the Grand Dome needs to be altered for this to happen. It is very easy to do. I told Accem I didn't make changes, so the Grand Dome is now useless as a weapon. Accem informed me he intended to kill me for my betrayal and added that he would kill Miriam if this explosion did not go as planned. I turned my focus to helping Miriam. I have tried to contact her, but it goes straight to voice mail. That is why I'm in Flint. I'm trying to find her."

"I'll call you back," Colton said abruptly and hung up.

CHAPTER 109
COLTON GRAY

Colton absorbed it briefly, then quickly recognized Taj was right—they were in the same spot. Anniston was supposed to be with Miriam! Despite calling her number, once again it went directly to her voice mailbox. Suddenly, a wave of sickness hit his stomach. Clear thinking was required. He had until 10:00 Wednesday morning to get a resolution. Obviously, if required, they would change the meeting to ensure no one gets hurt. However, Miriam and Anniston's lives were still at risk once Accem discovered no one had died. He decided to go to Flint but needed a quicker way than commercial airlines.

He called Special Agent Shapiro and quickly summarized everything Taj told him. "Quade, I need your help."

"Name it."

"I need to borrow one of your jets to get to Flint quickly."

"I will arrange it and will text you the address. The jet will be ready when you get there."

Colton also gave her a list of firearms he needed. She assured him she would provide all the weapons he needed and inform her liaison with the White House and other agencies about what was going on. She added she would notify the FBI field offices in Michigan and let them know that his fiancé and her friend were missing.

"Do you need anything else?" asked Quade.

"Nothing comes to mind right now. Thanks, you're awesome! This situation could get tricky as my fiancé and her friend may become pawns in some strategy. I'll contact you once I learn more."

"Good luck and let me know."

Colton then called Taj back. "Anniston is with Miriam. I'm flying to Flint and will call you when I land, which should be around 4:30 p.m.

The next call was to Knox. "I need your help. I'm taking a private jet to Flint. Something has come up. I'll explain on the way over."

"OK. What airport?"

Colton gave the address. They flew out shortly after Knox arrived. Colton explained everything to Knox. Knox let out a low whistle.

"Wow! I had no idea. Clever to substitute a liquid explosive in a component of the building and design the glass in the Grand Dome to become fragmented shards."

"They would have succeeded."

Colton saw Knox studying him from the side. "What are you looking at?"

"It looks like you are meditating."

"It's a breathing exercise the psychologist gave me to relax. No more hand tapping."

"I noticed that. So, it works, huh?"

"Yep, it helps me relax and focus."

"Glad for you, brother," Knox said nodding his head as he fist bumped Colton.

The next call Colton made was to Ali. Ali and Jacques LeClair had arrived in Flint early for the wedding and had a rental car. They would pick them up at the airport. The last call was to Jack Straw. He told him he was out on an emergency, and Jack needed to represent the Steering Committee at the Grand Opening. Jack told him he would take care of it and would text if he had questions.

CHAPTER 110
TAJ JILANI

Taj arrived in Flint at 2:30 p.m. and checked into the Holiday Inn Express he stayed at many times previously. Taking a quick shower helped him feel slightly refreshed. Sitting on the edge of the bed, he towel-dried his hair. Upon finishing, he glanced at his phone and noticed a missed call. When he pressed a button, the number matched the one from earlier today, which had a '312' area code. It automatically dialed and someone answered, "Hello."

"Yes, you have called my number twice. Who is speaking, please?"

"Captain! I've been trying to call you. This is Bob Collins. You leased my cab for a day, and we went to Flint together. Remember?"

"Yes, I do."

"Where are you?"

"I'm in Flint. Where are you?"

"I'm in Flint as well. Tell me where you are, and I'll meet you."

Taj told him and Bob promised he would be there shortly.

• • •

Approximately twenty minutes passed, and a knock sounded at the door. As Taj opened the door, in walked Bob Collins, the owner of the classic Checker cab with mag wheels and a red racing stripe.

Taj studied Bob Collins and thought he seemed uneasy. While motioning to a seat, Taj glanced outside and promptly shut the door. "Why are you in Flint, Bob?"

Bob quickly told of being hired for $2000 a day to provide transportation service for the same person who hired him previously whenever that person came to Chicago.

"Go on."

"I received instructions to pick him up at a hotel near O'Hare early this morning. We drove here to Flint and waited near your friend's house."

"How did you know she was my friend?"

"In the past, I was paid to follow you twice and knew you were friends, possibly more."

"Her name is Miriam. Continue."

"We arrived at her house just as she was pulling out of the driveway. We tailed her, and she picked up another woman and followed them to a grocery store. The man said my services were complete, gave me cash and told me to leave. But I didn't. I hid and watched him. He broke into your friend's car and hid out of sight. I knew this wasn't good. I followed them and was going to contact the police, but you called me back."

Taj abruptly interrupted. "Wait! Back up. You followed them? You know where they are?"

"Yes, I do. Captain, I believe this man is dangerous and I couldn't just watch those women get hurt."

The cab driver drew a map on paper, showing the way to Miriam's car. Taj thanked him, shook his hand and ushered him out the door. They now had a chance!

CHAPTER 111
COLTON GRAY / KNOX MCKENNA

It was 4:15 p.m. when the private jet touched down at a small airport outside of Flint. Colton called Taj as they taxied and told him they had landed. He got Taj's hotel address and said his team would meet him there. They walked into the small brick building that was clean and smelled of air freshener. It housed a lounge, restrooms, and a small dining area with vending machines. Two men were in the lounge watching TV when Knox and Colton entered.

"Jacques! Ali!"

Both men jumped up and came over. Jacques shook hands with Colton. "Monsieur, good to see you."

Jacques looked fit and fully recovered.

"Jacques, meet Knox McKenna. Knox, this is Jacques LeClair." The men shook hands. He turned to Ali. "And you remember Ali."

"Good to meet you Jacques and to see you again Ali."

"Let's sit a minute and I will explain what's going on."

Colton provided Knox with a little background about Jacques and credited him for alerting him to a plan to blow up the United Nations building. Colton then brought them up quickly to date, including the fact that Anniston and her best friend were missing.

"I know you guys did not come here to get involved, but I could use your help."

"No problem, boss," said Ali.

"At your service my friend. I have some—uh—quick personal business to take care of but I will meet you shortly. Ali can call me with an address, and I will take an Uber there. Do you have a weapon for me?" asked Jacques.

Colton handed over a pistol which Jacques quickly checked, rechecked, and then put in his waistband.

"Thank you. Let's go," said Colton.

They left the small FBO terminal building. Everyone but Jacques piled into the rental car. Colton gave directions to Ali to Taj's hotel, and they got there a few minutes later. Colton tapped on the door. Taj opened the door and shook Colton's hand. He gestured for everyone to enter.

Colton made the introductions, and they sat down in the small sitting area. Taj started as soon as everyone was seated, eager to tell them what he had just learned.

"I have information." He quickly told them what the taxi driver said. "The man with the taxi driver took Miriam and possibly Anniston. He told me two women were in the car."

"He gave you the address?" asked Colton.

"Yes. Here it is." He pulled a sheet of paper from his pocket, unfolded it, and smoothed it out on the small, round table where they were gathered. All eyes were on the map.

"I think it is about twenty miles from here," said Taj.

"Want to contact the FBI and get some help?" asked Knox, looking at Colton.

"I will call Special Agent Shapiro, our task force leader, on the way, and she will take care of that. Let's go check the house out."

Colton and Knox rode with Taj and Ali followed behind. Colton called Special Agent Shapiro, spoke briefly, and then finished.

They left the city heading south at almost 80 mph. Minutes later, they noticed the exit sign they needed and followed the directions by turning right. They drove almost two miles more when they suddenly came upon a rusty mailbox with reflective numbers—323. They passed by the driveway and found a spot to plan. It was bitterly cold outside, and it was getting dark.

"Ali, I want to see the house. Drop Knox and me just past the driveway and we'll check it out."

"I will go too. I can handle myself," said Taj in a no-nonsense fashion.

Knox looked at Colton and Colton nodded. "OK." Hidden by the trees, Colton, Knox, and Taj made their way through the woods. Colton pulled out a backup handgun tucked in his pants and handed the gun to Taj. Taj stopped and checked it in a way that showed he knew what he was doing. They continued walking around a slight curve when a wood frame house came into view. Smoke slowly curled out of the chimney. The house sat in a large clearing, which would not allow much cover.

"We should head to the back," suggested Knox.

Colton nodded. They finally got around to the back of the house where they squatted by the garage and watched the house for a full ten minutes. Colton looked at Knox. He gestured for Knox and Taj to go on one side, while he went to the other. They nodded.

• • •

Knox and Taj crept along the exterior wall until they came to the first set of windows. They couldn't see inside because the blinds were closed. Taj placed his ear against the window.

"What is it?" asked Knox.

"It sounds like Miriam—crying," said Taj.

Knox nodded, signaling it was time to return and join Colton behind the garage. The five minutes they had agreed to were up.

• • •

Colton stayed low and walked past a screened porch to reach the other side of the house. He moved past the first windows and reached the following ones beside the smoking chimney.

He slowly raised himself up and looked inside. A man, phone in hand, rotated towards the fire. The light generated by the fire was reflective to where Colton could now clearly see his face. Colton was stunned! He almost got caught staring as the man twisted his head and looked toward the window.

CHAPTER 112
ACCEM

Accem was small in stature with salt and pepper short hair. Standing a few blocks from the United Nations building, he waited. Wearing gray coveralls with the name of the *Hubinski Furnishings Since 1946* stenciled on the back, he carried a cloth tool bag. Once inside, he estimated he had approximately one hour of work. It was not if he got inside but when he got inside. He hoped the area he needed to be in was not under surveillance.

Pretty soon, a large delivery truck with Hubinski Furnishings Since 1946 painted on the side stopped at the curb. The back door rolled up, and Accem hopped in. At a cost of $10,000, he now had a job site security badge, which was handed to him once he got inside the truck, and transportation to the project site. He laid down his cloth bag. They would check it, but he had an explanation ready for what he would be doing.

Having cleared security, he headed to the elevator for the lowest three floors. He pushed the button BL3, which was the lowest level. The doors closed, and he heard someone shout, "Hold the door."

Accem pressed the button with the opposite triangle points and the doors reopened.

"Thank you," said the man wearing an FBI jacket.

"What level?" asked Accem.

"BL2 please."

Accem hit the button which was one floor above where he was going. A few seconds later, the doors opened at BL2. The agent got off. Accem could see that other FBI agents filled the corridor. *He wondered if it was the same for his floor. That would be a problem!* The doors closed and continued their descent to BL3. As the elevator dinged, the doors slid open. Nobody else seemed present on the floor. Relieved, he walked unhurriedly towards the electrical room that was written in the notes he had stolen from Taj's apartment. Without turning on the light, he secured the door behind him. From his bag, he took out a small penlight. He laid the 8½" x 11" spiral notebook on the floor and started to work. Despite his technical capability, it took him a while to comprehend Taj's writing. *Sometimes you must take matters in your own hands, he thought.* He removed the tools and devices from his bag and got to work. *Still odd he thought, what were all the agents doing on the floor above him?*

CHAPTER 113
COLTON GRAY / CK

Colton stepped back quickly before the man saw him. He darted to the garage to meet Knox and Taj.

"We think Anniston and Miriam are in the front room," Knox whispered to Colton. "What did you find?"

Colton said one word. "Wolf!"

"What did you say?"

"Wolf! He isn't dead!"

"How could he possibly be involved?"

"Who is Wolf?" asked Taj.

While Taj spoke, Knox asked. "You're sure it was him?"

Colton looked first in Knox's direction. "Yes, without a doubt. He looked my way, and I barely moved back in time."

Colton then looked at Taj. "He was formerly Chinese Special Ops that nearly killed Knox on a rescue mission years ago. I thought I killed him. Please go get Ali. We will strategize what to do next. I want to move soon," said Colton.

Taj discreetly used the woods for cover, moving alongside the driveway.

"We should have backup and medical care available," said Knox.

"Agree." Colton pressed a few buttons and got the voice mail Special Agent Shapiro. He left a detailed message.

"What's the plan?" Knox questioned.

"Create a diversion in back and charge through the front."

Colton suddenly looked up and turned his head slightly, hearing a noise near the porch.

"What?" whispered Knox.

"I heard a squeaking sound."

Moving quietly around the side of the garage, Colton peeked around the corner. The screen door from the porch was open and the door closer allowed the door to bounce several times before it shut.

Wolf had just left the house! He searched with his eyes and ears but found nothing to hear or see. Colton knew they had to move fast.

• • •

CK's (Wolf) senses were on high alert. Something suddenly drew him to look from the fire to the window. He must investigate, but before, he must secure an exit plan. He first attached a device to Miriam's head, then to Anniston's. Through the back screen porch, he exited the house.

• • •

Colton whispered, "Let's go around the driveway side and through the front door. I believe Wolf went to where I was standing first. I think we strike now while Wolf is outside. Without him in the house, our odds are better."

Knox nodded. He followed Colton as they sprinted to the front. They rapidly climbed the short set of steps to the doorway. Colton opened the screen door and Knox followed by kicking the door right above the doorknob. The door jamb splintered, and the front door swung open. Knox crouched with his pistol drawn and Colton ran in beside him. They cleared the den. Colton went straight to the left bedroom, assuming Anniston and Miriam would be there. Knox returned shortly after.

"I cleared the kitchen and then locked the kitchen door that led to the screened porch," said Knox.

"Come look," Colton said, finishing cutting the zip ties from hands and feet. Both women were crying. Colton told them to remain still as he was studying the small gadgets attached to their heads. Knox walked over and said, "What do you think?"

"I haven't seen this before. We need an explosives expert."

"I'm an expert," said a voice behind Knox.

Colton looked up and Knox whirled around to stare at Wolf's dark eyes. In his left hand, he held a pistol, and in his right, a push-button device.

Wolf spoke in perfect English while looking at Knox, "It has been a long time since I stuck my knife in you. Drop your weapons and kick them over here."

Colton stood slowly and raised his pistol to eye level, cocked his head to the right slightly and looked through the sights at Wolf's forehead. Knox did the same.

"I will push the button and kill the women," threatened Wolf.

"You flinch and you'll be dead," said Knox.

Wolf hesitated which Colton read he had not counted on getting any pushback since he had the women as his bargaining chip.

"Put the device and pistol down, and hope I don't shoot your other knee," said Colton taking offense at Wolf's reference to burying his knife into Knox years ago.

Wolf finally spoke looking at Colton, "I will drop the detonator, keep my gun and leave. This will get settled another day."

Wolf laid down the controller, backed out until he reached the front door. He spun around and walked unhurriedly around the house. Colton stepped out onto the small porch and peered around the corner. He saw Wolf slip the firearm in his waistband and slowly jog to the garage.

Right now, Colton had no interest in pursuing him. He was glad Anniston and Miriam were unharmed though they still had to deal with the device strapped to their heads.

Suddenly, Colton saw Wolf backing out of the garage with his hands up as Ali and Taj followed him with Taj's gun pointed at Wolf. Colton ran to them and took the pistol from Wolf's waistband. They all walked back into the house. Knox's face showed surprise when they walked back in with Wolf. Both women whispered and sniffled in conversation.

Taj located rope, bound Wolf's hands, and seated him on the couch.

"Ali, please finish tying his feet. I want to check on Miriam."

"Colton!" yelled Ali.

When Colton came out, he looked at Ali. "It's him—he was in the elevator in Venice."

Colton acknowledged with a nod, "I know."

Wolf said, "You were lucky. I'm not finished with you yet either."

"You keep making threats like you have a future. You're done," Colton stated as he walked back to the bedroom.

Ali seemed intimidated and backed away before securing Wolf's feet.

Suddenly, they heard sirens in the distance. Knox announced he would go to the road and direct them in. After briefly stepping outside, he quickly returned and called for Colton.

Colton walked back out of the bedroom. "Yeah?"

"You had better stay with Ali and monitor Wolf."

Wolf had already taken advantage of that slight distraction to pull his tied hands under his butt and thread his legs through the circle his arms and bound hands created. Ali had turned away from Wolf while Knox was talking. Wolf leaped from the sofa and got his hands over Ali's head and created a choke hold.

Wolf started backing out using a gasping Ali as a shield. Knox and Colton followed with their weapons drawn. Wolf kept moving. It was impossible to get a good sight line as Wolf kept moving Ali's body to be a shield to their sight lines. He unlocked the kitchen back door and moved out onto the porch. Knox flipped on the porch light so they could see. Wolf quickly positioned his arms differently. Colton knew what was about to happen.

Colton screamed, "No!" He started to take a shot, but he was too late.

• • •

Wolf smiled. Snapping #3's (Ali's) neck was going to be a pleasure. He started the motion when the screen door behind him suddenly opened and caused him to be distracted and turn his head momentarily. What he saw shocked him! *It can't be – he's dead! Kill count back to 99...*

CHAPTER 114
COLTON GRAY

A single shot rang out and Wolf's head exploded. Blood, bone, and brain matter splattered everywhere. He dropped immediately, taking Ali, now covered with blood, down with him. Through the screen door walked Jacques LeClair!

He looked at Wolf and finally lowered his gun. "Sorry my friend," he said to Ali. "He was about to end your life. I couldn't have that, could I?"

He smiled and helped a clearly shaken Ali off the floor.

"Jacques, perfect timing!" exclaimed Colton.

"Monsieur, he nearly killed me in the alley that night. It is fitting he should die this way."

All four men quietly stood for a minute. Colton reflected that Knox, Ali, Jacques, and himself almost lost their lives at the hands of Wolf. Another evil man eliminated, ensuring no more terror or murder.

Police cars, ambulances, unmarked FBI black SUV's all with flashing blue lights raced up the driveway to the house. Men opened doors and descended upon the house. Colton hurried back to be with Anniston. Taj led an FBI explosives expert into the bedroom. The expert studied the devices attached to both women's heads.

"Hmmm—," said the expert. He suddenly pulled the device off Aniston's head. Everyone in the room gasped.

"It's harmless—a bogus device."

Colton and Taj both walked over to their respective mate and wrapped their arms around them and held them tight. Tears were flowing freely. The paramedics insisted they go to the hospital to be checked out. They reluctantly agreed to go, and both men accompanied them in the ambulance. Before the ambulance left with, Colton grabbed Wolf's cell phone.

CHAPTER 115
ACCEM

January 10, 2024

It was 5:00 a.m. Accem got up and was jubilant. The alterations to the electrical panel were a success and everything was working as he planned, despite Pakistan's actions. He left his hotel room for a long walk. It was cold outside, but he didn't notice. Today, the world will go into cardiac arrest.

After walking roughly five miles he returned to his room, undressed, and took a warm bath. After being soothed and relaxed from the water, he wrapped a huge, thick terry-cloth robe around his body and sat in one of the comfortable wing-backed chairs that was in his room. He crossed his legs and rested them on the footrest.

He thought about his life and career. *Standing 5'7", he still had a lean body and smooth skin that made him appear younger than his 65 years. After the personal tragedy of losing his wife to cancer, it left him the responsibility to single-handedly raise Lang, their two-year-old son, just as he had success in his profession. He consistently achieved incredible wins in his career because of his well-planned and executed missions. Only one assignment had failed in his 40-year career. His mind drifted back to 1998. If the extraction of the Taiwanese scientist had succeeded, he could have retired early. But it did not go as planned, and retribution was coming soon to the man that help mess his otherwise perfect record.*

Creating and taking on the identity of Accem had been quite easy. At every step, Lang (Wolf) was there with him. It was amusing thinking back about Pakistan helping him get his cart out of the crack in the sidewalk before their first meeting. Lang was hidden inside the cart, which made it so heavy. It was entertaining to see Pakistan's expression while trying to lift the buggy.

Sitting with Accem behind the darkened bullet proof glass when meeting with Pakistan, Lang confirmed Pakistan was telling the truth since he tailed him to Chicago and other places. He still reveled at how Lang had done so many smart, tactical maneuvers to get them where they were. He showed brilliance in handling the Steering Committee votes, particularly with the Saudi Arabian representative. The Saudi was told Dunhill St. James would be selected if the Saudi representative voted for them. It had been pointed out to him that his country's architectural firm, Sayedd, owned Dunhill St. James. The Saudi Arabian representative had quickly agreed.

Accem also had many skill sets. The intelligence sector had plucked him early in his life within the Chinese government and spent years training in covert operations and different languages. Lang had been his most important achievement. Accem personally provided all his initial training as an assassin.

He still had to kill and dispose of the bodies of the two women he had captured and then Pakistan. With all witnesses eliminated – his beloved China, would benefit from this event in several ways. He would call him in a little while to check on his progress.

He was told the President of the People's Republic of China would be late for the meeting in the Grand Dome. His friend and partner, the General, had managed that part of the plan. The General – he smiled to himself at the mention of the title.

The General was not really a General. On a mission once in Europe, his friend had hidden in a General Electric refrigerator to avoid capture. As he would humorously retell that story, he would say a brave American officer named General Electric had saved him. From then on, Accem referred to him as General.

But Accem's biggest accomplishment in his entire career would be this current assignment.

Accem felt a nap coming on and drifted slowly off into a deep, comfortable sleep. He would call Lang for an update after his nap. They would richly reward him for being part of shaping world history. In the chess game in his mind, he softly spoke the word, 'Checkmate.'

CHAPTER 116
TAJ JILANI / COLTON GRAY / QING POW

The meeting for the national leaders of the nations, represented by the UN Security Council, remained scheduled to take place at 10:00 a.m. in the Grand Dome. Special Agent Shapiro and other alphabet agencies had adequately proven that they had addressed and neutralized all threats related to the new building.

Between 9:45 and 10:00, the plan was for heads of state to arrive and gather in the lobby of the new building.

They'd go to the Grand Dome from there. The NYC police department, in cooperation with the Secret Service, managed all traffic to the UN with intersections being closed as necessary. Traffic barricades were strategically located, and sharpshooters positioned in places that would not be apparent to the untrained eye.

At 9:05, a huge Airbus carrying the Chinese President landed at JFK. As the plane slowed to a stop, people watching the landing witnessed a shocking disaster—

• • •

Taj remained at the hospital with Miriam throughout the night. When she finally woke for a moment, the next morning he whispered in her ear, "I was so worried about you."

She smiled and fell back to sleep. Settling back in his chair, he relaxed. As emotional and physical exhaustion had taken its toll, he closed his eyes when his cell phone started buzzing. It was his contact at ISI confirming the actual cause of the explosion, killing his wife and daughter, was a suicide vest worn by his wife. Taj thanked his friend for this information and hung up.

He was relieved his wife wasn't a suicide bomber but still heartbroken he lost both her and his daughter at the hands of an evil man. Ready to close the chapter of the last five years, he needed to follow Amal's advice and rebuild his life with Miriam.

• • •

The Airbus carrying the President of China suddenly split apart in three separate sections with the middle piece exploding into small pieces. The other two pieces of the Airbus rolled independently and stopped on their own. Within minutes, emergency vehicles sped to the scene. The pilots, the Chinese president and his closest staff were all unharmed and removed quickly to safety. None survived in the plane's middle section. Body parts littered the runway. It was a gruesome sight.

Word quickly spread that a bomb had exploded on board the President of China's plane. The Secret Service quickly briefed the President of the United States. The president urged the continuation of plans unless the Secret Service had information on imminent danger. They did not. The American president insisted on being kept up-to-date and declared that he would include any information they had about the explosion when he addressed the UN in his 2:00 speech.

All leaders, except the President of China, walked over to the Grand Dome and sat down around the large mahogany conference table and looked at the large screen TV. They watched the news coverage of the explosion. Telephone calls quickly confirmed the safety of the President of China, and he would not be attending the 10:00 celebratory meeting.

• • •

• • •

At 9:55, Colton asked Taj to join him for breakfast in the hospital cafeteria. Anniston and Miriam were still resting. Suddenly, the phone that Colton had taken from Wolf's pocket vibrated. Colton pulled it out of his pocket and showed the screen Taj. A New York City area code flashed on the screen. Taj held up a finger that Colton read as 'hang on before answering' and quickly started scrolling on his own phone screen.

"It's Accem! He called from that number yesterday," he said.

He held his hand out as a gesture he would answer it, so Colton handed Taj the phone. Pushing the screen's speakerphone button he said, "Hello," quickly and slightly muffled.

There was silence for almost three seconds while Colton wrote the number and sent a quick text to Special Agent Shapiro.

"Son?"

"Yes?"

"Who is this?"

"32."

Curse words spewed out followed by, "Where is he?"

"Last night, the owner of this phone was killed."

Silence for maybe ten seconds.

"Impossible."

"It's over."

"Far from it. In a few minutes the Grand Dome will explode."

"How?"

"You fool! Do you think you are the only one capable of changing the electrical panel? I took care of it! Chaos will ensue in a few minutes. The President of the United States and other global leaders will be dead!"

Colton eyes suddenly got big, and he held his hands up and open as two revelations shocked him. *We failed to stop them and that is the voice of Qing Pow!*

Taj raised his hand, motioning Colton to wait, and asked a specific question, "How would you know what changes to make?"

"The notebook in your apartment told me everything I needed to know."

"Nothing will happen."

Silence. Taj continued, "The reason is, you made changes at the wrong location. You altered the electrical panel at the lowest level. The panel you should have worked on is one floor above. I had written it down wrong. Accem—checkmate!" Taj immediately hit the 'end call' button. *Hanging up on Accem felt amazing!*

Taj asked Colton, "What's next?"

"We need to get to New York. I just followed up with another text to Special Agent Shapiro with Homeland Security with both contact and hotel information that goes with this number. I told her to have the FBI arrest the person belonging to this phone number and hotel address—it will be a Chinese national."

Taj seemed to be surprised. "Chinese? I was sure he was Arabic."

"Nope. Accem is Qing Pow, the Chinese representative that served on my Steering Committee. It makes sense now. He suggested we check if the sequence of letters and numbers in the 4th clue were the same sequence as a NYC vehicle plate. They were, and it is how we caught the terrorists. He knew because he wrote the note!"

"Fooled me as well." *He was the little Chinese man pushing the cleaning cart years ago!*

They left to inform Aniston and Miriam that they had to return promptly to New York. They arrived back at the FBO and boarded the jet Special Agent Shapiro had provided. After taking off, they backtracked the entire story. Starting with Colton's history with Wolf, they discovered their paths had inadvertently crossed many years before related to the rescue of a laser scientist by the name of Wang Soo!

• • •

Qing Pow slammed down the phone. Sadness immediately washed over him. *His only son, Lang, was dead. How could that happen? But, how else could they have his phone? If Pakistan was telling the truth about the location of the electrical panel, then he accomplished nothing and had a devastating, personal loss. The reason agents were stationed on the floor above is now clear.* He compartmentalized his emotions and returned to the present. *Got to go – disappear. He knew it was over for him.* He called General.

General answered immediately and listened for one word. Green – success. Red – failure.

"Red," said Qing. He followed with, "I'm sorry old friend." He hung up.

Qing got dressed and threw all his clothes in a duffel bag and was ready to leave fifteen minutes later. Unexpectedly, a knock on the door and he heard the words, "Housekeeping."

Opening the door, a man stepped in wearing a navy-blue wind breaker, surrounded by several other men with their pistols drawn, and announced, "F-B-I, you're under arrest!"

They handcuffed him and led him away. Qing decided right then what his course of action would be: *defect and trade information for protection.*

CHAPTER 117
US PRESIDENT

January 11, 2024

A meeting was being conducted in the Oval Office which included the President's closest advisors and heads of the different alphabet agencies for security and intelligence. They all listened closely as the Director of the FBI told the story.

When he finished, the President cleared his throat to speak. "Let me see if I can summarize. A Chinese national, who we arrested, cooperated fully with our team after being debriefed. Someone murdered a group of young Muslim men. The life insurance policies, taken out on each of the young men by their parents, funded the operation. Before I continue, I am struggling to understand why the parents would be involved in this scheme?"

The Director scanned his notes quickly. "Many Muslim majority countries operating under Sharia law can use the death penalty for crimes such as abandonment of Islam, adultery, witchcraft, same-sex relations, murder, rape, and publishing pornography. All victims were reportedly guilty of at least one crime, as per the informer. A persuasive mullah convinced parents to adopt Sharia law for Islam's benefit and monetary gain."

"Thanks. It's just hard to comprehend. OK, I'll continue. A Steering Committee, set up by the United Nations, was controlled in such a way that certain building components were included in the design which allowed their strategy to move forward. The first component was the floor heating system composed of tubing in the concrete slab that was pumped full of nitromethane smuggled in from China."

"That's correct, sir."

"Then, a backup plan ultimately became the primary plan, and that was to have the Grand Dome glass explode and kill all in attendance. The Muslim terrorist group would have been able to take credit, which also provided cover for whomever planned this whole affair. But the terrorist group became a liability. They leaked information about what was being planned, so they executed their 'Plan B' which included killing or causing to be killed, the terrorist group. The terrorist group, in either event would get the credit and the blame."

"Yes sir."

"Most important. The country behind this plot was China. Their government could take advantage of the sudden vacuum of leadership in the West ranging from financial to military."

"Again, that is accurate."

"But I am still unclear what proof we have the Chinese government was involved versus a rogue group within the Chinese government."

"The Chinese national we have in custody did not know who inside the Chinese government knew about this or was involved. He only dealt with a man that is senior in their intelligence agency."

"It's quite convenient," the CIA Director interjected, "that the Chinese President wasn't present at the supposed explosion at the Grand Dome."

"I agree," said the Director of the FBI. "Also, according to the eyewitness accounts, the Airbus separated into three separate pieces several seconds before the explosion occurred giving rise to the possibility that it was all planned. The official response stated that the plane had blast walls designed to protect and isolate the president. We checked on one other curious anomaly. The results were just texted to me. Analyzing body parts from the Airbus revealed significant formaldehyde levels. Those reported dead were deceased prior to their arrival. The bodies were prepared for burial and contrived to look like victims of the plane explosion."

The door quietly opened, and the Secretary of State's assistant slipped her a note. Everyone paused because of the interruption. The President's face seemed to express annoyance when someone interrupted his meeting. The Secretary of State read the lengthy note twice.

"Mr. President, I apologize for the interruption. The note I just received helps answer your question concerning China's involvement. We received a communication from our embassy in Beijing. Yesterday, a man, and his family entered the embassy, seeking protection and asylum. He told our staff he worked on the airplane that blew apart in three sections. Witnessing the Chinese President observing the plane at the plant, he overheard who he believed was a high-ranking military official, tell the Chinese President that all workers were to be executed upon completion and how that would play into the overall scheme. He and one other worker escaped. Just a thought, the workers that were killed may have been the bodies blown up in the plane."

The room was silent as everyone soaked in this latest little tidbit. The President sat with his hands forming a steeple in front of his mouth. Finally, he spoke. "So, what do we do about China?" said the President to no one in particular. The room was quiet. Everyone waited to see if the President had finished speaking. He wasn't. "Armed with most of the story, we confront China with a press conference. I think we call them out and let them prove they weren't involved."

"Sir, may I?" said the Director of the FBI.

"Go ahead."

"I would suggest you lead off with you have found the culprits who blew up the President of China's plane and it's the Chinese themselves."

The President processed that thought. "Not a bad angle. Anyway, that's a good start but we need to get our allies also involved in a long-term solution."

He put his hands on his knees and said, "I've got a ceremony in just a few minutes to honor the heroes that prevented this catastrophe. Good work all!"

The President stood, and the meeting ended with the Director of the FBI, Secretary of Homeland Security remaining behind.

The room attendant showed Colton Gray, Quade Shapiro, Chester Lagod, and the President of Interpol into the room. Colton, Chester, and Quade stood facing the President's desk. The President read his notes:

"Mr. Gray, Ms. Shapiro, and Mr. Lagod:
On behalf of my office and the people of the United States of America we salute and commend you for your leadership, bravery, hard work, and untiring commitment to prevent what would have been the greatest disaster the world has ever experienced in modern times.

To Colton Gray: I present you the highest U.S. civilian award, the Presidential Medal of Freedom.
To Quade Shapiro: DHS's Exceptional Service Gold Medal
To Chester Lagod: The FBI's Medal of Valor

As we have some strategies in play, I cannot disclose your awards and the reasons for them just yet, but I personally thank each of you," the President concluded. The President presented each award in an open leather box and shook each person's hand.

• • •

As the Secretary of Homeland Security and the Director of the FBI left the Oval Office together, they spoke briefly before going their separate ways.

"Wow, what a hornet's nest," said the FBI Director.

"Yep, incredible set of events. This story would be a great book," said the Secretary of DHS.

"Or movie—," added the FBI Director.

CHAPTER 118
CHINA PRESIDENT

In a secret location in China, the Chinese President, and other top leaders, sat around an intricately carved conference room table. All were quiet waiting for the president to speak since it was his meeting.

The President directly stared at Jung Pan, the Minister responsible for MSS, China's CIA equivalent. "You have failed us. We had excellent strategies in place to take advantage of America and their European counterparts. You assured me personally our stratagem would work."

The man in the spotlight nodded to show respect for the President and acknowledge his failure. The President continued as he glared at the intelligence head. "I just heard the President of the United States say at a news conference that we blew up our own plane and were behind a plot to assassinate the world leaders meeting at the UN Grand Opening."

The man the President was addressing continued to look down.

"I will, of course, deny that we were part of this. Aside from us, who else is aware of this plan? And how do you intend to handle the mess you've caused?"

The man looked up. "Xi Haugh (General) never let Qing Pow (Accem) know who was aware of this plan or of our future strategy had the plot been successful. I have ordered two, two-person assassination teams to exterminate them both."

The President nodded. "I would like your resignation after you clean this up."

He bowed, nodded, and left.

The President cut his eyes toward the Deputy Minister of MSS and nodded his head slightly toward the door Jung Pan departed through. *Jung Pan was to be eliminated also!*

"We must be careful now. This incident must not affect our long-term plans for the U.S. and the world," finished the President.

CHAPTER 119
COLTON GRAY

January 13, 2024

Colton couldn't have asked for a more beautiful day for a wedding—frigid outside but a clear, blue sky. The small white church was filled as he and Anniston exchanged their marriage vows. Knox was best man and Miriam was the maid of honor. Nobody objected, and the newlyweds were happy to put this important event behind them. The week was extraordinary, but the ending was perfect.

After, there was food, drink, and a live band at the local events hall. Miriam and a few others sat at the same table with Ali, Jacques LeClair, and Taj. Colton walked up to Taj and whispered for him to follow him. Taj rose and headed towards a side door, which opened to a small room.

Upon opening the door, Chester Lagod with the FBI was there. After being released from the hospital a week ago, he was able to attend the wedding. Two chairs were in the room. He motioned for them to sit. Colton introduced them.

"Colton has explained all your circumstances and your role in preventing a disaster. Since I was attending the wedding, the Attorney General's office elected me to deliver this message. After several agencies discussed and agreed, they decided not to file any charges against you. We will expedite your citizenship if you desire to become one, and you will keep ownership and investment in the companies you are involved with here. On behalf of America, we thank you," said Chester.

"I would very much like to become a citizen—and thank you—." Emotion overwhelmed him. "May I ask you a question?"

"Sure."

"Where's the man I know as Accem?"

"He's in our 'Witness Protection Program'."

THE END

ABOUT THE AUTHOR

Born in Opelika, Alabama, Dwight Morgan Jr. graduated from Auburn University with a Bachelor of Science in building construction. He has been in the commercial construction industry for 48 years and worked on projects in Saudi Arabia, San Antonio, Chicago, and Atlanta. He owns a commercial construction company in the metro Atlanta area. He and his wife, Patti, have two adult sons.

When not on a project's jobsite or writing, he is an enthusiastic follower of college football and is learning to paint portraits.

NOTE TO THE READER

Word-of-mouth is crucial for any author to succeed. If you enjoyed *Heat of Hydration*, please leave a review online—anywhere you are able. Even if it's just a sentence or two. It would make all the difference and would be very much appreciated.

Please visit my website at *dwightmorganjrauthor.com* for upcoming books and other information.

    Thanks!
    Dwight Morgan, Jr.

We hope you enjoyed reading this title from:

BLACK ROSE writing

www.blackrosewriting.com

Subscribe to our mailing list – *The Rosevine* – and receive **FREE** books, daily deals, and stay current with news about upcoming releases and our hottest authors. Scan the QR code below to sign up.

Already a subscriber? Please accept a sincere thank you for being a fan of Black Rose Writing authors.

View other Black Rose Writing titles at www.blackrosewriting.com/books and use promo code **PRINT** to receive a **20% discount** when purchasing.